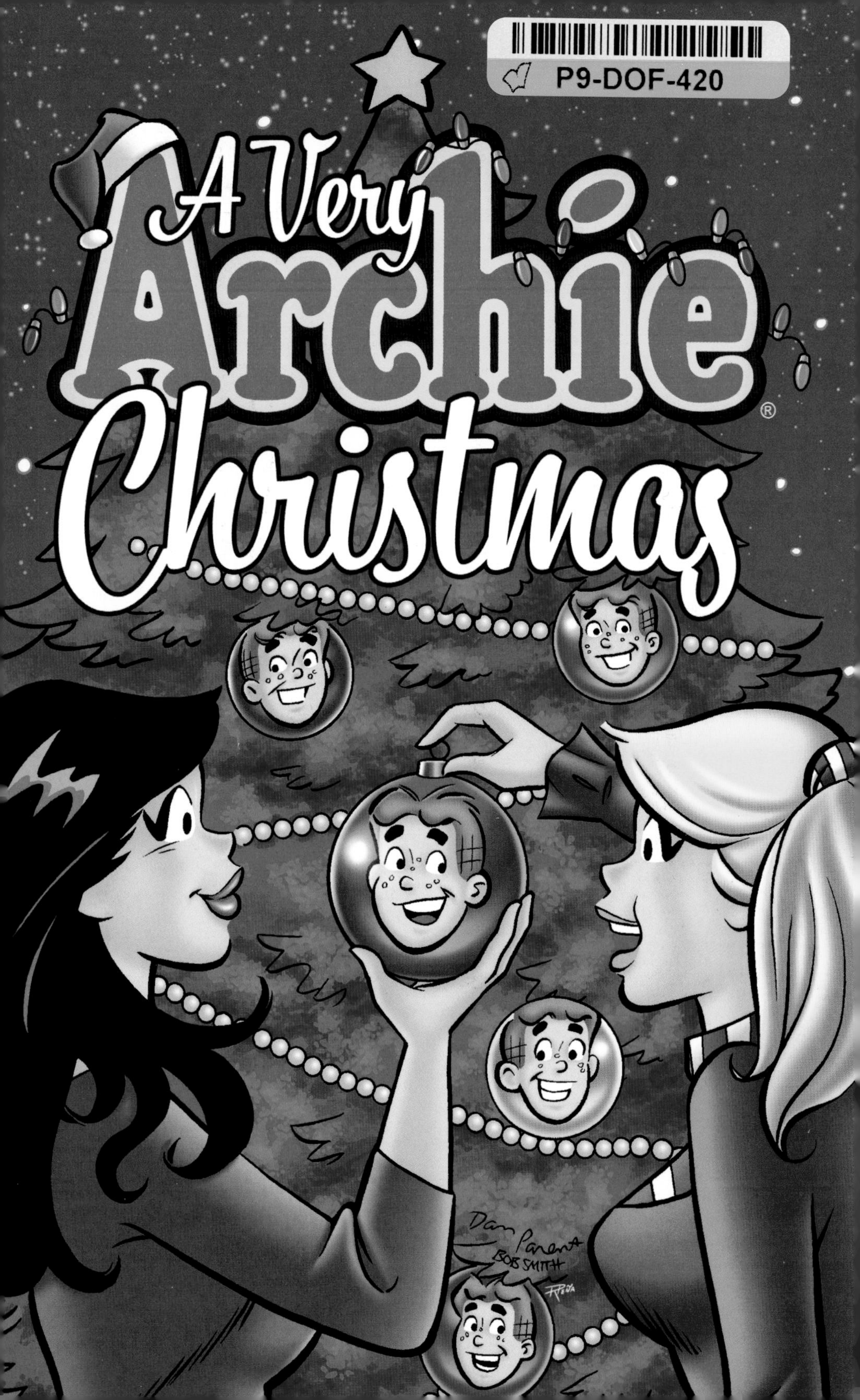
A Very
Archie®
Christmas
Dan Parent
BOB SMITH

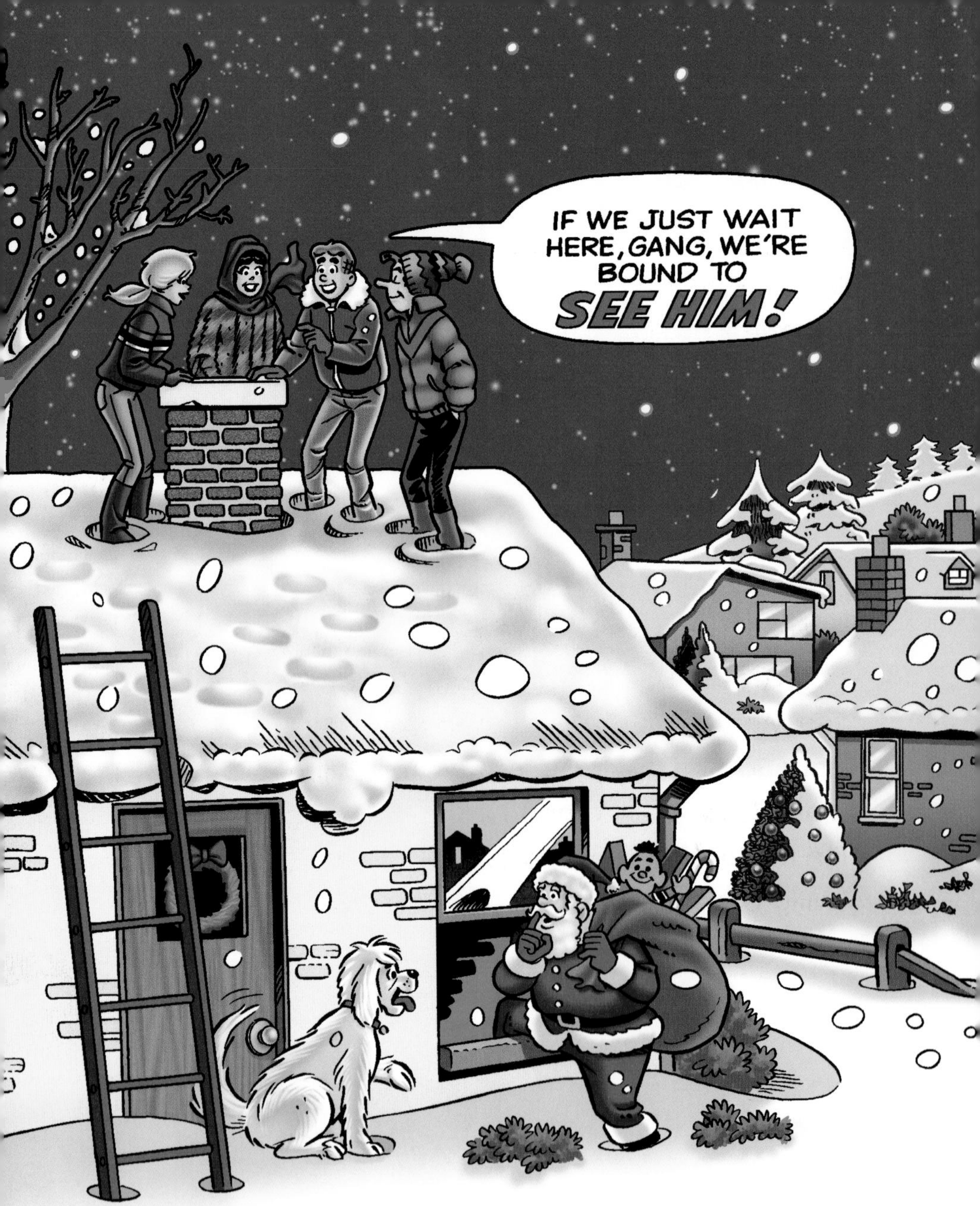
IF WE JUST WAIT HERE, GANG, WE'RE BOUND TO SEE HIM!

Publisher / Co-CEO: Jon Goldwater
President / Editor-In-Chief: Mike Pellerito
Chief Creative Officer: Roberto Aguirre-Sacasa
Chief Operating Officer: William Mooar
Chief Financial Officer: Robert Wintle
Director: Jonathan Betancourt
Senior Director of Editorial: Jamie Lee Rotante
Production Manager: Stephen Oswald
Art Director: Vincent Lovallo
Lead Designer: Kari McLachlan
Associate Editor: Carlos Antunes
Co-CEO: Nancy Silberkleit

STORIES BY

Frank Doyle, George Gladir, Al Hartley, Rich Margopoulos, Kathleen Webb, Dan Parent, Bill Golliher, & Ron Robbins

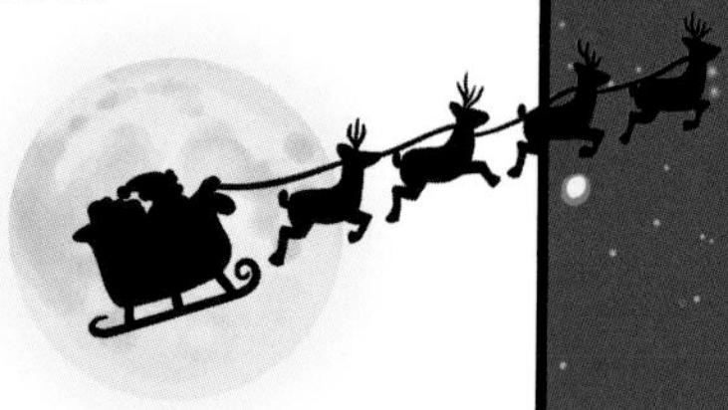

ART BY

Harry Lucey, Dan DeCarlo, Al Hartley, Jon D'Agostino, Bill Yoshida, Barry Grossman, Rudy Lapick, Bob Bolling, Dan DeCarlo Jr, Alisa Merrill, Jim DeCarlo, Stan Goldberg, Henry Scarpelli, Dan Parent, Alison Flood, Dexter Taylor, Pat Kennedy, Tim Kennedy, Rich Koslowski, Jack Morelli, Jeff Shultz, Al Milgrom, Jim Amash, & Glenn Whitmore

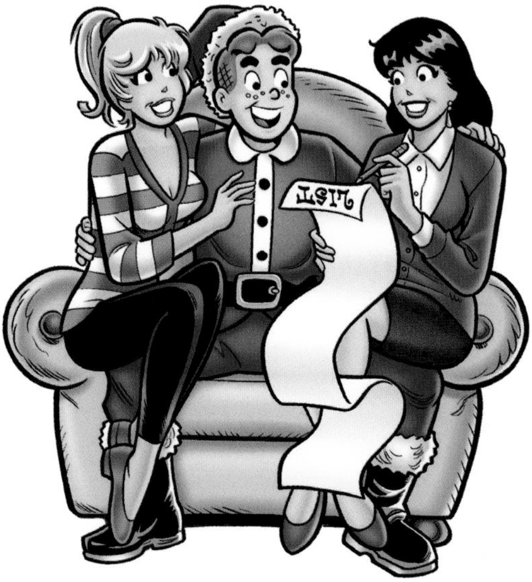

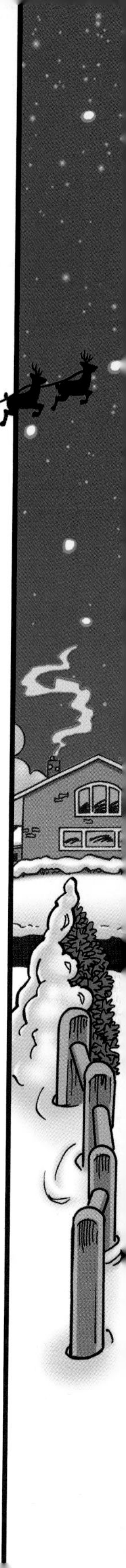

TABLE OF CONTENTS

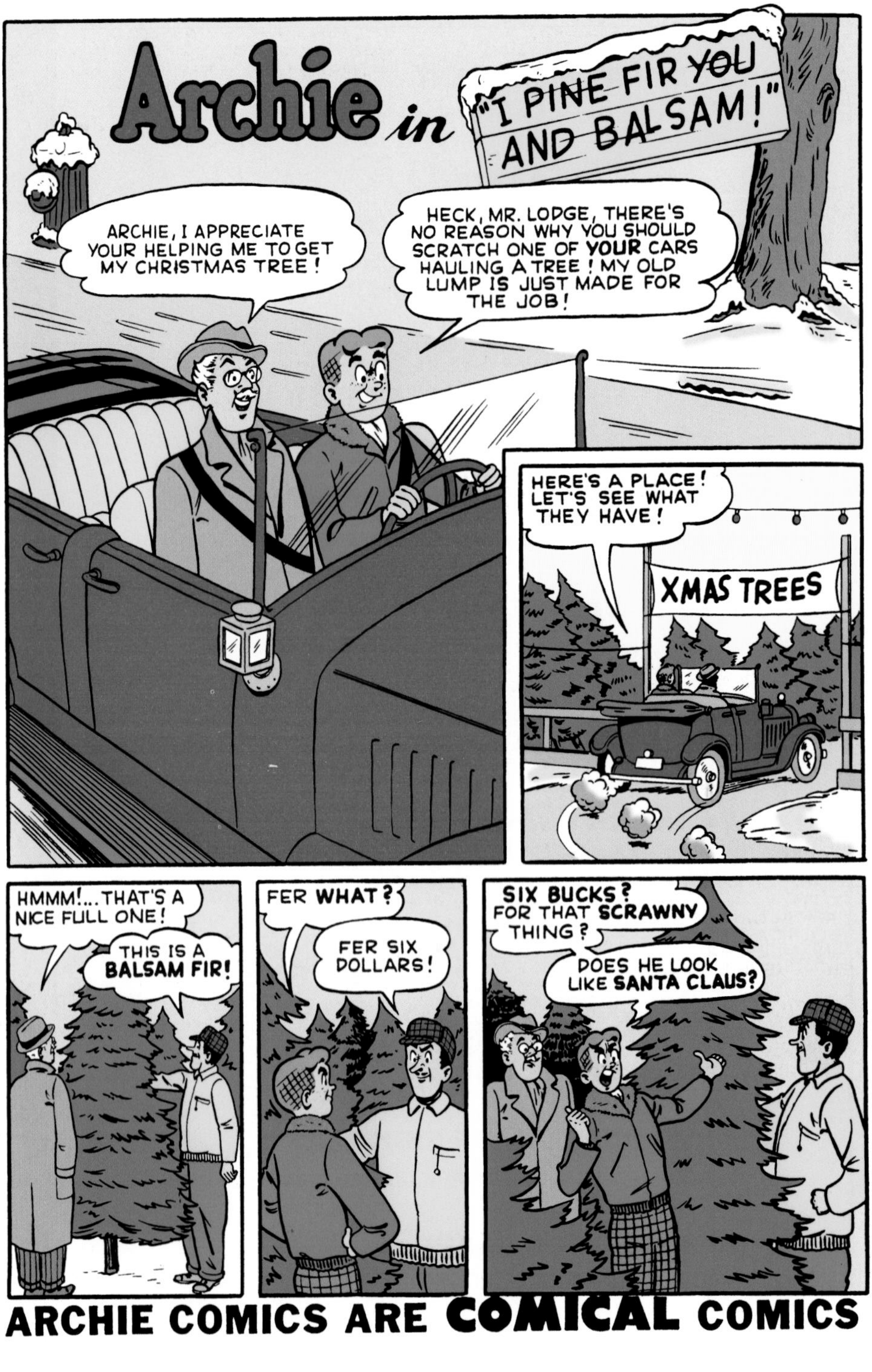
Archie in
"I PINE FIR YOU AND BALSAM!"
ARCHIE, I APPRECIATE YOUR HELPING ME TO GET MY CHRISTMAS TREE!
HECK, MR. LODGE, THERE'S NO REASON WHY YOU SHOULD SCRATCH ONE OF YOUR CARS HAULING A TREE! MY OLD LUMP IS JUST MADE FOR THE JOB!
HERE'S A PLACE! LET'S SEE WHAT THEY HAVE!
XMAS TREES
HMMM!... THAT'S A NICE FULL ONE!
THIS IS A BALSAM FIR!
FER WHAT?
FER SIX DOLLARS!
SIX BUCKS? FOR THAT SCRAWNY THING?
DOES HE LOOK LIKE SANTA CLAUS?
ARCHIE COMICS ARE COMICAL COMICS

Harry Lucey

Originally printed in ARCHIE GIANT SERIES MAGAZINE #4, 1957

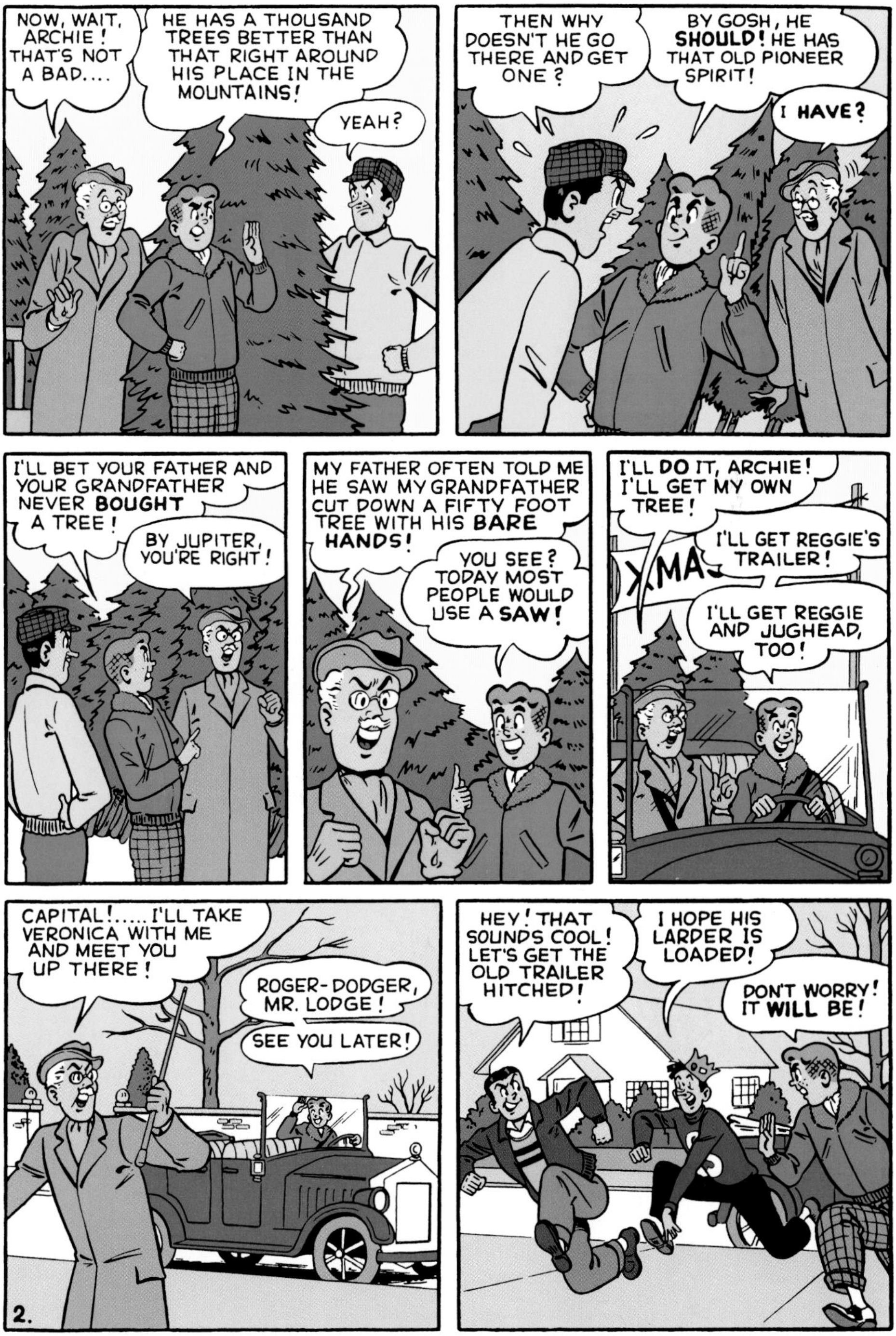
NOW, WAIT, ARCHIE! THAT'S NOT A BAD....
HE HAS A THOUSAND TREES BETTER THAN THAT RIGHT AROUND HIS PLACE IN THE MOUNTAINS!
YEAH?
THEN WHY DOESN'T HE GO THERE AND GET ONE?
BY GOSH, HE SHOULD! HE HAS THAT OLD PIONEER SPIRIT!
I HAVE?
I'LL BET YOUR FATHER AND YOUR GRANDFATHER NEVER BOUGHT A TREE!
BY JUPITER, YOU'RE RIGHT!
MY FATHER OFTEN TOLD ME HE SAW MY GRANDFATHER CUT DOWN A FIFTY FOOT TREE WITH HIS BARE HANDS!
YOU SEE? TODAY MOST PEOPLE WOULD USE A SAW!
I'LL DO IT, ARCHIE! I'LL GET MY OWN TREE!
I'LL GET REGGIE'S TRAILER!
I'LL GET REGGIE AND JUGHEAD, TOO!
CAPITAL!..... I'LL TAKE VERONICA WITH ME AND MEET YOU UP THERE!
ROGER-DODGER, MR. LODGE!
SEE YOU LATER!
2.
HEY! THAT SOUNDS COOL! LET'S GET THE OLD TRAILER HITCHED!
I HOPE HIS LARDER IS LOADED!
DON'T WORRY! IT WILL BE!

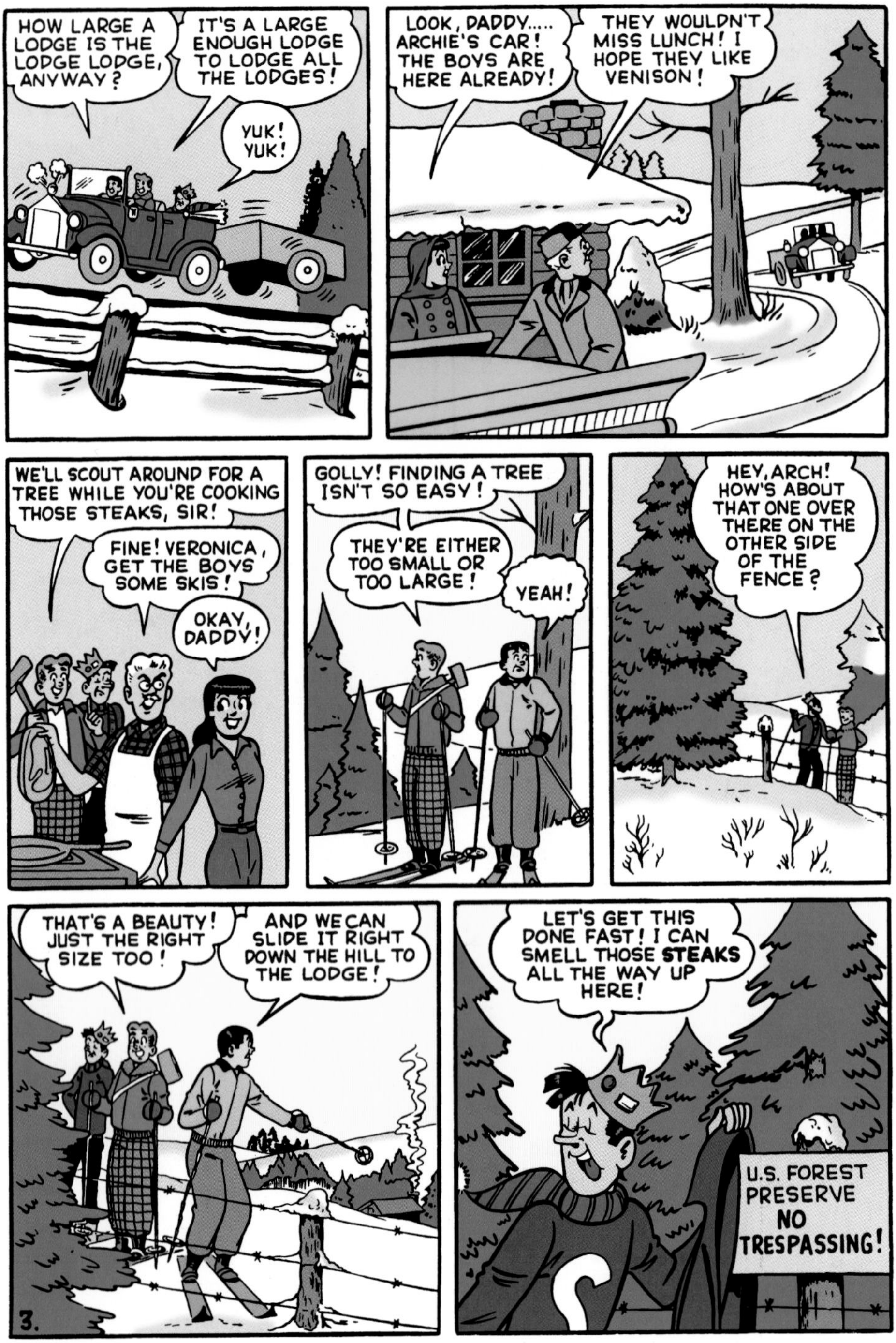
HOW LARGE A LODGE IS THE LODGE LODGE, ANYWAY?
IT'S A LARGE ENOUGH LODGE TO LODGE ALL THE LODGES!
YUK! YUK!
LOOK, DADDY..... ARCHIE'S CAR! THE BOYS ARE HERE ALREADY!
THEY WOULDN'T MISS LUNCH! I HOPE THEY LIKE VENISON!
WE'LL SCOUT AROUND FOR A TREE WHILE YOU'RE COOKING THOSE STEAKS, SIR!
FINE! VERONICA, GET THE BOYS SOME SKIS!
OKAY, DADDY!
GOLLY! FINDING A TREE ISN'T SO EASY!
THEY'RE EITHER TOO SMALL OR TOO LARGE!
YEAH!
HEY, ARCH! HOW'S ABOUT THAT ONE OVER THERE ON THE OTHER SIDE OF THE FENCE?
THAT'S A BEAUTY! JUST THE RIGHT SIZE TOO!
AND WE CAN SLIDE IT RIGHT DOWN THE HILL TO THE LODGE!
3.
LET'S GET THIS DONE FAST! I CAN SMELL THOSE STEAKS ALL THE WAY UP HERE!
U.S. FOREST PRESERVE
NO TRESPASSING!

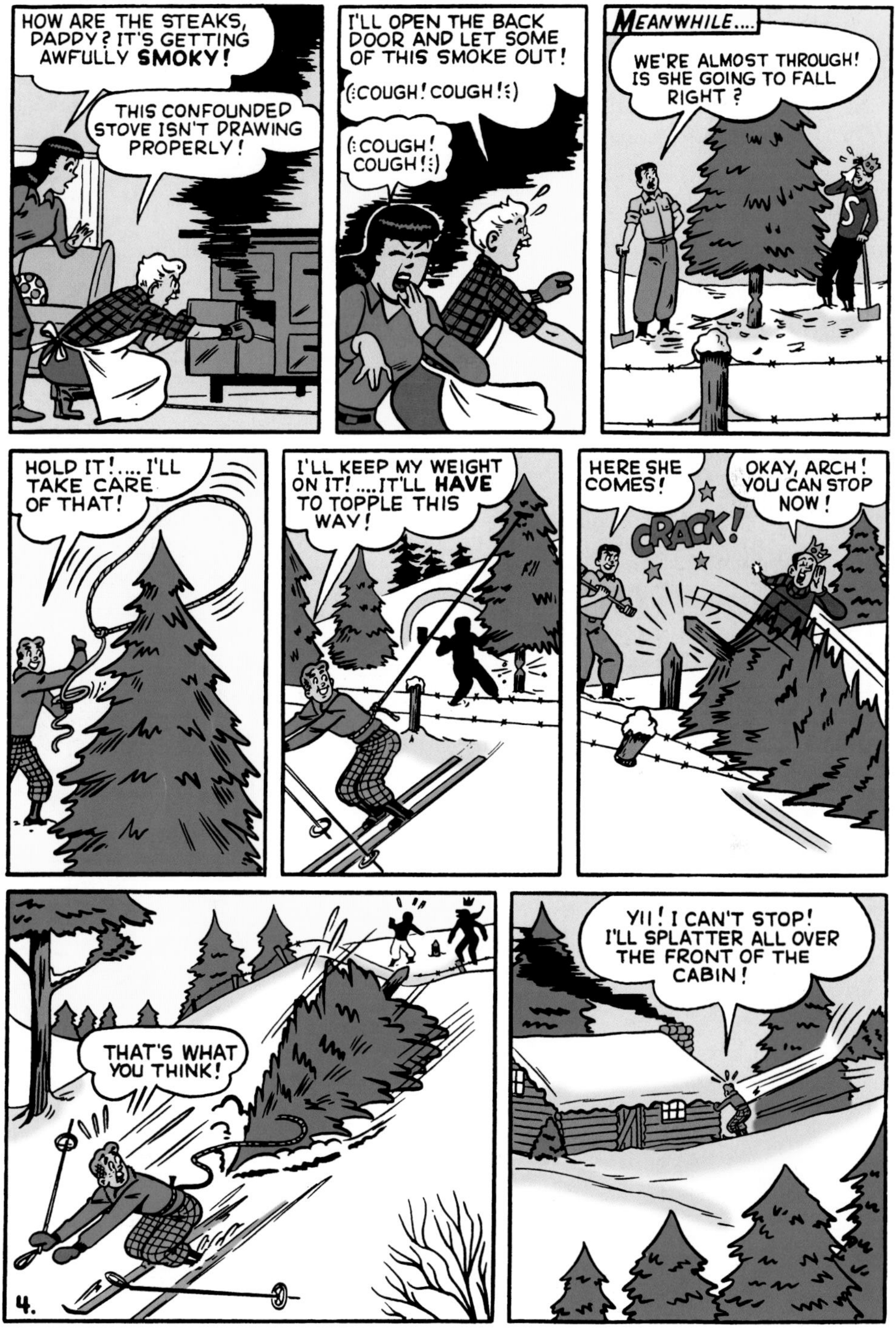
HOW ARE THE STEAKS, DADDY? IT'S GETTING AWFULLY SMOKY!
THIS CONFOUNDED STOVE ISN'T DRAWING PROPERLY!
I'LL OPEN THE BACK DOOR AND LET SOME OF THIS SMOKE OUT!
(COUGH! COUGH!)
(COUGH! COUGH!)
MEANWHILE....
WE'RE ALMOST THROUGH! IS SHE GOING TO FALL RIGHT?
HOLD IT!.... I'LL TAKE CARE OF THAT!
I'LL KEEP MY WEIGHT ON IT! ....IT'LL HAVE TO TOPPLE THIS WAY!
HERE SHE COMES!
OKAY, ARCH! YOU CAN STOP NOW!
CRACK!
THAT'S WHAT YOU THINK!
4.
YII! I CAN'T STOP! I'LL SPLATTER ALL OVER THE FRONT OF THE CABIN!

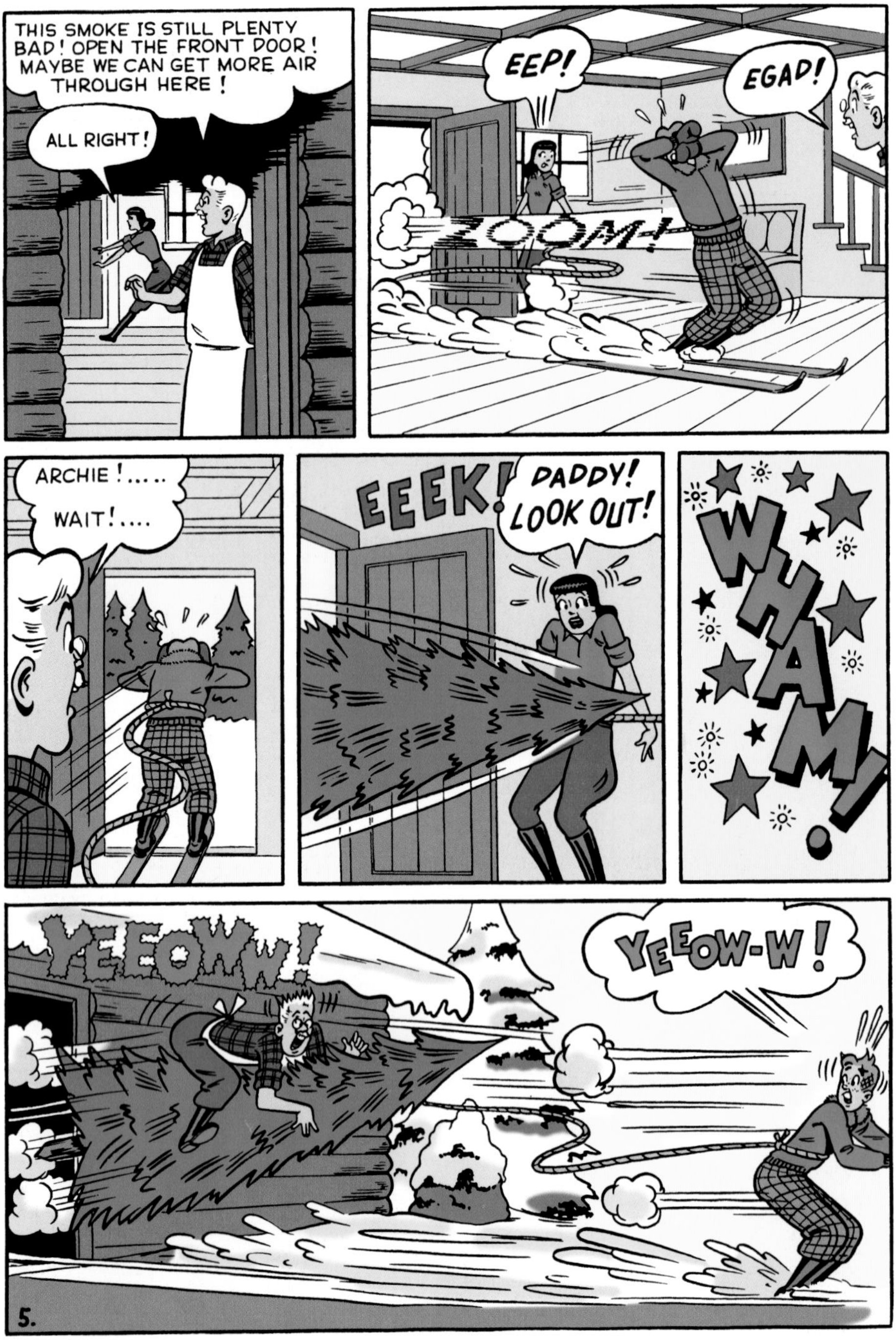
THIS SMOKE IS STILL PLENTY BAD! OPEN THE FRONT DOOR! MAYBE WE CAN GET MORE AIR THROUGH HERE!
ALL RIGHT!
EEP!
EGAD!
ZOOM!
ARCHIE!.....
WAIT!....
EEEK!
DADDY! LOOK OUT!
WHAM!
YEEOWW!
YEEOW-W!
5.

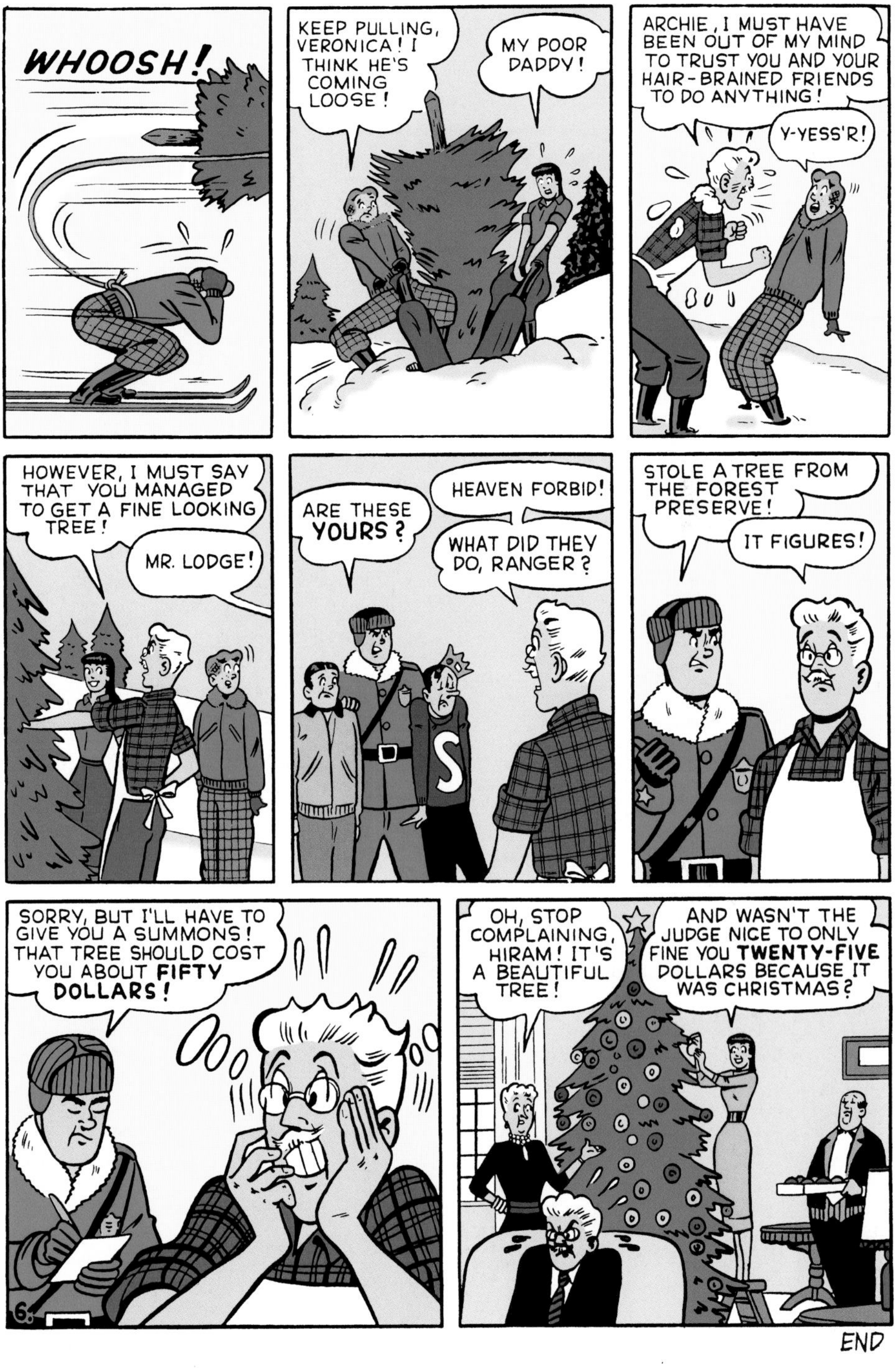
WHOOSH!
KEEP PULLING, VERONICA! I THINK HE'S COMING LOOSE!
MY POOR DADDY!
ARCHIE, I MUST HAVE BEEN OUT OF MY MIND TO TRUST YOU AND YOUR HAIR-BRAINED FRIENDS TO DO ANYTHING!
Y-YESS'R!
HOWEVER, I MUST SAY THAT YOU MANAGED TO GET A FINE LOOKING TREE!
MR. LODGE!
ARE THESE YOURS?
HEAVEN FORBID!
WHAT DID THEY DO, RANGER?
STOLE A TREE FROM THE FOREST PRESERVE!
IT FIGURES!
SORRY, BUT I'LL HAVE TO GIVE YOU A SUMMONS! THAT TREE SHOULD COST YOU ABOUT FIFTY DOLLARS!
6
OH, STOP COMPLAINING, HIRAM! IT'S A BEAUTIFUL TREE!
AND WASN'T THE JUDGE NICE TO ONLY FINE YOU TWENTY-FIVE DOLLARS BECAUSE IT WAS CHRISTMAS?
END

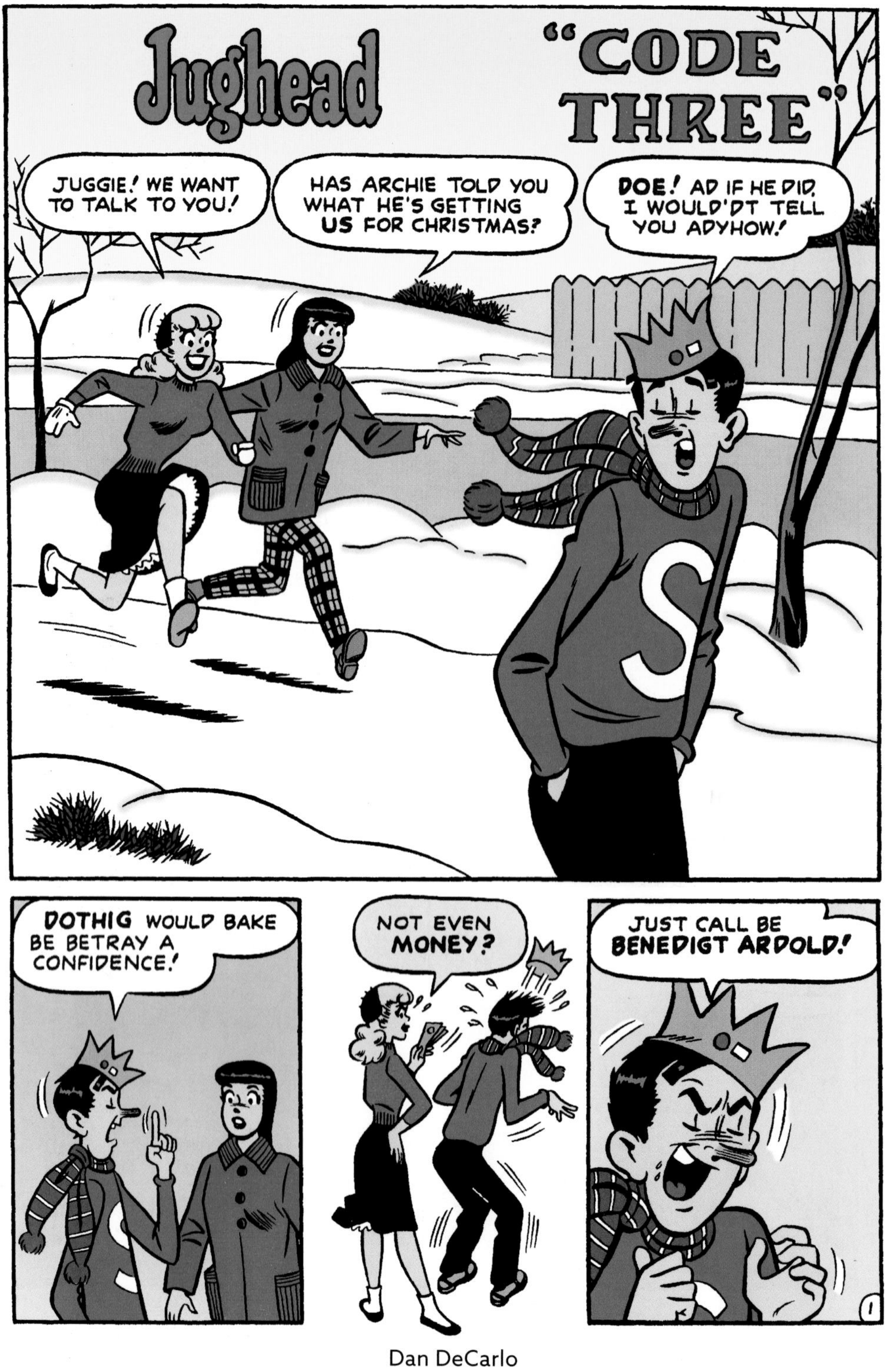
Jughead
"CODE THREE"
JUGGIE! WE WANT TO TALK TO YOU!
HAS ARCHIE TOLD YOU WHAT HE'S GETTING US FOR CHRISTMAS?
DOE! AD IF HE DID, I WOULD'DT TELL YOU ADYHOW!
DOTHIG WOULD BAKE BE BETRAY A CONFIDENCE!
NOT EVEN MONEY?
JUST CALL BE BENEDIGT ARDOLD!
1

Dan DeCarlo

Originally printed in ARCHIE GIANT SERIES MAGAZINE #10, 1961

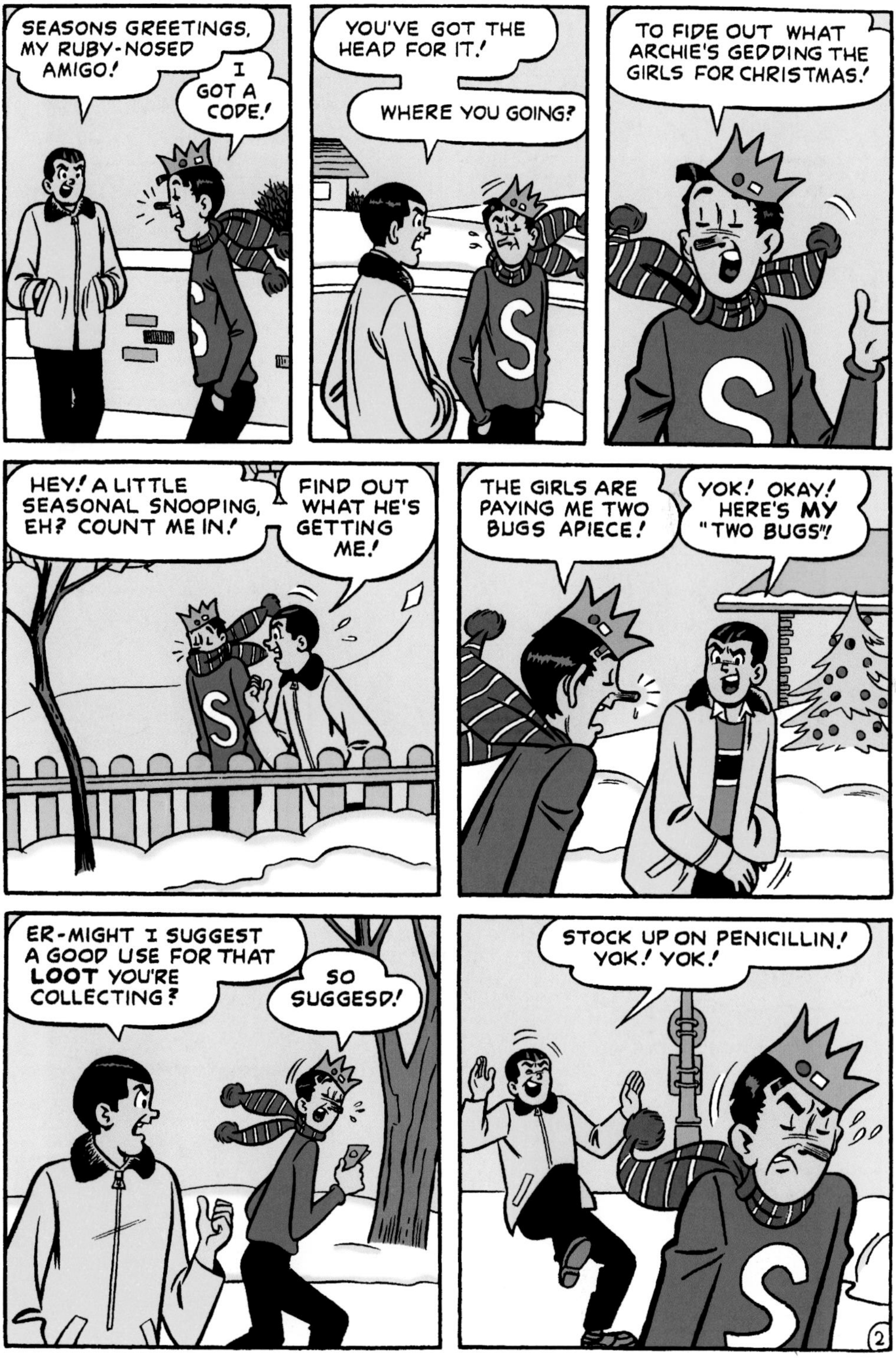
SEASONS GREETINGS, MY RUBY-NOSED AMIGO!
I GOT A CODE!
YOU'VE GOT THE HEAD FOR IT!
WHERE YOU GOING?
TO FIDE OUT WHAT ARCHIE'S GEDDING THE GIRLS FOR CHRISTMAS!
HEY! A LITTLE SEASONAL SNOOPING, EH? COUNT ME IN!
FIND OUT WHAT HE'S GETTING ME!
THE GIRLS ARE PAYING ME TWO BUGS APIECE!
YOK! OKAY! HERE'S MY "TWO BUGS"!
ER-MIGHT I SUGGEST A GOOD USE FOR THAT LOOT YOU'RE COLLECTING?
SO SUGGESD!
STOCK UP ON PENICILLIN! YOK! YOK!
2

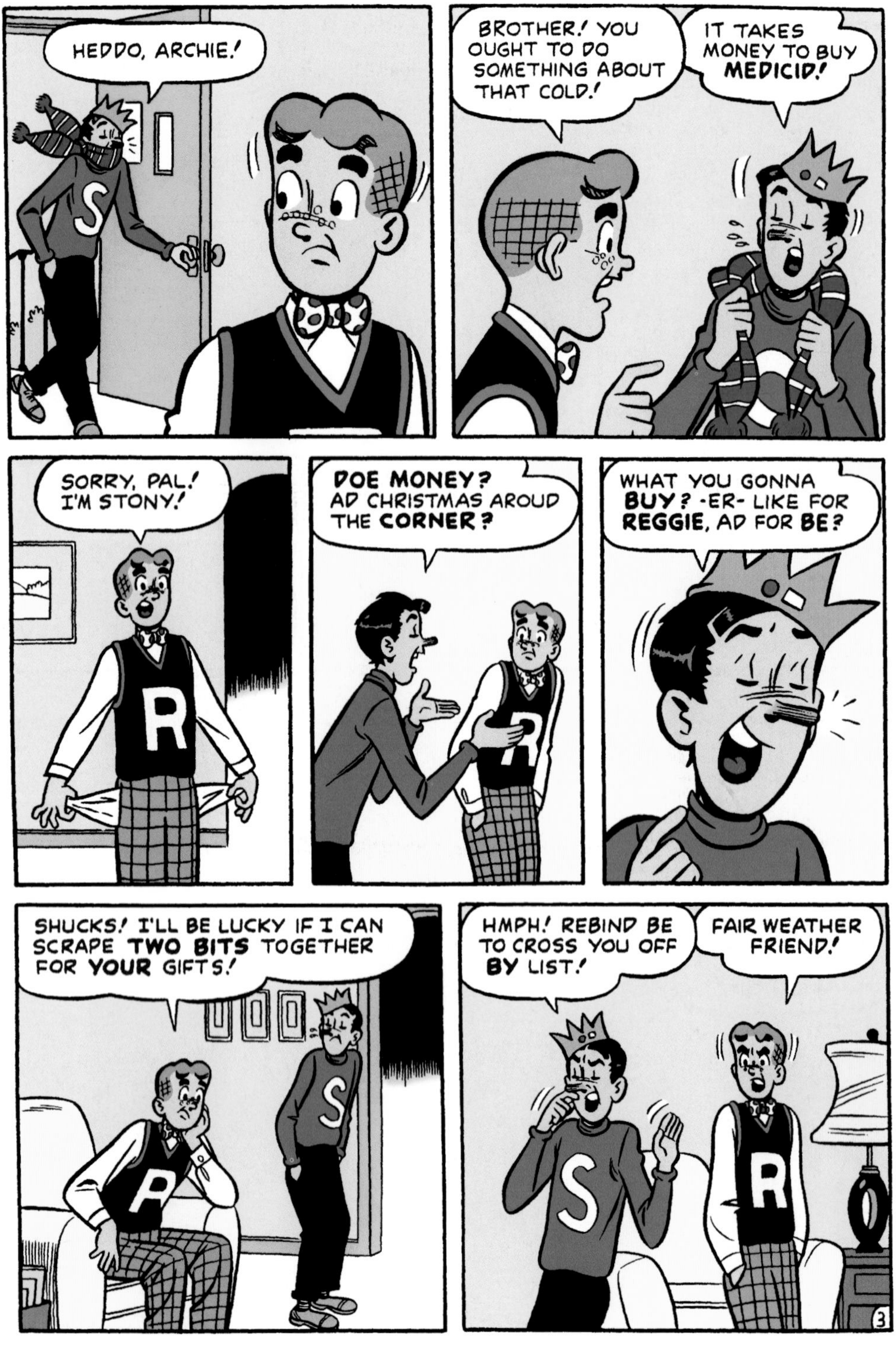
HEDDO, ARCHIE!
BROTHER! YOU OUGHT TO DO SOMETHING ABOUT THAT COLD!
IT TAKES MONEY TO BUY MEDICID!
SORRY, PAL! I'M STONY!
DOE MONEY? AD CHRISTMAS AROUD THE CORNER?
WHAT YOU GONNA BUY? -ER- LIKE FOR REGGIE, AD FOR BE?
SHUCKS! I'LL BE LUCKY IF I CAN SCRAPE TWO BITS TOGETHER FOR YOUR GIFTS!
HMPH! REBIND BE TO CROSS YOU OFF BY LIST!
FAIR WEATHER FRIEND!
3

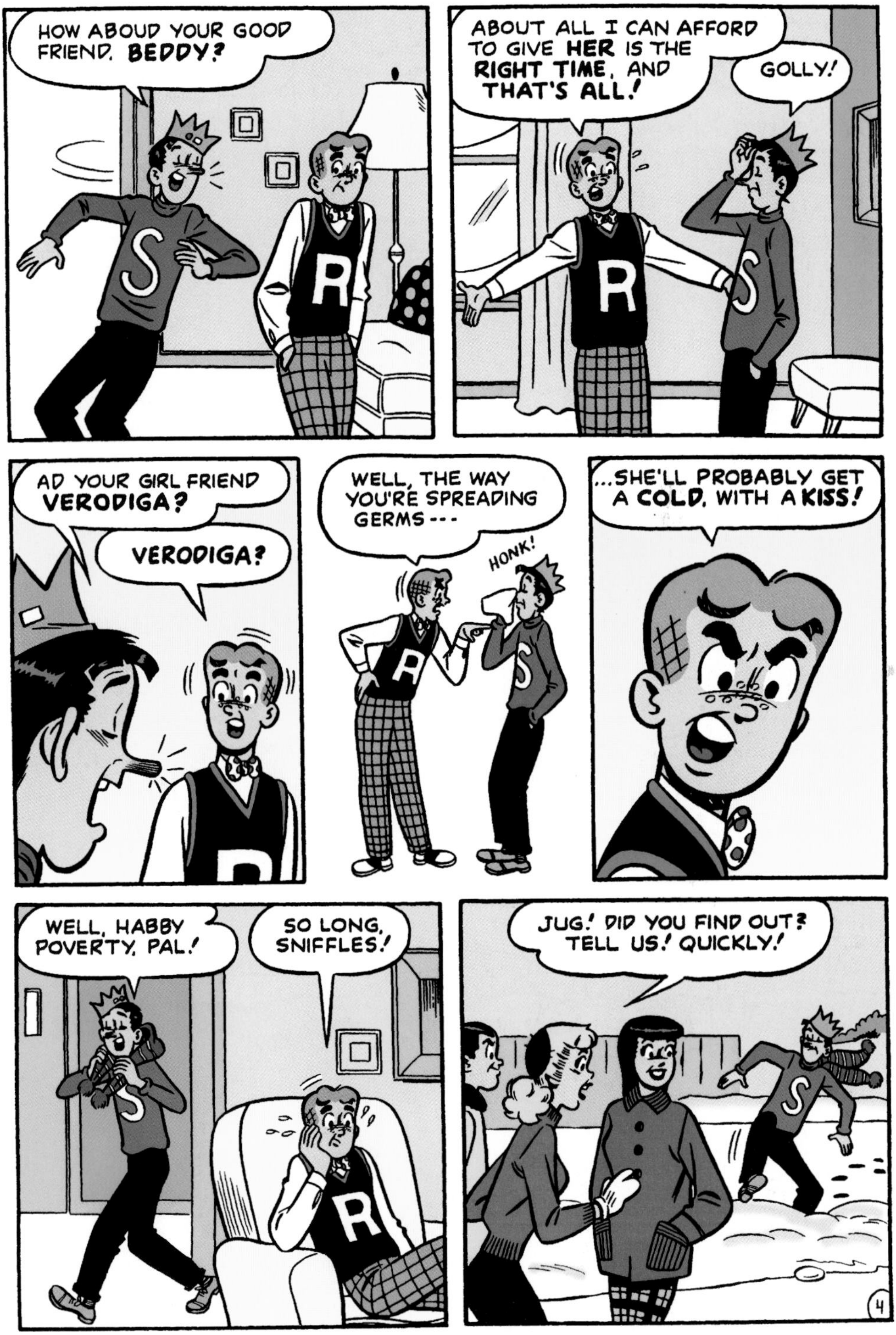
HOW ABOUD YOUR GOOD FRIEND. BEDDY?
ABOUT ALL I CAN AFFORD TO GIVE HER IS THE RIGHT TIME, AND THAT'S ALL!
GOLLY!
AD YOUR GIRL FRIEND VERODIGA?
VERODIGA?
WELL, THE WAY YOU'RE SPREADING GERMS ---
HONK!
...SHE'LL PROBABLY GET A COLD, WITH A KISS!
WELL, HABBY POVERTY, PAL!
SO LONG, SNIFFLES!
JUG! DID YOU FIND OUT? TELL US! QUICKLY!
4

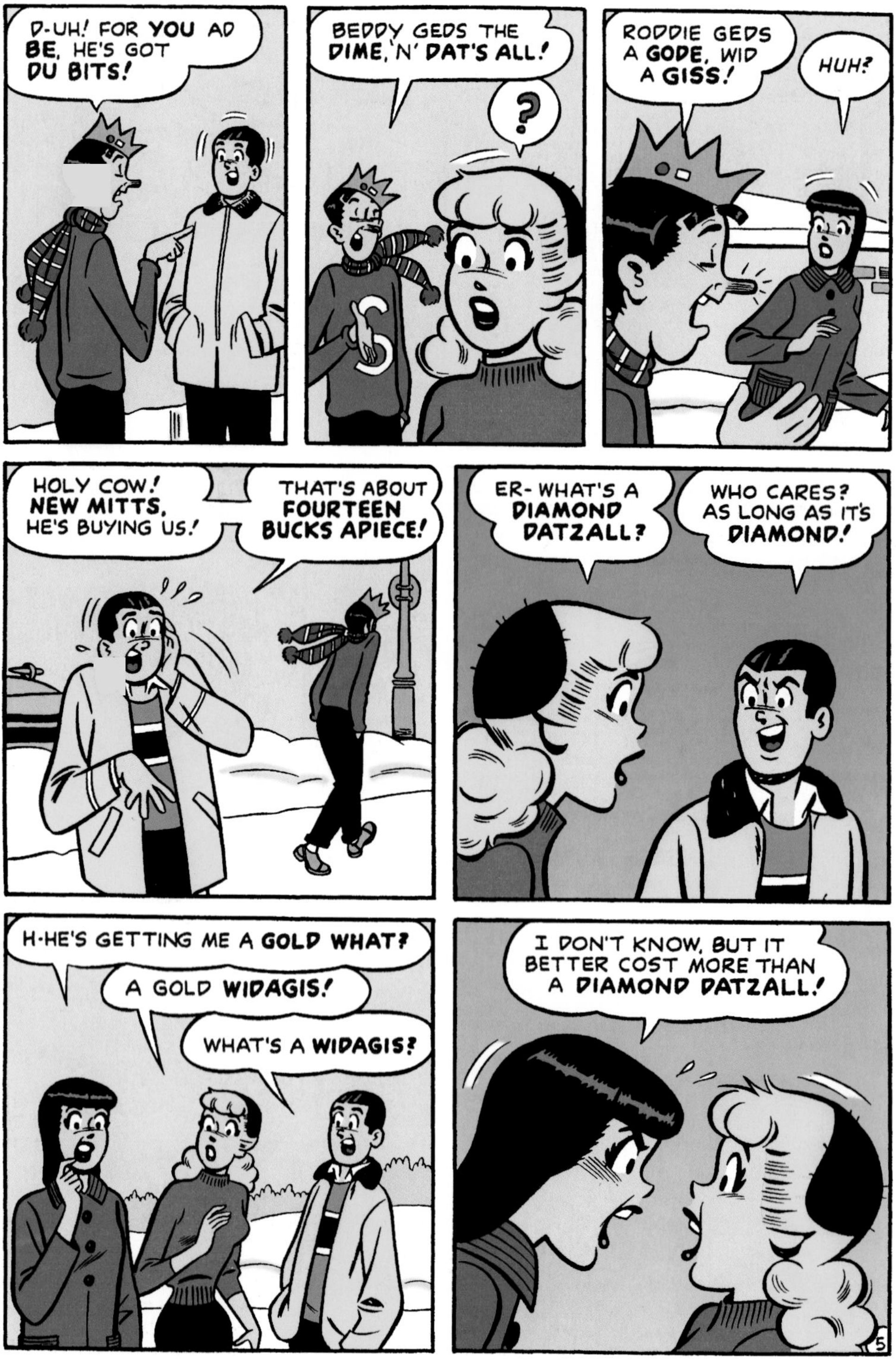
D-UH! FOR **YOU** AD **BE**, HE'S GOT **DU BITS!**
BEDDY GEDS THE **DIME**, 'N' **DAT'S ALL!**
?
RODDIE GEDS A **GODE**, WID A **GISS!**
HUH?
HOLY COW! **NEW MITTS**, HE'S BUYING US!
THAT'S ABOUT **FOURTEEN BUCKS APIECE!**
ER- WHAT'S A **DIAMOND DATZALL?**
WHO CARES? AS LONG AS IT'S **DIAMOND!**
H-HE'S GETTING ME A **GOLD WHAT?**
A GOLD **WIDAGIS!**
WHAT'S A **WIDAGIS?**
I DON'T KNOW, BUT IT BETTER COST MORE THAN A **DIAMOND DATZALL!**
5

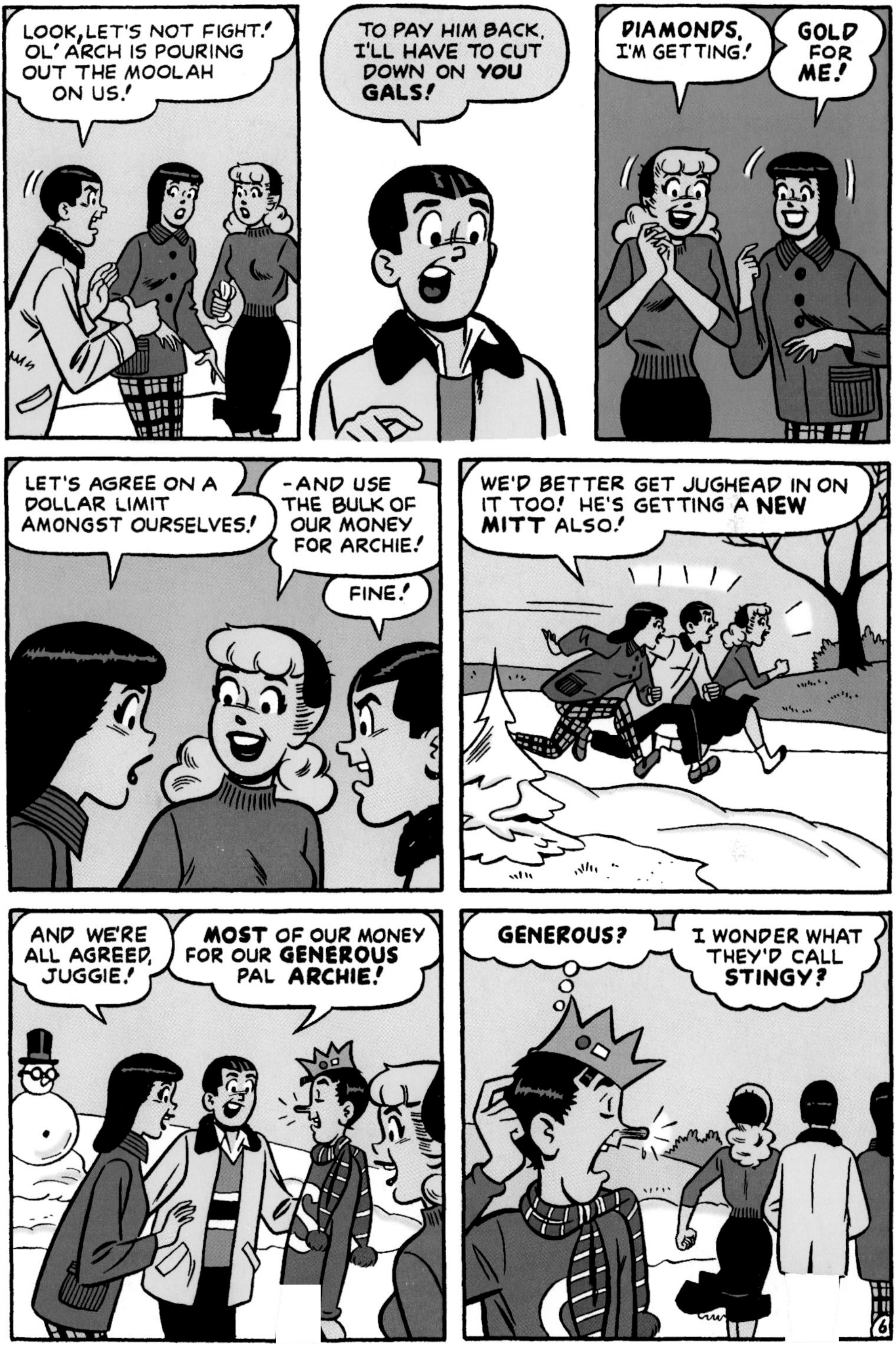
LOOK, LET'S NOT FIGHT! OL' ARCH IS POURING OUT THE MOOLAH ON US!
TO PAY HIM BACK, I'LL HAVE TO CUT DOWN ON YOU GALS!
DIAMONDS, I'M GETTING!
GOLD FOR ME!
LET'S AGREE ON A DOLLAR LIMIT AMONGST OURSELVES!
-AND USE THE BULK OF OUR MONEY FOR ARCHIE!
FINE!
WE'D BETTER GET JUGHEAD IN ON IT TOO! HE'S GETTING A NEW MITT ALSO!
AND WE'RE ALL AGREED, JUGGIE!
MOST OF OUR MONEY FOR OUR GENEROUS PAL ARCHIE!
GENEROUS?
I WONDER WHAT THEY'D CALL STINGY?
6

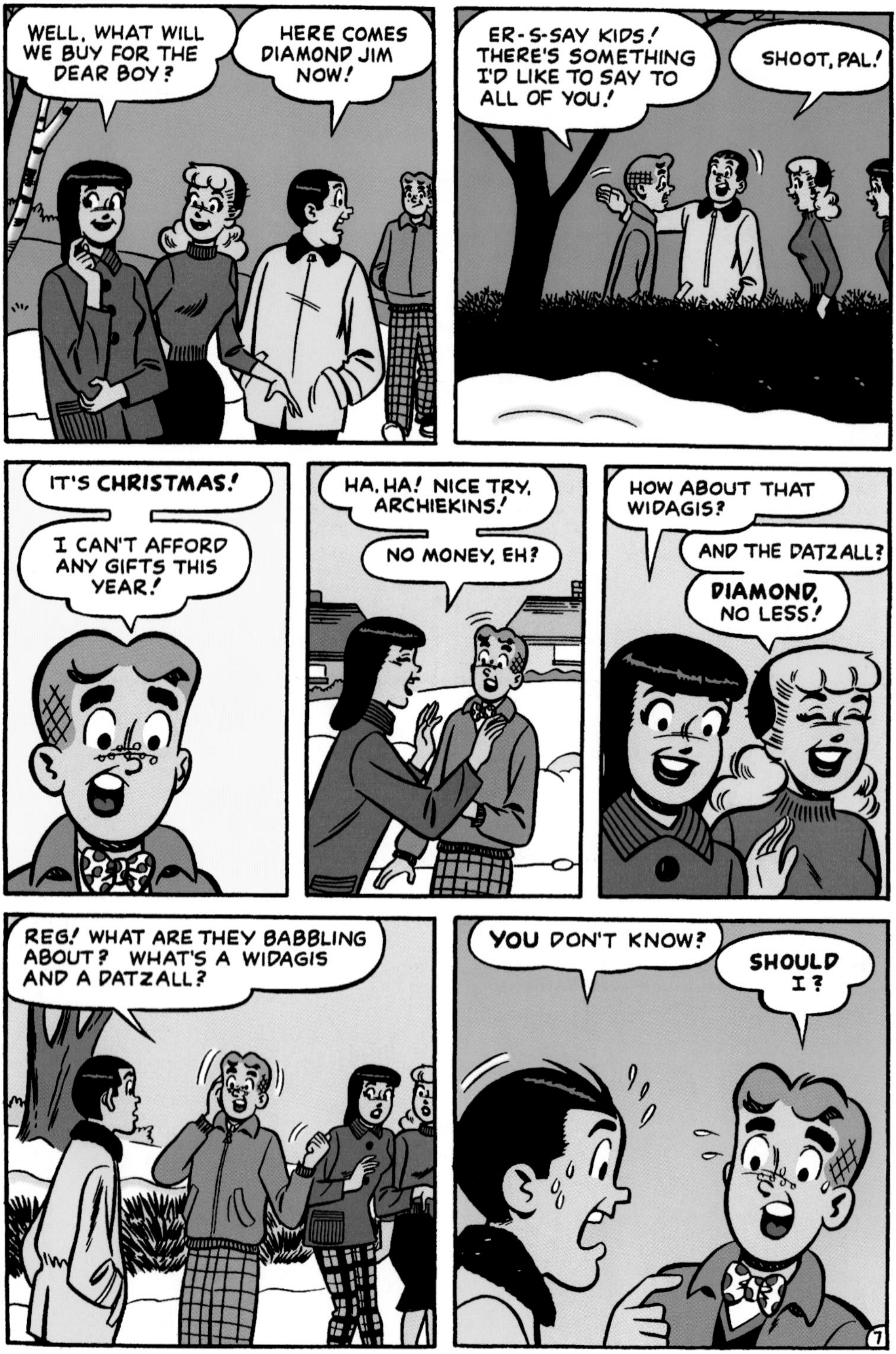
WELL, WHAT WILL WE BUY FOR THE DEAR BOY?
HERE COMES DIAMOND JIM NOW!
ER-S-SAY KIDS! THERE'S SOMETHING I'D LIKE TO SAY TO ALL OF YOU!
SHOOT, PAL!
IT'S CHRISTMAS!
I CAN'T AFFORD ANY GIFTS THIS YEAR!
HA, HA! NICE TRY, ARCHIEKINS!
NO MONEY, EH?
HOW ABOUT THAT WIDAGIS?
AND THE DATZALL?
DIAMOND, NO LESS!
REG! WHAT ARE THEY BABBLING ABOUT? WHAT'S A WIDAGIS AND A DATZALL?
YOU DON'T KNOW?
SHOULD I?
7

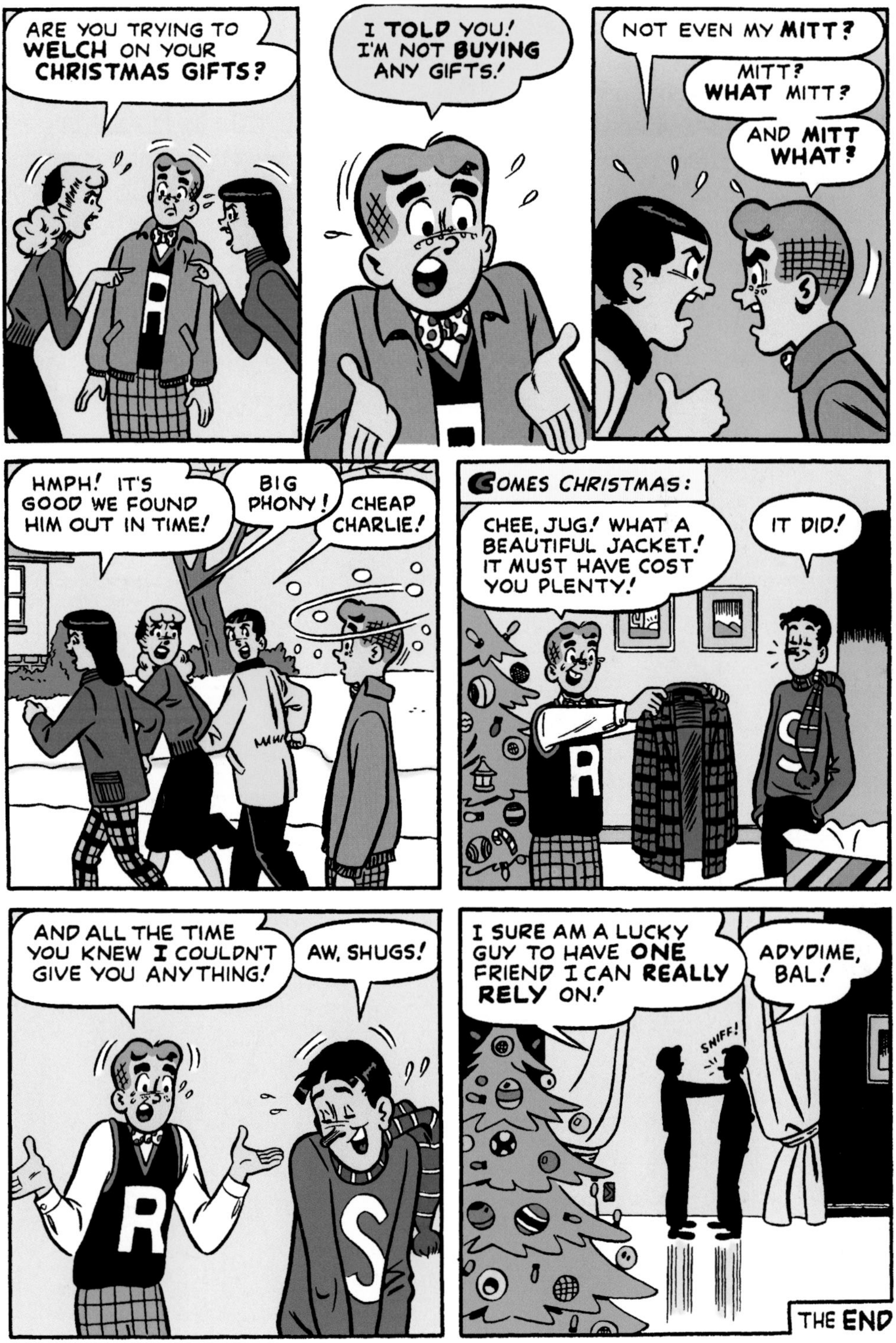
ARE YOU TRYING TO WELCH ON YOUR CHRISTMAS GIFTS?
I TOLD YOU! I'M NOT BUYING ANY GIFTS!
NOT EVEN MY MITT?
MITT? WHAT MITT?
AND MITT WHAT?
HMPH! IT'S GOOD WE FOUND HIM OUT IN TIME!
BIG PHONY!
CHEAP CHARLIE!
COMES CHRISTMAS:
CHEE, JUG! WHAT A BEAUTIFUL JACKET! IT MUST HAVE COST YOU PLENTY!
IT DID!
AND ALL THE TIME YOU KNEW I COULDN'T GIVE YOU ANYTHING!
AW, SHUGS!
I SURE AM A LUCKY GUY TO HAVE ONE FRIEND I CAN REALLY RELY ON!
ADYDIME, BAL!
SNIFF!
THE END

Betty and Veronica in "Yule Tide Fool Time"

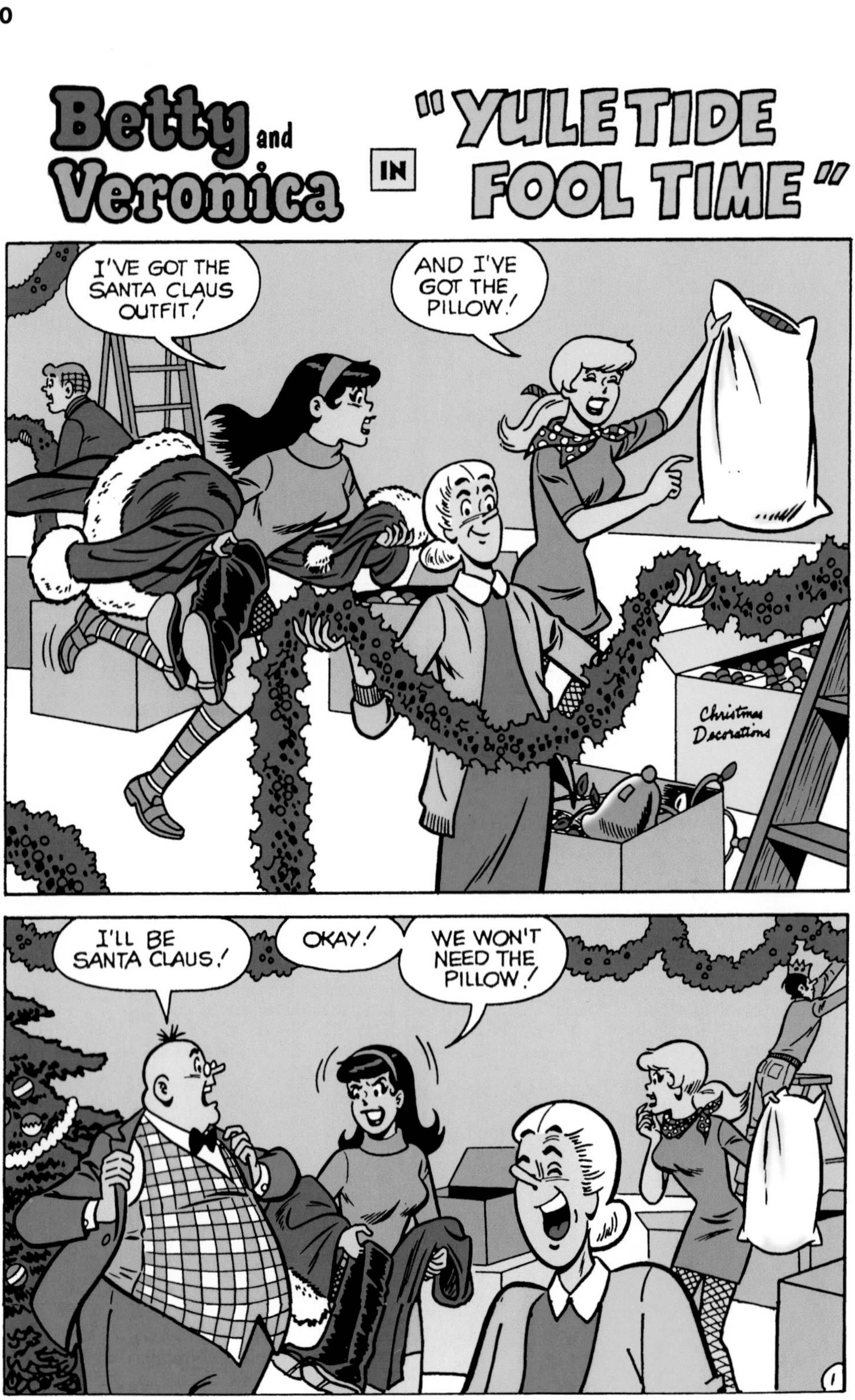
I'VE GOT THE SANTA CLAUS OUTFIT!
AND I'VE GOT THE PILLOW!
Christmas Decorations
I'LL BE SANTA CLAUS!
OKAY!
WE WON'T NEED THE PILLOW!
1

Al Hartley • Jon D'Agostino • Bill Yoshida • Barry Grossman

Originally printed in ARCHIE GIANT SERIES MAGAZINE #168, 1970

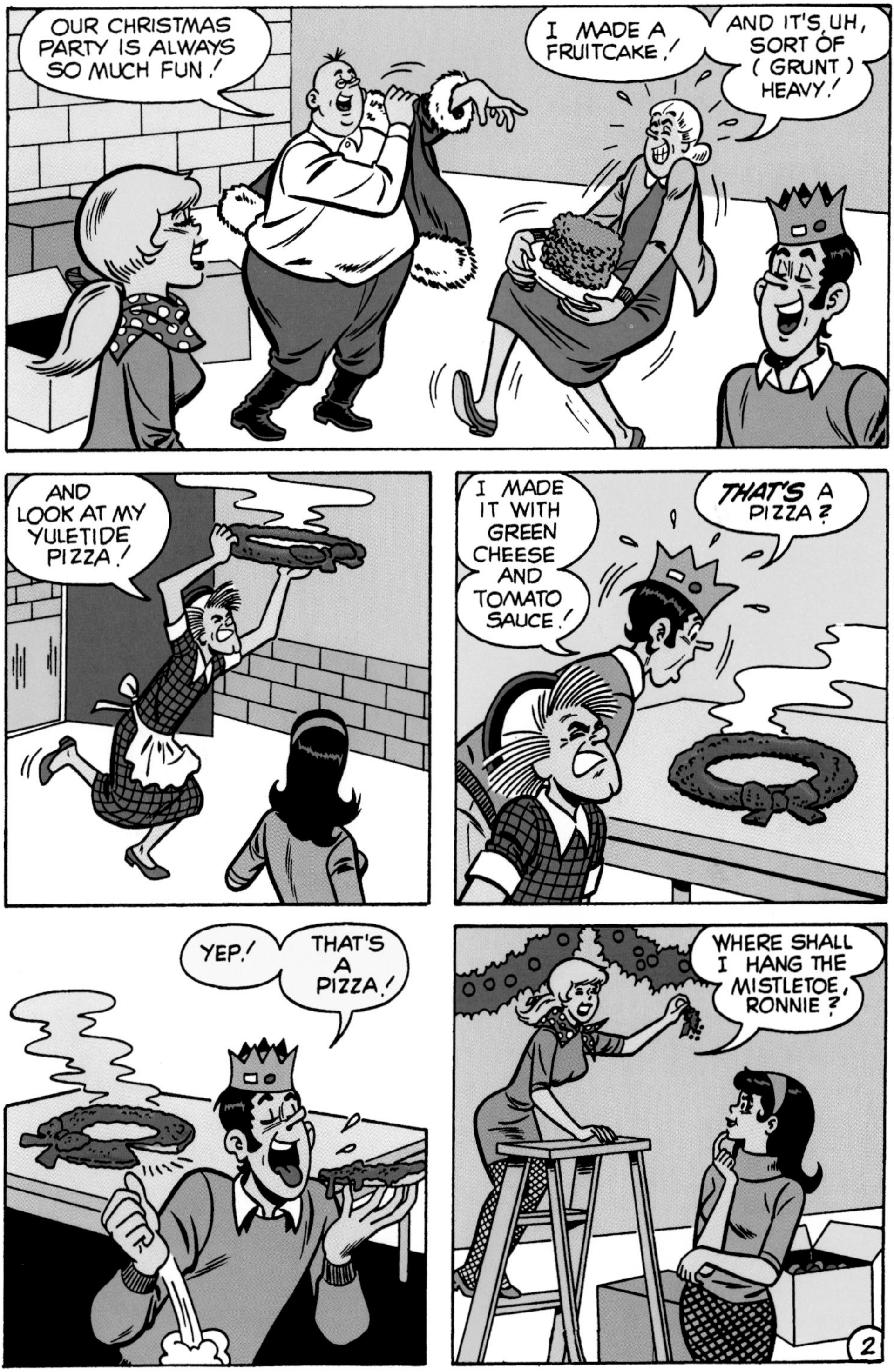
OUR CHRISTMAS PARTY IS ALWAYS SO MUCH FUN!
I MADE A FRUITCAKE!
AND IT'S, UH, SORT OF (GRUNT) HEAVY!
AND LOOK AT MY YULETIDE PIZZA!
I MADE IT WITH GREEN CHEESE AND TOMATO SAUCE!
THAT'S A PIZZA?
YEP!
THAT'S A PIZZA!
WHERE SHALL I HANG THE MISTLETOE, RONNIE?
2

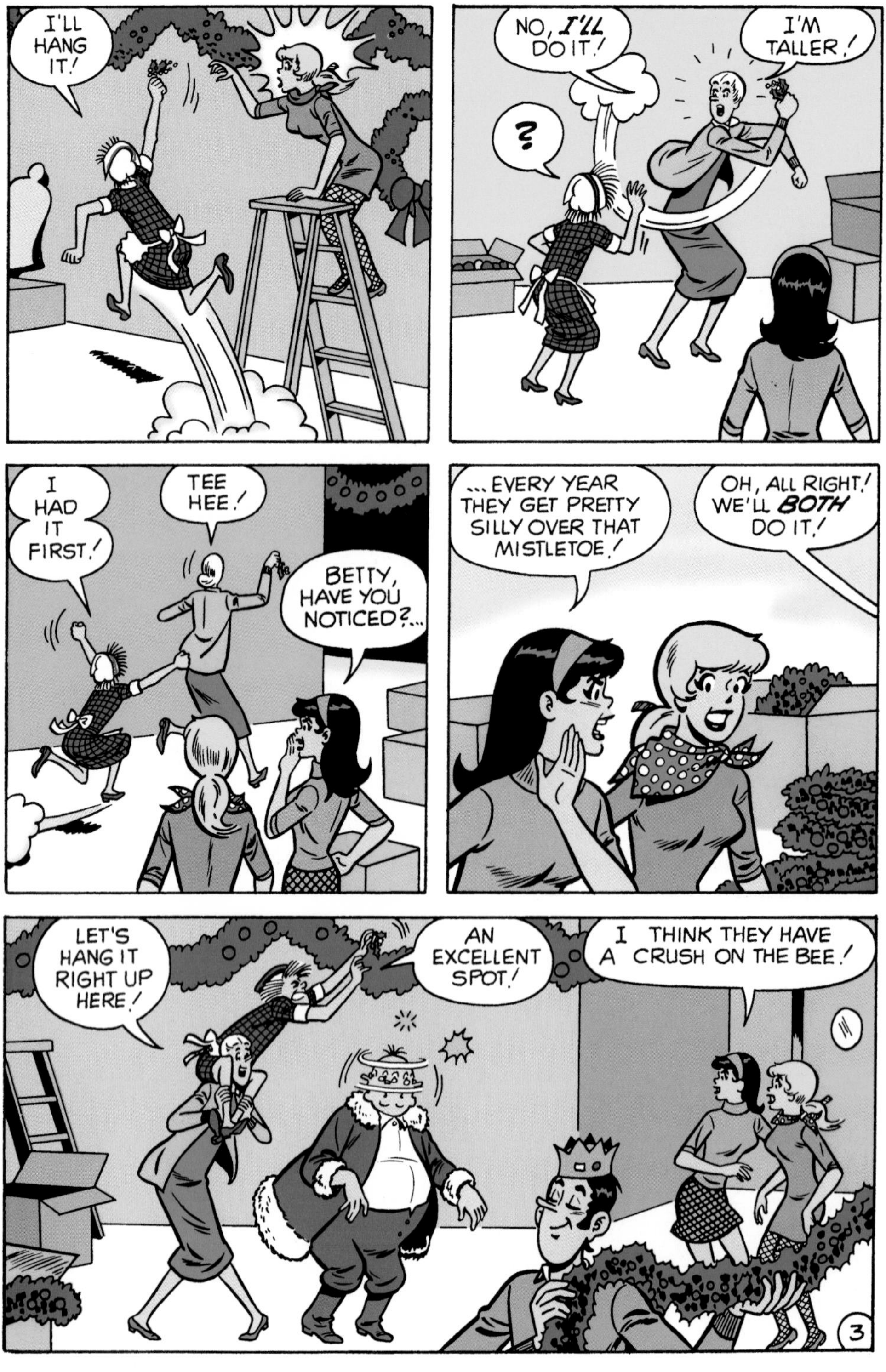
I'LL HANG IT!
NO, I'LL DO IT!
I'M TALLER!
?
I HAD IT FIRST!
TEE HEE!
BETTY, HAVE YOU NOTICED?...
...EVERY YEAR THEY GET PRETTY SILLY OVER THAT MISTLETOE!
OH, ALL RIGHT! WE'LL BOTH DO IT!
LET'S HANG IT RIGHT UP HERE!
AN EXCELLENT SPOT!
I THINK THEY HAVE A CRUSH ON THE BEE!
3

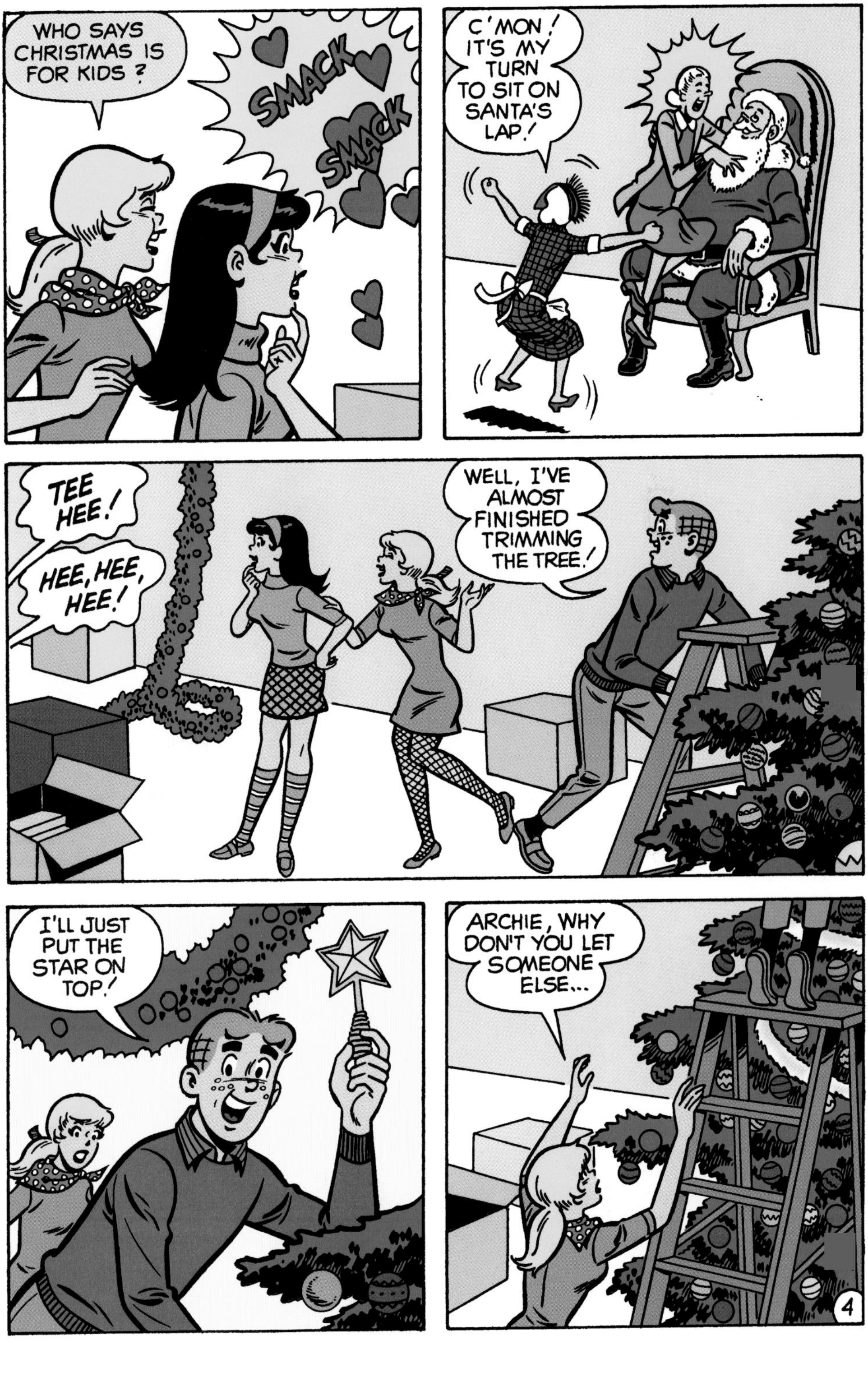
WHO SAYS CHRISTMAS IS FOR KIDS ?
SMACK
SMACK
C'MON! IT'S MY TURN TO SIT ON SANTA'S LAP!
TEE HEE!
HEE, HEE, HEE!
WELL, I'VE ALMOST FINISHED TRIMMING THE TREE!
I'LL JUST PUT THE STAR ON TOP!
ARCHIE, WHY DON'T YOU LET SOMEONE ELSE...
4

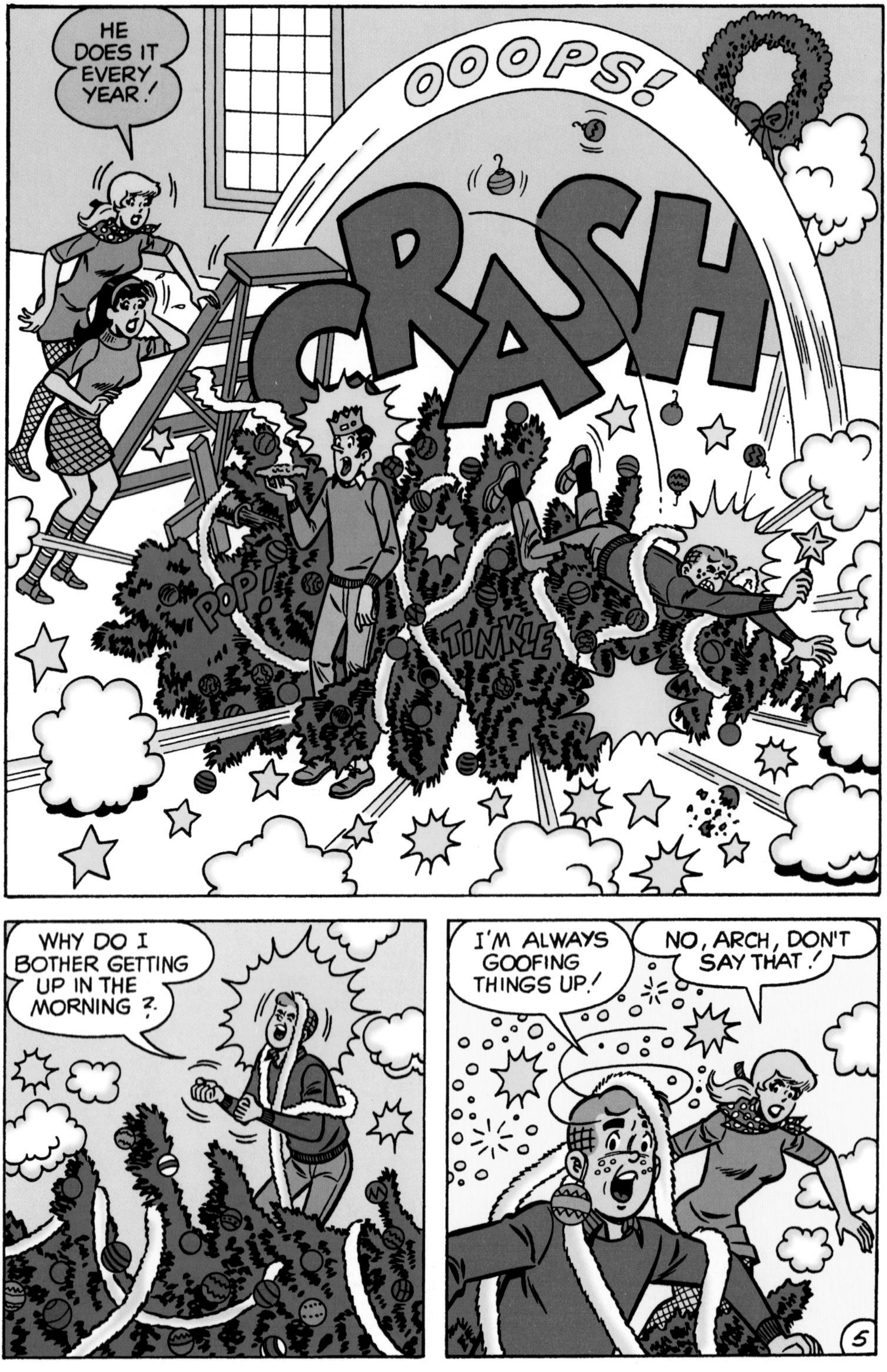
HE DOES IT EVERY YEAR!
OOOPS!
CRASH
POP!
TINKLE
WHY DO I BOTHER GETTING UP IN THE MORNING ?.
I'M ALWAYS GOOFING THINGS UP!
NO, ARCH, DON'T SAY THAT!
5

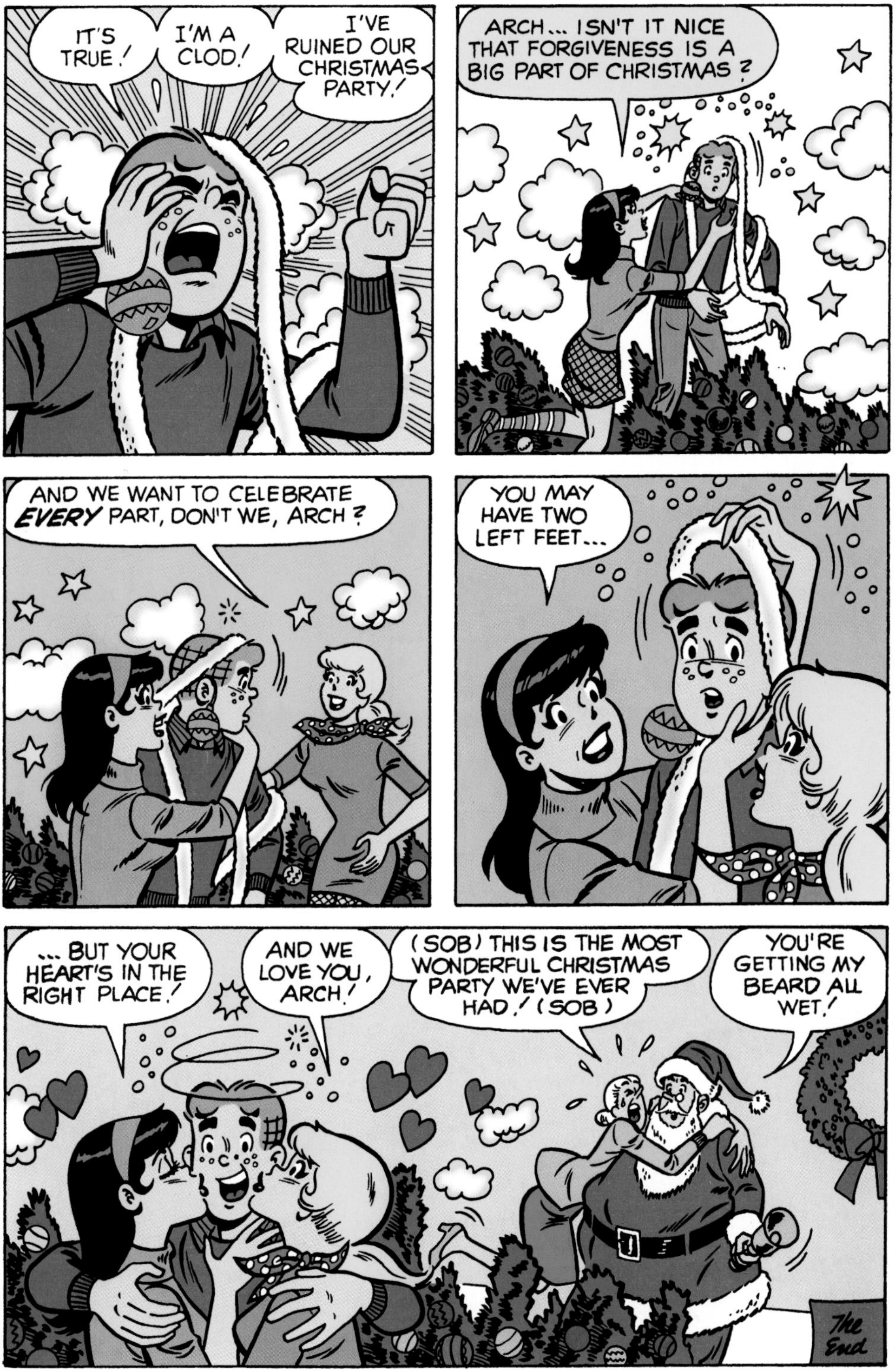
IT'S TRUE!
I'M A CLOD!
I'VE RUINED OUR CHRISTMAS PARTY!
ARCH... ISN'T IT NICE THAT FORGIVENESS IS A BIG PART OF CHRISTMAS?
AND WE WANT TO CELEBRATE EVERY PART, DON'T WE, ARCH?
YOU MAY HAVE TWO LEFT FEET...
... BUT YOUR HEART'S IN THE RIGHT PLACE!
AND WE LOVE YOU, ARCH!
(SOB) THIS IS THE MOST WONDERFUL CHRISTMAS PARTY WE'VE EVER HAD! (SOB)
YOU'RE GETTING MY BEARD ALL WET!
The End

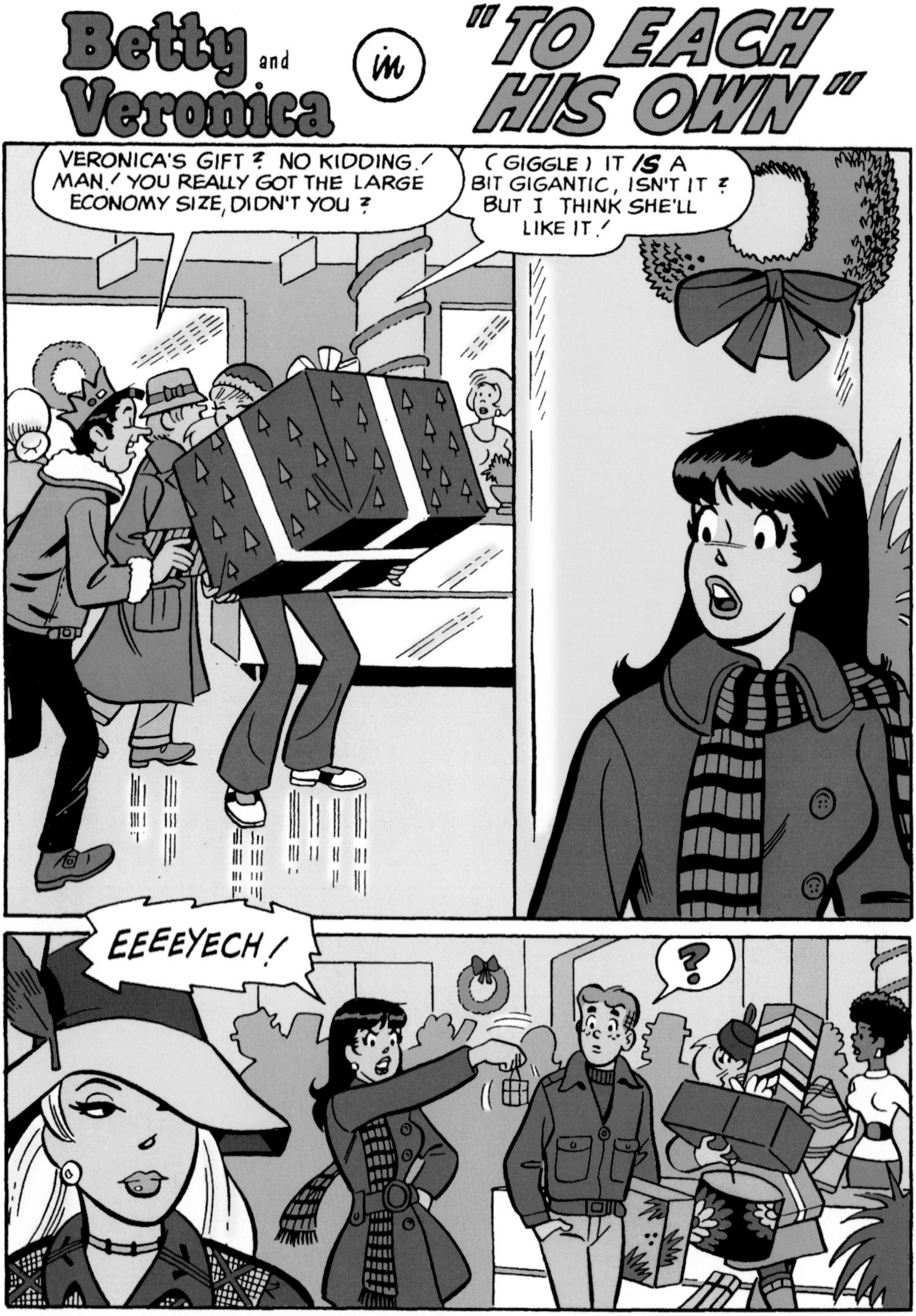
Betty and Veronica in "TO EACH HIS OWN"
VERONICA'S GIFT? NO KIDDING! MAN! YOU REALLY GOT THE LARGE ECONOMY SIZE, DIDN'T YOU?
(GIGGLE) IT IS A BIT GIGANTIC, ISN'T IT? BUT I THINK SHE'LL LIKE IT!
EEEEYECH!
?

Frank Doyle • Dan DeCarlo • Rudy Lapick • Bill Yoshida • Barry Grossman

Originally printed in ARCHIE GIANT SERIES MAGAZINE #191, 1972

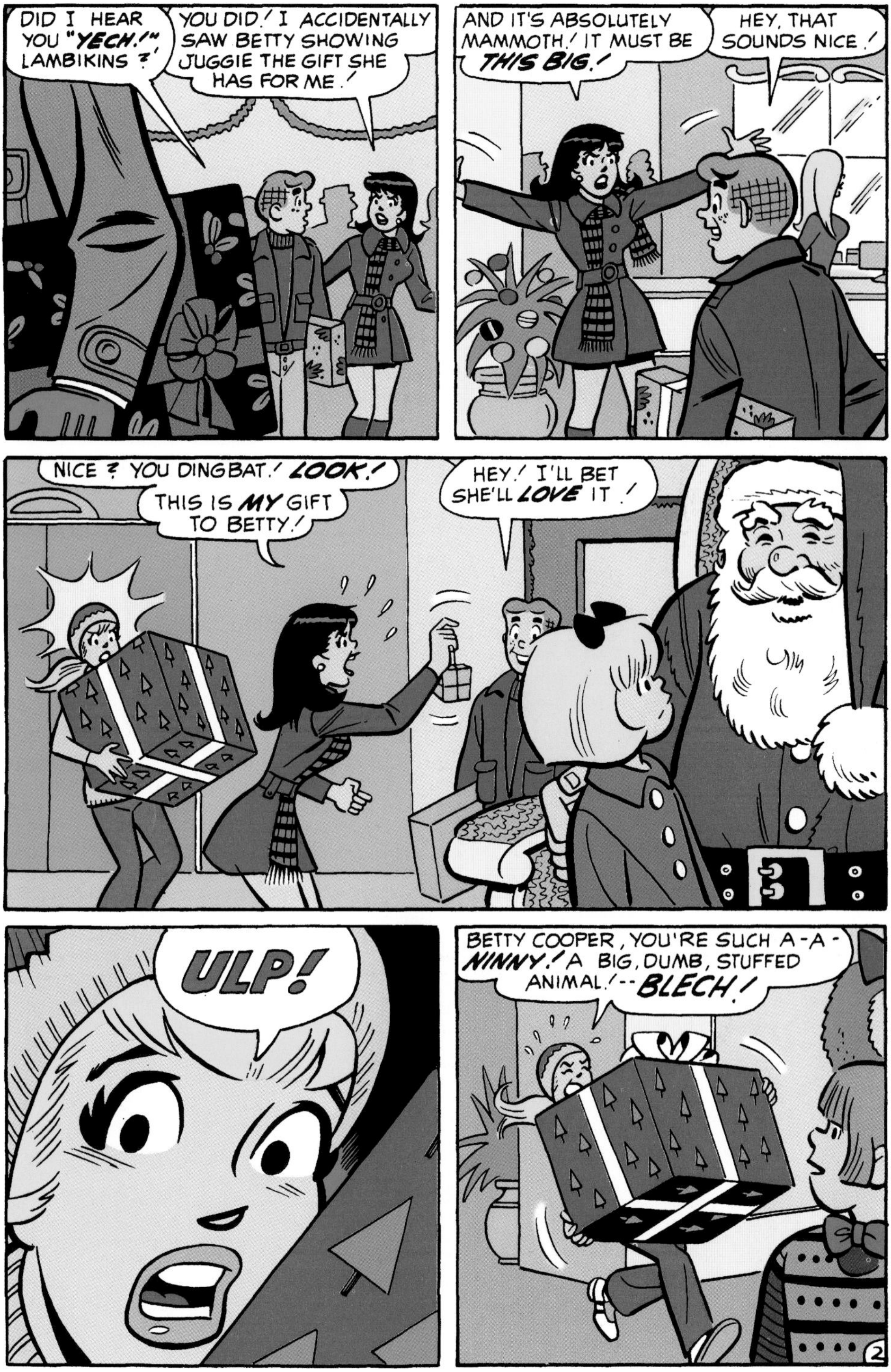
DID I HEAR YOU "YECH!" LAMBIKINS ?
YOU DID! I ACCIDENTALLY SAW BETTY SHOWING JUGGIE THE GIFT SHE HAS FOR ME!
AND IT'S ABSOLUTELY MAMMOTH! IT MUST BE THIS BIG!
HEY, THAT SOUNDS NICE!
NICE ? YOU DINGBAT! LOOK!
THIS IS MY GIFT TO BETTY!
HEY! I'LL BET SHE'LL LOVE IT!
ULP!
BETTY COOPER, YOU'RE SUCH A-A-NINNY! A BIG, DUMB, STUFFED ANIMAL!--BLECH!
2

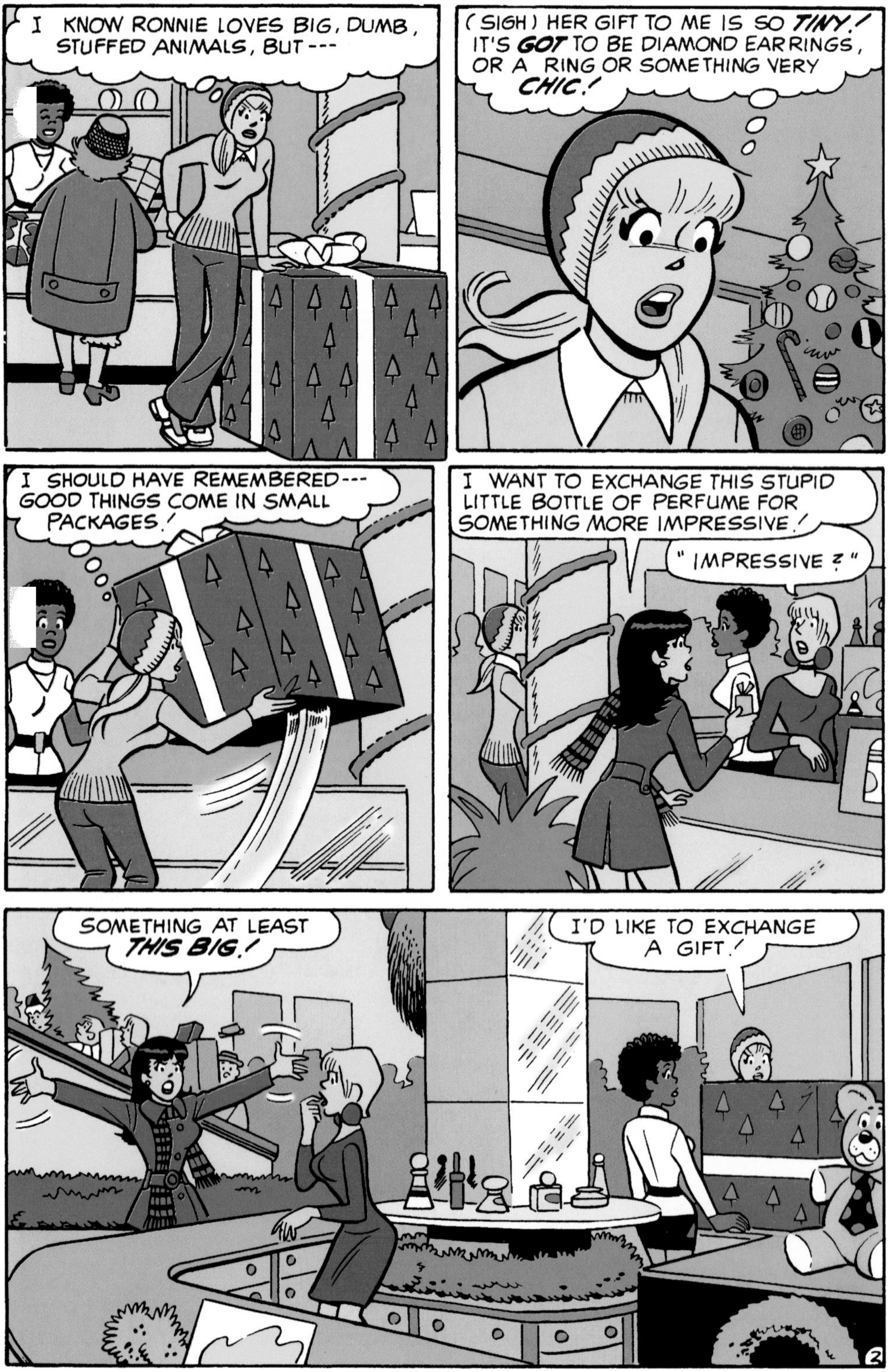
I KNOW RONNIE LOVES BIG, DUMB, STUFFED ANIMALS, BUT---
(SIGH) HER GIFT TO ME IS SO *TINY!* IT'S *GOT* TO BE DIAMOND EARRINGS, OR A RING OR SOMETHING VERY *CHIC!*
I SHOULD HAVE REMEMBERED--- GOOD THINGS COME IN SMALL PACKAGES!
I WANT TO EXCHANGE THIS STUPID LITTLE BOTTLE OF PERFUME FOR SOMETHING MORE IMPRESSIVE!
"IMPRESSIVE?"
SOMETHING AT LEAST *THIS BIG!*
I'D LIKE TO EXCHANGE A GIFT!
2

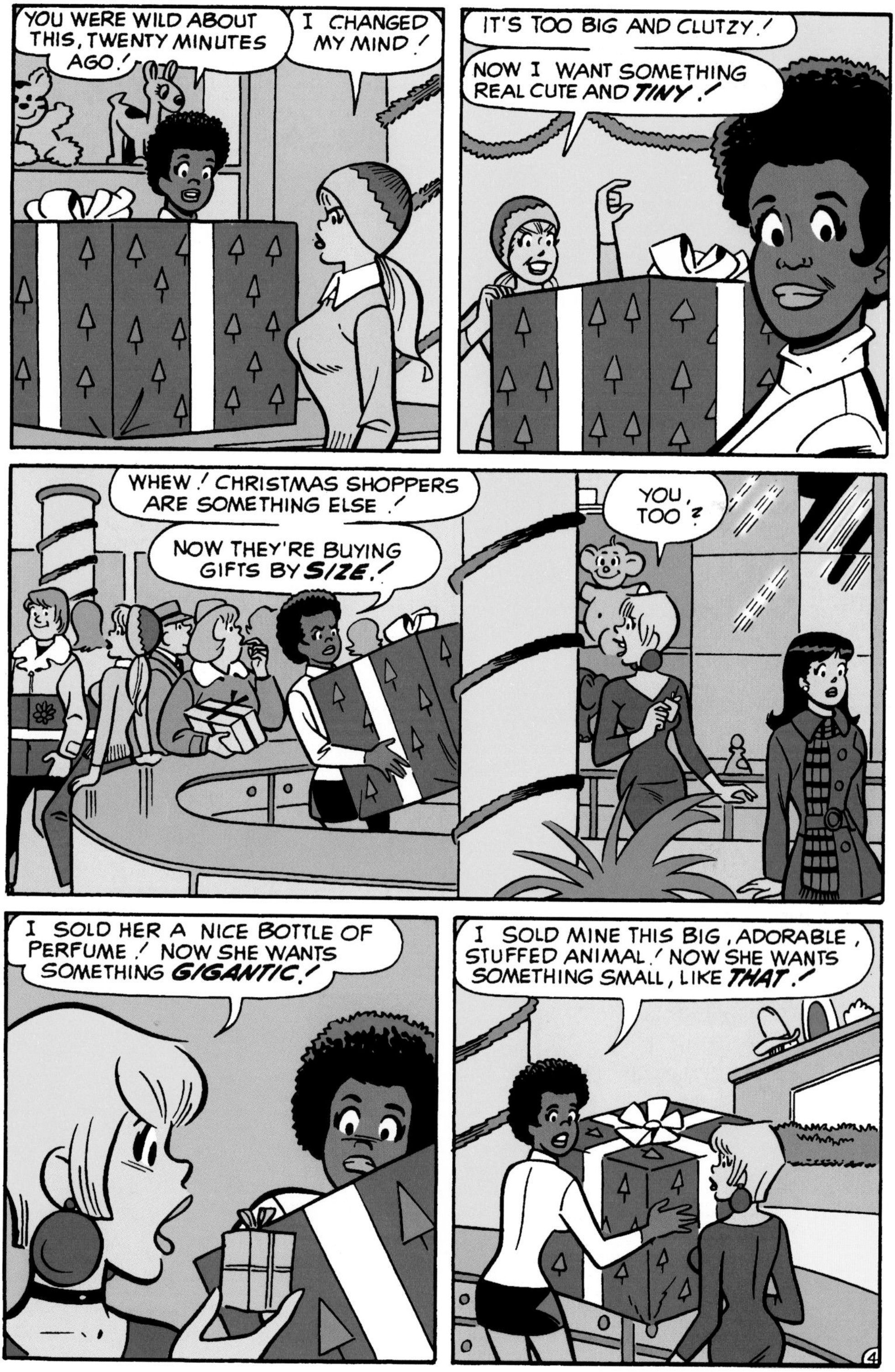
YOU WERE WILD ABOUT THIS, TWENTY MINUTES AGO!
I CHANGED MY MIND!
IT'S TOO BIG AND CLUTZY!
NOW I WANT SOMETHING REAL CUTE AND TINY!
WHEW! CHRISTMAS SHOPPERS ARE SOMETHING ELSE!
NOW THEY'RE BUYING GIFTS BY SIZE!
YOU, TOO?
I SOLD HER A NICE BOTTLE OF PERFUME! NOW SHE WANTS SOMETHING GIGANTIC!
I SOLD MINE THIS BIG, ADORABLE, STUFFED ANIMAL! NOW SHE WANTS SOMETHING SMALL, LIKE THAT!
4

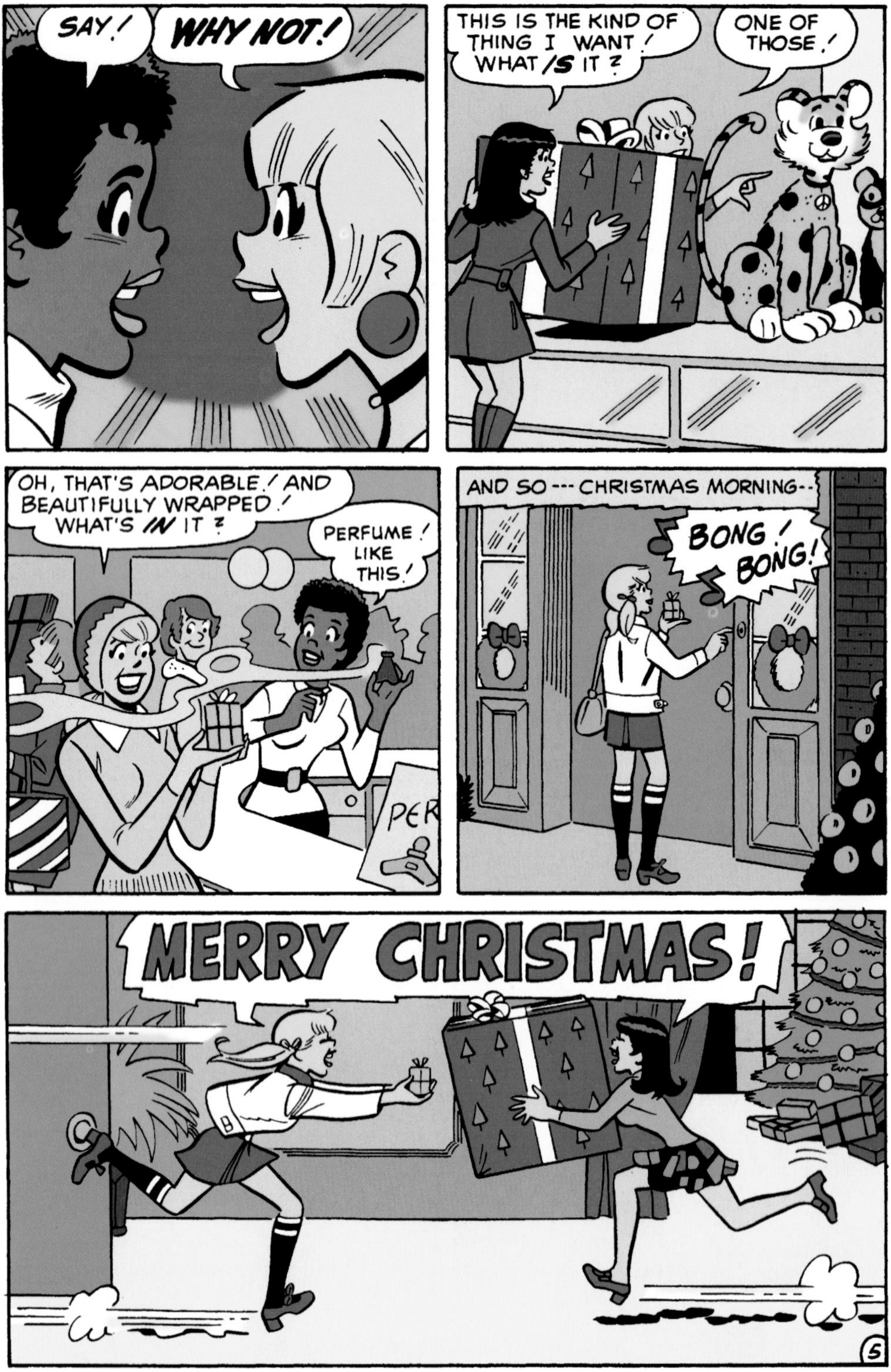
SAY!
WHY NOT!
THIS IS THE KIND OF THING I WANT! WHAT IS IT?
ONE OF THOSE!
OH, THAT'S ADORABLE! AND BEAUTIFULLY WRAPPED! WHAT'S IN IT?
PERFUME! LIKE THIS!
PER
AND SO --- CHRISTMAS MORNING--
BONG! BONG!
MERRY CHRISTMAS!
5

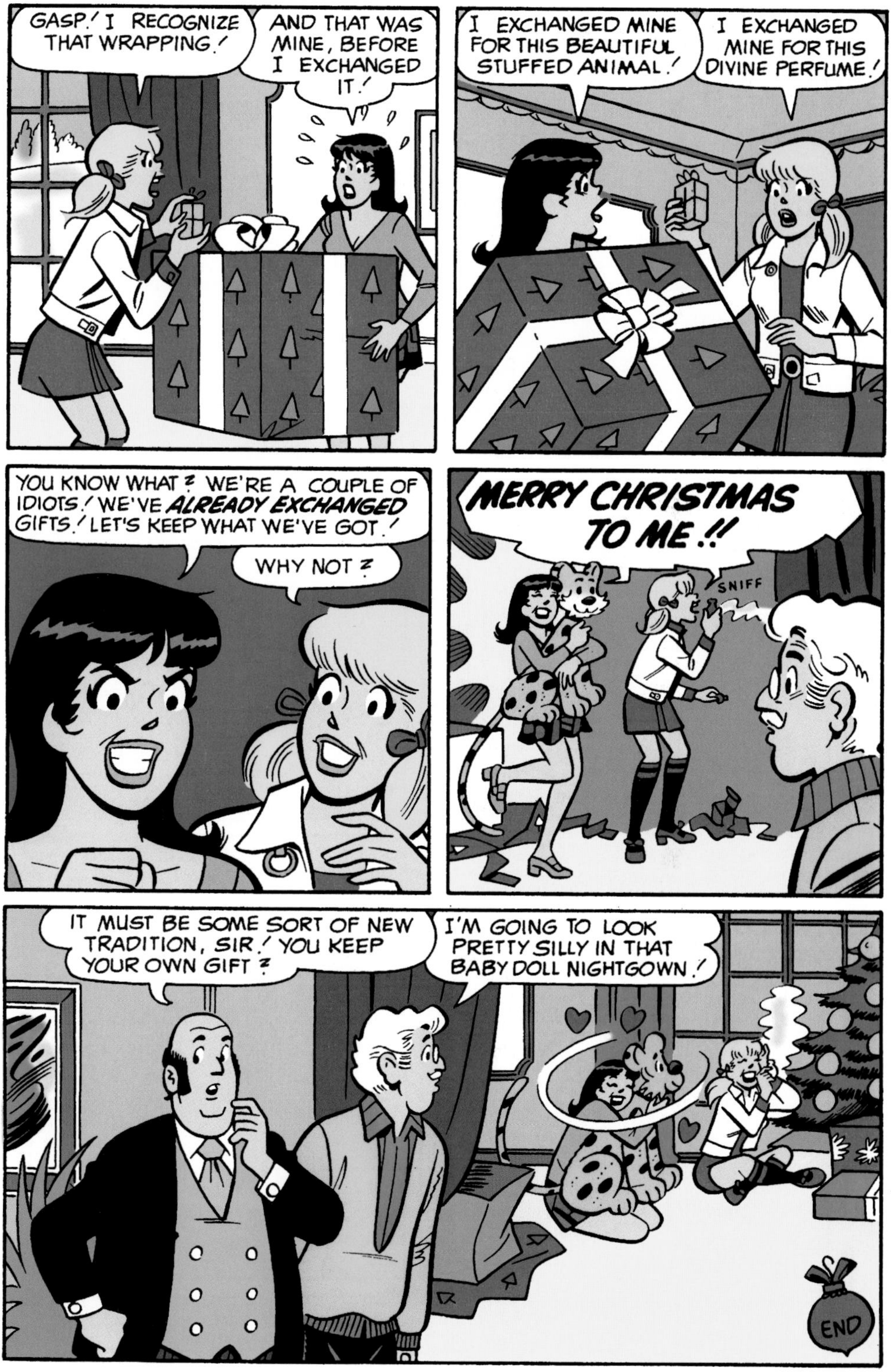
GASP! I RECOGNIZE THAT WRAPPING!
AND THAT WAS MINE, BEFORE I EXCHANGED IT!
I EXCHANGED MINE FOR THIS BEAUTIFUL STUFFED ANIMAL!
I EXCHANGED MINE FOR THIS DIVINE PERFUME!
YOU KNOW WHAT? WE'RE A COUPLE OF IDIOTS! WE'VE ALREADY EXCHANGED GIFTS! LET'S KEEP WHAT WE'VE GOT!
WHY NOT?
MERRY CHRISTMAS TO ME!!
SNIFF
IT MUST BE SOME SORT OF NEW TRADITION, SIR! YOU KEEP YOUR OWN GIFT?
I'M GOING TO LOOK PRETTY SILLY IN THAT BABY DOLL NIGHTGOWN!
END

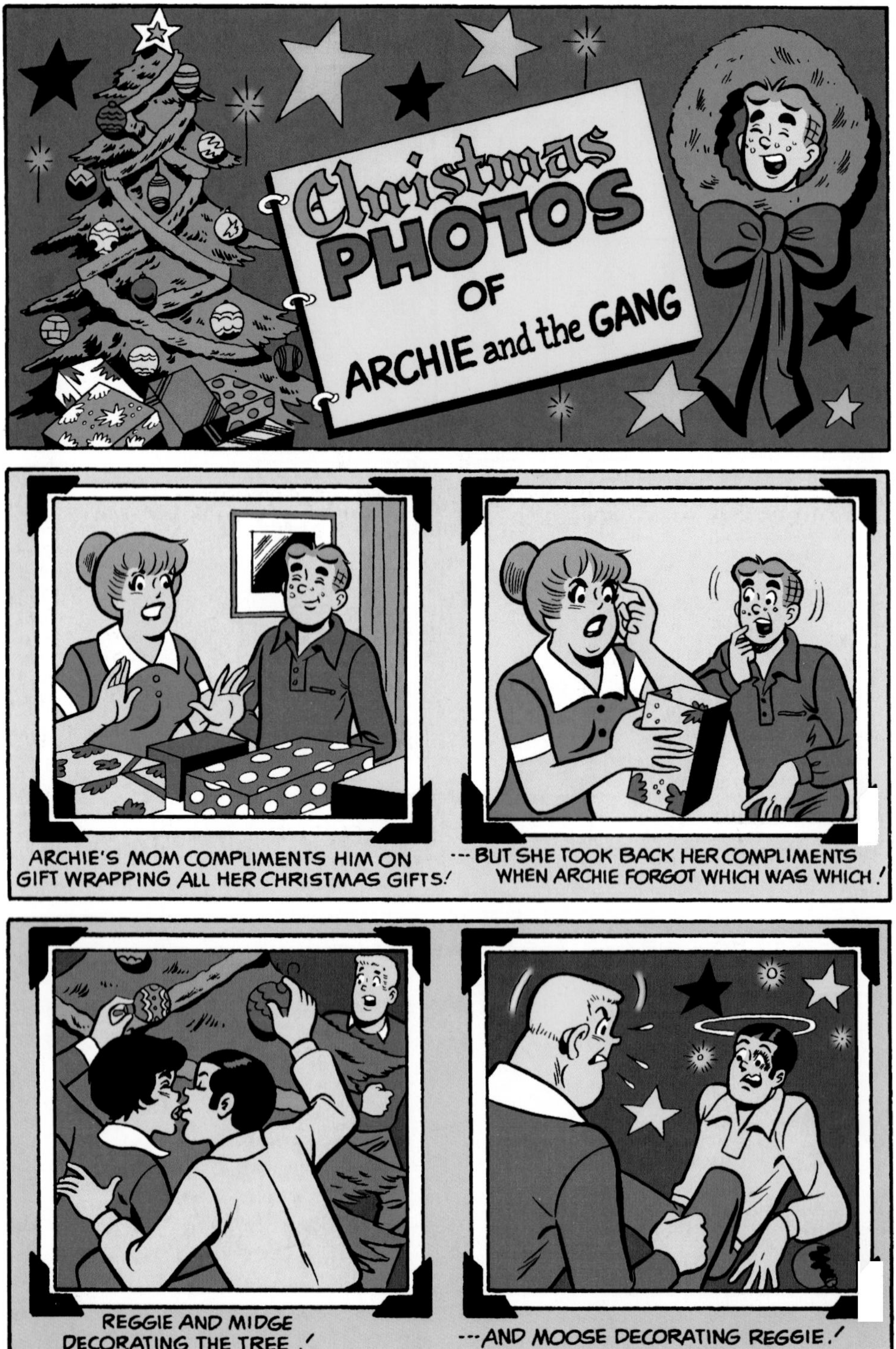
Christmas PHOTOS OF ARCHIE and the GANG
ARCHIE'S MOM COMPLIMENTS HIM ON GIFT WRAPPING ALL HER CHRISTMAS GIFTS!
--- BUT SHE TOOK BACK HER COMPLIMENTS WHEN ARCHIE FORGOT WHICH WAS WHICH!
REGGIE AND MIDGE DECORATING THE TREE!
---AND MOOSE DECORATING REGGIE!

Originally printed in ARCHIE'S JOKE BOOK MAGAZINE #169, 1972

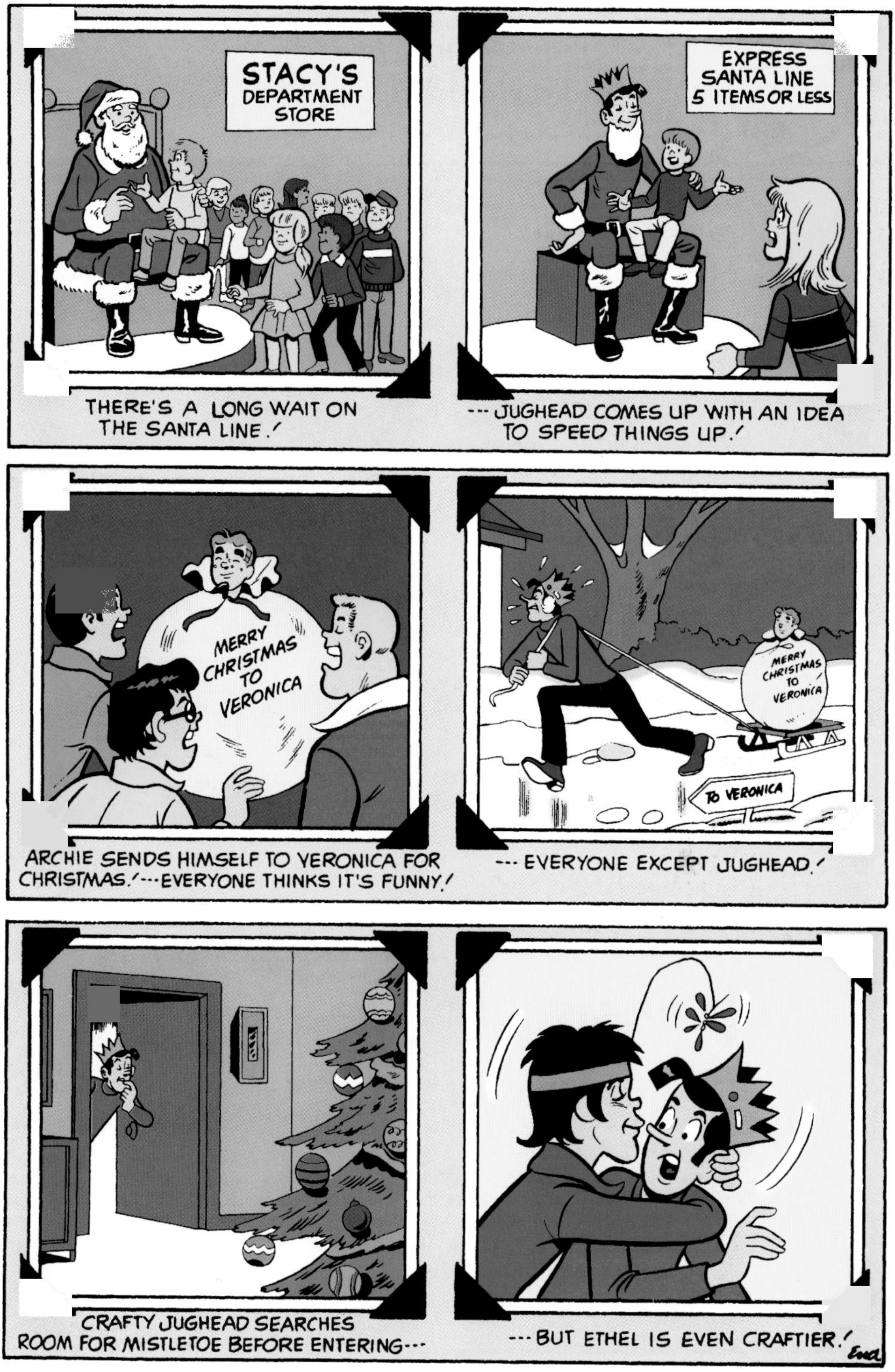
STACY'S DEPARTMENT STORE
THERE'S A LONG WAIT ON THE SANTA LINE!
EXPRESS SANTA LINE 5 ITEMS OR LESS
--- JUGHEAD COMES UP WITH AN IDEA TO SPEED THINGS UP!
MERRY CHRISTMAS TO VERONICA
ARCHIE SENDS HIMSELF TO VERONICA FOR CHRISTMAS! --- EVERYONE THINKS IT'S FUNNY!
MERRY CHRISTMAS TO VERONICA
TO VERONICA
--- EVERYONE EXCEPT JUGHEAD!
CRAFTY JUGHEAD SEARCHES ROOM FOR MISTLETOE BEFORE ENTERING---
--- BUT ETHEL IS EVEN CRAFTIER!
End

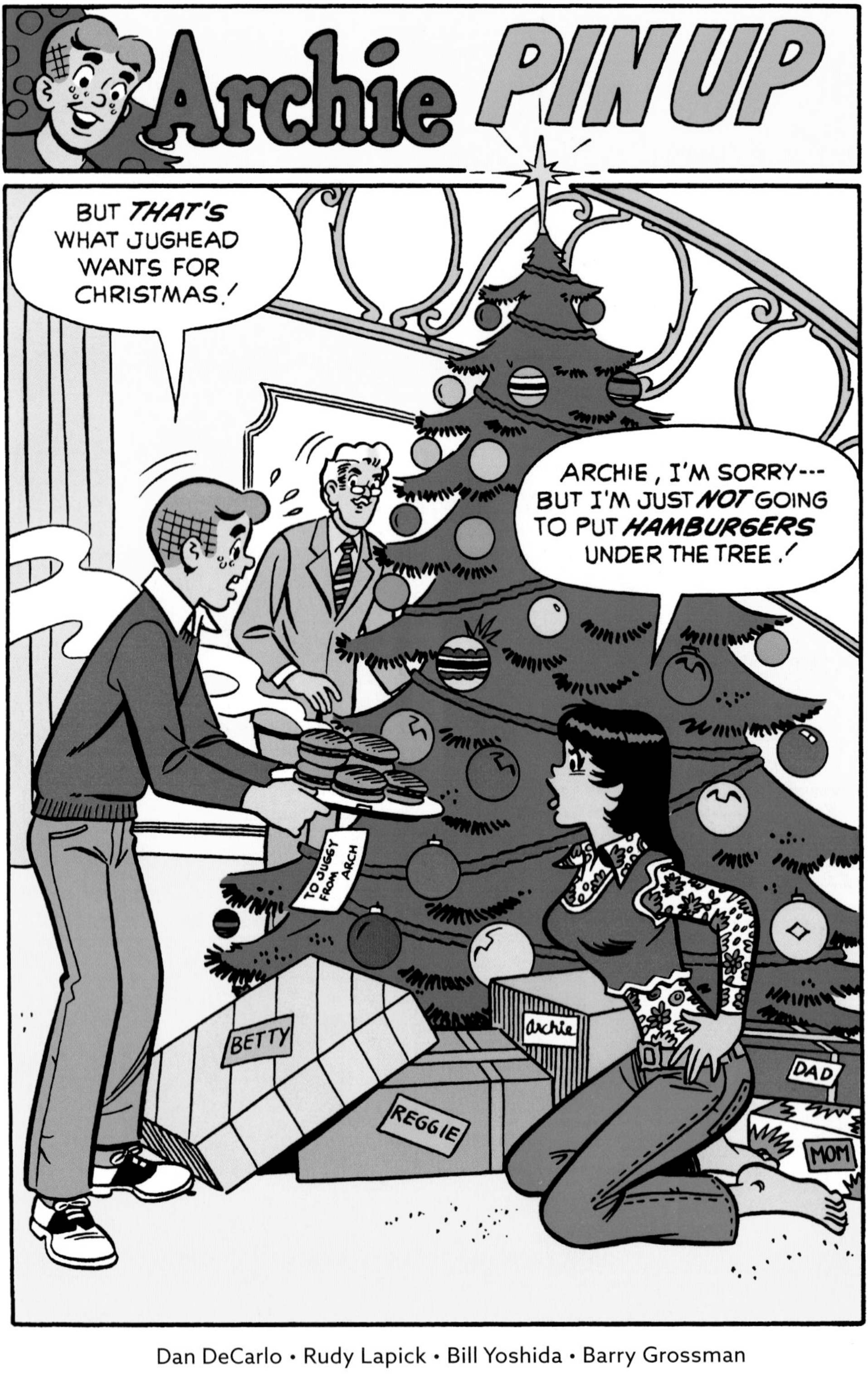
Archie PINUP
BUT THAT'S WHAT JUGHEAD WANTS FOR CHRISTMAS!
ARCHIE, I'M SORRY--- BUT I'M JUST NOT GOING TO PUT HAMBURGERS UNDER THE TREE!
TO JUGGY FROM ARCH
BETTY
archie
REGGIE
DAD
MOM

Dan DeCarlo • Rudy Lapick • Bill Yoshida • Barry Grossman

Originally printed in ARCHIE'S PALS'N'GALS #75, 1973

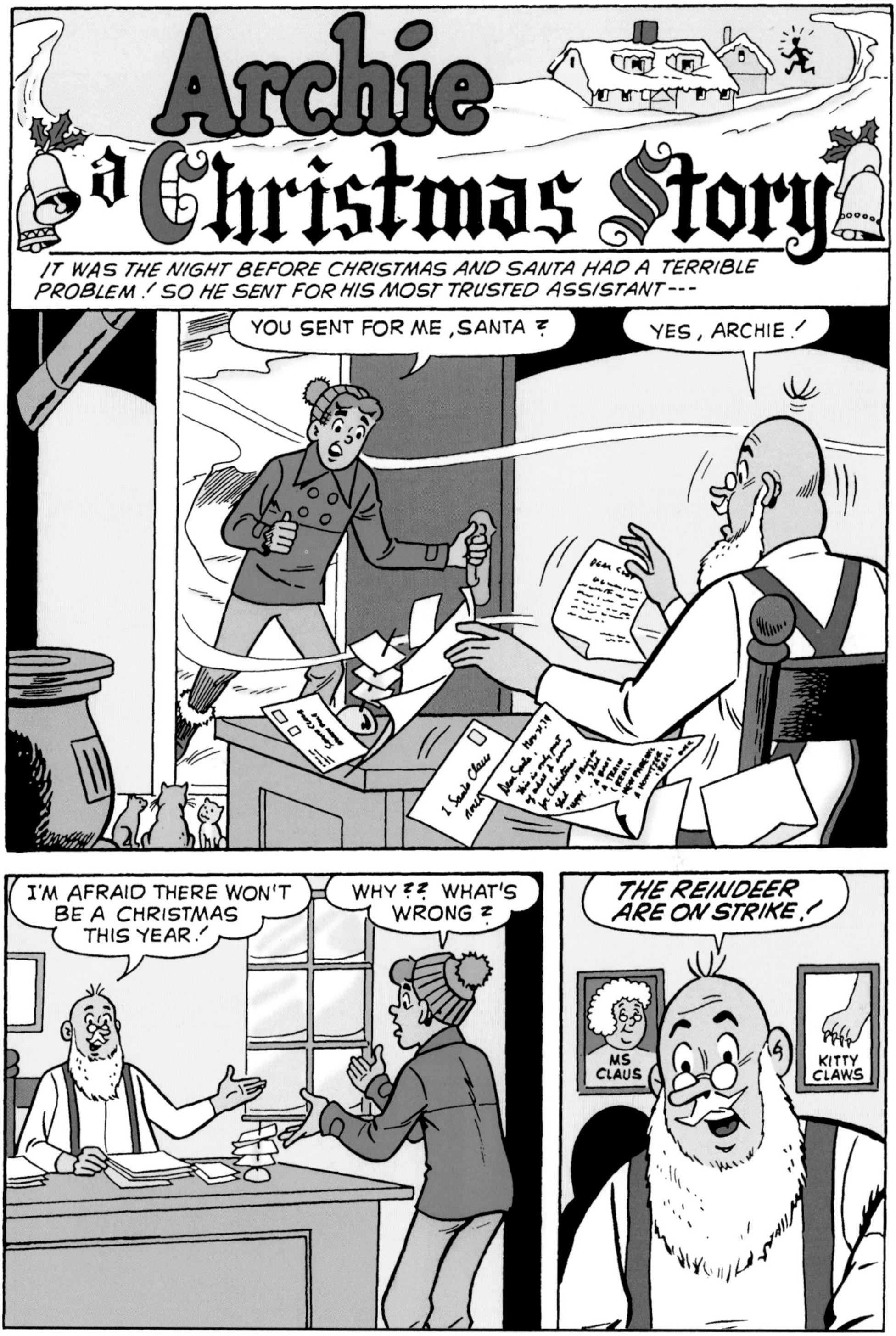
Archie
a Christmas Story
IT WAS THE NIGHT BEFORE CHRISTMAS AND SANTA HAD A TERRIBLE PROBLEM! SO HE SENT FOR HIS MOST TRUSTED ASSISTANT---
YOU SENT FOR ME, SANTA?
YES, ARCHIE!
I'M AFRAID THERE WON'T BE A CHRISTMAS THIS YEAR!
WHY?? WHAT'S WRONG?
THE REINDEER ARE ON STRIKE!
MS CLAUS
KITTY CLAWS

George Gladir • Bob Bolling • Jon D'Agostino • Bill Yoshida • Barry Grossman

Originally printed in ARCHIE AND ME #72, 1975

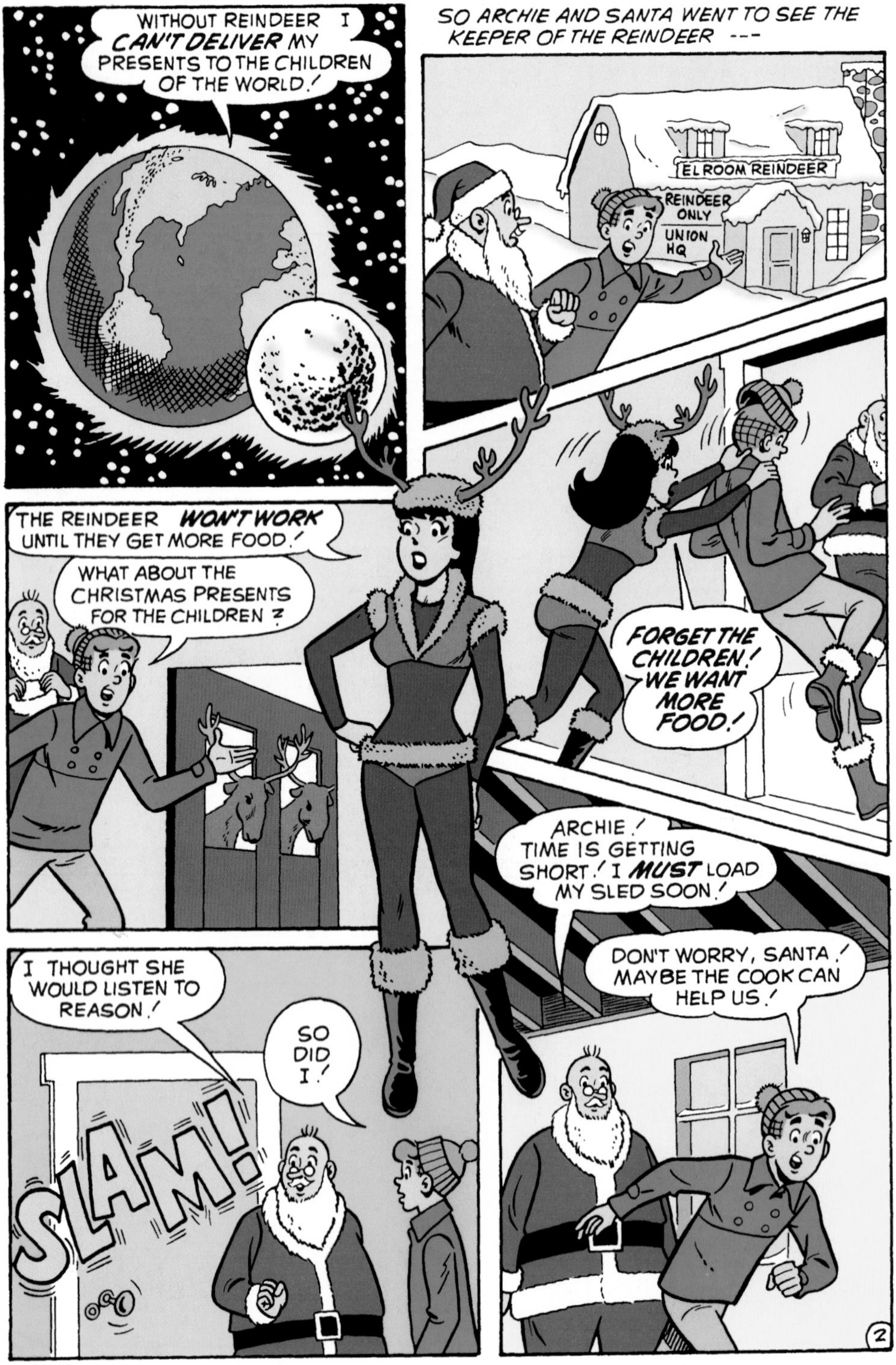
WITHOUT REINDEER I CAN'T DELIVER MY PRESENTS TO THE CHILDREN OF THE WORLD!
SO ARCHIE AND SANTA WENT TO SEE THE KEEPER OF THE REINDEER ---
EL ROOM REINDEER
REINDEER ONLY
UNION HQ
THE REINDEER WON'T WORK UNTIL THEY GET MORE FOOD!
WHAT ABOUT THE CHRISTMAS PRESENTS FOR THE CHILDREN ?
FORGET THE CHILDREN! WE WANT MORE FOOD!
ARCHIE! TIME IS GETTING SHORT! I MUST LOAD MY SLED SOON!
I THOUGHT SHE WOULD LISTEN TO REASON!
SO DID I!
SLAM!
DON'T WORRY, SANTA! MAYBE THE COOK CAN HELP US!
2

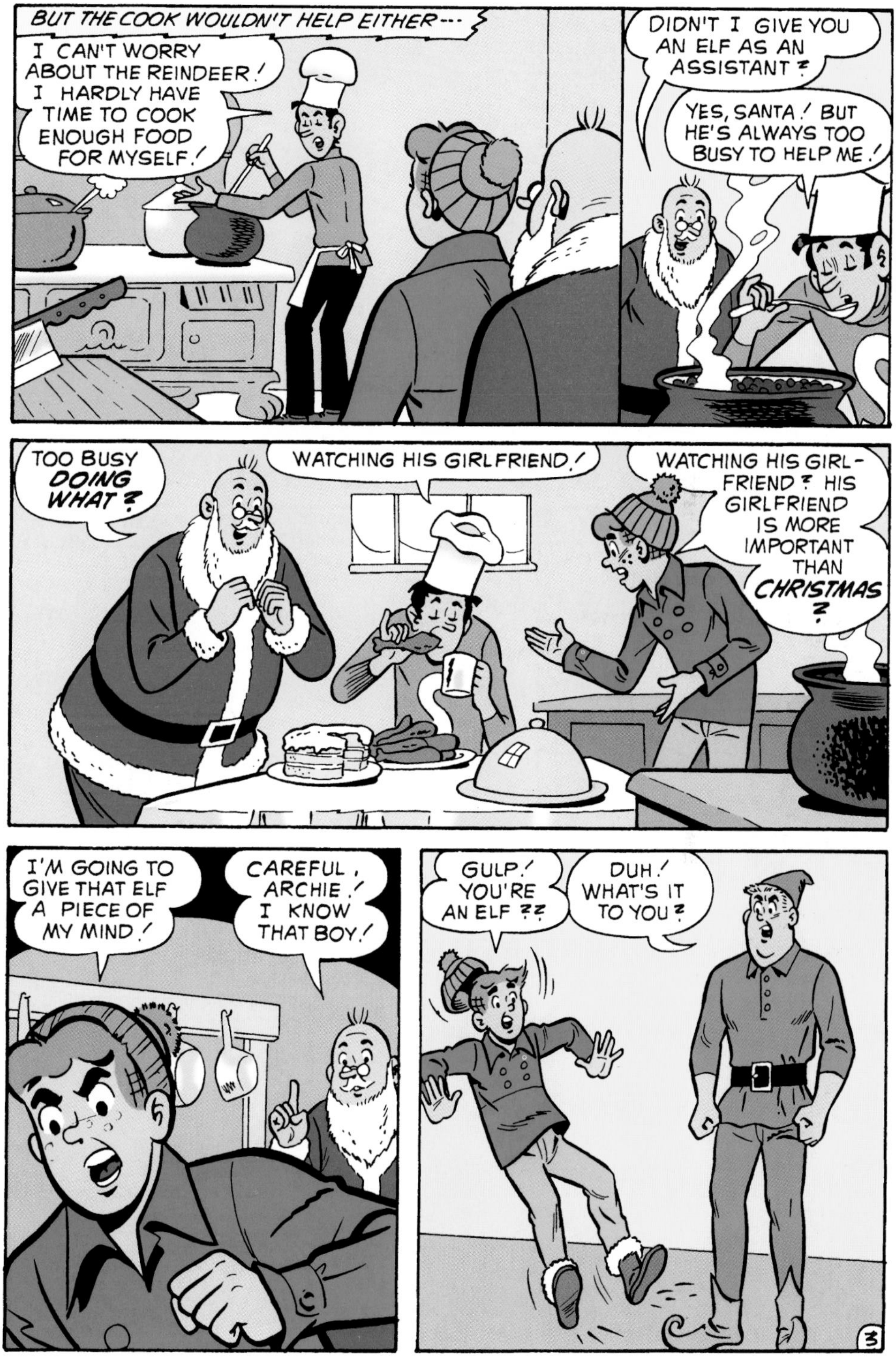
BUT THE COOK WOULDN'T HELP EITHER---
I CAN'T WORRY ABOUT THE REINDEER! I HARDLY HAVE TIME TO COOK ENOUGH FOOD FOR MYSELF!
DIDN'T I GIVE YOU AN ELF AS AN ASSISTANT?
YES, SANTA! BUT HE'S ALWAYS TOO BUSY TO HELP ME!
TOO BUSY DOING WHAT?
WATCHING HIS GIRLFRIEND!
WATCHING HIS GIRL-FRIEND? HIS GIRLFRIEND IS MORE IMPORTANT THAN CHRISTMAS?
I'M GOING TO GIVE THAT ELF A PIECE OF MY MIND!
CAREFUL, ARCHIE! I KNOW THAT BOY!
GULP! YOU'RE AN ELF??
DUH! WHAT'S IT TO YOU?
3

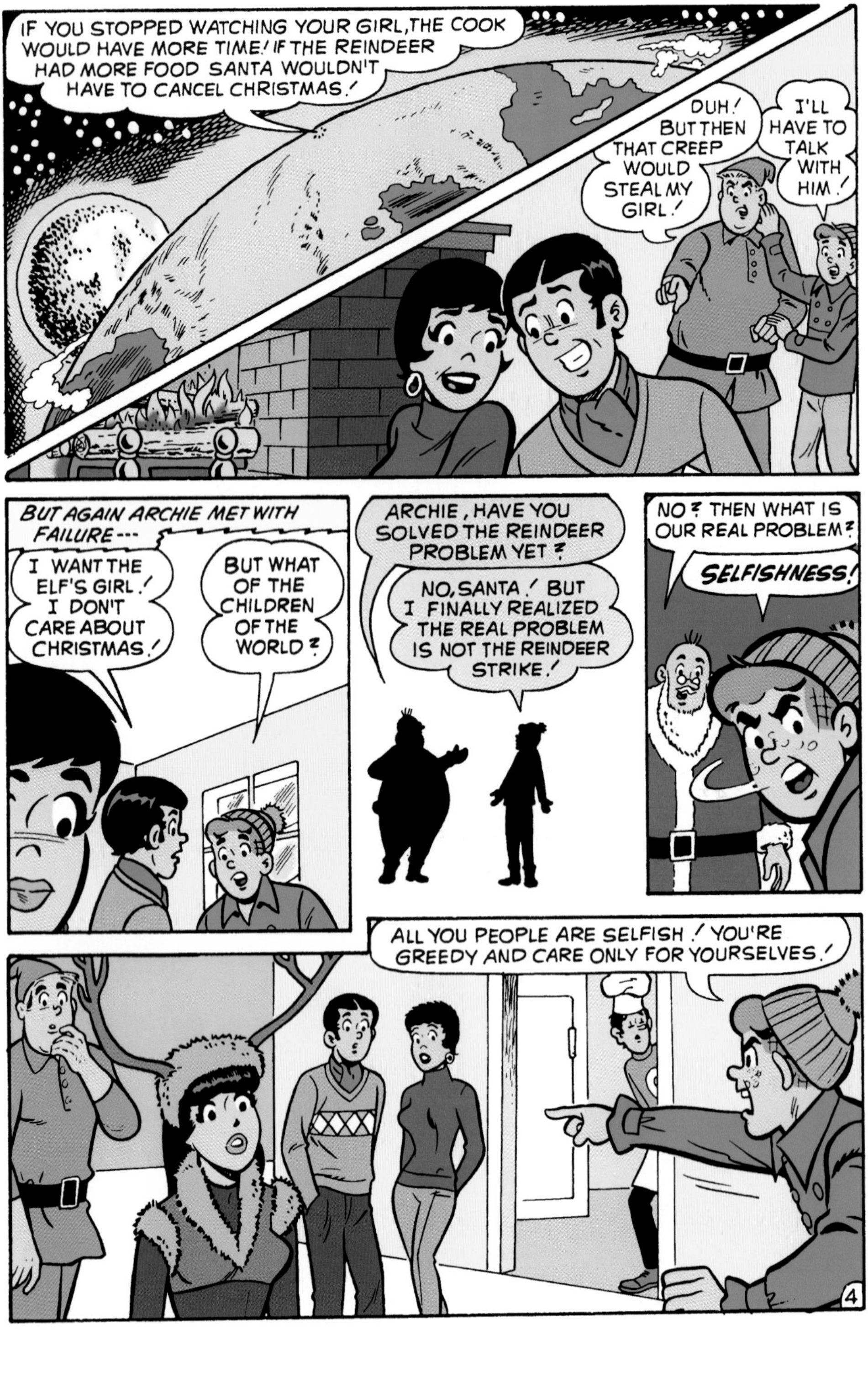
IF YOU STOPPED WATCHING YOUR GIRL, THE COOK WOULD HAVE MORE TIME! IF THE REINDEER HAD MORE FOOD SANTA WOULDN'T HAVE TO CANCEL CHRISTMAS!
DUH! BUT THEN THAT CREEP WOULD STEAL MY GIRL!
I'LL HAVE TO TALK WITH HIM!
BUT AGAIN ARCHIE MET WITH FAILURE---
I WANT THE ELF'S GIRL! I DON'T CARE ABOUT CHRISTMAS!
BUT WHAT OF THE CHILDREN OF THE WORLD?
ARCHIE, HAVE YOU SOLVED THE REINDEER PROBLEM YET?
NO, SANTA! BUT I FINALLY REALIZED THE REAL PROBLEM IS NOT THE REINDEER STRIKE!
NO? THEN WHAT IS OUR REAL PROBLEM?
SELFISHNESS!
ALL YOU PEOPLE ARE SELFISH! YOU'RE GREEDY AND CARE ONLY FOR YOURSELVES!
4

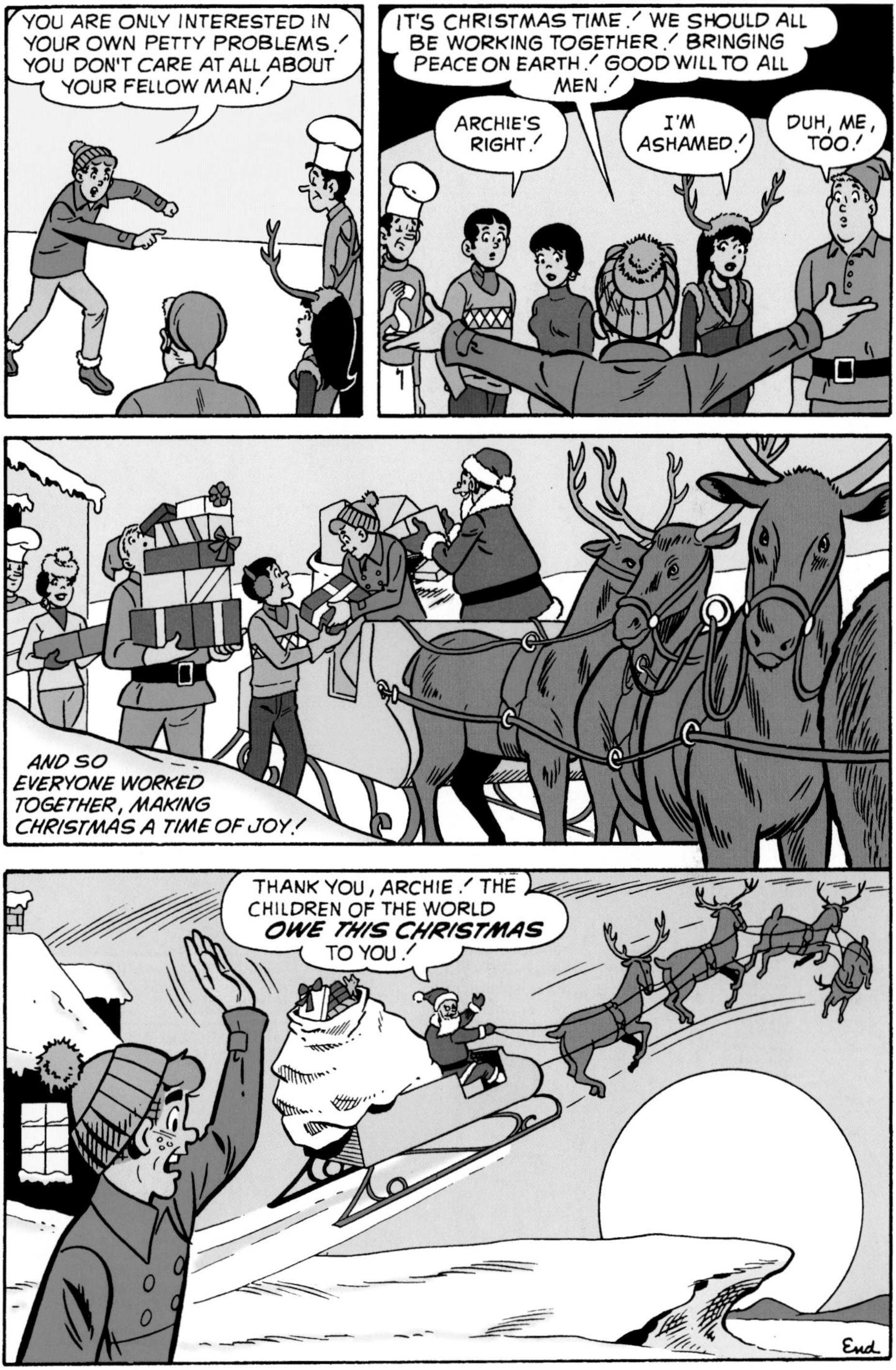
YOU ARE ONLY INTERESTED IN YOUR OWN PETTY PROBLEMS! YOU DON'T CARE AT ALL ABOUT YOUR FELLOW MAN!
IT'S CHRISTMAS TIME! WE SHOULD ALL BE WORKING TOGETHER! BRINGING PEACE ON EARTH! GOOD WILL TO ALL MEN!
ARCHIE'S RIGHT!
I'M ASHAMED!
DUH, ME, TOO!
AND SO EVERYONE WORKED TOGETHER, MAKING CHRISTMAS A TIME OF JOY!
THANK YOU, ARCHIE! THE CHILDREN OF THE WORLD OWE THIS CHRISTMAS TO YOU!
End

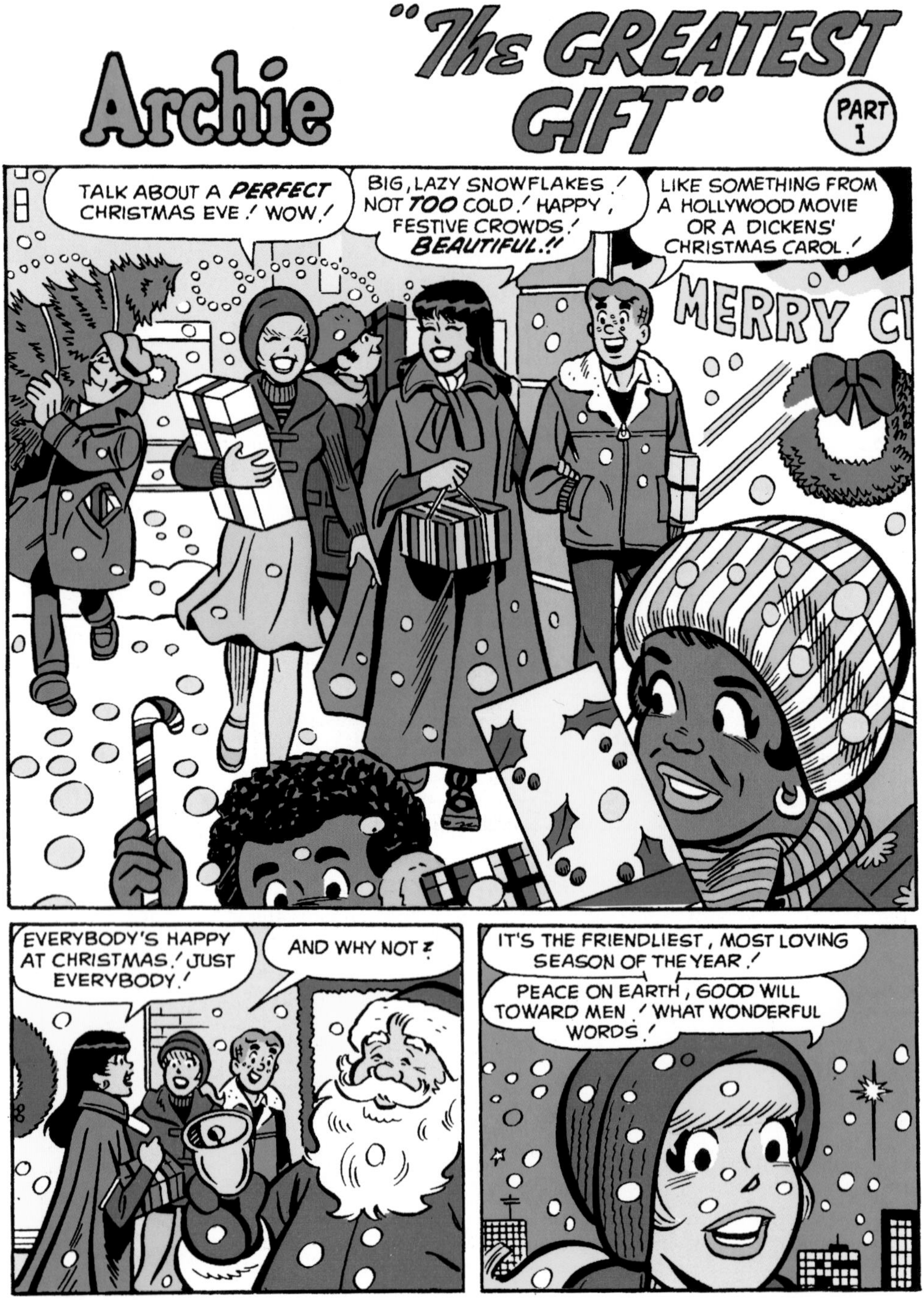
Archie
"The GREATEST GIFT"
PART I
TALK ABOUT A PERFECT CHRISTMAS EVE! WOW!
BIG, LAZY SNOWFLAKES! NOT TOO COLD! HAPPY, FESTIVE CROWDS! BEAUTIFUL!!
LIKE SOMETHING FROM A HOLLYWOOD MOVIE OR A DICKENS' CHRISTMAS CAROL!
EVERYBODY'S HAPPY AT CHRISTMAS! JUST EVERYBODY!
AND WHY NOT?
IT'S THE FRIENDLIEST, MOST LOVING SEASON OF THE YEAR!
PEACE ON EARTH, GOOD WILL TOWARD MEN! WHAT WONDERFUL WORDS!

Frank Doyle • Dan DeCarlo • Rudy Lapick • Bill Yoshida • Barry Grossman

Originally printed in LIFE WITH ARCHIE #154, 1975

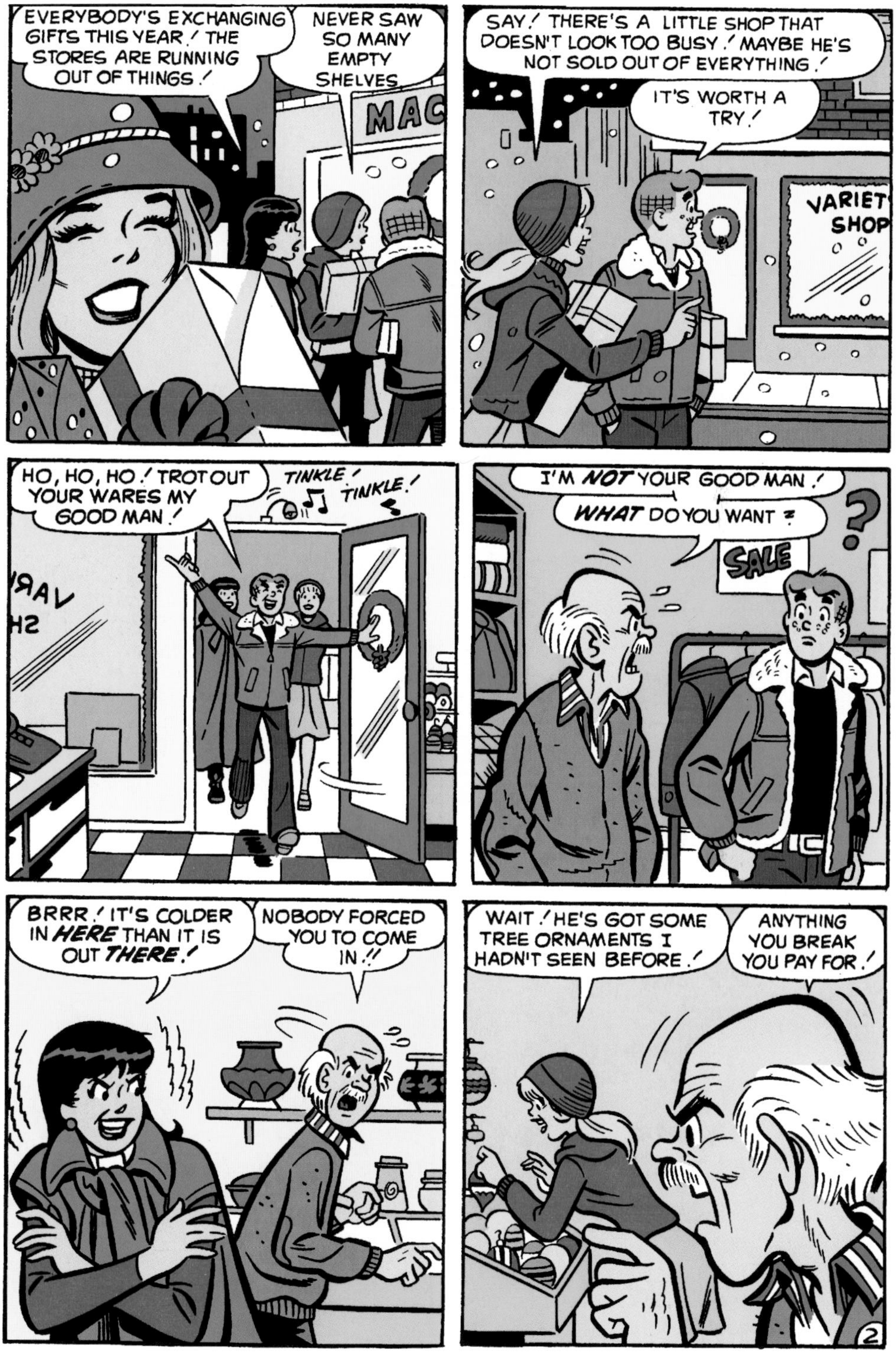
EVERYBODY'S EXCHANGING GIFTS THIS YEAR! THE STORES ARE RUNNING OUT OF THINGS!
NEVER SAW SO MANY EMPTY SHELVES
MAC
SAY! THERE'S A LITTLE SHOP THAT DOESN'T LOOK TOO BUSY! MAYBE HE'S NOT SOLD OUT OF EVERYTHING!
IT'S WORTH A TRY!
VARIET SHOP
HO, HO, HO! TROT OUT YOUR WARES MY GOOD MAN!
TINKLE! TINKLE!
I'M NOT YOUR GOOD MAN!
WHAT DO YOU WANT?
SALE
BRRR! IT'S COLDER IN HERE THAN IT IS OUT THERE!
NOBODY FORCED YOU TO COME IN!!
WAIT! HE'S GOT SOME TREE ORNAMENTS I HADN'T SEEN BEFORE!
ANYTHING YOU BREAK YOU PAY FOR!
2

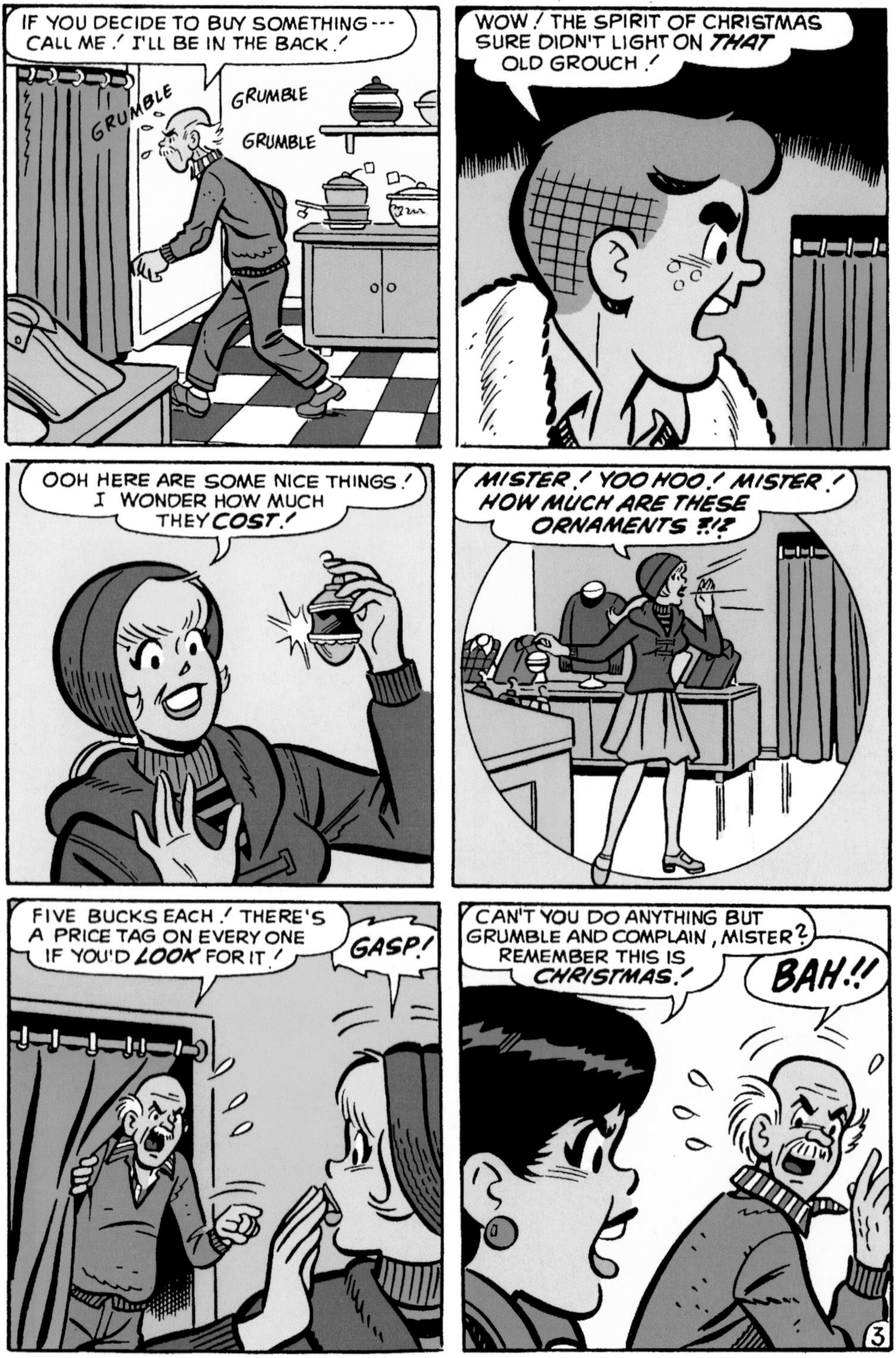
IF YOU DECIDE TO BUY SOMETHING--- CALL ME! I'LL BE IN THE BACK!
GRUMBLE
GRUMBLE
GRUMBLE
WOW! THE SPIRIT OF CHRISTMAS SURE DIDN'T LIGHT ON THAT OLD GROUCH!
OOH HERE ARE SOME NICE THINGS! I WONDER HOW MUCH THEY COST!
MISTER! YOO HOO! MISTER! HOW MUCH ARE THESE ORNAMENTS ?!?
FIVE BUCKS EACH! THERE'S A PRICE TAG ON EVERY ONE IF YOU'D LOOK FOR IT!
GASP!
CAN'T YOU DO ANYTHING BUT GRUMBLE AND COMPLAIN, MISTER? REMEMBER THIS IS CHRISTMAS!
BAH!!
3

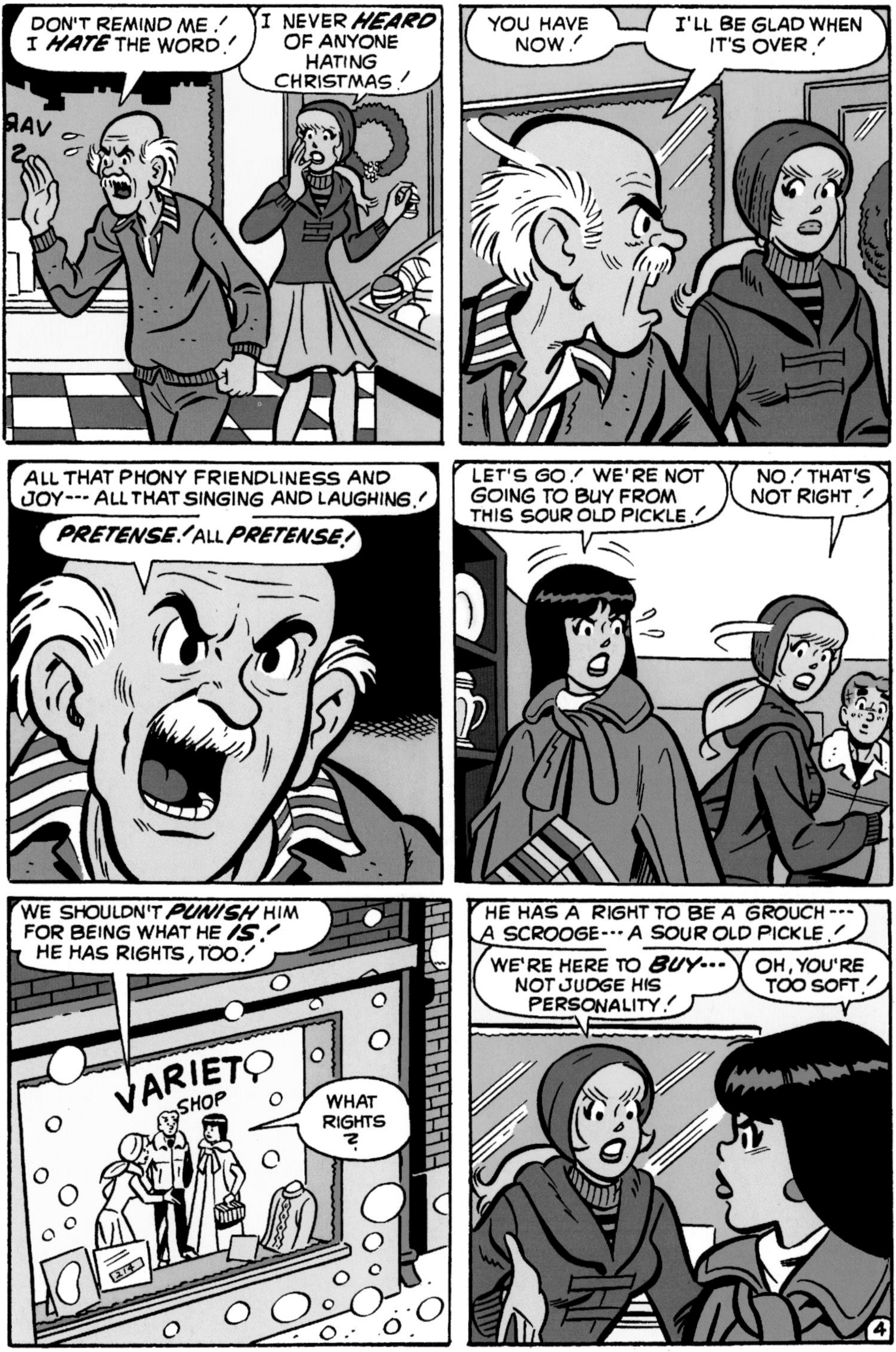
DON'T REMIND ME! I HATE THE WORD!
I NEVER HEARD OF ANYONE HATING CHRISTMAS!
GRAVL
YOU HAVE NOW!
I'LL BE GLAD WHEN IT'S OVER!
ALL THAT PHONY FRIENDLINESS AND JOY--- ALL THAT SINGING AND LAUGHING!
PRETENSE! ALL PRETENSE!
LET'S GO! WE'RE NOT GOING TO BUY FROM THIS SOUR OLD PICKLE!
NO! THAT'S NOT RIGHT!
WE SHOULDN'T PUNISH HIM FOR BEING WHAT HE IS! HE HAS RIGHTS, TOO!
WHAT RIGHTS?
VARIETY SHOP
HE HAS A RIGHT TO BE A GROUCH--- A SCROOGE--- A SOUR OLD PICKLE!
WE'RE HERE TO BUY--- NOT JUDGE HIS PERSONALITY!
OH, YOU'RE TOO SOFT!
4

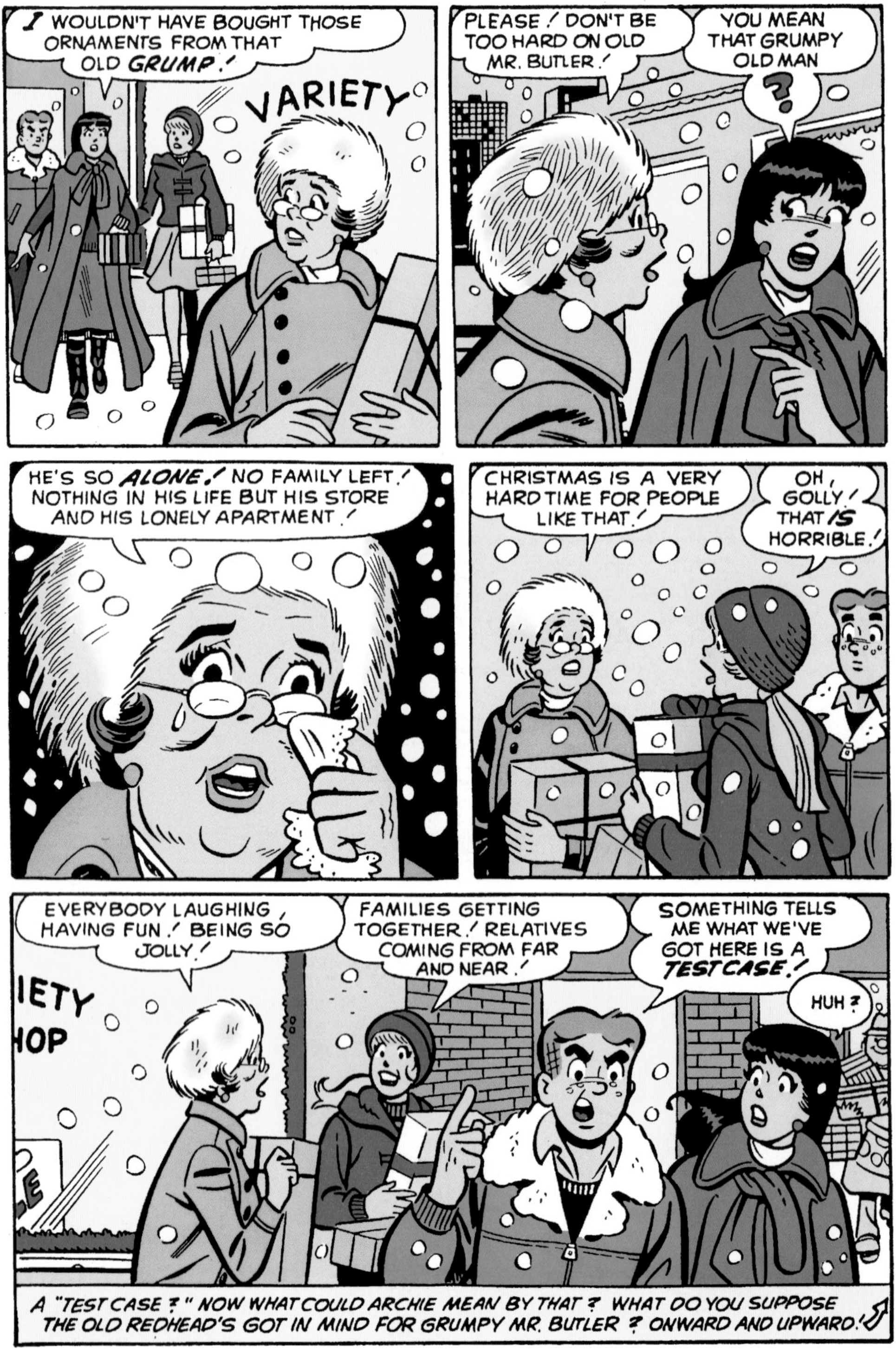
I WOULDN'T HAVE BOUGHT THOSE ORNAMENTS FROM THAT OLD GRUMP!
VARIETY
PLEASE! DON'T BE TOO HARD ON OLD MR. BUTLER!
YOU MEAN THAT GRUMPY OLD MAN
?
HE'S SO ALONE! NO FAMILY LEFT! NOTHING IN HIS LIFE BUT HIS STORE AND HIS LONELY APARTMENT!
CHRISTMAS IS A VERY HARD TIME FOR PEOPLE LIKE THAT!
OH, GOLLY! THAT IS HORRIBLE!
EVERYBODY LAUGHING, HAVING FUN! BEING SO JOLLY!
FAMILIES GETTING TOGETHER! RELATIVES COMING FROM FAR AND NEAR!
SOMETHING TELLS ME WHAT WE'VE GOT HERE IS A TEST CASE!
HUH?
IETY
HOP
A "TEST CASE?" NOW WHAT COULD ARCHIE MEAN BY THAT? WHAT DO YOU SUPPOSE THE OLD REDHEAD'S GOT IN MIND FOR GRUMPY MR. BUTLER? ONWARD AND UPWARD!

Archie "The GREATEST GIFT" PART II

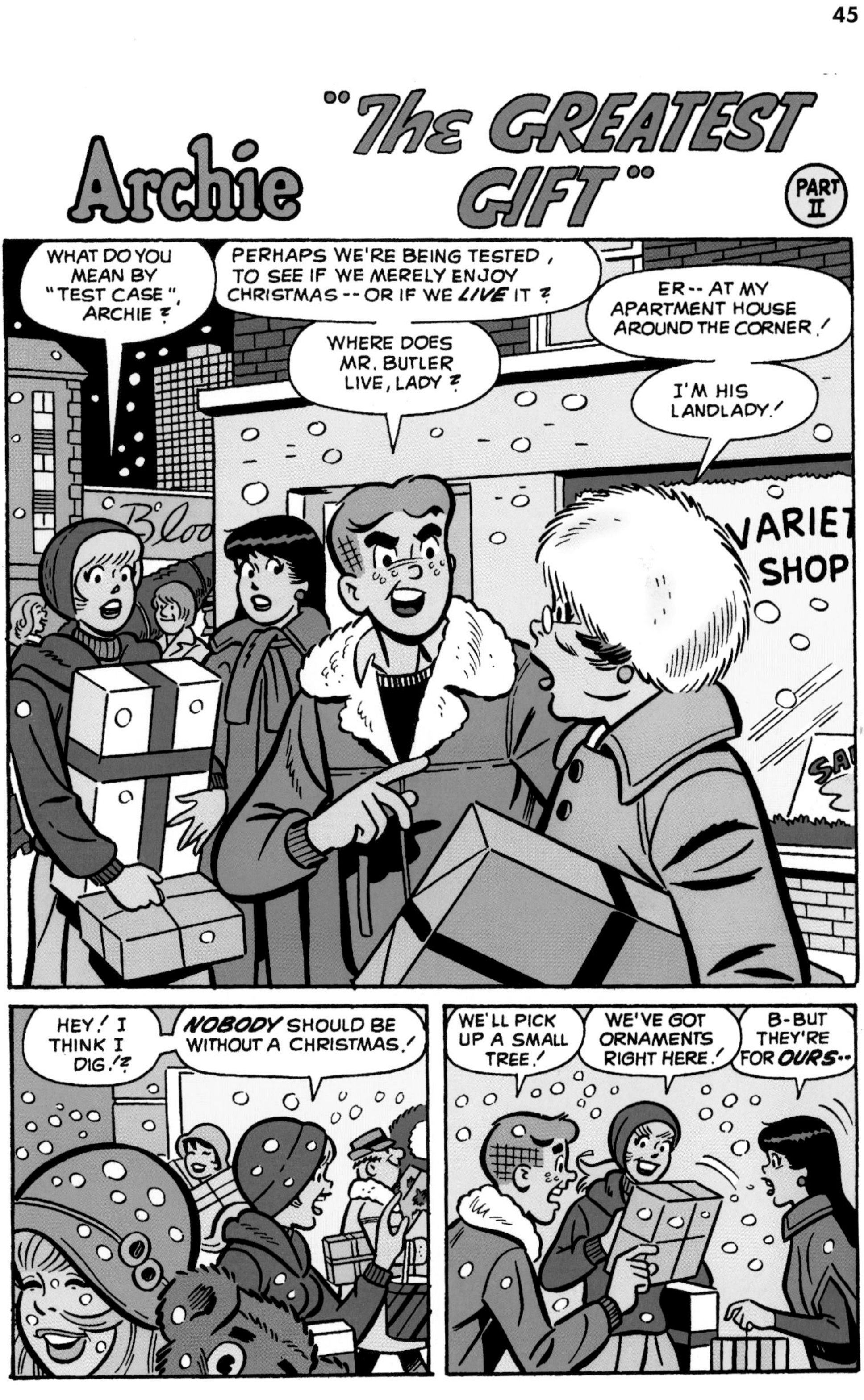
WHAT DO YOU MEAN BY "TEST CASE", ARCHIE?
PERHAPS WE'RE BEING TESTED, TO SEE IF WE MERELY ENJOY CHRISTMAS -- OR IF WE LIVE IT?
WHERE DOES MR. BUTLER LIVE, LADY?
ER -- AT MY APARTMENT HOUSE AROUND THE CORNER!
I'M HIS LANDLADY!
VARIET
SHOP
HEY! I THINK I DIG!?
NOBODY SHOULD BE WITHOUT A CHRISTMAS!
WE'LL PICK UP A SMALL TREE!
WE'VE GOT ORNAMENTS RIGHT HERE!
B-BUT THEY'RE FOR OURS--

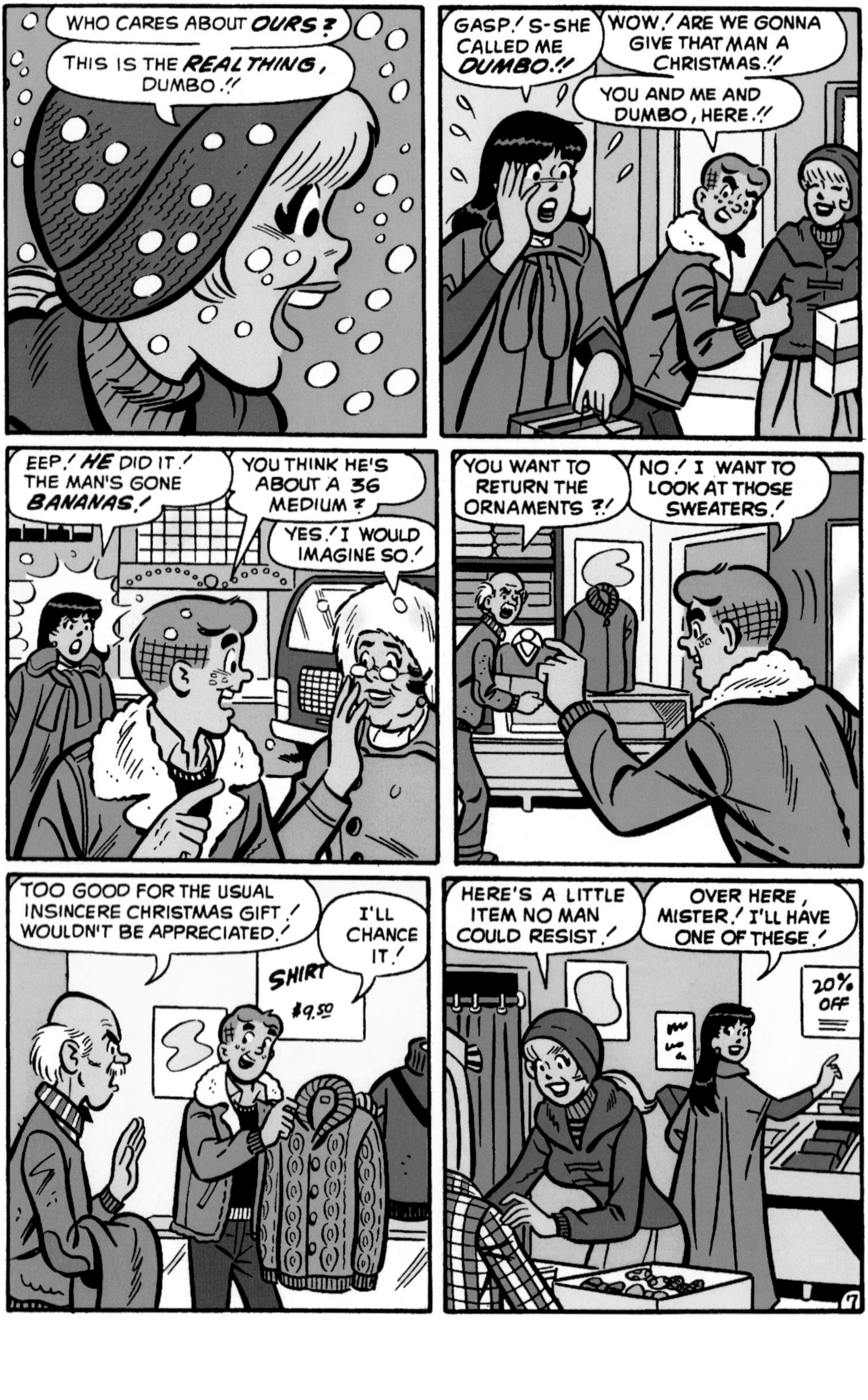
WHO CARES ABOUT OURS ?
THIS IS THE REAL THING, DUMBO.!!
GASP! S-SHE CALLED ME DUMBO.!!
WOW! ARE WE GONNA GIVE THAT MAN A CHRISTMAS.!!
YOU AND ME AND DUMBO, HERE.!!
EEP! HE DID IT! THE MAN'S GONE BANANAS!
YOU THINK HE'S ABOUT A 36 MEDIUM ?
YES! I WOULD IMAGINE SO!
YOU WANT TO RETURN THE ORNAMENTS ?!
NO! I WANT TO LOOK AT THOSE SWEATERS!
TOO GOOD FOR THE USUAL INSINCERE CHRISTMAS GIFT! WOULDN'T BE APPRECIATED!
I'LL CHANCE IT!
SHIRT
$9.50
HERE'S A LITTLE ITEM NO MAN COULD RESIST!
OVER HERE, MISTER! I'LL HAVE ONE OF THESE!
20% OFF
7

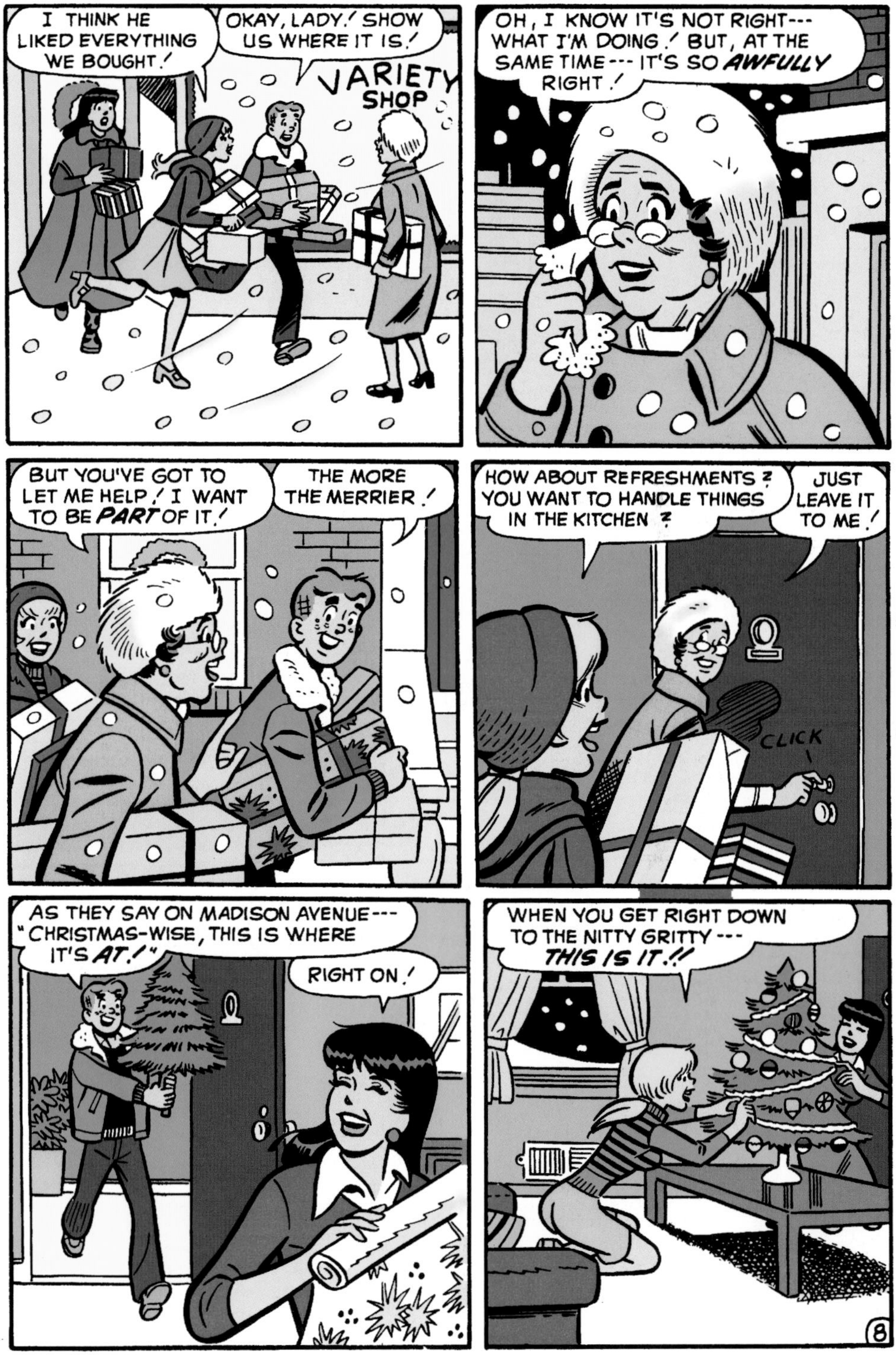
I THINK HE LIKED EVERYTHING WE BOUGHT!
OKAY, LADY! SHOW US WHERE IT IS!
VARIETY SHOP
OH, I KNOW IT'S NOT RIGHT--- WHAT I'M DOING! BUT, AT THE SAME TIME--- IT'S SO AWFULLY RIGHT!
BUT YOU'VE GOT TO LET ME HELP! I WANT TO BE PART OF IT!
THE MORE THE MERRIER!
HOW ABOUT REFRESHMENTS? YOU WANT TO HANDLE THINGS IN THE KITCHEN?
JUST LEAVE IT TO ME!
CLICK
AS THEY SAY ON MADISON AVENUE--- "CHRISTMAS-WISE, THIS IS WHERE IT'S AT!"
RIGHT ON!
WHEN YOU GET RIGHT DOWN TO THE NITTY GRITTY--- THIS IS IT!!
8

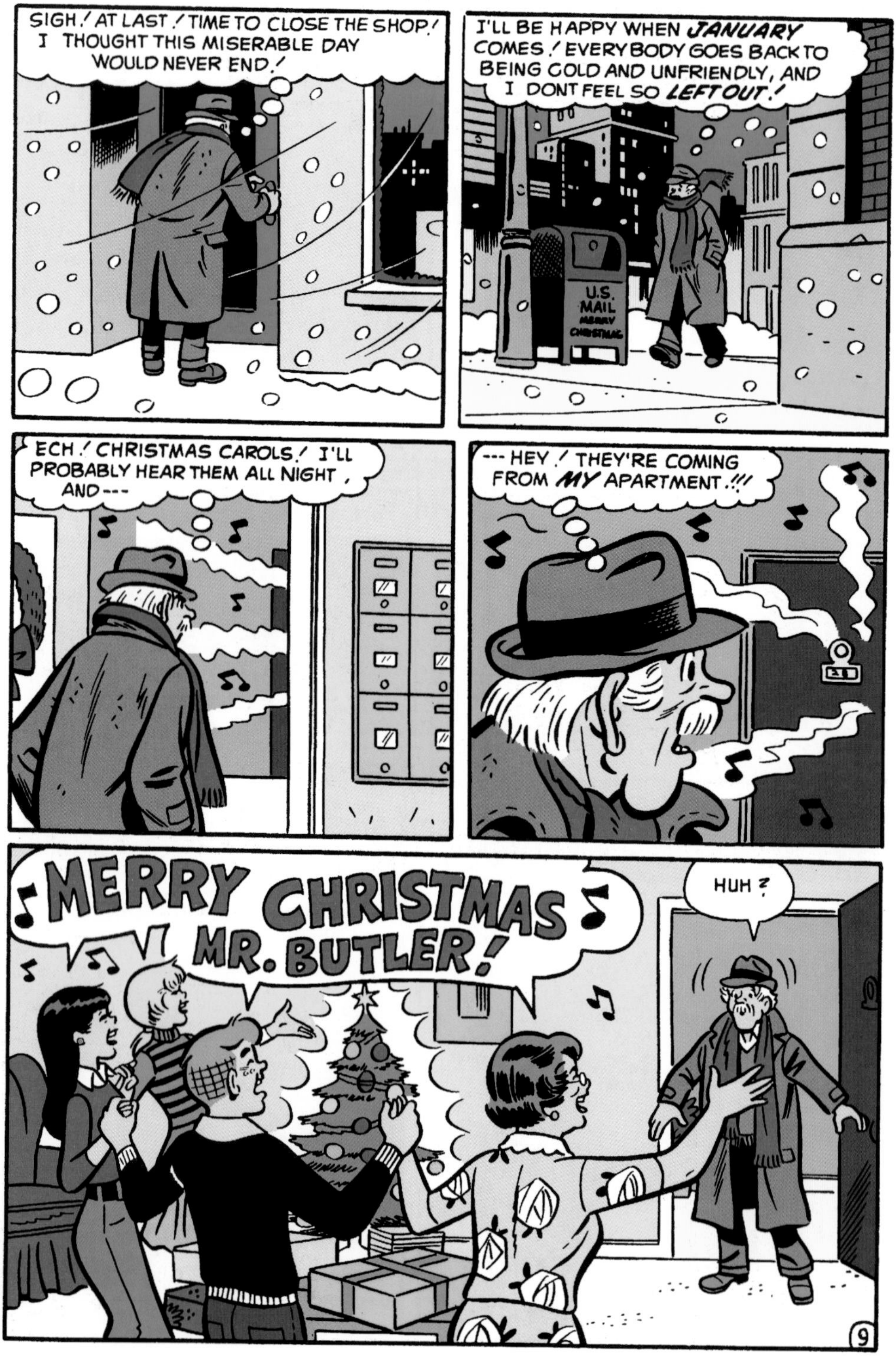
SIGH! AT LAST! TIME TO CLOSE THE SHOP! I THOUGHT THIS MISERABLE DAY WOULD NEVER END!
I'LL BE HAPPY WHEN JANUARY COMES! EVERYBODY GOES BACK TO BEING COLD AND UNFRIENDLY, AND I DONT FEEL SO LEFT OUT!
U.S. MAIL
MERRY CHRISTMAS
ECH! CHRISTMAS CAROLS! I'LL PROBABLY HEAR THEM ALL NIGHT, AND---
--- HEY! THEY'RE COMING FROM MY APARTMENT!!!
MERRY CHRISTMAS MR. BUTLER!
HUH?
9

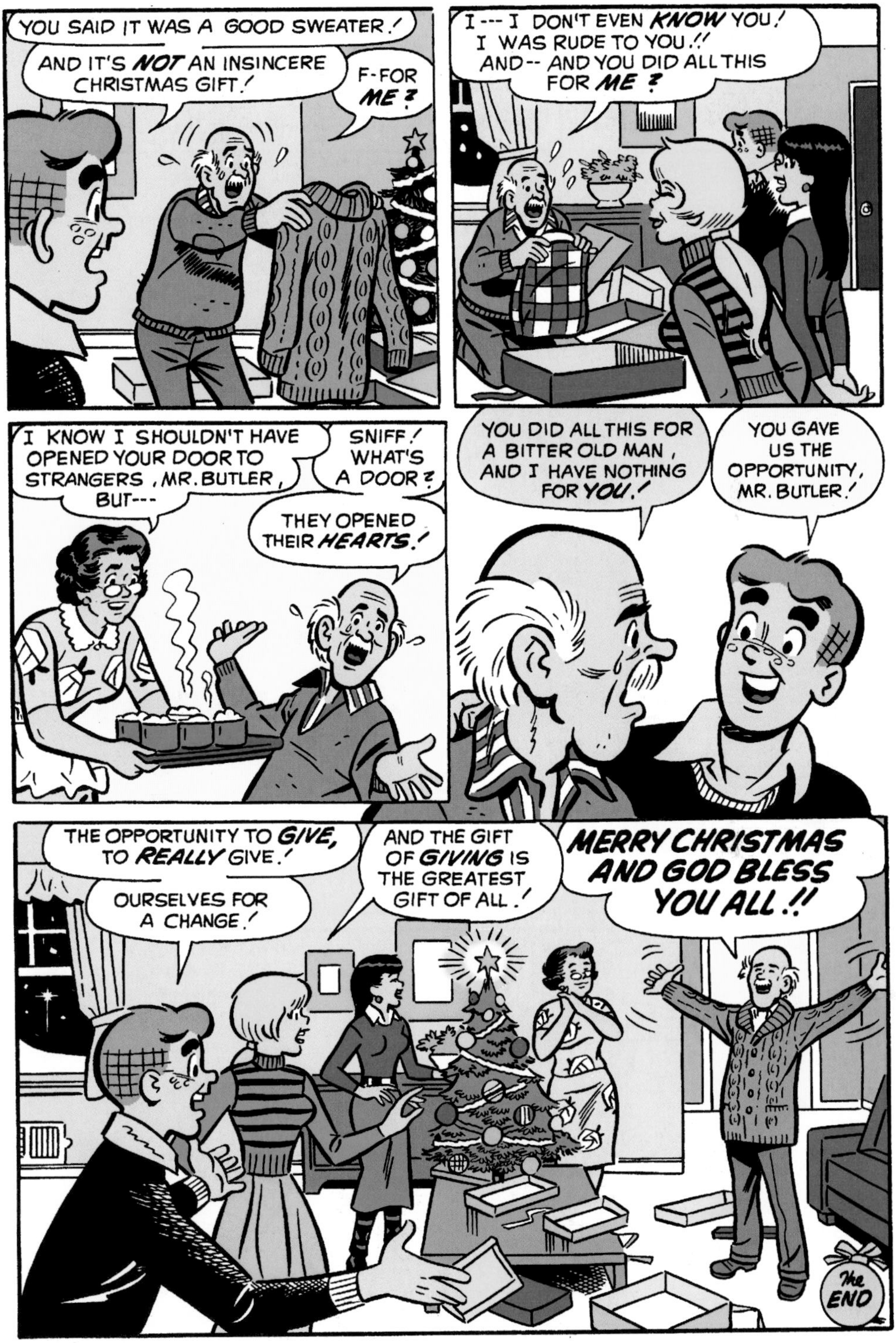
YOU SAID IT WAS A GOOD SWEATER!
AND IT'S NOT AN INSINCERE CHRISTMAS GIFT!
F-FOR ME?
I--- I DON'T EVEN KNOW YOU! I WAS RUDE TO YOU!! AND-- AND YOU DID ALL THIS FOR ME?
I KNOW I SHOULDN'T HAVE OPENED YOUR DOOR TO STRANGERS, MR. BUTLER, BUT---
SNIFF! WHAT'S A DOOR?
THEY OPENED THEIR HEARTS!
YOU DID ALL THIS FOR A BITTER OLD MAN, AND I HAVE NOTHING FOR YOU!
YOU GAVE US THE OPPORTUNITY, MR. BUTLER!
THE OPPORTUNITY TO GIVE, TO REALLY GIVE!
OURSELVES FOR A CHANGE!
AND THE GIFT OF GIVING IS THE GREATEST GIFT OF ALL!
MERRY CHRISTMAS AND GOD BLESS YOU ALL!!
The END

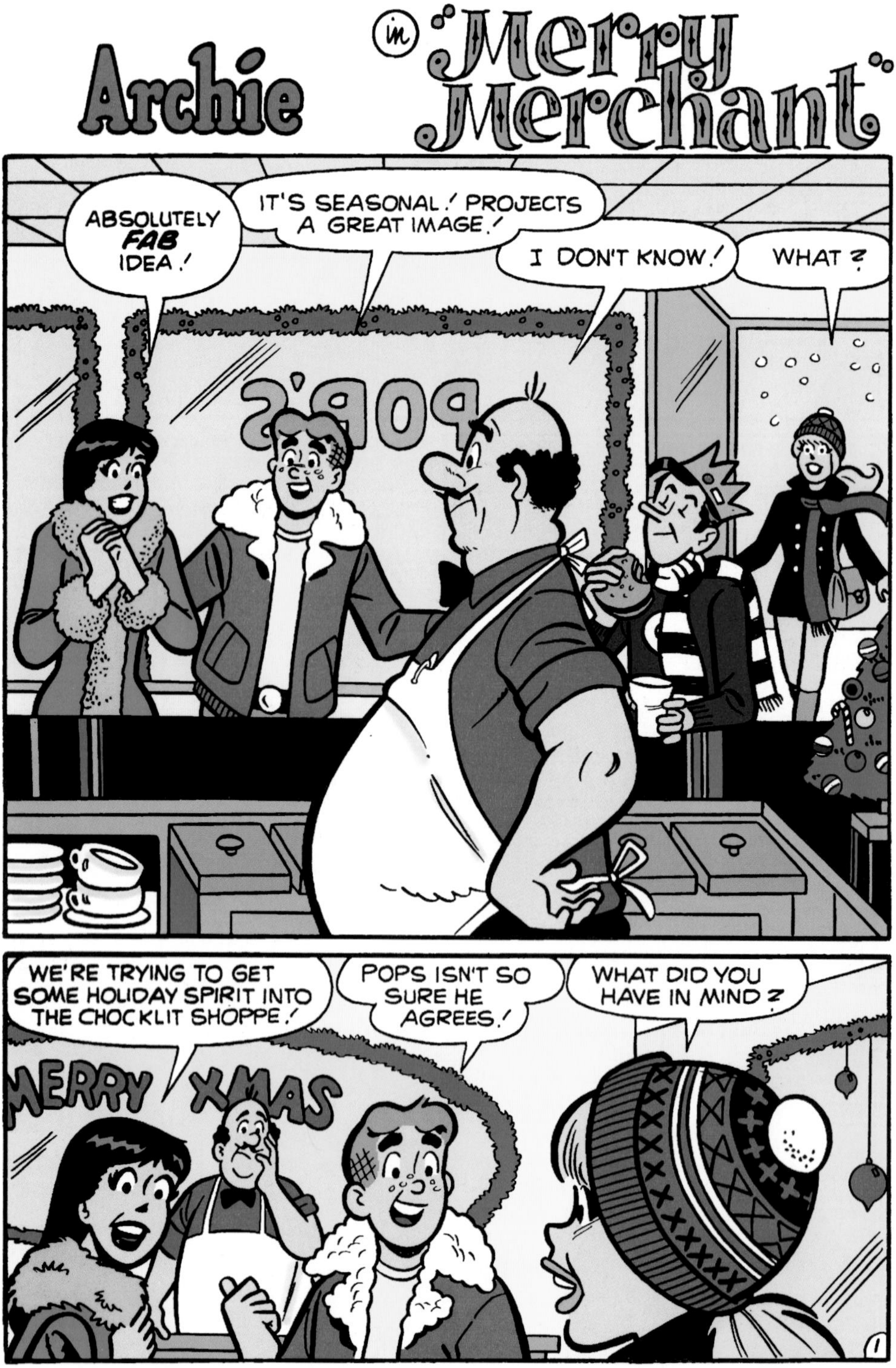
Archie in "Merry Merchant"
ABSOLUTELY FAB IDEA!
IT'S SEASONAL! PROJECTS A GREAT IMAGE!
I DON'T KNOW!
WHAT?
POP'S
WE'RE TRYING TO GET SOME HOLIDAY SPIRIT INTO THE CHOCKLIT SHOPPE!
POPS ISN'T SO SURE HE AGREES!
WHAT DID YOU HAVE IN MIND?
MERRY XMAS
1

Frank Doyle • Dan DeCarlo • Rudy Lapick • Bill Yoshida • Barry Grossman

Originally printed in ARCHIE GIANT SERIES MAGAZINE #453, 1976

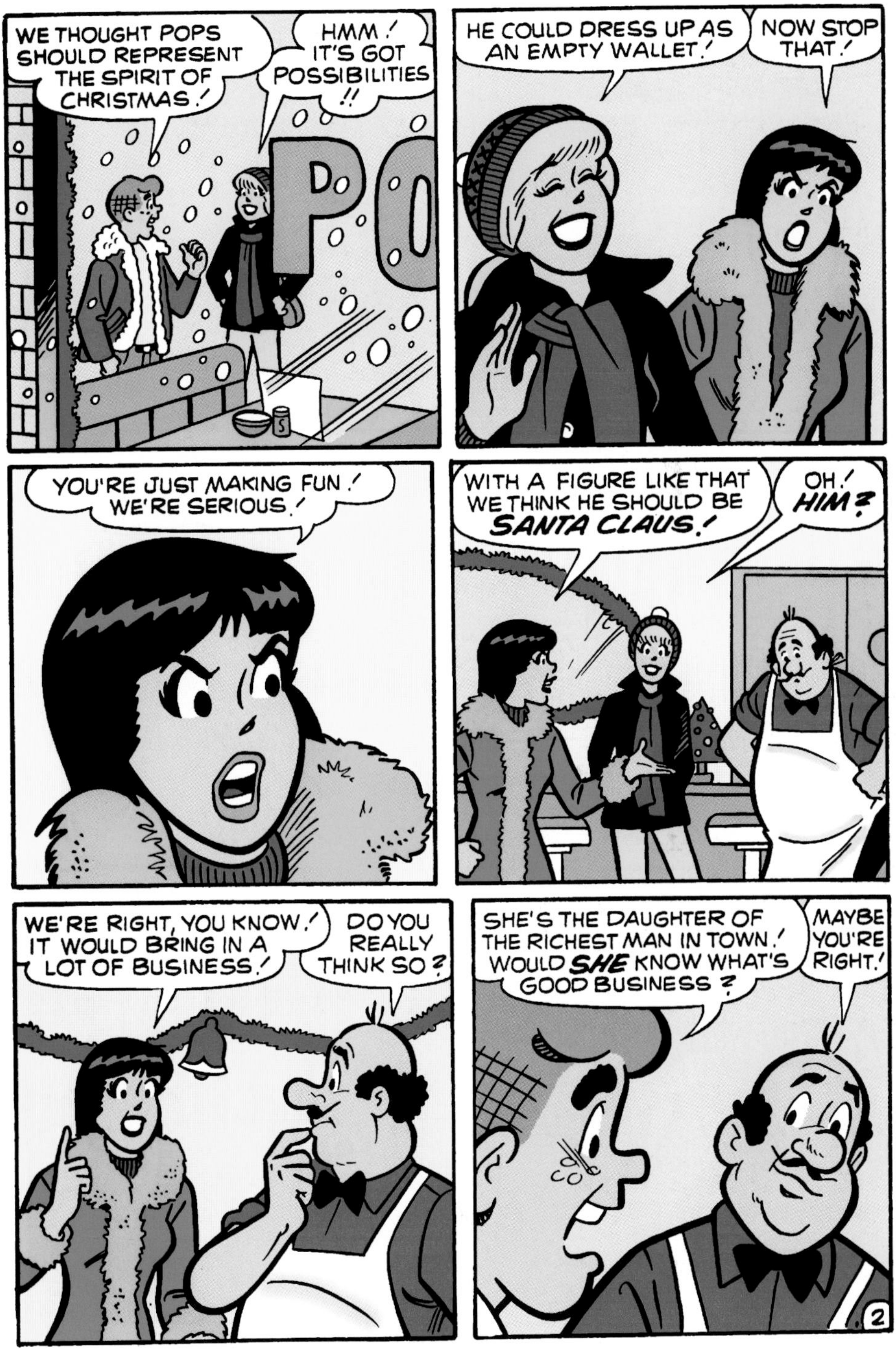
WE THOUGHT POPS SHOULD REPRESENT THE SPIRIT OF CHRISTMAS!
HMM! IT'S GOT POSSIBILITIES!!
PO
HE COULD DRESS UP AS AN EMPTY WALLET!
NOW STOP THAT!
YOU'RE JUST MAKING FUN! WE'RE SERIOUS!
WITH A FIGURE LIKE THAT WE THINK HE SHOULD BE SANTA CLAUS!
OH! HIM?
WE'RE RIGHT, YOU KNOW! IT WOULD BRING IN A LOT OF BUSINESS!
DO YOU REALLY THINK SO?
SHE'S THE DAUGHTER OF THE RICHEST MAN IN TOWN! WOULD SHE KNOW WHAT'S GOOD BUSINESS?
MAYBE YOU'RE RIGHT!
2

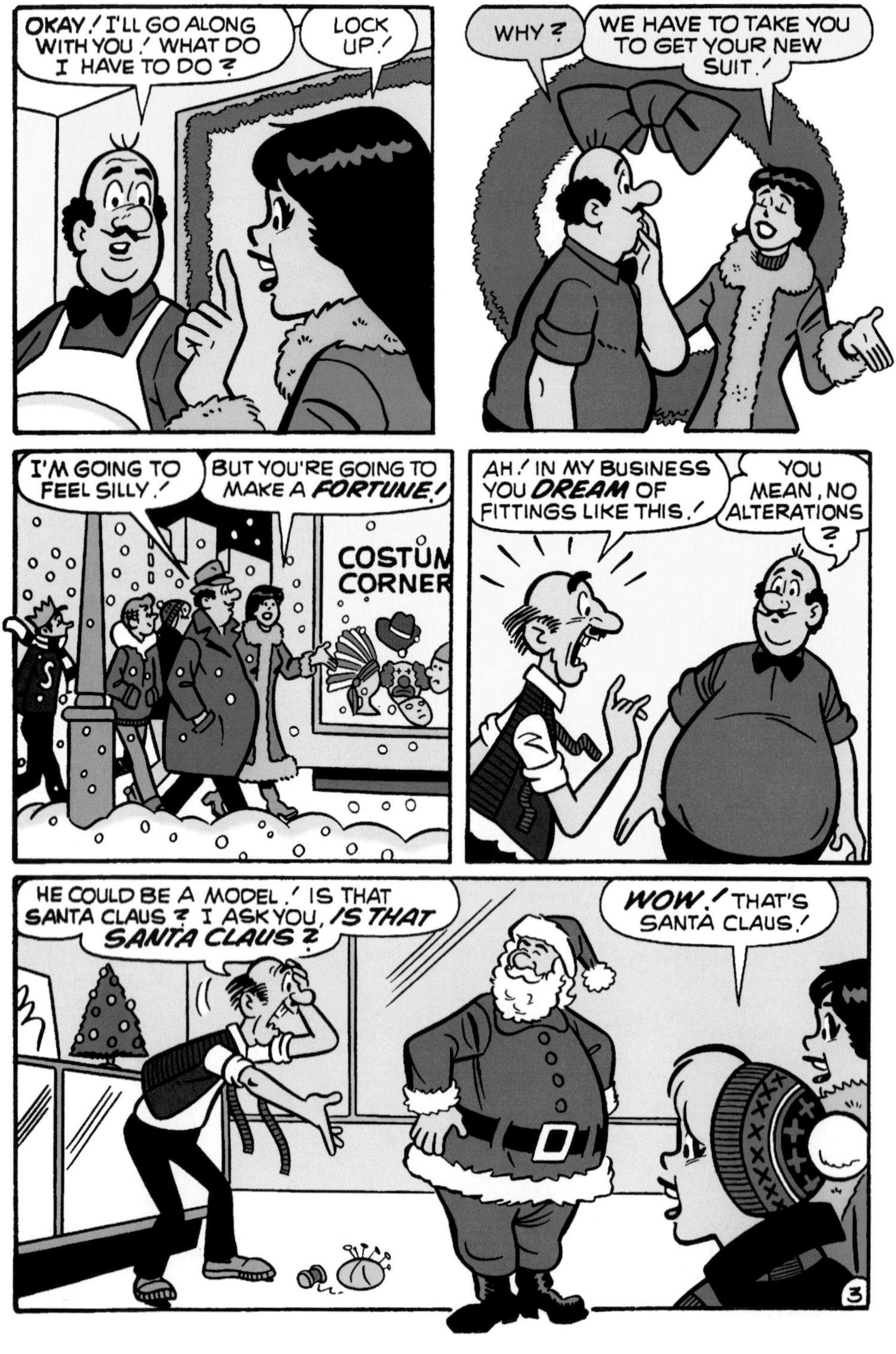
OKAY! I'LL GO ALONG WITH YOU! WHAT DO I HAVE TO DO?
LOCK UP!
WHY?
WE HAVE TO TAKE YOU TO GET YOUR NEW SUIT!
I'M GOING TO FEEL SILLY!
BUT YOU'RE GOING TO MAKE A FORTUNE!
COSTUM CORNER
AH! IN MY BUSINESS YOU DREAM OF FITTINGS LIKE THIS!
YOU MEAN, NO ALTERATIONS?
HE COULD BE A MODEL! IS THAT SANTA CLAUS? I ASK YOU, IS THAT SANTA CLAUS?
WOW! THAT'S SANTA CLAUS!
3

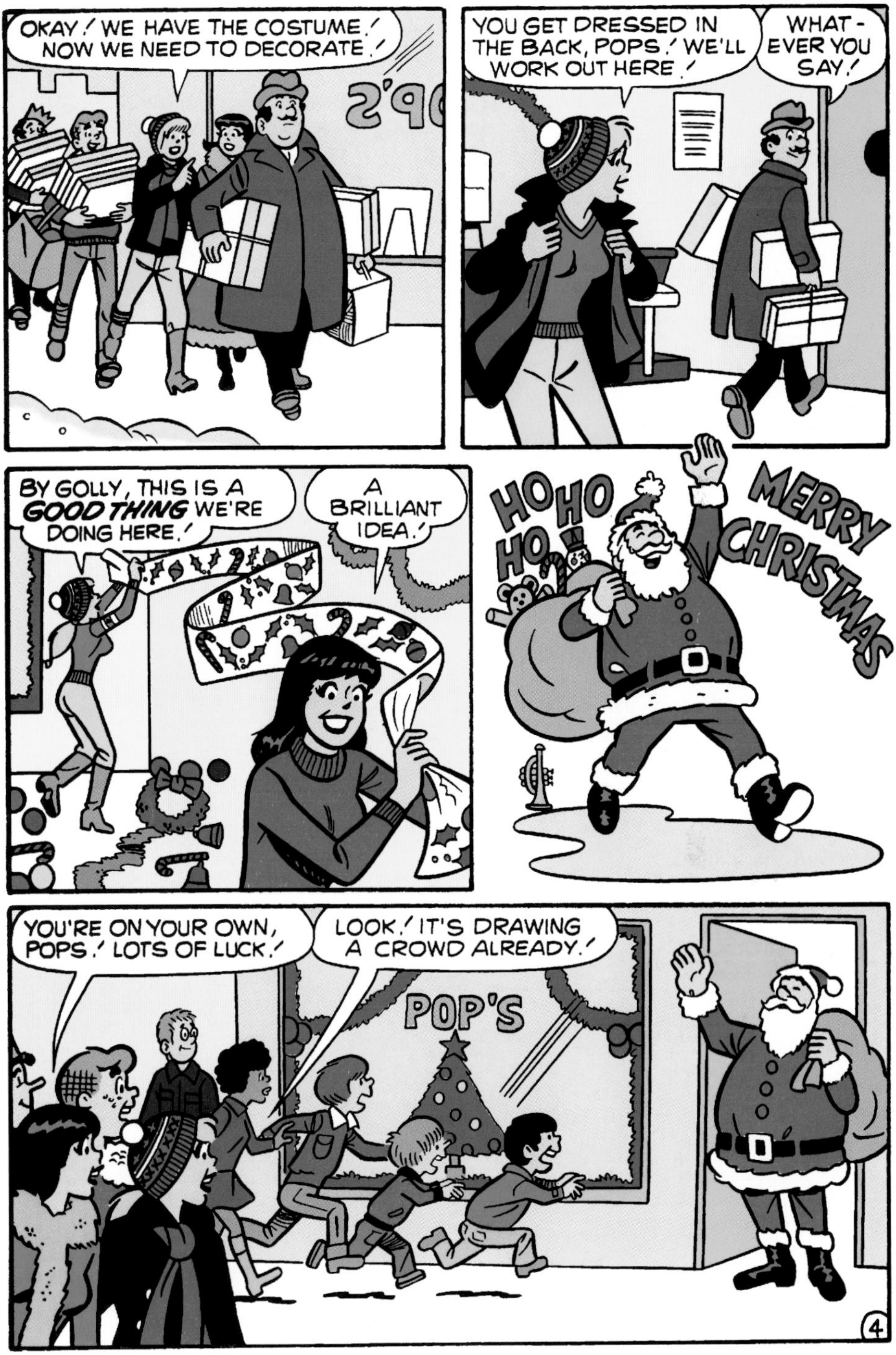
OKAY! WE HAVE THE COSTUME! NOW WE NEED TO DECORATE!
YOU GET DRESSED IN THE BACK, POPS! WE'LL WORK OUT HERE!
WHAT-EVER YOU SAY!
BY GOLLY, THIS IS A GOOD THING WE'RE DOING HERE!
A BRILLIANT IDEA!
HO HO HO
MERRY CHRISTMAS
YOU'RE ON YOUR OWN, POPS! LOTS OF LUCK!
LOOK! IT'S DRAWING A CROWD ALREADY!
POP'S
4

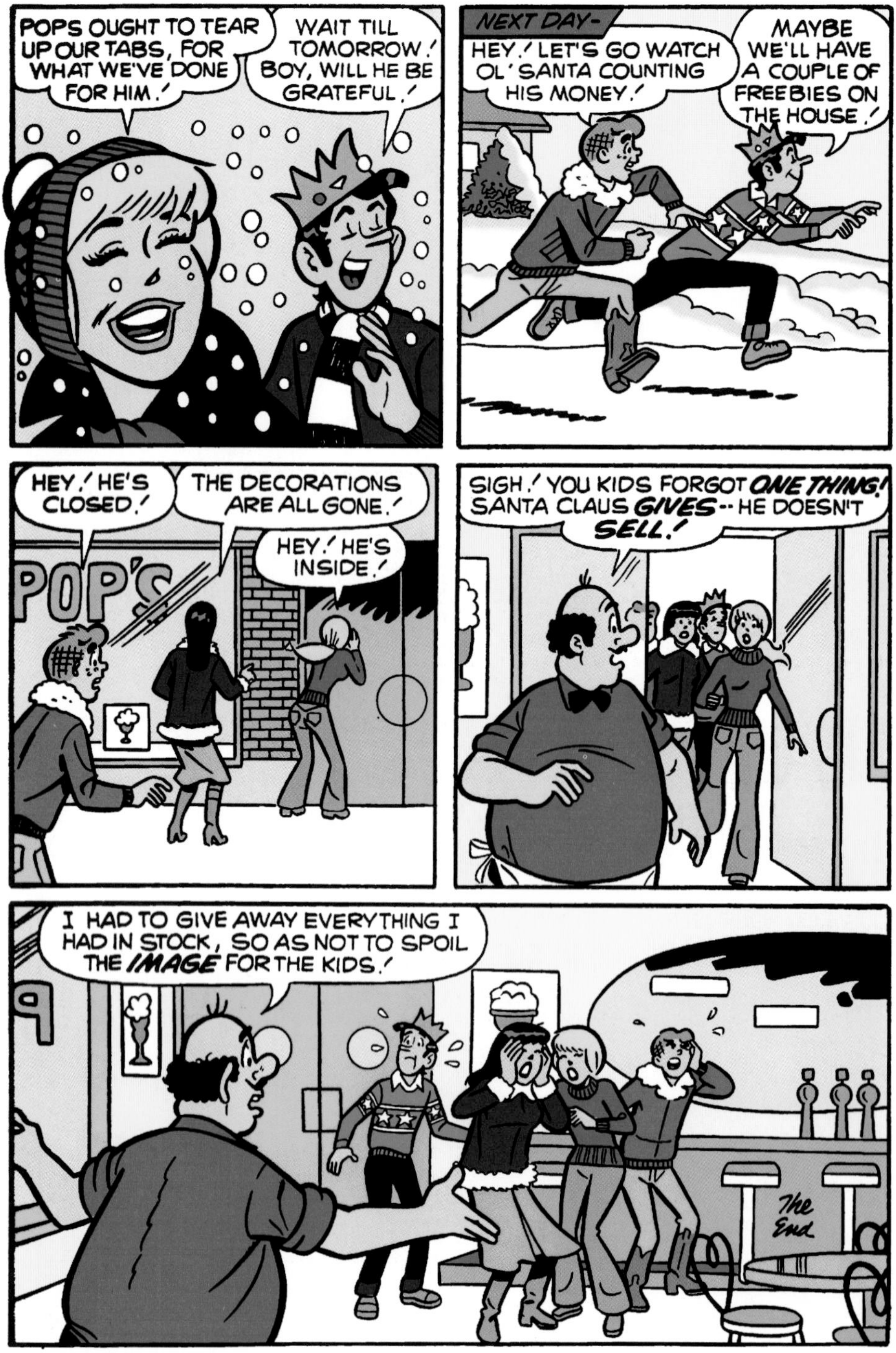
POPS OUGHT TO TEAR UP OUR TABS, FOR WHAT WE'VE DONE FOR HIM.!
WAIT TILL TOMORROW.! BOY, WILL HE BE GRATEFUL.!
NEXT DAY-
HEY.! LET'S GO WATCH OL' SANTA COUNTING HIS MONEY.!
MAYBE WE'LL HAVE A COUPLE OF FREEBIES ON THE HOUSE.!
HEY.! HE'S CLOSED.!
THE DECORATIONS ARE ALL GONE.!
POP'S
HEY.! HE'S INSIDE.!
SIGH.! YOU KIDS FORGOT ONE THING! SANTA CLAUS GIVES-- HE DOESN'T SELL.!
I HAD TO GIVE AWAY EVERYTHING I HAD IN STOCK, SO AS NOT TO SPOIL THE IMAGE FOR THE KIDS.!
The End

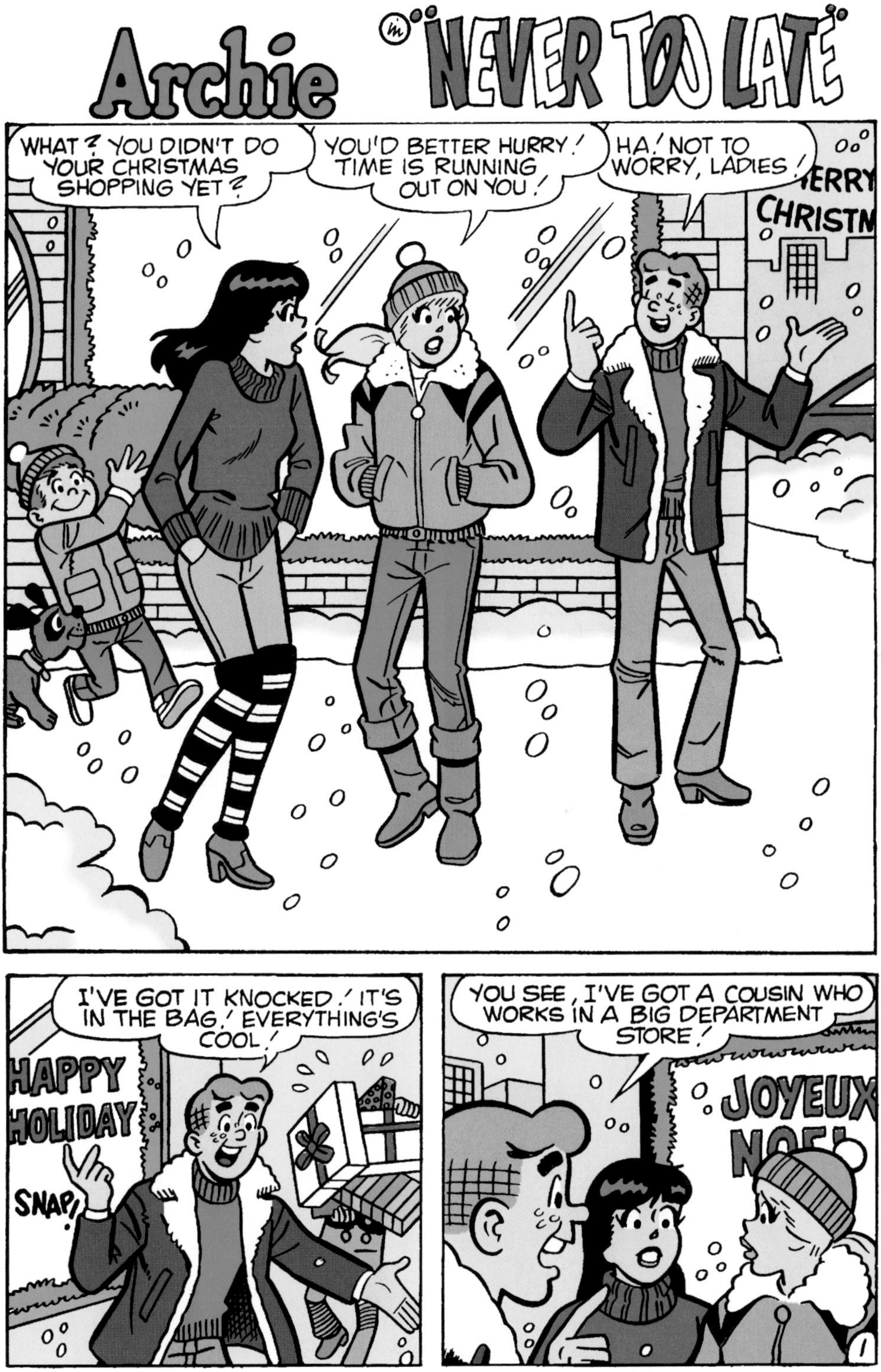
Archie in "NEVER TOO LATE"
WHAT? YOU DIDN'T DO YOUR CHRISTMAS SHOPPING YET?
YOU'D BETTER HURRY! TIME IS RUNNING OUT ON YOU!
HA! NOT TO WORRY, LADIES!
I'VE GOT IT KNOCKED! IT'S IN THE BAG! EVERYTHING'S COOL!
HAPPY HOLIDAY
SNAP!
YOU SEE, I'VE GOT A COUSIN WHO WORKS IN A BIG DEPARTMENT STORE!
JOYEUX
1

Frank Doyle • Dan DeCarlo Jr. • Rudy Lapick • Bill Yoshida • Alisa Merrill

Originally printed in LAUGH COMICS #371, 1982

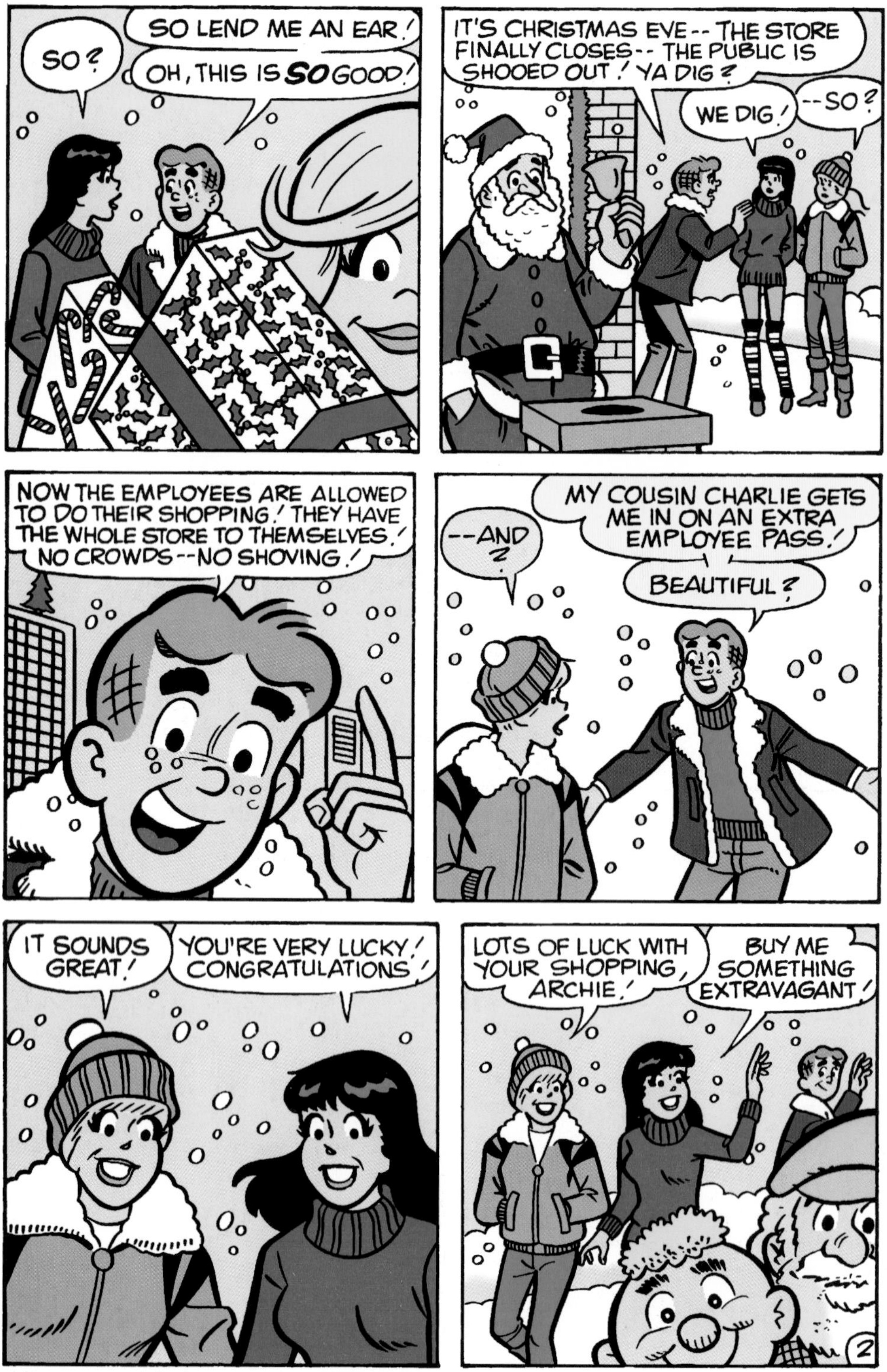
SO?
SO LEND ME AN EAR!
OH, THIS IS **SO** GOOD!
IT'S CHRISTMAS EVE -- THE STORE FINALLY CLOSES -- THE PUBLIC IS SHOOED OUT! YA DIG?
WE DIG!
--SO?
NOW THE EMPLOYEES ARE ALLOWED TO DO THEIR SHOPPING! THEY HAVE THE WHOLE STORE TO THEMSELVES! NO CROWDS--NO SHOVING!
--AND?
MY COUSIN CHARLIE GETS ME IN ON AN EXTRA EMPLOYEE PASS!
BEAUTIFUL?
IT SOUNDS GREAT!
YOU'RE VERY LUCKY! CONGRATULATIONS!
LOTS OF LUCK WITH YOUR SHOPPING, ARCHIE!
BUY ME SOMETHING EXTRAVAGANT!
2

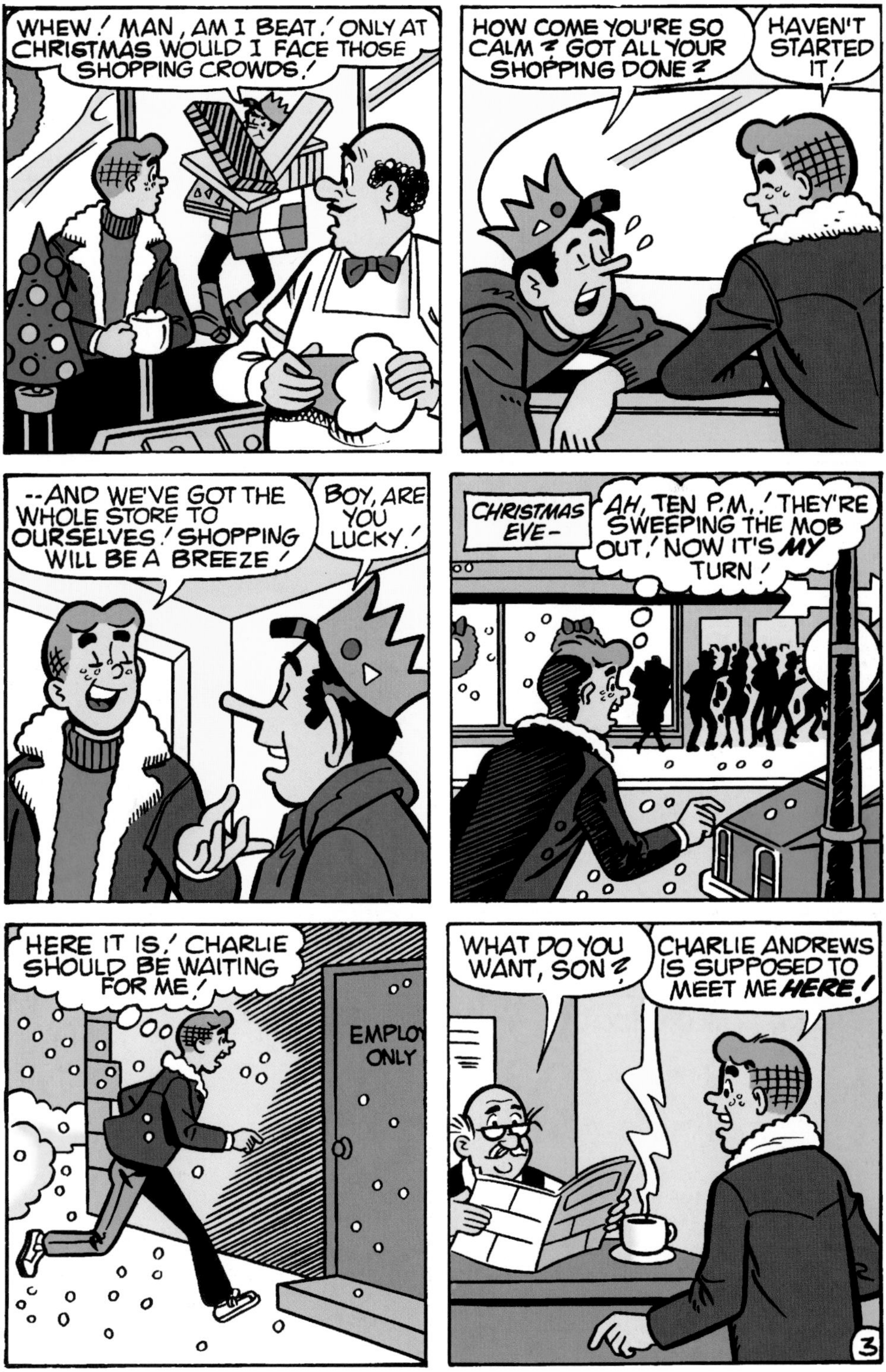
WHEW! MAN, AM I BEAT! ONLY AT CHRISTMAS WOULD I FACE THOSE SHOPPING CROWDS!
HOW COME YOU'RE SO CALM? GOT ALL YOUR SHOPPING DONE?
HAVEN'T STARTED IT!
--AND WE'VE GOT THE WHOLE STORE TO OURSELVES! SHOPPING WILL BE A BREEZE!
BOY, ARE YOU LUCKY!
CHRISTMAS EVE-
AH, TEN P.M.! THEY'RE SWEEPING THE MOB OUT! NOW IT'S MY TURN!
HERE IT IS! CHARLIE SHOULD BE WAITING FOR ME!
ONLY
WHAT DO YOU WANT, SON?
CHARLIE ANDREWS IS SUPPOSED TO MEET ME HERE!
3

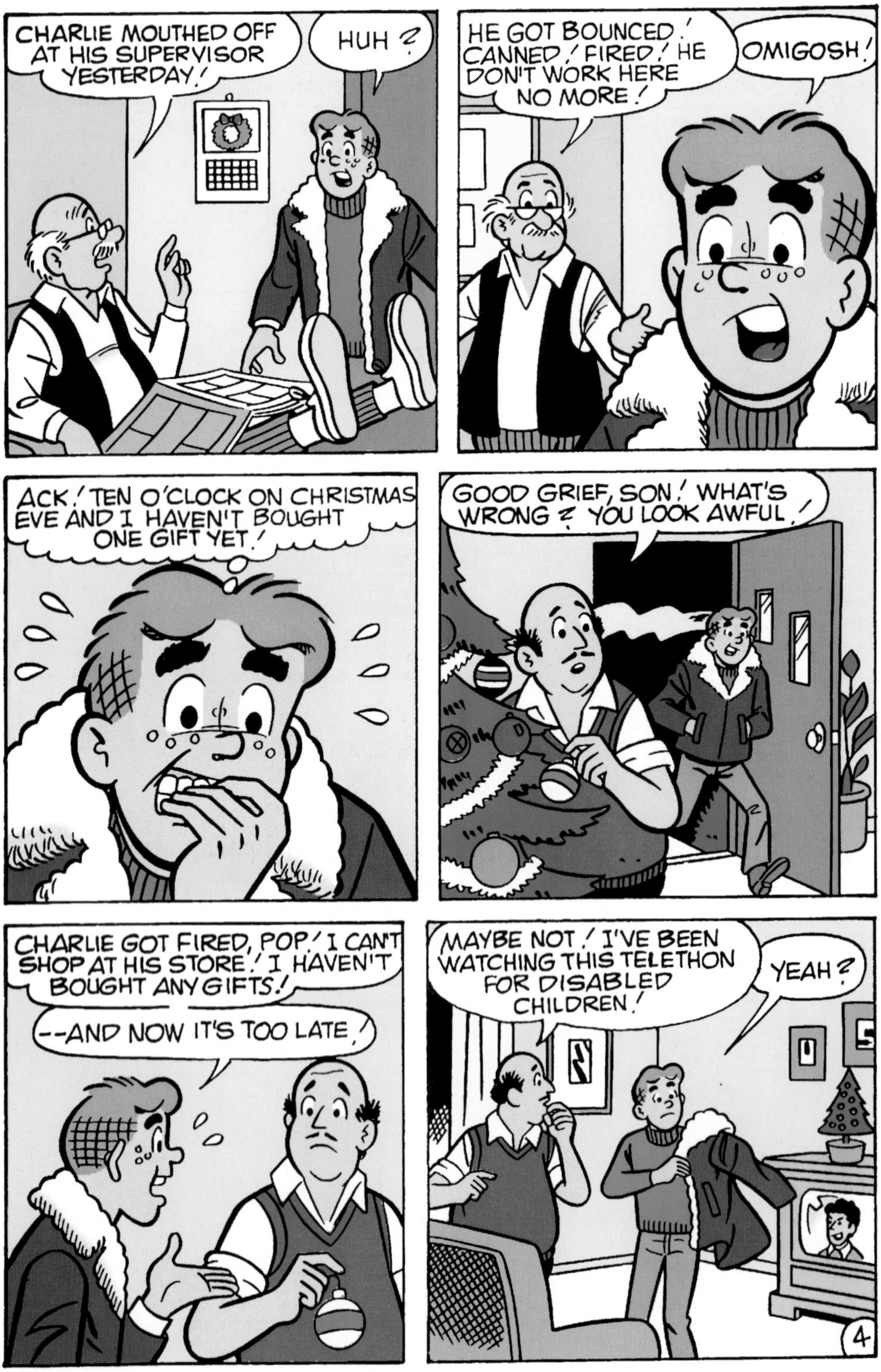
CHARLIE MOUTHED OFF AT HIS SUPERVISOR YESTERDAY!
HUH?
HE GOT BOUNCED! CANNED! FIRED! HE DON'T WORK HERE NO MORE!
OMIGOSH!
ACK! TEN O'CLOCK ON CHRISTMAS EVE AND I HAVEN'T BOUGHT ONE GIFT YET!
GOOD GRIEF, SON! WHAT'S WRONG? YOU LOOK AWFUL!
CHARLIE GOT FIRED, POP! I CAN'T SHOP AT HIS STORE! I HAVEN'T BOUGHT ANY GIFTS!
--AND NOW IT'S TOO LATE!
MAYBE NOT! I'VE BEEN WATCHING THIS TELETHON FOR DISABLED CHILDREN!
YEAH?
4

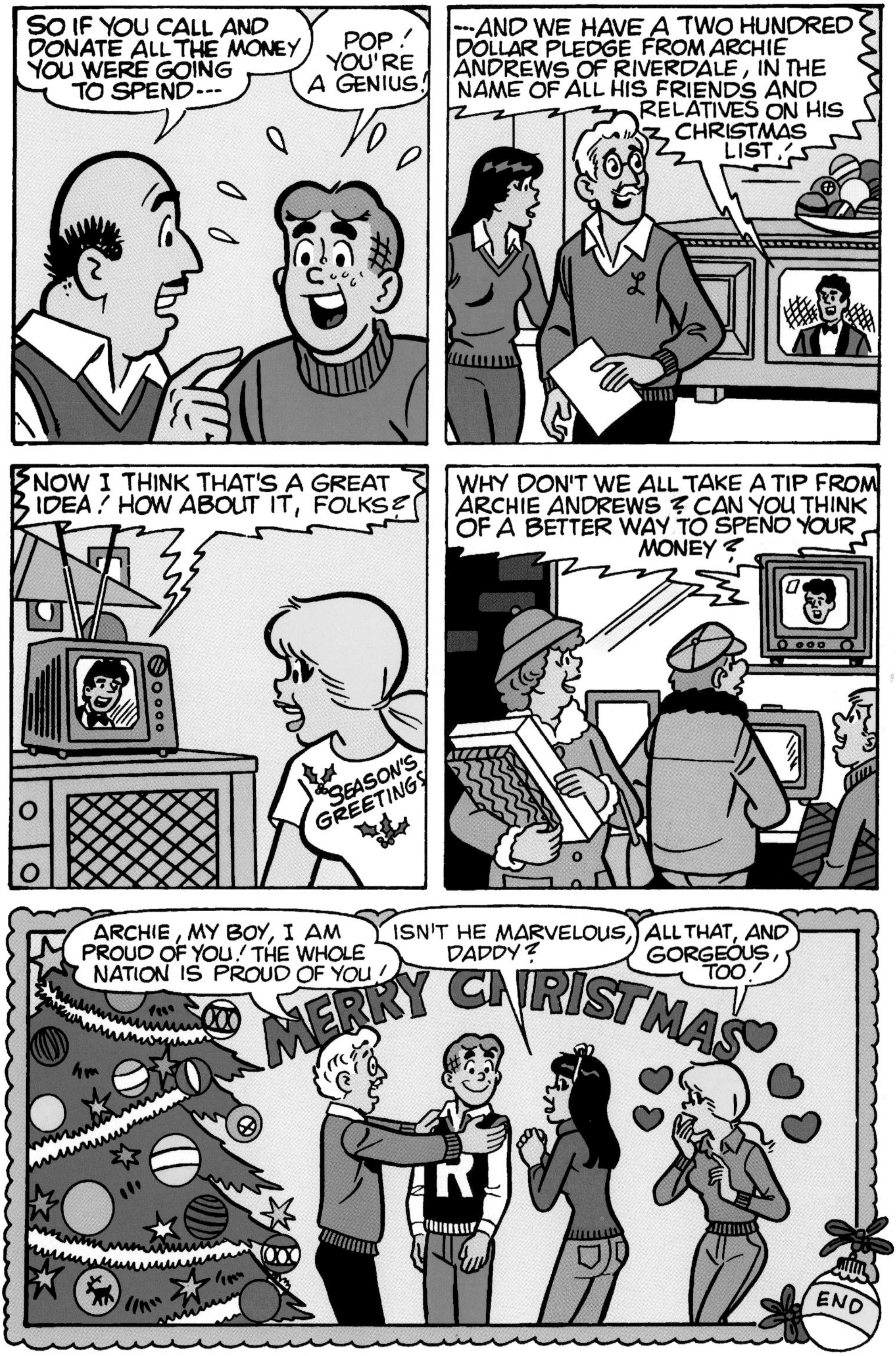
SO IF YOU CALL AND DONATE ALL THE MONEY YOU WERE GOING TO SPEND---
POP! YOU'RE A GENIUS!
---AND WE HAVE A TWO HUNDRED DOLLAR PLEDGE FROM ARCHIE ANDREWS OF RIVERDALE, IN THE NAME OF ALL HIS FRIENDS AND RELATIVES ON HIS CHRISTMAS LIST!
NOW I THINK THAT'S A GREAT IDEA! HOW ABOUT IT, FOLKS?
SEASON'S GREETINGS
WHY DON'T WE ALL TAKE A TIP FROM ARCHIE ANDREWS? CAN YOU THINK OF A BETTER WAY TO SPEND YOUR MONEY?
ARCHIE, MY BOY, I AM PROUD OF YOU! THE WHOLE NATION IS PROUD OF YOU!
ISN'T HE MARVELOUS, DADDY?
ALL THAT, AND GORGEOUS, TOO!
MERRY CHRISTMAS
END

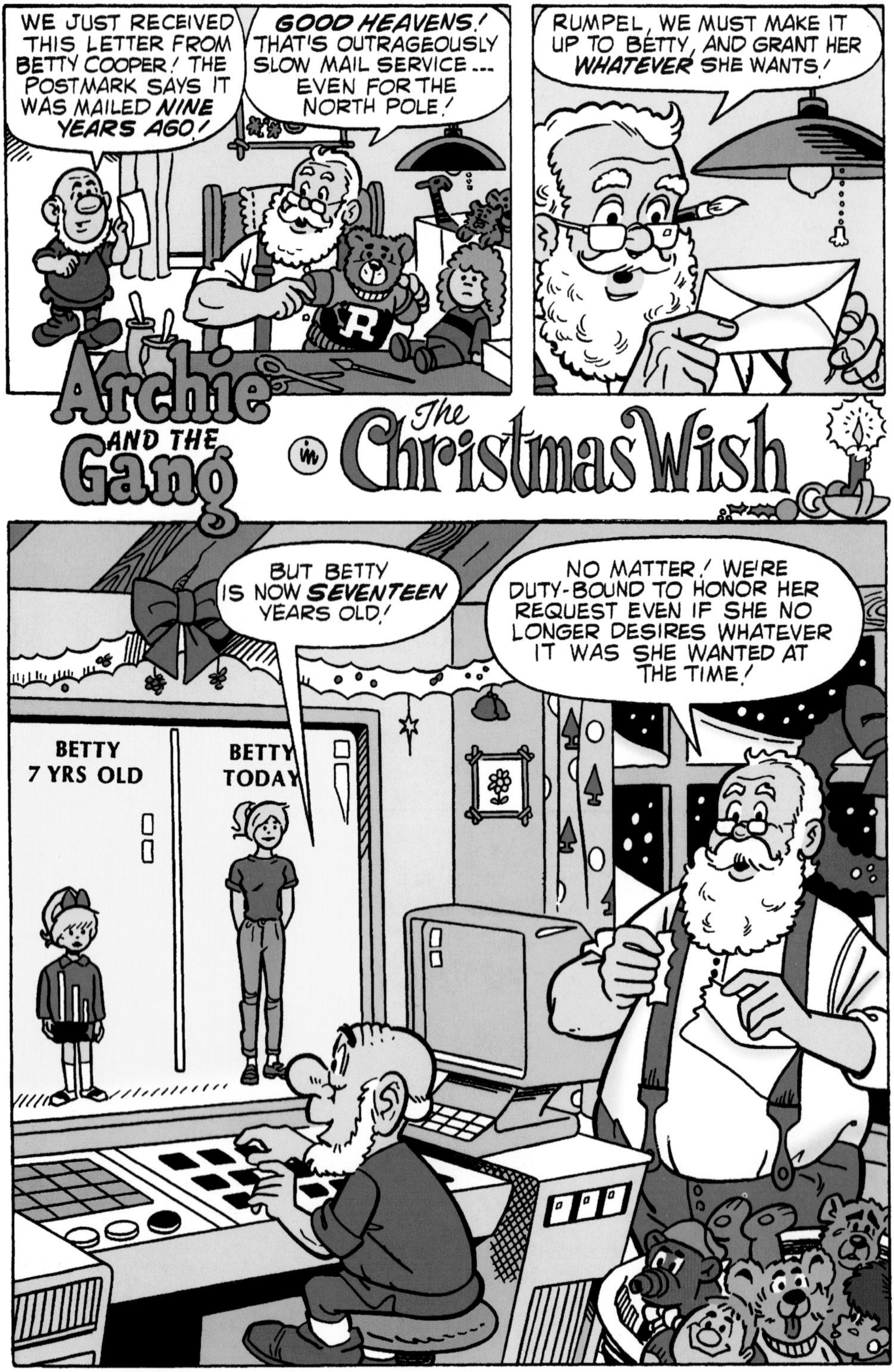
WE JUST RECEIVED THIS LETTER FROM BETTY COOPER! THE POSTMARK SAYS IT WAS MAILED NINE YEARS AGO!
GOOD HEAVENS! THAT'S OUTRAGEOUSLY SLOW MAIL SERVICE... EVEN FOR THE NORTH POLE!
RUMPEL, WE MUST MAKE IT UP TO BETTY, AND GRANT HER WHATEVER SHE WANTS!
Archie AND THE Gang in The Christmas Wish
BUT BETTY IS NOW SEVENTEEN YEARS OLD!
NO MATTER! WE'RE DUTY-BOUND TO HONOR HER REQUEST EVEN IF SHE NO LONGER DESIRES WHATEVER IT WAS SHE WANTED AT THE TIME!
BETTY 7 YRS OLD
BETTY TODAY

George Gladir • Dan DeCarlo • Jim DeCarlo • Bill Yoshida • Barry Grossman

Originally printed in BETTY & VERONICA #8, 1988

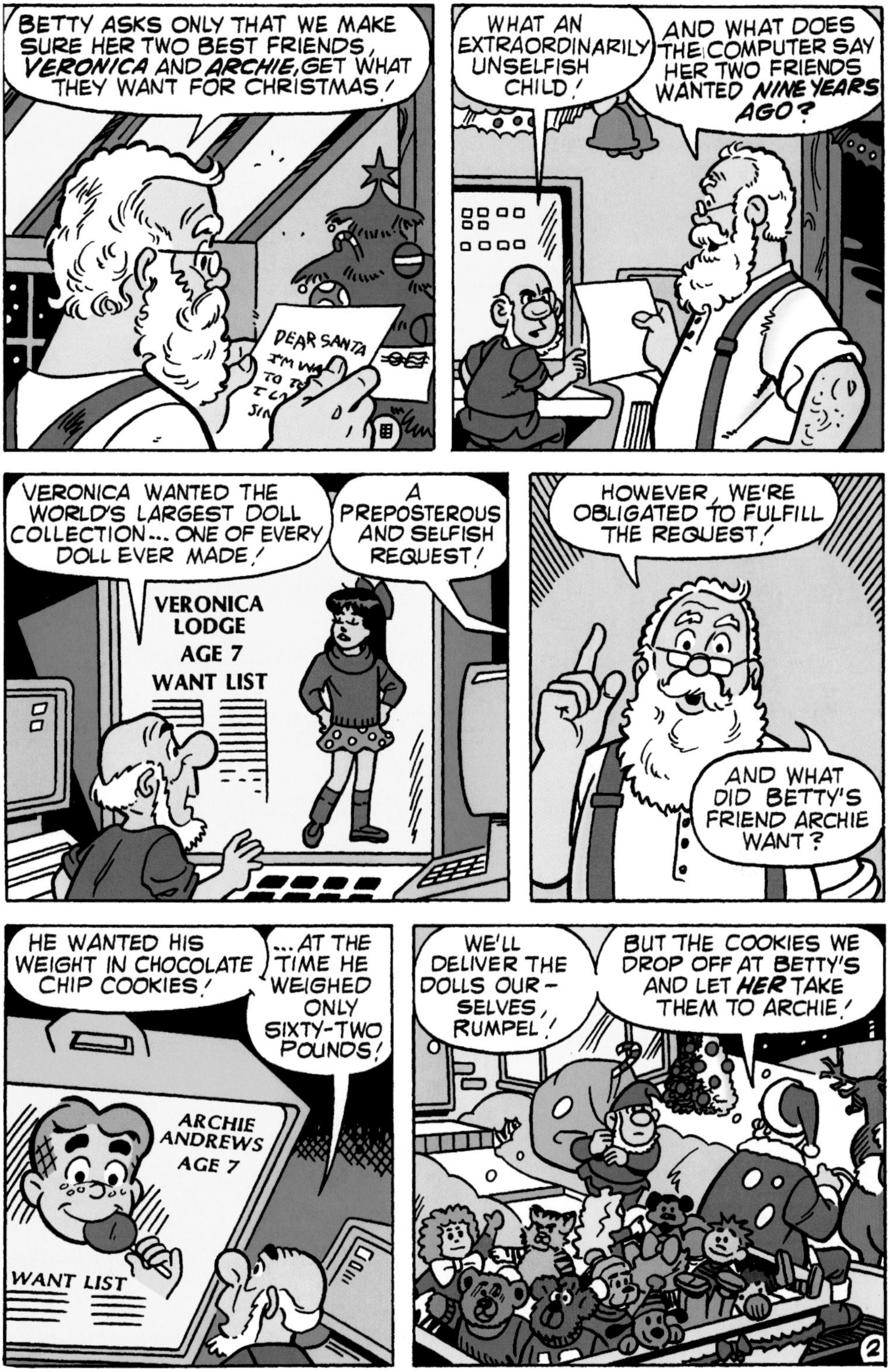
BETTY ASKS ONLY THAT WE MAKE SURE HER TWO BEST FRIENDS, VERONICA AND ARCHIE, GET WHAT THEY WANT FOR CHRISTMAS!
DEAR SANTA
WHAT AN EXTRAORDINARILY UNSELFISH CHILD!
AND WHAT DOES THE COMPUTER SAY HER TWO FRIENDS WANTED NINE YEARS AGO?
VERONICA WANTED THE WORLD'S LARGEST DOLL COLLECTION... ONE OF EVERY DOLL EVER MADE!
A PREPOSTEROUS AND SELFISH REQUEST!
VERONICA LODGE AGE 7 WANT LIST
HOWEVER, WE'RE OBLIGATED TO FULFILL THE REQUEST!
AND WHAT DID BETTY'S FRIEND ARCHIE WANT?
HE WANTED HIS WEIGHT IN CHOCOLATE CHIP COOKIES!
...AT THE TIME HE WEIGHED ONLY SIXTY-TWO POUNDS!
ARCHIE ANDREWS AGE 7
WANT LIST
WE'LL DELIVER THE DOLLS OURSELVES, RUMPEL!
BUT THE COOKIES WE DROP OFF AT BETTY'S AND LET HER TAKE THEM TO ARCHIE!
2

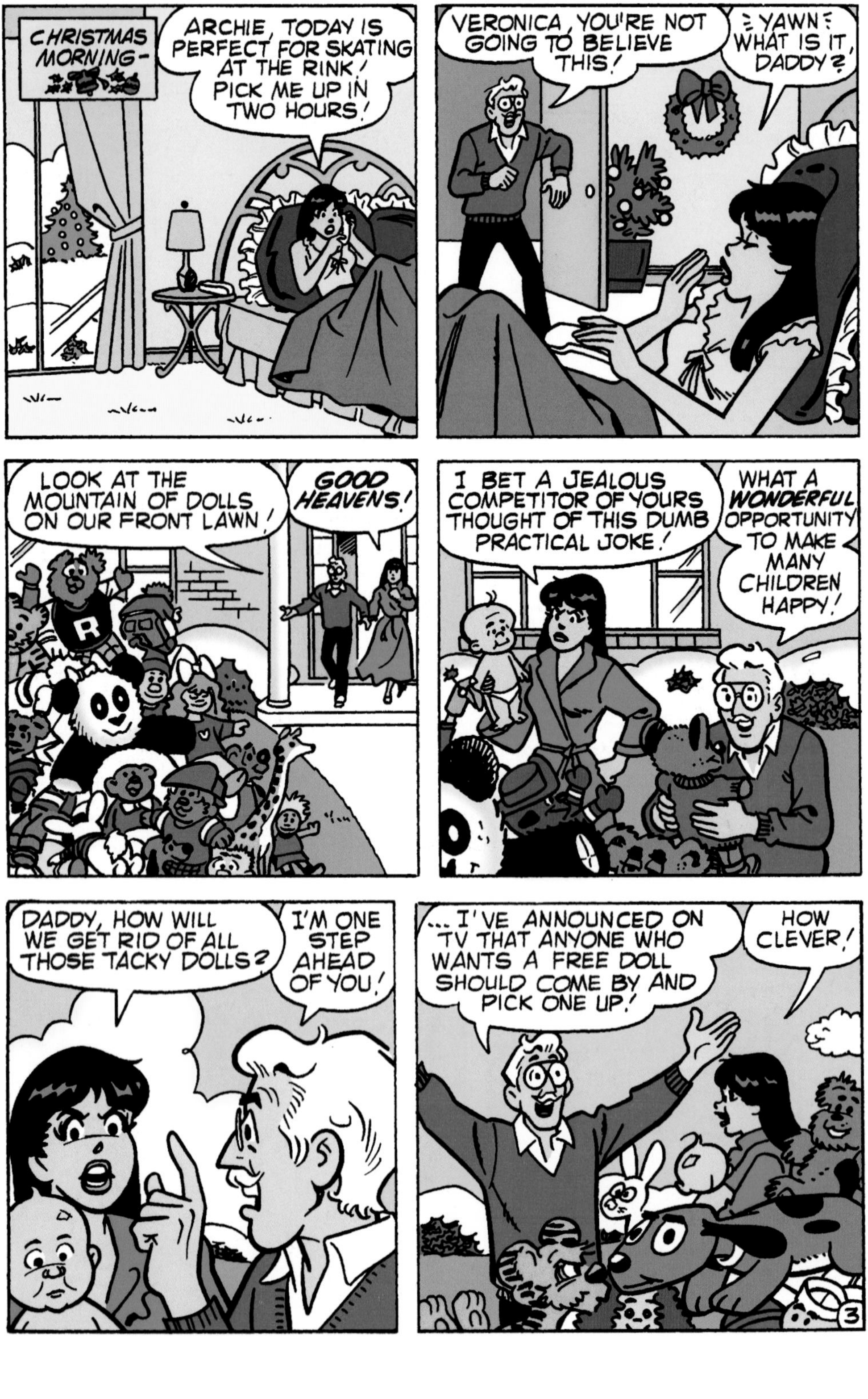
CHRISTMAS MORNING -
ARCHIE, TODAY IS PERFECT FOR SKATING AT THE RINK! PICK ME UP IN TWO HOURS!
VERONICA, YOU'RE NOT GOING TO BELIEVE THIS!
YAWN WHAT IS IT, DADDY?
LOOK AT THE MOUNTAIN OF DOLLS ON OUR FRONT LAWN!
GOOD HEAVENS!
I BET A JEALOUS COMPETITOR OF YOURS THOUGHT OF THIS DUMB PRACTICAL JOKE!
WHAT A WONDERFUL OPPORTUNITY TO MAKE MANY CHILDREN HAPPY!
DADDY, HOW WILL WE GET RID OF ALL THOSE TACKY DOLLS?
I'M ONE STEP AHEAD OF YOU!
... I'VE ANNOUNCED ON TV THAT ANYONE WHO WANTS A FREE DOLL SHOULD COME BY AND PICK ONE UP!
HOW CLEVER!
3

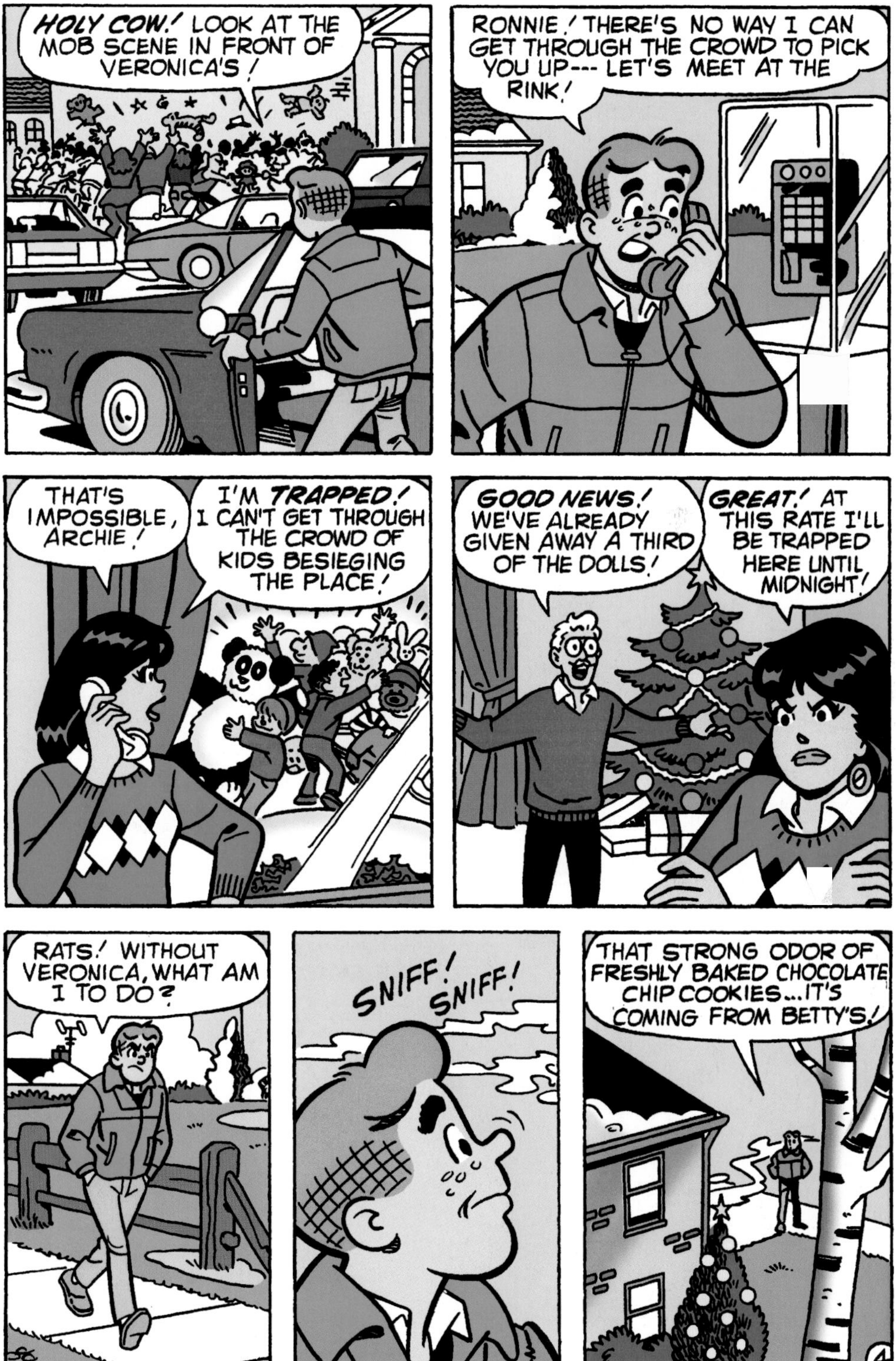
HOLY COW! LOOK AT THE MOB SCENE IN FRONT OF VERONICA'S!
RONNIE! THERE'S NO WAY I CAN GET THROUGH THE CROWD TO PICK YOU UP--- LET'S MEET AT THE RINK!
THAT'S IMPOSSIBLE, ARCHIE!
I'M TRAPPED! I CAN'T GET THROUGH THE CROWD OF KIDS BESIEGING THE PLACE!
GOOD NEWS! WE'VE ALREADY GIVEN AWAY A THIRD OF THE DOLLS!
GREAT! AT THIS RATE I'LL BE TRAPPED HERE UNTIL MIDNIGHT!
RATS! WITHOUT VERONICA, WHAT AM I TO DO?
SNIFF! SNIFF!
THAT STRONG ODOR OF FRESHLY BAKED CHOCOLATE CHIP COOKIES...IT'S COMING FROM BETTY'S!
4

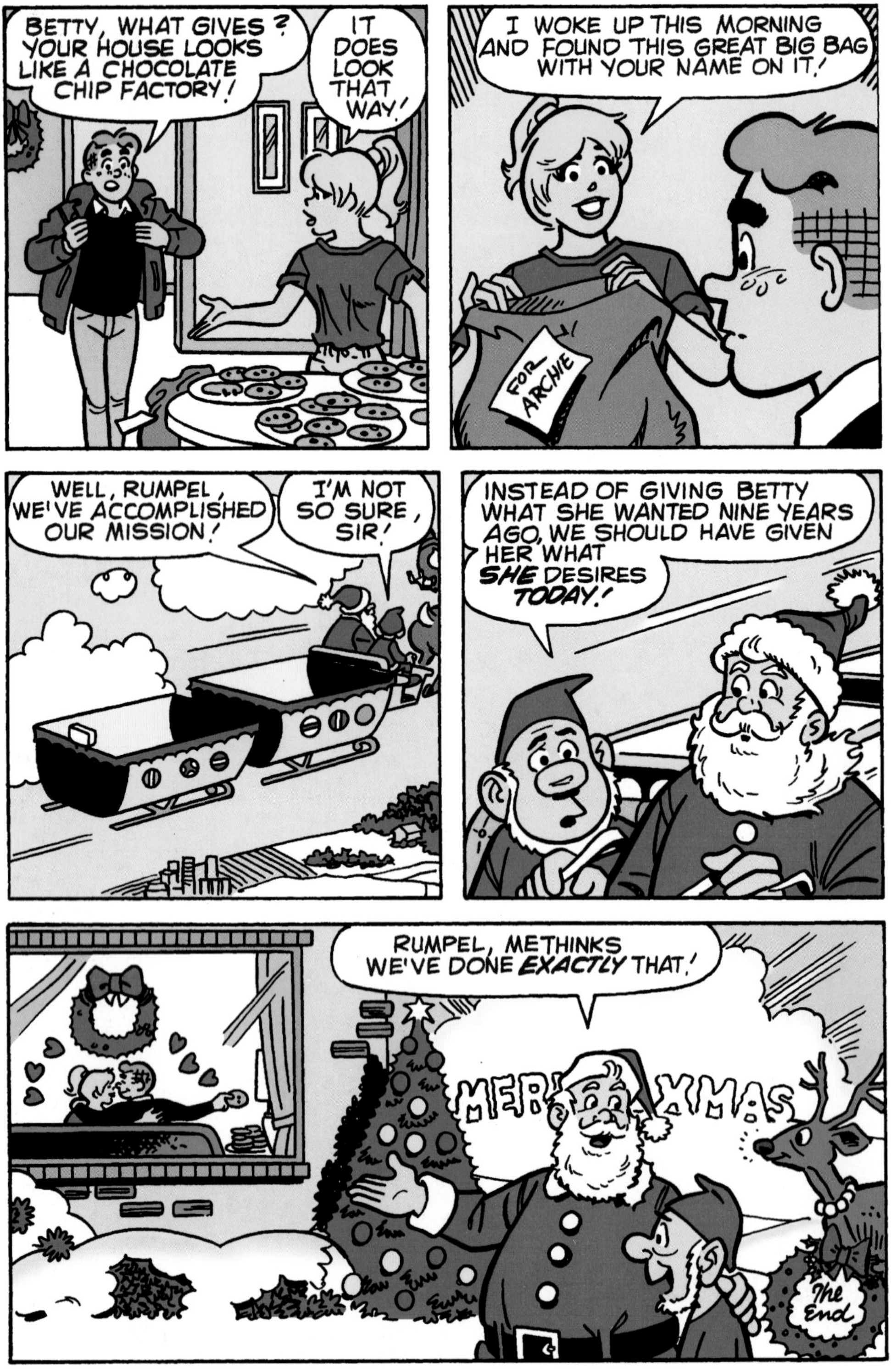
BETTY, WHAT GIVES? YOUR HOUSE LOOKS LIKE A CHOCOLATE CHIP FACTORY!
IT DOES LOOK THAT WAY!
I WOKE UP THIS MORNING AND FOUND THIS GREAT BIG BAG WITH YOUR NAME ON IT!
FOR ARCHIE
WELL, RUMPEL, WE'VE ACCOMPLISHED OUR MISSION!
I'M NOT SO SURE, SIR!
INSTEAD OF GIVING BETTY WHAT SHE WANTED NINE YEARS AGO, WE SHOULD HAVE GIVEN HER WHAT SHE DESIRES TODAY!
RUMPEL, METHINKS WE'VE DONE EXACTLY THAT!
The End

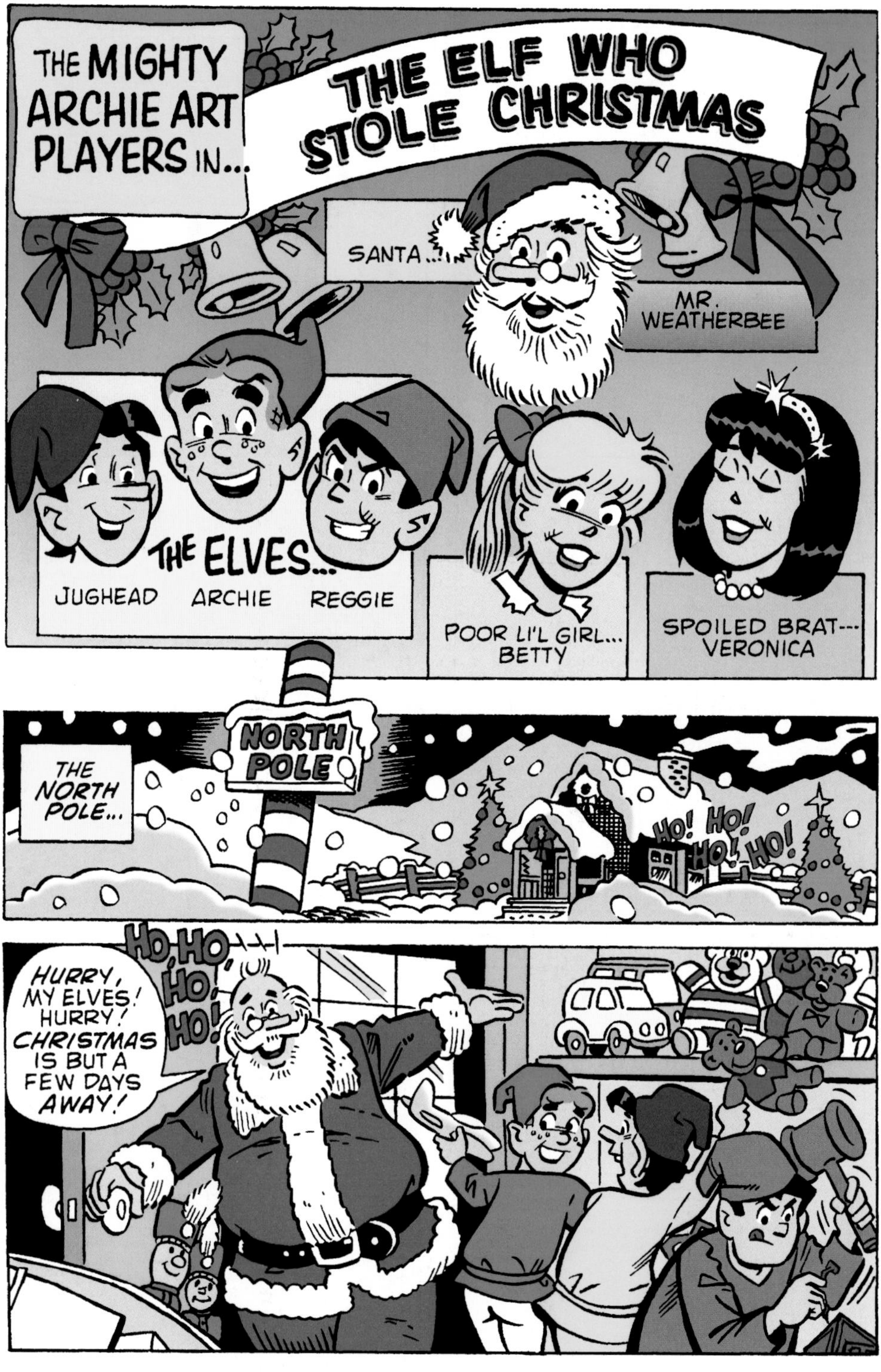
THE MIGHTY ARCHIE ART PLAYERS IN...
THE ELF WHO STOLE CHRISTMAS
SANTA...
MR. WEATHERBEE
THE ELVES...
JUGHEAD
ARCHIE
REGGIE
POOR LI'L GIRL... BETTY
SPOILED BRAT--- VERONICA
THE NORTH POLE...
NORTH POLE
HO! HO! HO! HO!
HO, HO, HO, HO!
HURRY, MY ELVES! HURRY! CHRISTMAS IS BUT A FEW DAYS AWAY!

Rich Margopoulos • Stan Goldberg • Rudy Lapick • Bill Yoshida • Barry Grossman

Originally printed in LAUGH #26, 1991

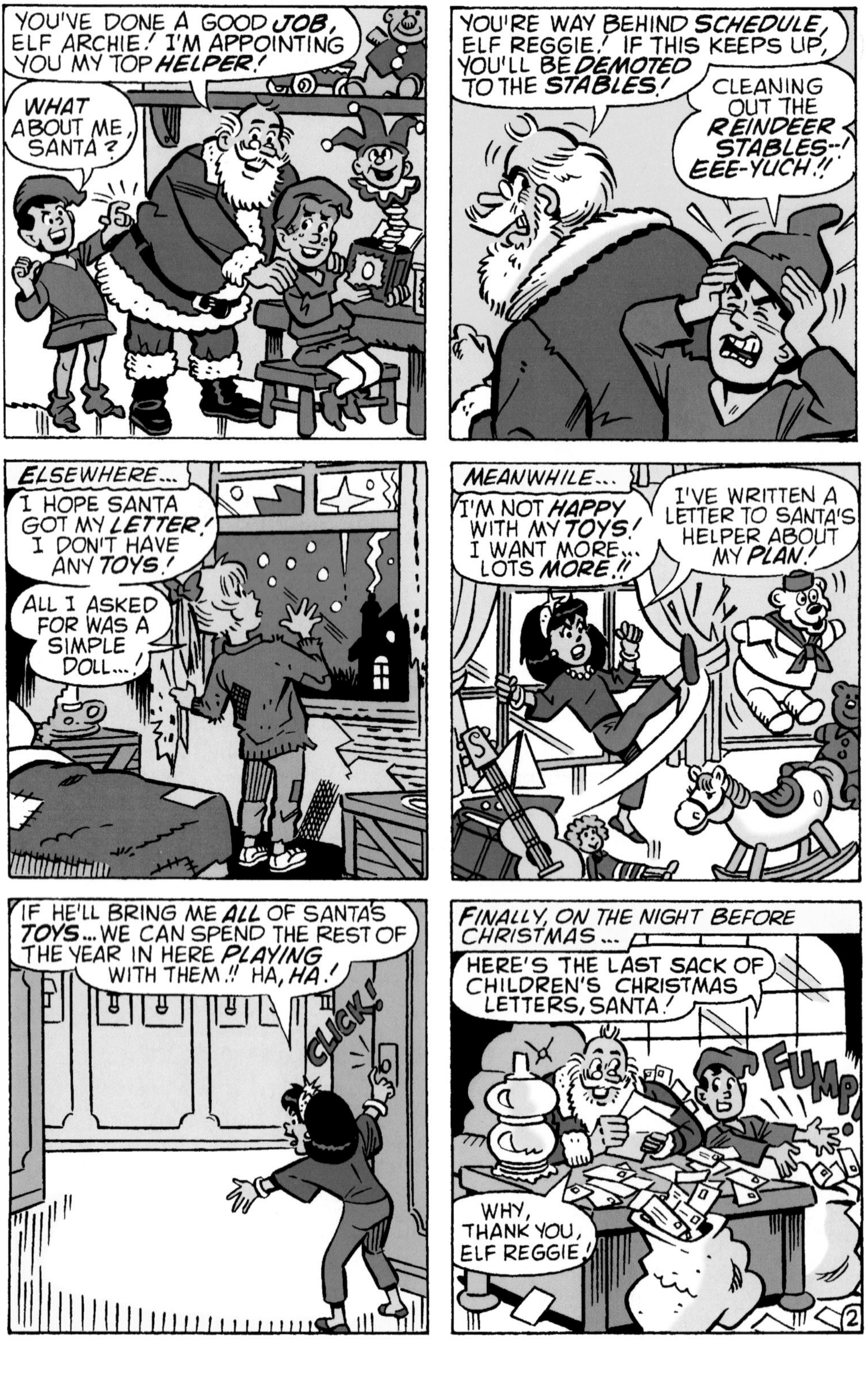
YOU'VE DONE A GOOD JOB, ELF ARCHIE! I'M APPOINTING YOU MY TOP HELPER!
WHAT ABOUT ME, SANTA?
YOU'RE WAY BEHIND SCHEDULE, ELF REGGIE! IF THIS KEEPS UP, YOU'LL BE DEMOTED TO THE STABLES!
CLEANING OUT THE REINDEER STABLES--! EEE-YUCH!!
ELSEWHERE...
I HOPE SANTA GOT MY LETTER! I DON'T HAVE ANY TOYS!
ALL I ASKED FOR WAS A SIMPLE DOLL...!
MEANWHILE...
I'M NOT HAPPY WITH MY TOYS! I WANT MORE... LOTS MORE!!
I'VE WRITTEN A LETTER TO SANTA'S HELPER ABOUT MY PLAN!
IF HE'LL BRING ME ALL OF SANTA'S TOYS... WE CAN SPEND THE REST OF THE YEAR IN HERE PLAYING WITH THEM!! HA, HA!
CLICK!
FINALLY, ON THE NIGHT BEFORE CHRISTMAS...
HERE'S THE LAST SACK OF CHILDREN'S CHRISTMAS LETTERS, SANTA!
FUMP!
WHY, THANK YOU, ELF REGGIE!
2

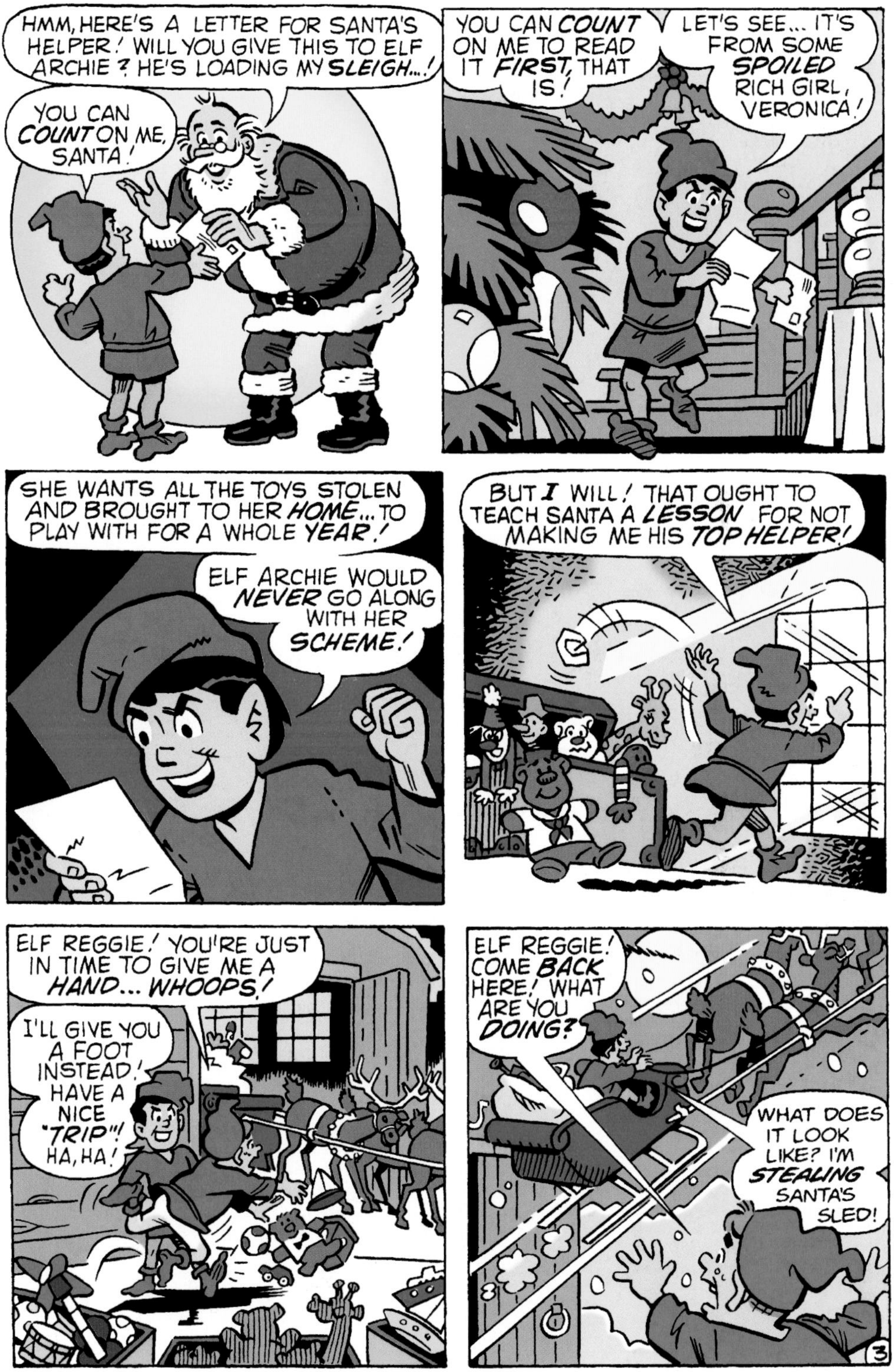
HMM, HERE'S A LETTER FOR SANTA'S HELPER! WILL YOU GIVE THIS TO ELF ARCHIE? HE'S LOADING MY SLEIGH...!
YOU CAN COUNT ON ME, SANTA!
YOU CAN COUNT ON ME TO READ IT FIRST, THAT IS!
LET'S SEE... IT'S FROM SOME SPOILED RICH GIRL, VERONICA!
SHE WANTS ALL THE TOYS STOLEN AND BROUGHT TO HER HOME... TO PLAY WITH FOR A WHOLE YEAR!
ELF ARCHIE WOULD NEVER GO ALONG WITH HER SCHEME!
BUT I WILL! THAT OUGHT TO TEACH SANTA A LESSON FOR NOT MAKING ME HIS TOP HELPER!
ELF REGGIE! YOU'RE JUST IN TIME TO GIVE ME A HAND... WHOOPS!
I'LL GIVE YOU A FOOT INSTEAD! HAVE A NICE "TRIP"! HA, HA!
ELF REGGIE! COME BACK HERE! WHAT ARE YOU DOING?
WHAT DOES IT LOOK LIKE? I'M STEALING SANTA'S SLED!
3

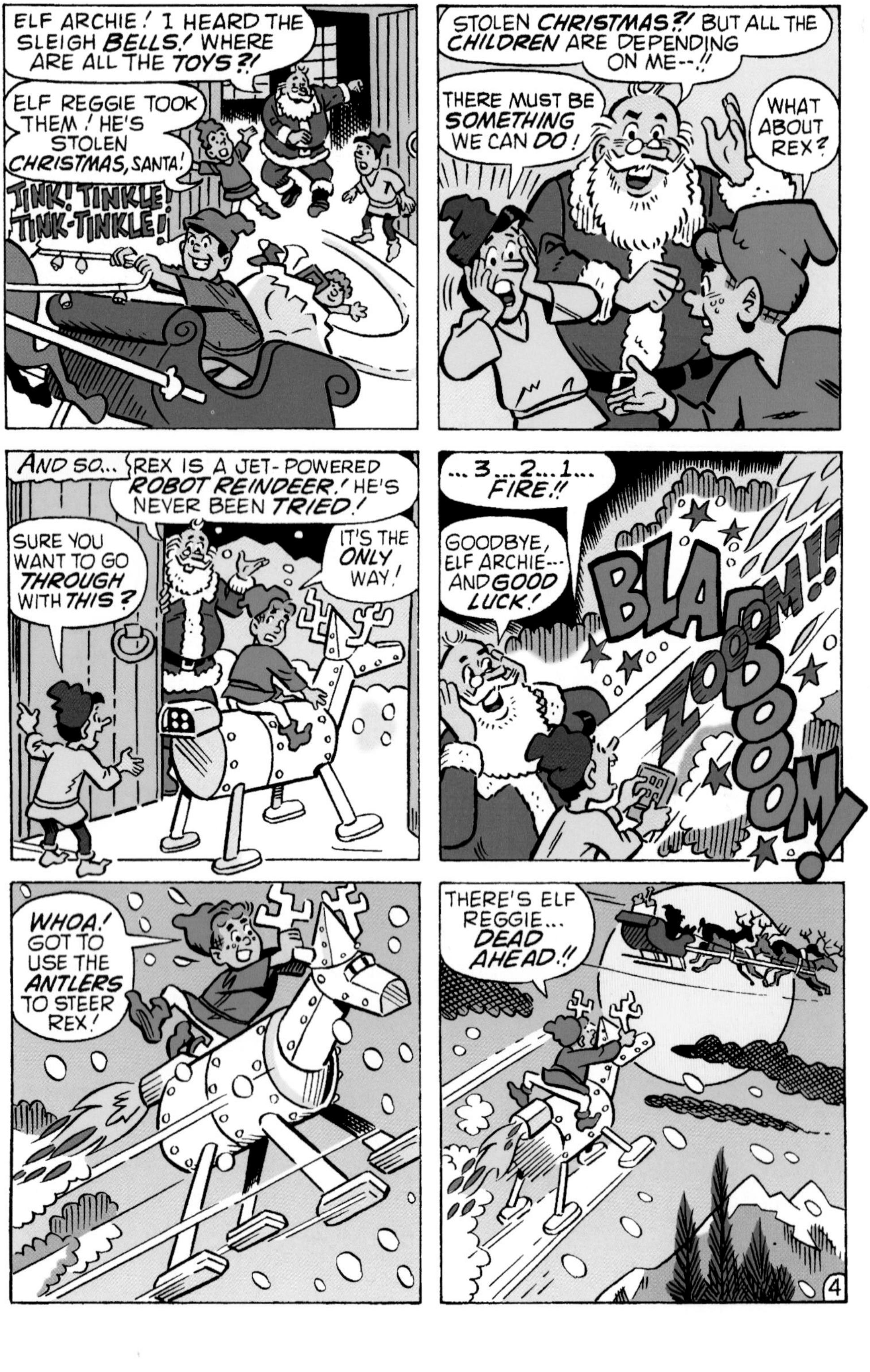
ELF ARCHIE! I HEARD THE SLEIGH BELLS! WHERE ARE ALL THE TOYS?!
ELF REGGIE TOOK THEM! HE'S STOLEN CHRISTMAS, SANTA!
TINK! TINKLE! TINK-TINKLE!
STOLEN CHRISTMAS?! BUT ALL THE CHILDREN ARE DEPENDING ON ME--!!
THERE MUST BE SOMETHING WE CAN DO!
WHAT ABOUT REX?
AND SO...
REX IS A JET-POWERED ROBOT REINDEER! HE'S NEVER BEEN TRIED!
SURE YOU WANT TO GO THROUGH WITH THIS?
IT'S THE ONLY WAY!
...3...2...1... FIRE!!
GOODBYE, ELF ARCHIE--- AND GOOD LUCK!
BLAM!!
ZOOOOOOM!
WHOA! GOT TO USE THE ANTLERS TO STEER REX!
THERE'S ELF REGGIE... DEAD AHEAD!!
4

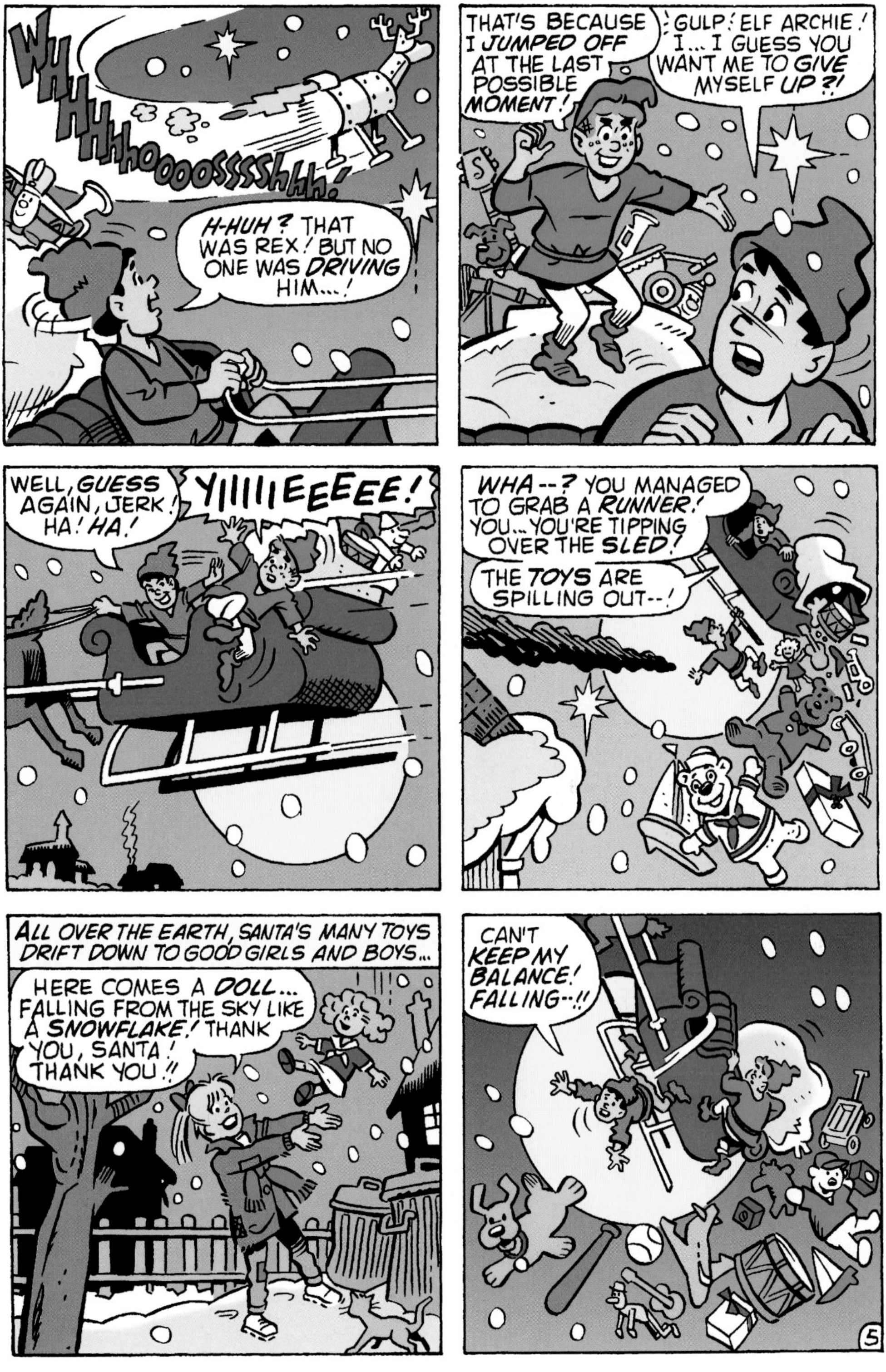
WHHHhhoooossssshhh!
H-HUH? THAT WAS REX! BUT NO ONE WAS DRIVING HIM...!
THAT'S BECAUSE I JUMPED OFF AT THE LAST POSSIBLE MOMENT!
GULP! ELF ARCHIE! I... I GUESS YOU WANT ME TO GIVE MYSELF UP?!
WELL, GUESS AGAIN, JERK! HA! HA!
YIIIIIEEEEE!
WHA--? YOU MANAGED TO GRAB A RUNNER! YOU...YOU'RE TIPPING OVER THE SLED!
THE TOYS ARE SPILLING OUT--!
ALL OVER THE EARTH, SANTA'S MANY TOYS DRIFT DOWN TO GOOD GIRLS AND BOYS...
HERE COMES A DOLL... FALLING FROM THE SKY LIKE A SNOWFLAKE! THANK YOU, SANTA! THANK YOU!!
CAN'T KEEP MY BALANCE! FALLING--!!
5

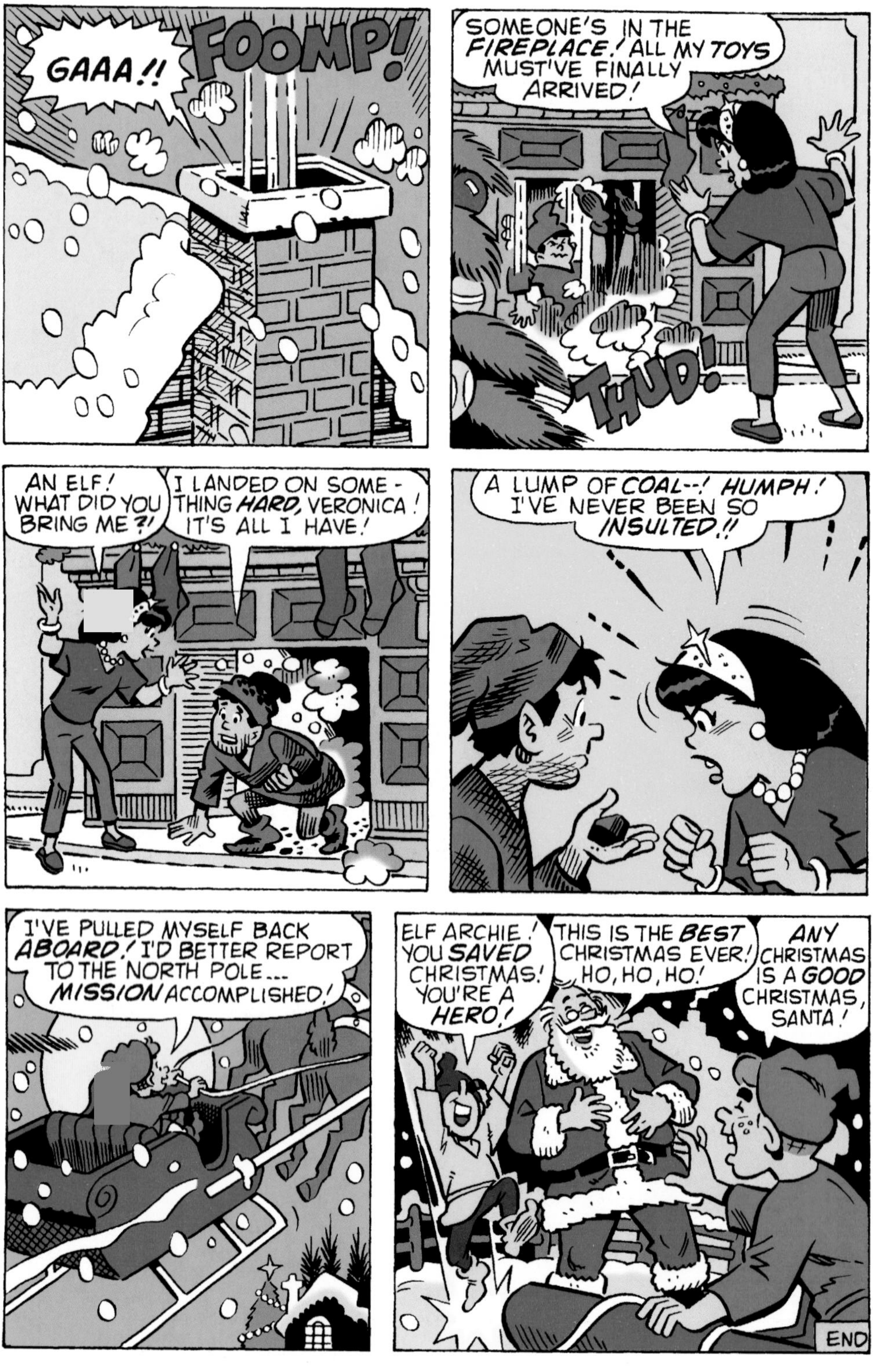
GAAA!!
FOOMP!
SOMEONE'S IN THE FIREPLACE! ALL MY TOYS MUST'VE FINALLY ARRIVED!
THUD!
AN ELF! WHAT DID YOU BRING ME?!
I LANDED ON SOMETHING HARD, VERONICA! IT'S ALL I HAVE!
A LUMP OF COAL--! HUMPH! I'VE NEVER BEEN SO INSULTED!!
I'VE PULLED MYSELF BACK ABOARD! I'D BETTER REPORT TO THE NORTH POLE... MISSION ACCOMPLISHED!
ELF ARCHIE! YOU SAVED CHRISTMAS! YOU'RE A HERO!
THIS IS THE BEST CHRISTMAS EVER! HO, HO, HO!
ANY CHRISTMAS IS A GOOD CHRISTMAS, SANTA!
END

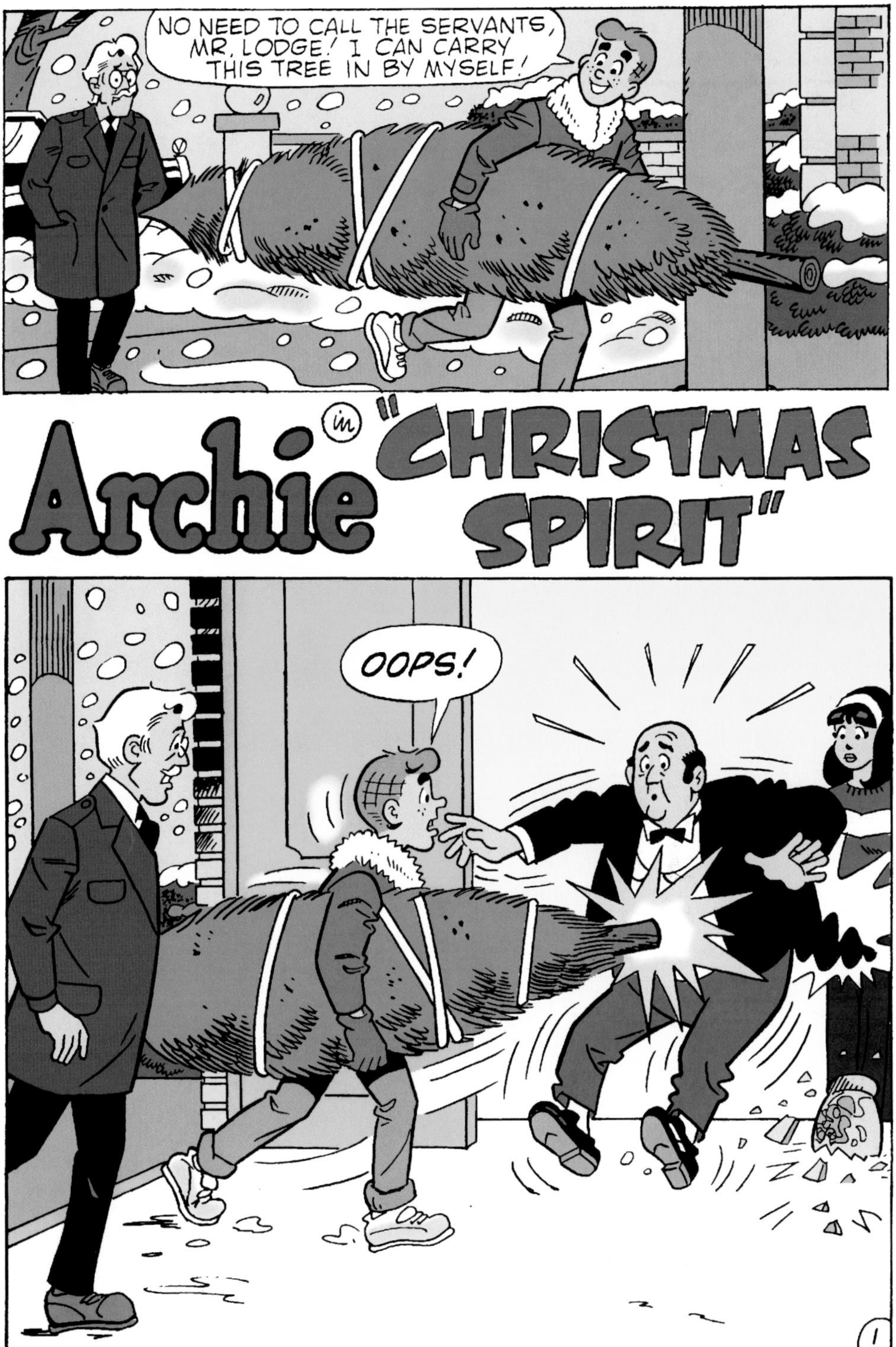
NO NEED TO CALL THE SERVANTS, MR. LODGE! I CAN CARRY THIS TREE IN BY MYSELF!
Archie in "CHRISTMAS SPIRIT"
OOPS!
1

George Gladir • Henry Scarpelli • Bill Yoshida • Barry Grossman

Originally printed in ARCHIE'S STORY & GAME DIGEST MAGAZINE #18, 1991

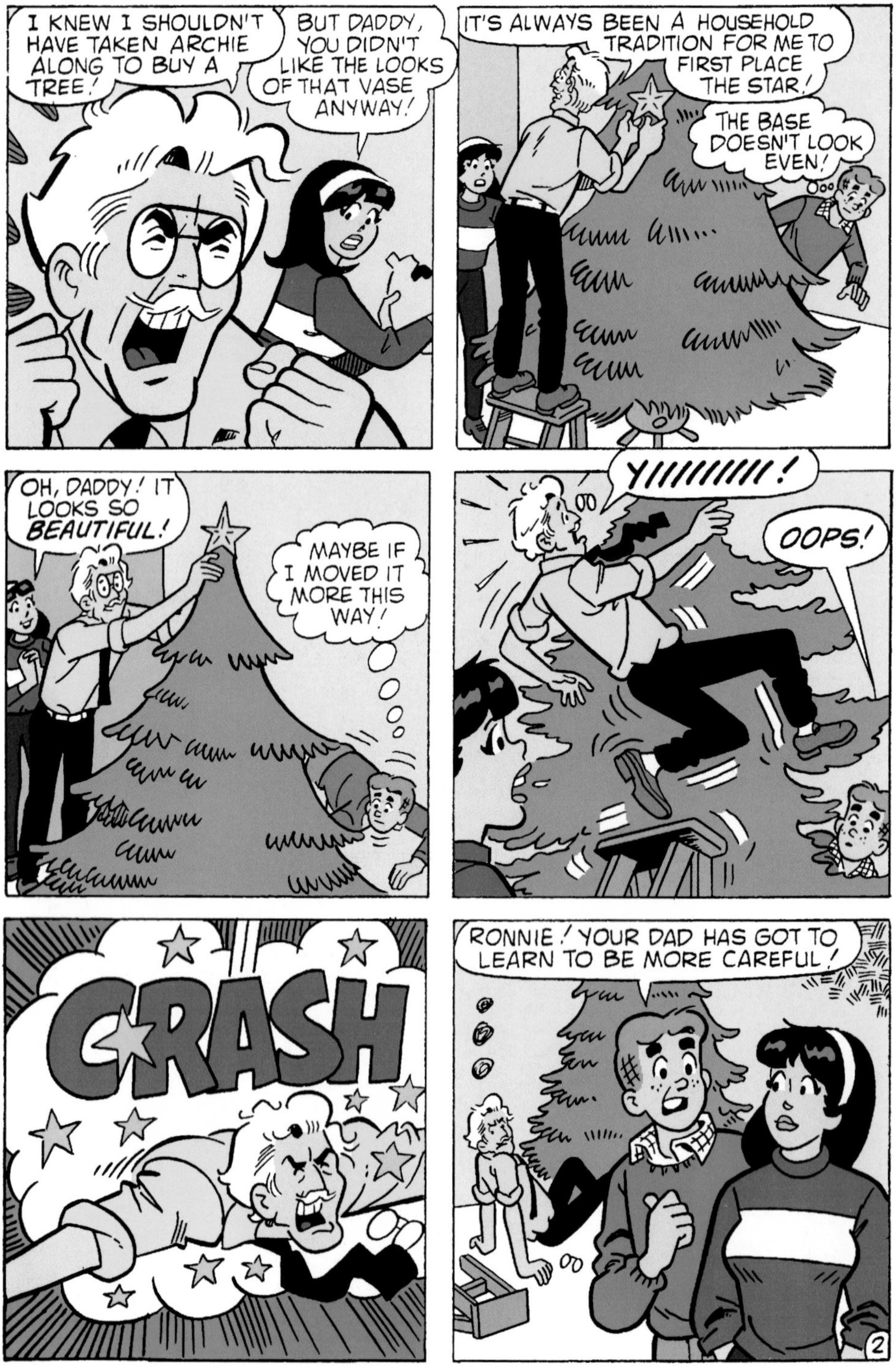
I KNEW I SHOULDN'T HAVE TAKEN ARCHIE ALONG TO BUY A TREE!
BUT DADDY, YOU DIDN'T LIKE THE LOOKS OF THAT VASE ANYWAY!
IT'S ALWAYS BEEN A HOUSEHOLD TRADITION FOR ME TO FIRST PLACE THE STAR!
THE BASE DOESN'T LOOK EVEN!
OH, DADDY! IT LOOKS SO *BEAUTIFUL*!
MAYBE IF I MOVED IT MORE THIS WAY!
YIIIIIIIII!
OOPS!
CRASH
RONNIE! YOUR DAD HAS GOT TO LEARN TO BE MORE CAREFUL!
2

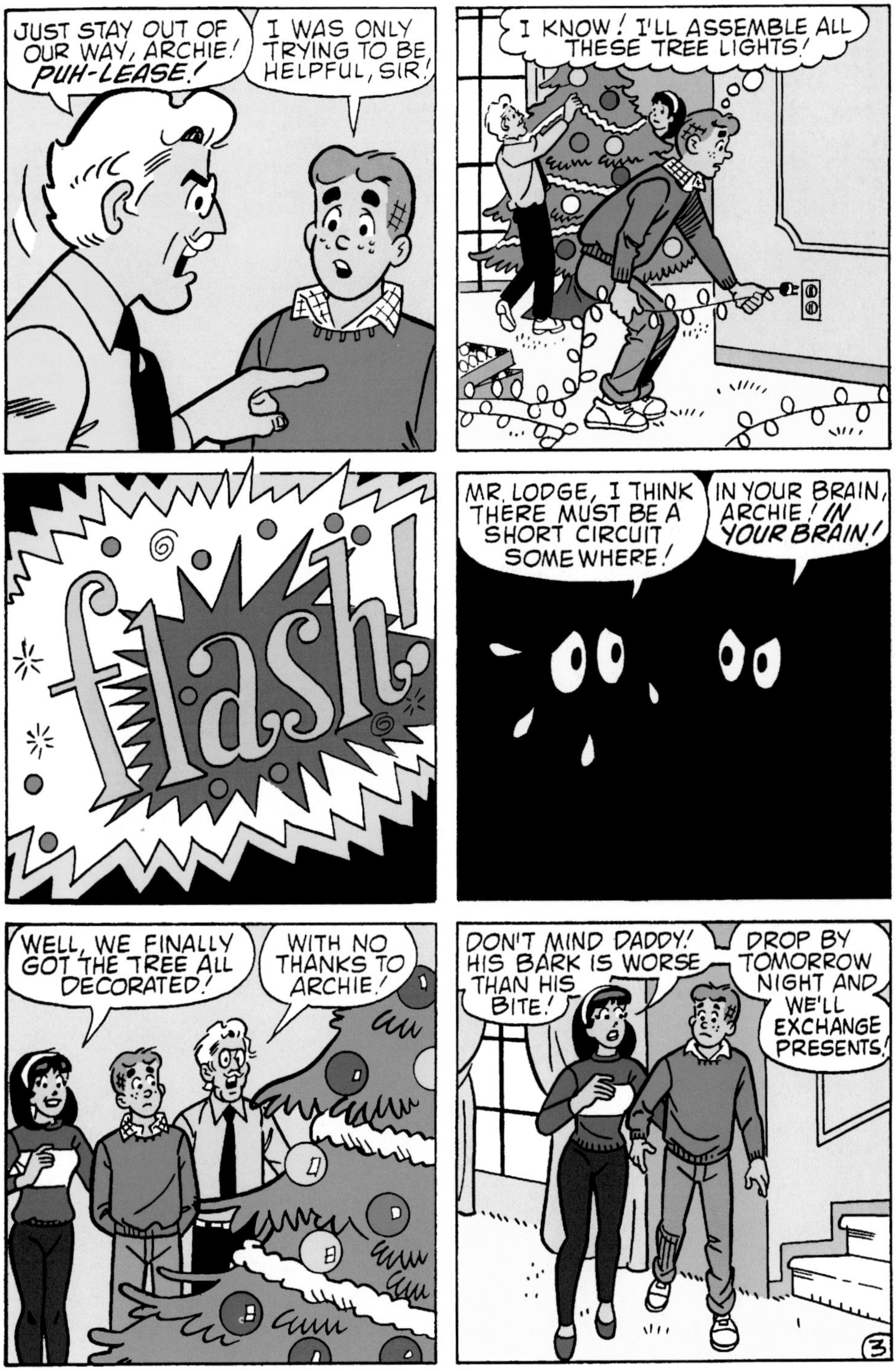
JUST STAY OUT OF OUR WAY, ARCHIE! PUH-LEASE!
I WAS ONLY TRYING TO BE HELPFUL, SIR!
I KNOW! I'LL ASSEMBLE ALL THESE TREE LIGHTS!
flash!
MR. LODGE, I THINK THERE MUST BE A SHORT CIRCUIT SOMEWHERE!
IN YOUR BRAIN, ARCHIE! IN YOUR BRAIN!
WELL, WE FINALLY GOT THE TREE ALL DECORATED!
WITH NO THANKS TO ARCHIE!
DON'T MIND DADDY! HIS BARK IS WORSE THAN HIS BITE!
DROP BY TOMORROW NIGHT AND WE'LL EXCHANGE PRESENTS!
3

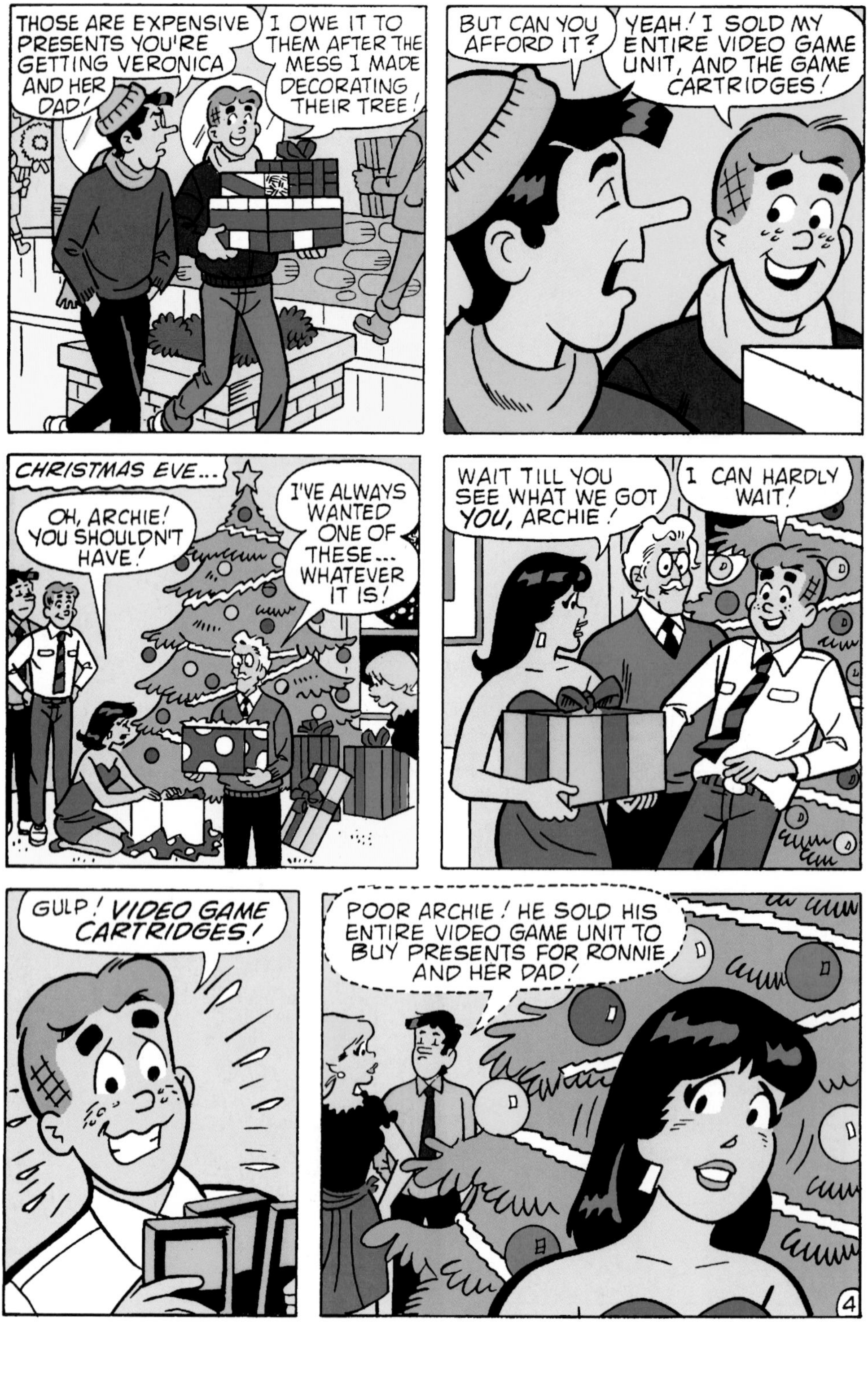
THOSE ARE EXPENSIVE PRESENTS YOU'RE GETTING VERONICA AND HER DAD!
I OWE IT TO THEM AFTER THE MESS I MADE DECORATING THEIR TREE!
BUT CAN YOU AFFORD IT?
YEAH! I SOLD MY ENTIRE VIDEO GAME UNIT, AND THE GAME CARTRIDGES!
CHRISTMAS EVE...
OH, ARCHIE! YOU SHOULDN'T HAVE!
I'VE ALWAYS WANTED ONE OF THESE... WHATEVER IT IS!
WAIT TILL YOU SEE WHAT WE GOT *YOU*, ARCHIE!
I CAN HARDLY WAIT!
GULP! *VIDEO GAME CARTRIDGES!*
POOR ARCHIE! HE SOLD HIS ENTIRE VIDEO GAME UNIT TO BUY PRESENTS FOR RONNIE AND HER DAD!
4

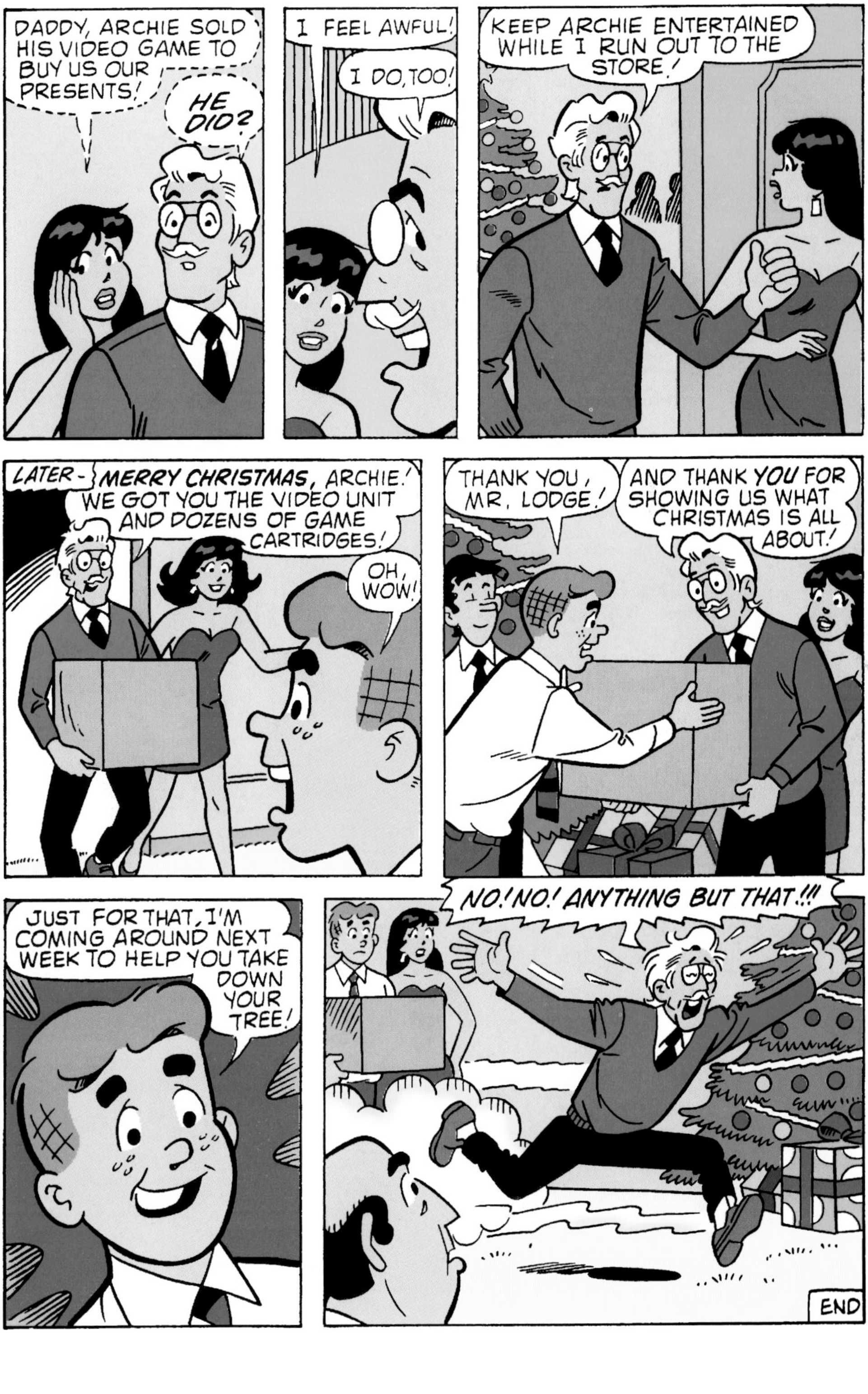
DADDY, ARCHIE SOLD HIS VIDEO GAME TO BUY US OUR PRESENTS!
HE DID?
I FEEL AWFUL!
I DO, TOO!
KEEP ARCHIE ENTERTAINED WHILE I RUN OUT TO THE STORE!
LATER-
MERRY CHRISTMAS, ARCHIE! WE GOT YOU THE VIDEO UNIT AND DOZENS OF GAME CARTRIDGES!
OH, WOW!
THANK YOU, MR. LODGE!
AND THANK YOU FOR SHOWING US WHAT CHRISTMAS IS ALL ABOUT!
JUST FOR THAT, I'M COMING AROUND NEXT WEEK TO HELP YOU TAKE DOWN YOUR TREE!
NO! NO! ANYTHING BUT THAT!!!
END

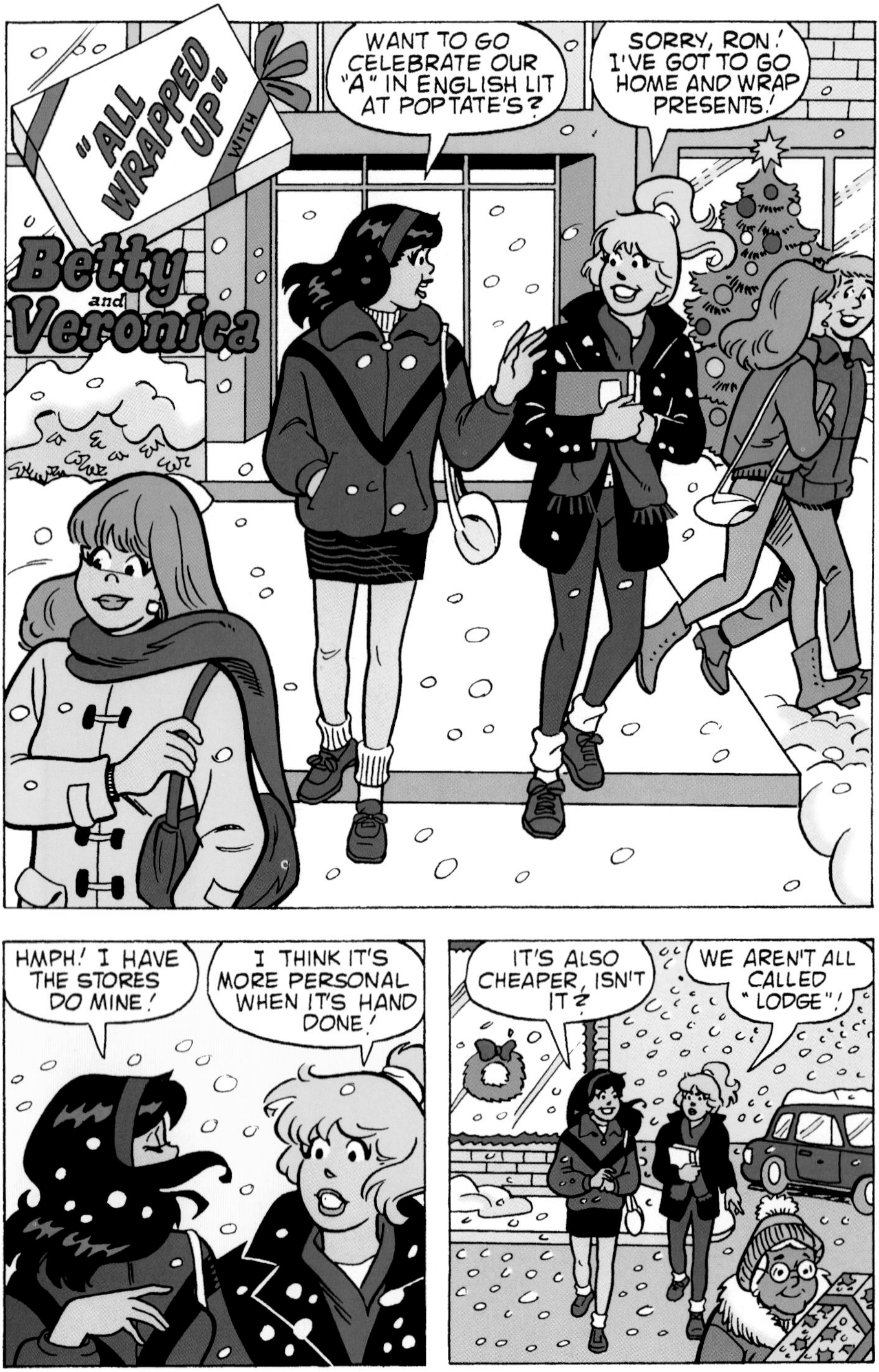
"ALL WRAPPED UP"
WITH
Betty and Veronica
WANT TO GO CELEBRATE OUR "A" IN ENGLISH LIT AT POPTATE'S?
SORRY, RON! I'VE GOT TO GO HOME AND WRAP PRESENTS!
HMPH! I HAVE THE STORES DO MINE!
I THINK IT'S MORE PERSONAL WHEN IT'S HAND DONE!
IT'S ALSO CHEAPER, ISN'T IT?
WE AREN'T ALL CALLED "LODGE"!

Kathleen Webb • Dan DeCarlo • Dan Parent • Alison Flood • Bill Yoshida

Originally printed in ARCHIE GIANT SERIES MAGAZINE #629, 1992

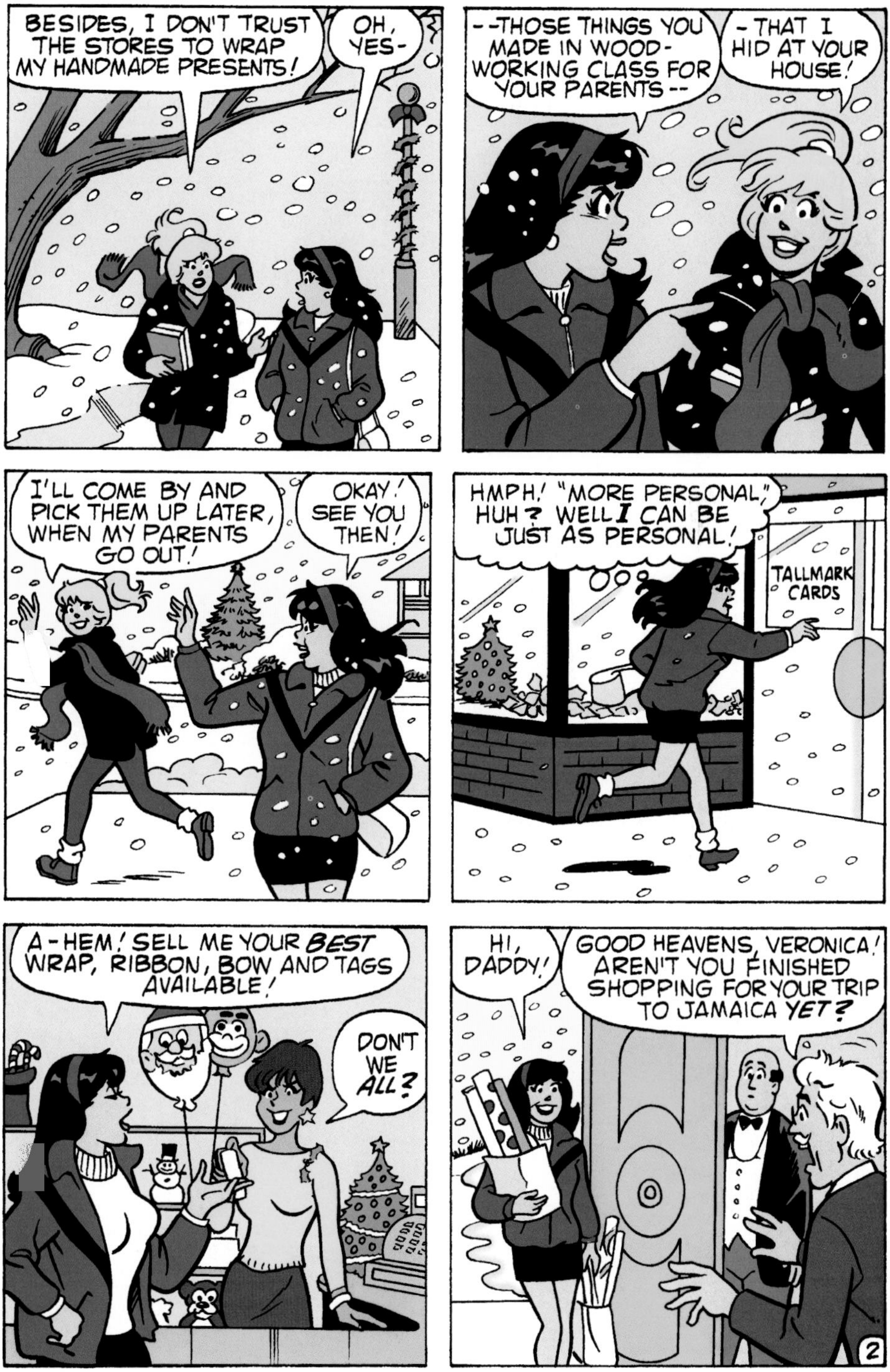
BESIDES, I DON'T TRUST THE STORES TO WRAP MY HANDMADE PRESENTS!
OH, YES-
--THOSE THINGS YOU MADE IN WOOD-WORKING CLASS FOR YOUR PARENTS --
- THAT I HID AT YOUR HOUSE!
I'LL COME BY AND PICK THEM UP LATER, WHEN MY PARENTS GO OUT!
OKAY! SEE YOU THEN!
HMPH! "MORE PERSONAL," HUH? WELL I CAN BE JUST AS PERSONAL!
TALLMARK CARDS
A-HEM! SELL ME YOUR BEST WRAP, RIBBON, BOW AND TAGS AVAILABLE!
DON'T WE ALL?
HI, DADDY!
GOOD HEAVENS, VERONICA! AREN'T YOU FINISHED SHOPPING FOR YOUR TRIP TO JAMAICA YET?
2

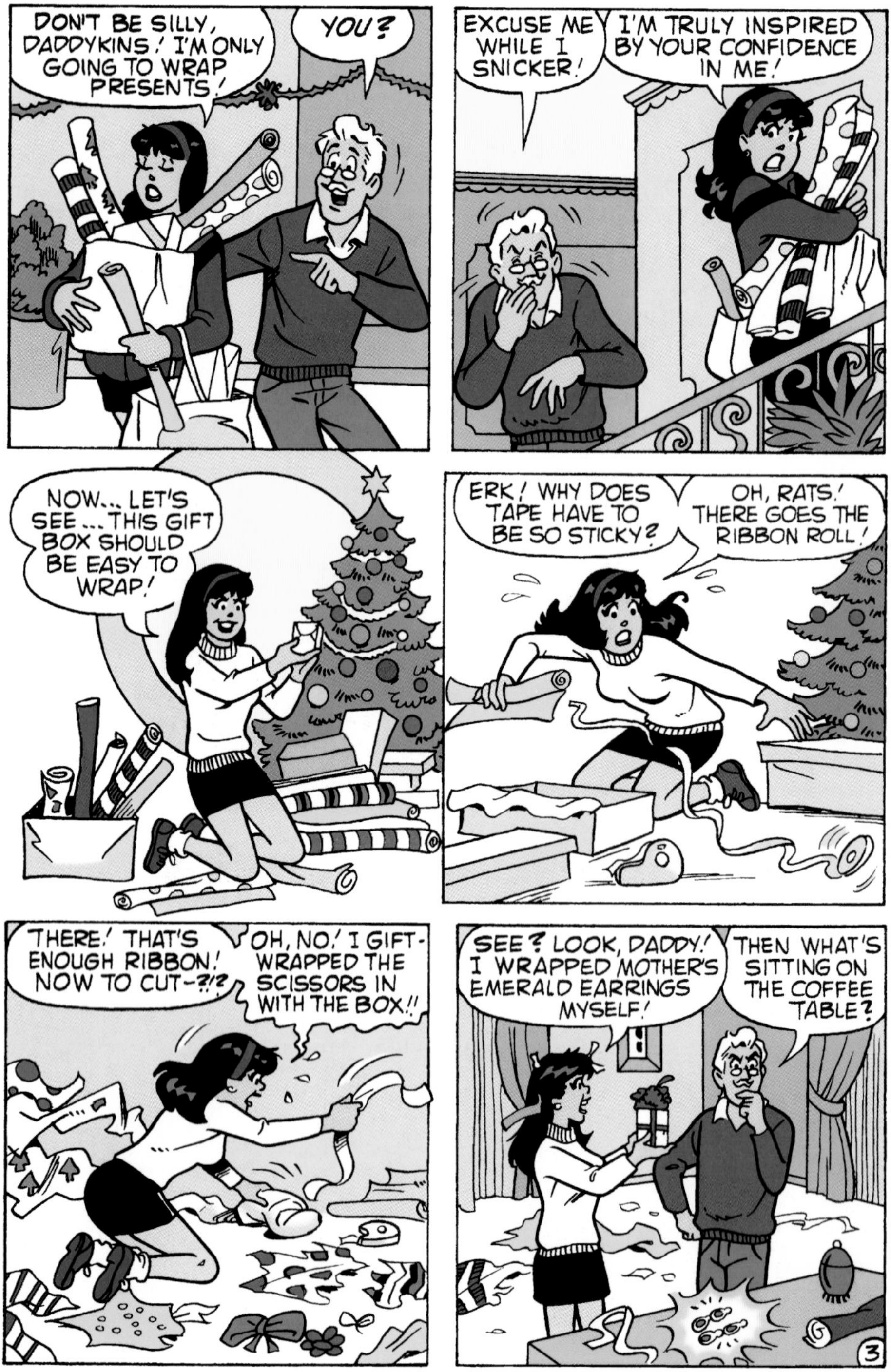
DON'T BE SILLY, DADDYKINS! I'M ONLY GOING TO WRAP PRESENTS!
YOU?
EXCUSE ME WHILE I SNICKER!
I'M TRULY INSPIRED BY YOUR CONFIDENCE IN ME!
NOW... LET'S SEE ... THIS GIFT BOX SHOULD BE EASY TO WRAP!
ERK! WHY DOES TAPE HAVE TO BE SO STICKY?
OH, RATS! THERE GOES THE RIBBON ROLL!
THERE! THAT'S ENOUGH RIBBON! NOW TO CUT-?!?
OH, NO! I GIFT-WRAPPED THE SCISSORS IN WITH THE BOX!!
SEE? LOOK, DADDY! I WRAPPED MOTHER'S EMERALD EARRINGS MYSELF!
THEN WHAT'S SITTING ON THE COFFEE TABLE?
3

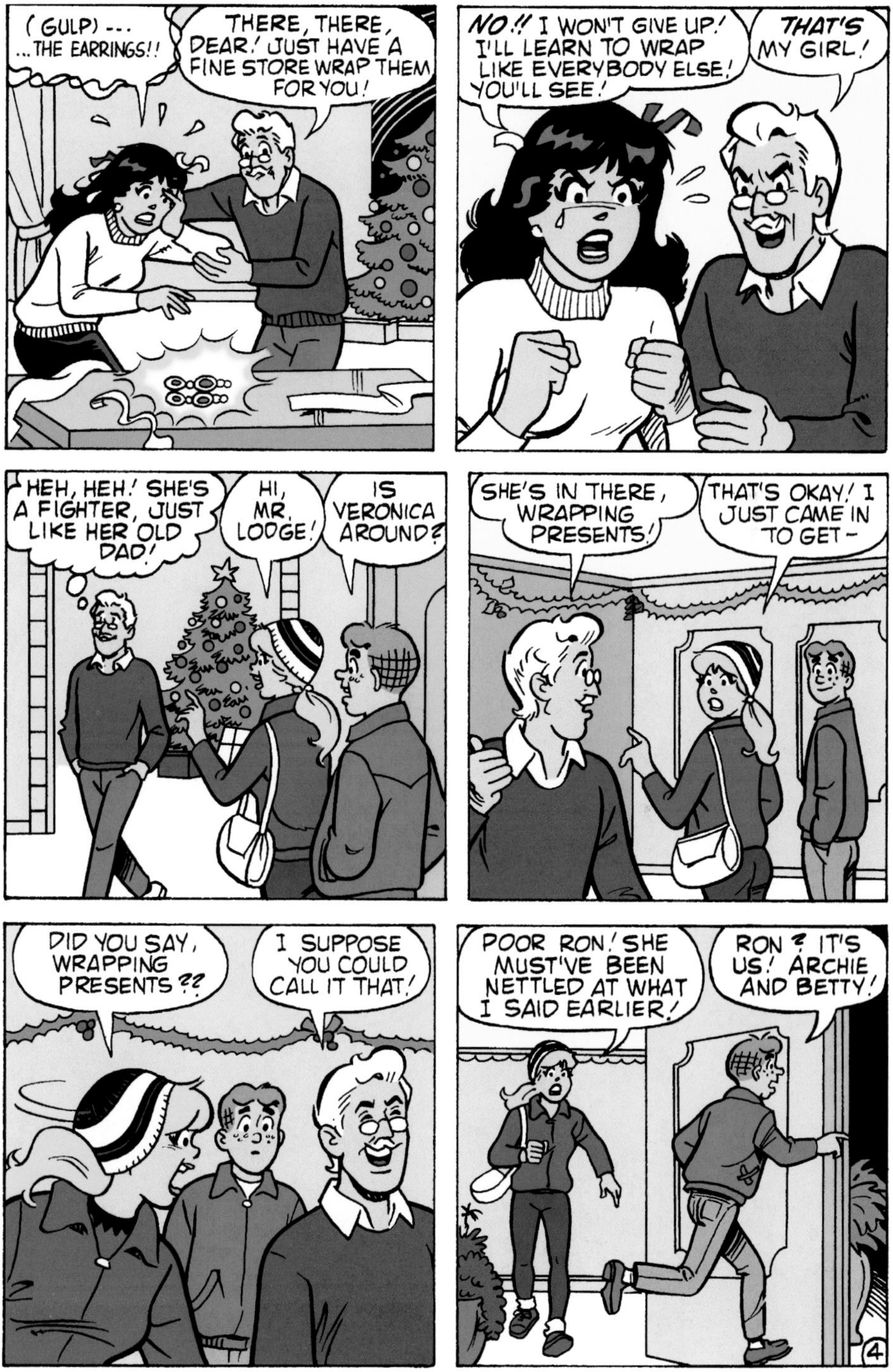
(GULP) ---
...THE EARRINGS!!
THERE, THERE, DEAR! JUST HAVE A FINE STORE WRAP THEM FOR YOU!
NO!! I WON'T GIVE UP! I'LL LEARN TO WRAP LIKE EVERYBODY ELSE! YOU'LL SEE!
THAT'S MY GIRL!
HEH, HEH! SHE'S A FIGHTER, JUST LIKE HER OLD DAD!
HI, MR. LODGE!
IS VERONICA AROUND?
SHE'S IN THERE, WRAPPING PRESENTS!
THAT'S OKAY! I JUST CAME IN TO GET -
DID YOU SAY, WRAPPING PRESENTS??
I SUPPOSE YOU COULD CALL IT THAT!
POOR RON! SHE MUST'VE BEEN NETTLED AT WHAT I SAID EARLIER!
RON? IT'S US! ARCHIE AND BETTY!
4

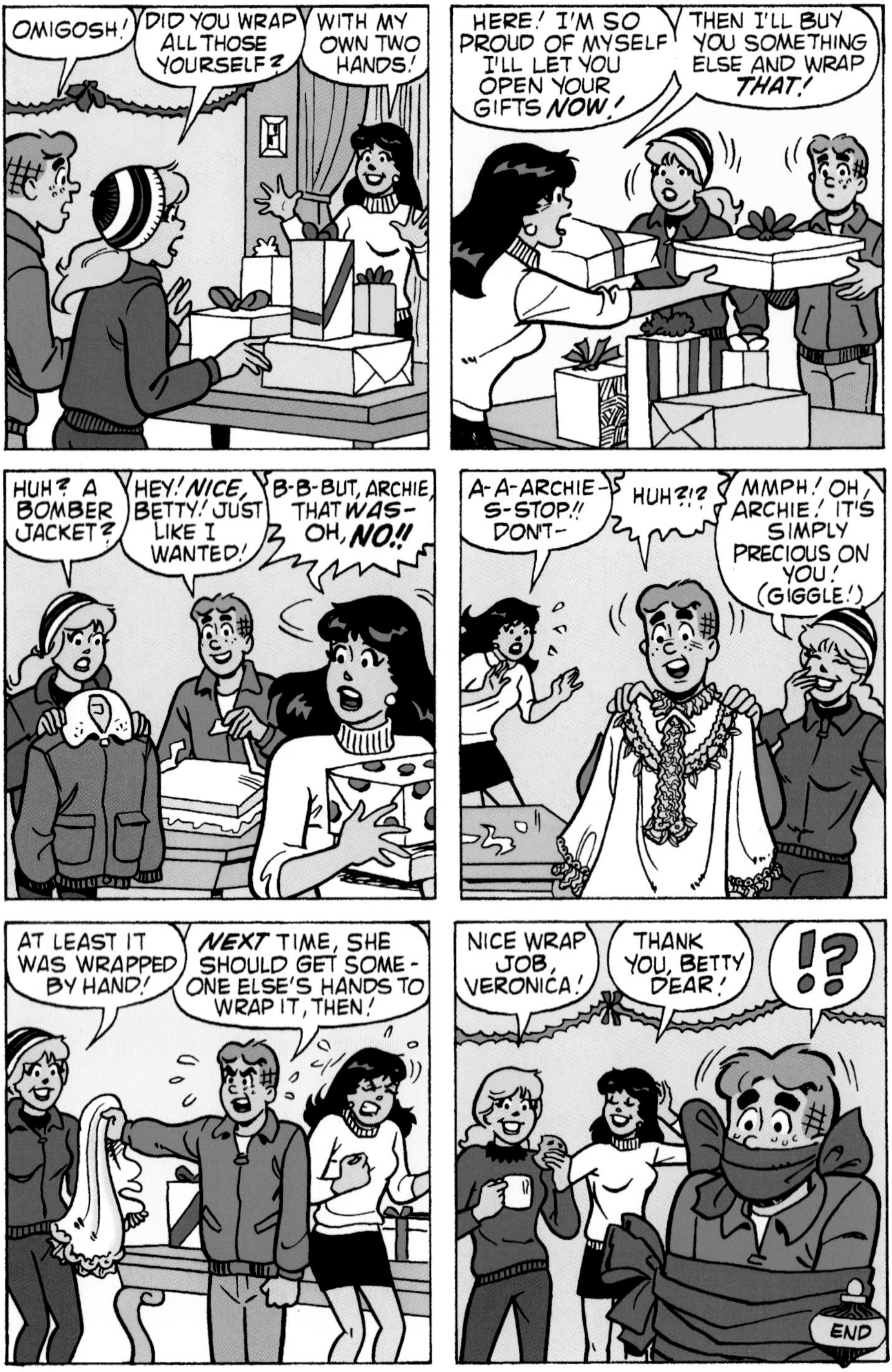

OMIGOSH!
DID YOU WRAP ALL THOSE YOURSELF?
WITH MY OWN TWO HANDS!
HERE! I'M SO PROUD OF MYSELF I'LL LET YOU OPEN YOUR GIFTS NOW!
THEN I'LL BUY YOU SOMETHING ELSE AND WRAP THAT!
HUH? A BOMBER JACKET?
HEY! NICE, BETTY! JUST LIKE I WANTED!
B-B-BUT, ARCHIE, THAT WAS- OH, NO!!
A-A-ARCHIE- S-STOP!! DON'T-
HUH?!?
MMPH! OH, ARCHIE! IT'S SIMPLY PRECIOUS ON YOU! (GIGGLE!)
AT LEAST IT WAS WRAPPED BY HAND!
NEXT TIME, SHE SHOULD GET SOMEONE ELSE'S HANDS TO WRAP IT, THEN!
NICE WRAP JOB, VERONICA!
THANK YOU, BETTY DEAR!
!?
END

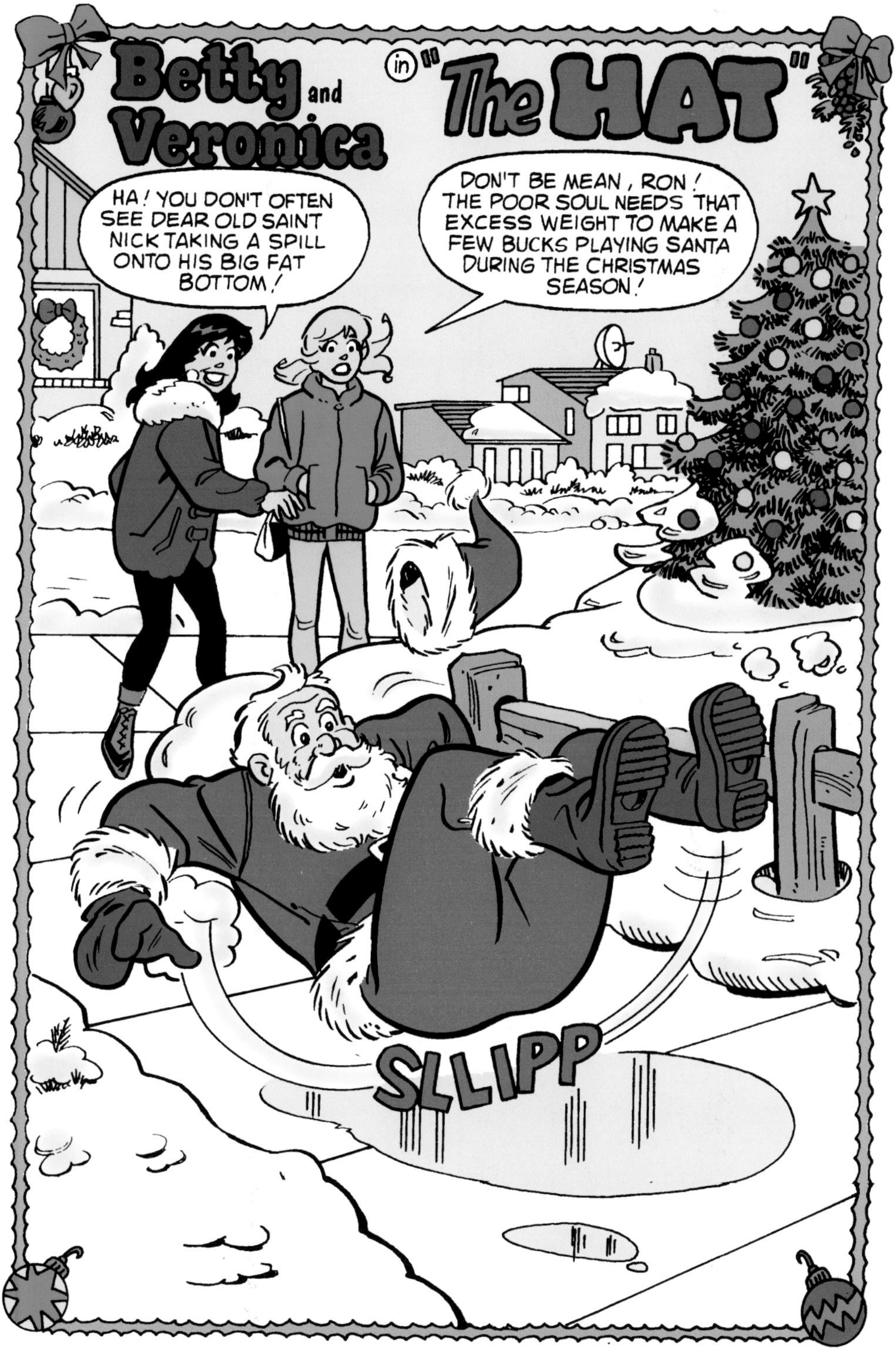
Betty and Veronica
in "The HAT"
HA! YOU DON'T OFTEN SEE DEAR OLD SAINT NICK TAKING A SPILL ONTO HIS BIG FAT BOTTOM!
DON'T BE MEAN, RON! THE POOR SOUL NEEDS THAT EXCESS WEIGHT TO MAKE A FEW BUCKS PLAYING SANTA DURING THE CHRISTMAS SEASON!
SLLIPP

Frank Doyle • Dan DeCarlo • Alison Flood • Bill Yoshida • Barry Grossman

Originally printed in BETTY AND VERONICA #72, 1994

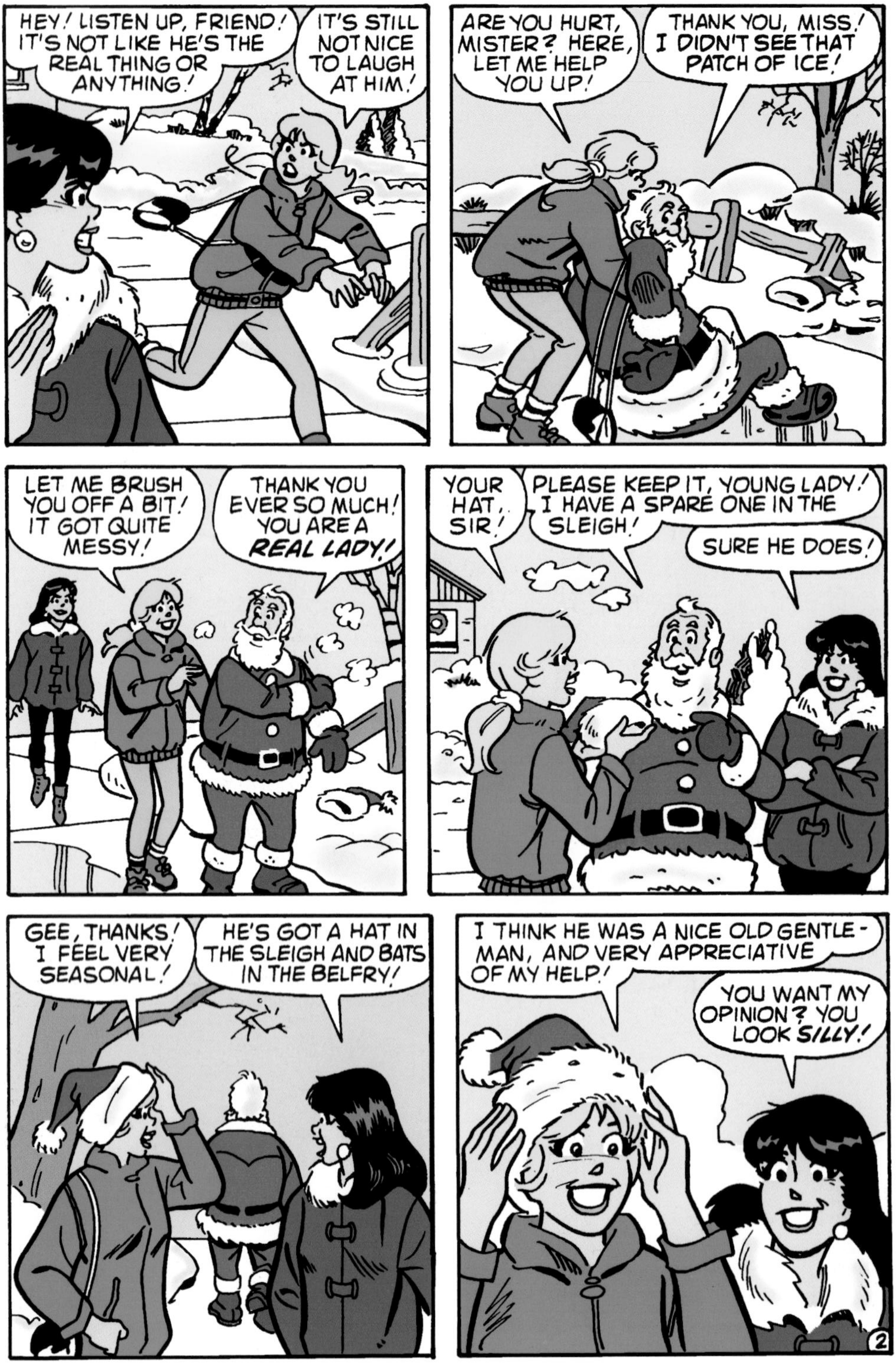
HEY! LISTEN UP, FRIEND! IT'S NOT LIKE HE'S THE REAL THING OR ANYTHING!
IT'S STILL NOT NICE TO LAUGH AT HIM!
ARE YOU HURT, MISTER? HERE, LET ME HELP YOU UP!
THANK YOU, MISS! I DIDN'T SEE THAT PATCH OF ICE!
LET ME BRUSH YOU OFF A BIT! IT GOT QUITE MESSY!
THANK YOU EVER SO MUCH! YOU ARE A REAL LADY!
YOUR HAT, SIR!
PLEASE KEEP IT, YOUNG LADY! I HAVE A SPARE ONE IN THE SLEIGH!
SURE HE DOES!
GEE, THANKS! I FEEL VERY SEASONAL!
HE'S GOT A HAT IN THE SLEIGH AND BATS IN THE BELFRY!
I THINK HE WAS A NICE OLD GENTLEMAN, AND VERY APPRECIATIVE OF MY HELP!
YOU WANT MY OPINION? YOU LOOK SILLY!
2

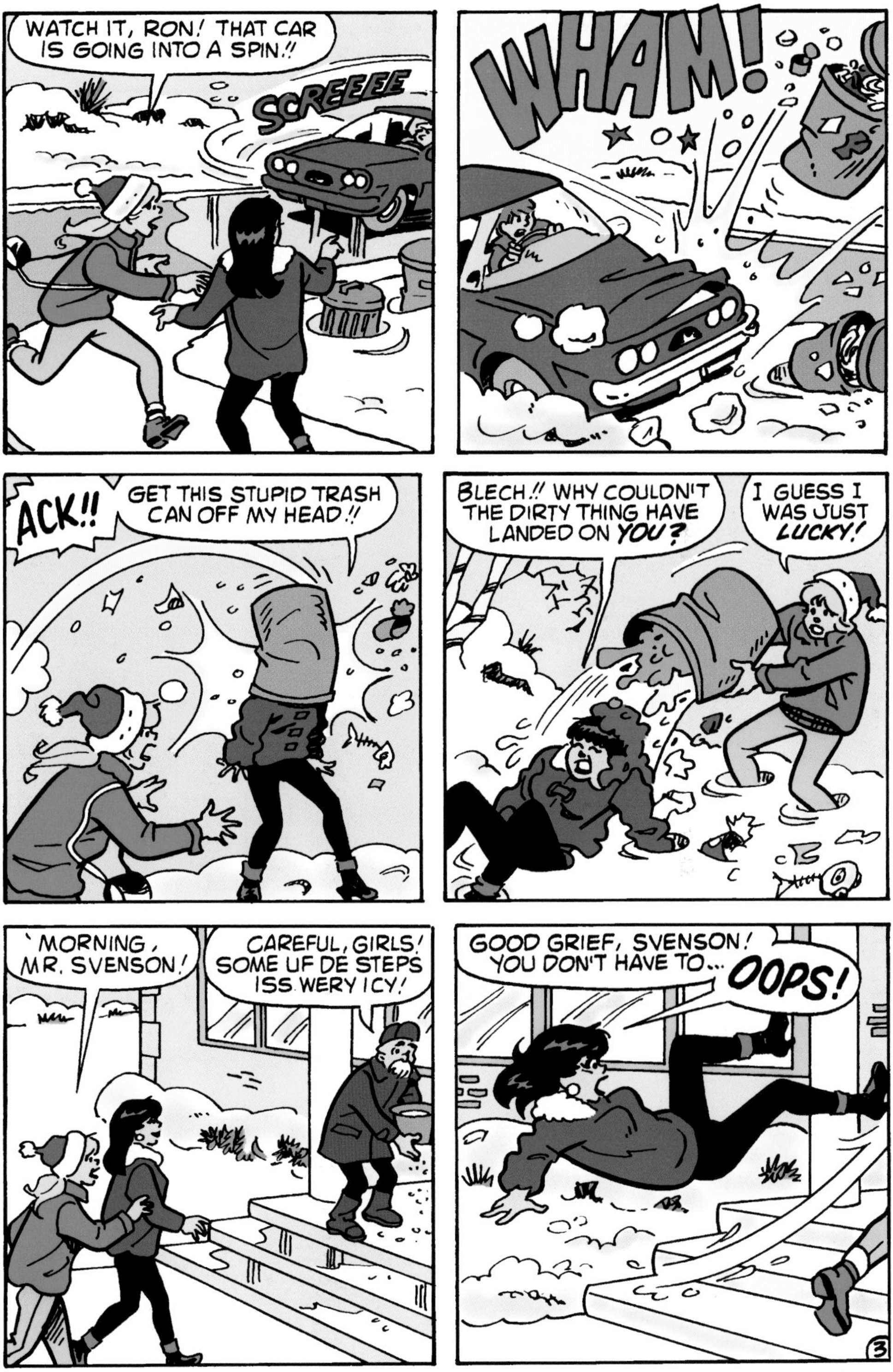
WATCH IT, RON! THAT CAR IS GOING INTO A SPIN!!
SCREEEEE
WHAM!
ACK!!
GET THIS STUPID TRASH CAN OFF MY HEAD!!
BLECH!! WHY COULDN'T THE DIRTY THING HAVE LANDED ON YOU?
I GUESS I WAS JUST LUCKY!
'MORNING, MR. SVENSON!
CAREFUL, GIRLS! SOME UF DE STEPS ISS WERY ICY!
GOOD GRIEF, SVENSON! YOU DON'T HAVE TO...
OOPS!
3

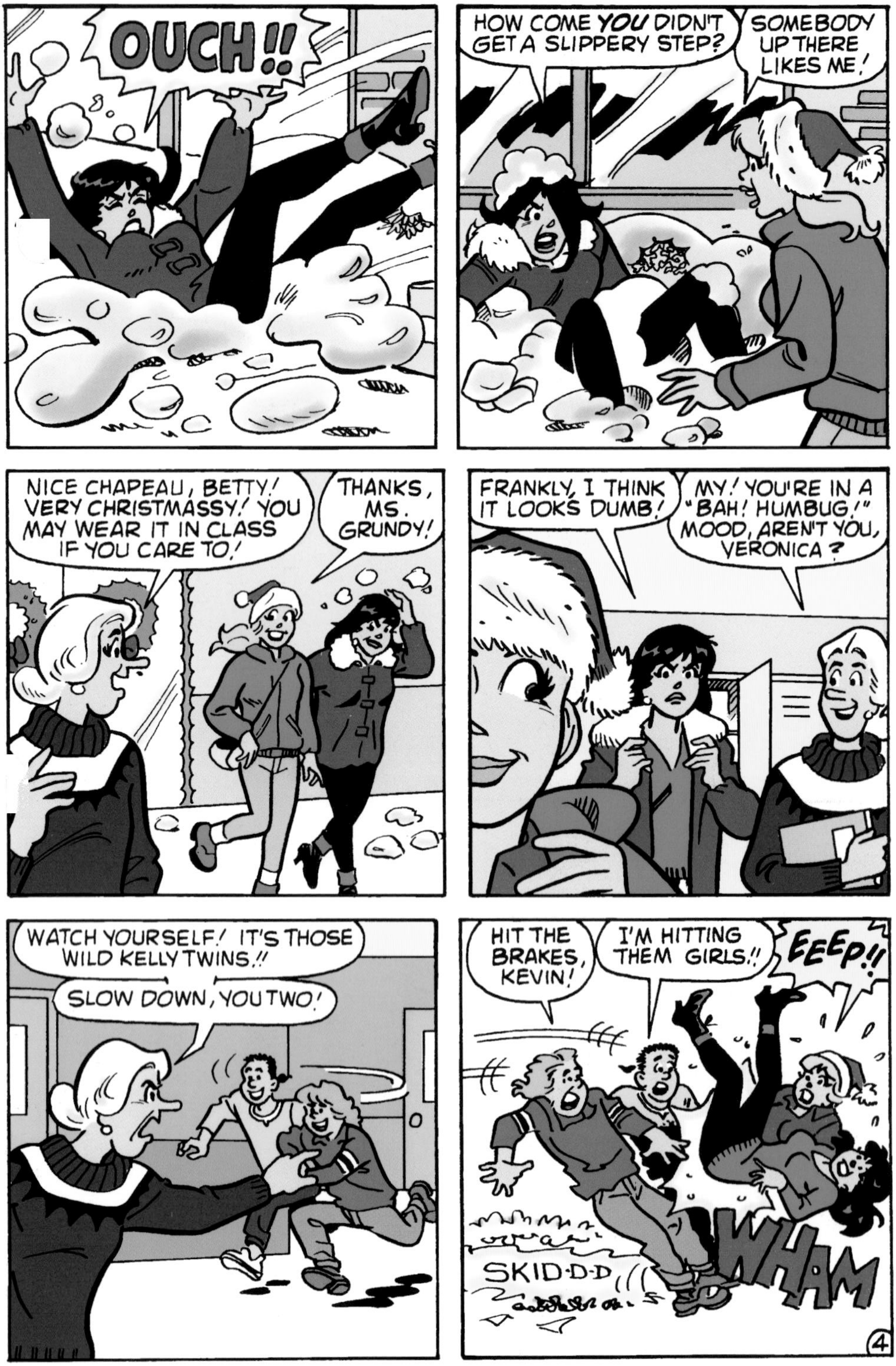
OUCH!!
HOW COME YOU DIDN'T GET A SLIPPERY STEP?
SOMEBODY UP THERE LIKES ME!
NICE CHAPEAU, BETTY! VERY CHRISTMASSY! YOU MAY WEAR IT IN CLASS IF YOU CARE TO!
THANKS, MS. GRUNDY!
FRANKLY, I THINK IT LOOKS DUMB!
MY! YOU'RE IN A "BAH! HUMBUG!" MOOD, AREN'T YOU, VERONICA?
WATCH YOURSELF! IT'S THOSE WILD KELLY TWINS!!
SLOW DOWN, YOU TWO!
HIT THE BRAKES, KEVIN!
I'M HITTING THEM GIRLS!!
EEEP!!
SKID-D-D
WHAM
4

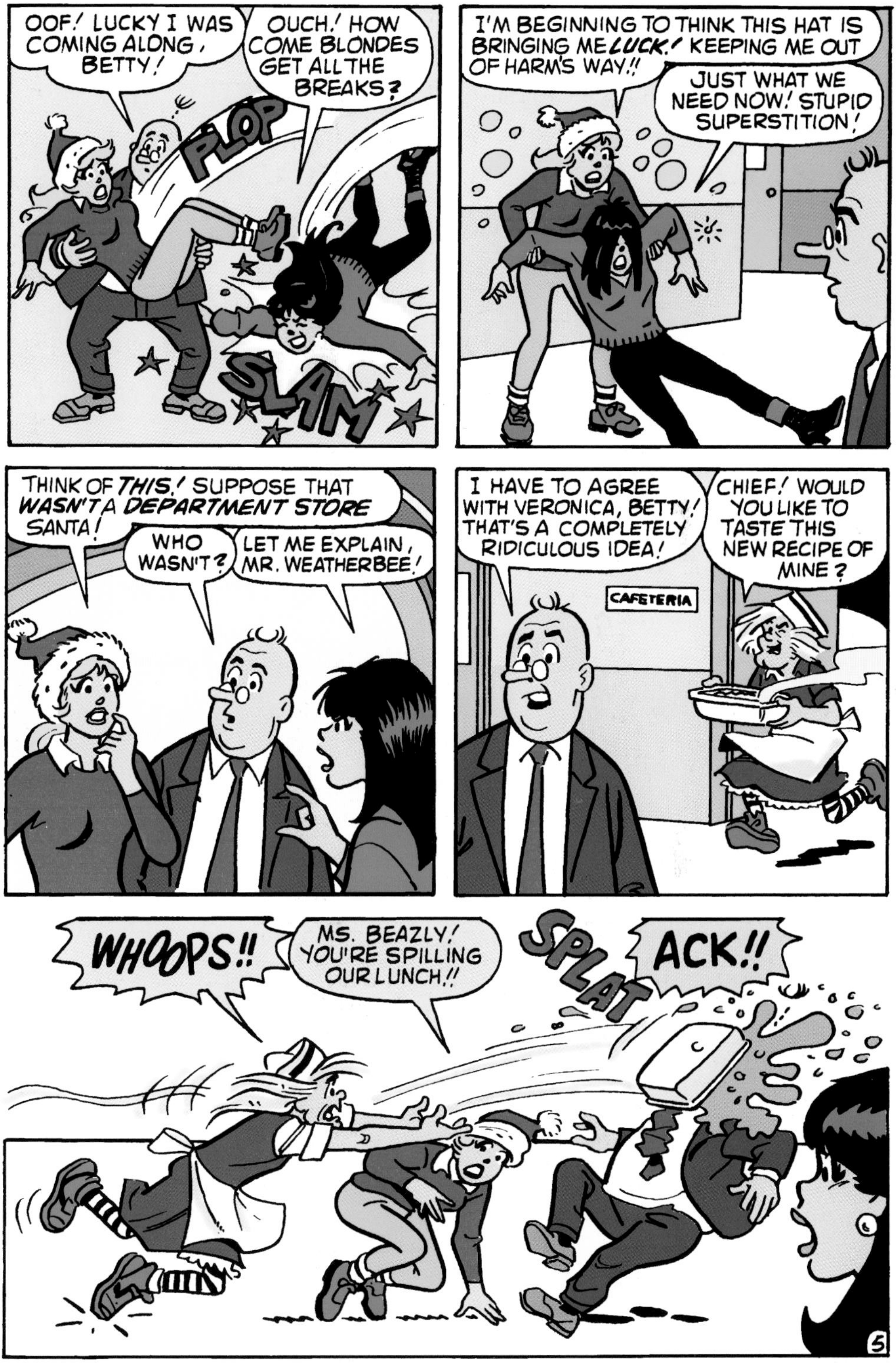
OOF! LUCKY I WAS COMING ALONG, BETTY!
OUCH! HOW COME BLONDES GET ALL THE BREAKS?
PLOP
SLAM
I'M BEGINNING TO THINK THIS HAT IS BRINGING ME LUCK! KEEPING ME OUT OF HARM'S WAY!!
JUST WHAT WE NEED NOW! STUPID SUPERSTITION!
THINK OF THIS! SUPPOSE THAT WASN'T A DEPARTMENT STORE SANTA!
WHO WASN'T?
LET ME EXPLAIN, MR. WEATHERBEE!
I HAVE TO AGREE WITH VERONICA, BETTY! THAT'S A COMPLETELY RIDICULOUS IDEA!
CAFETERIA
CHIEF! WOULD YOU LIKE TO TASTE THIS NEW RECIPE OF MINE?
WHOOPS!!
MS. BEAZLY! YOU'RE SPILLING OUR LUNCH!!
SPLAT
ACK!!
5

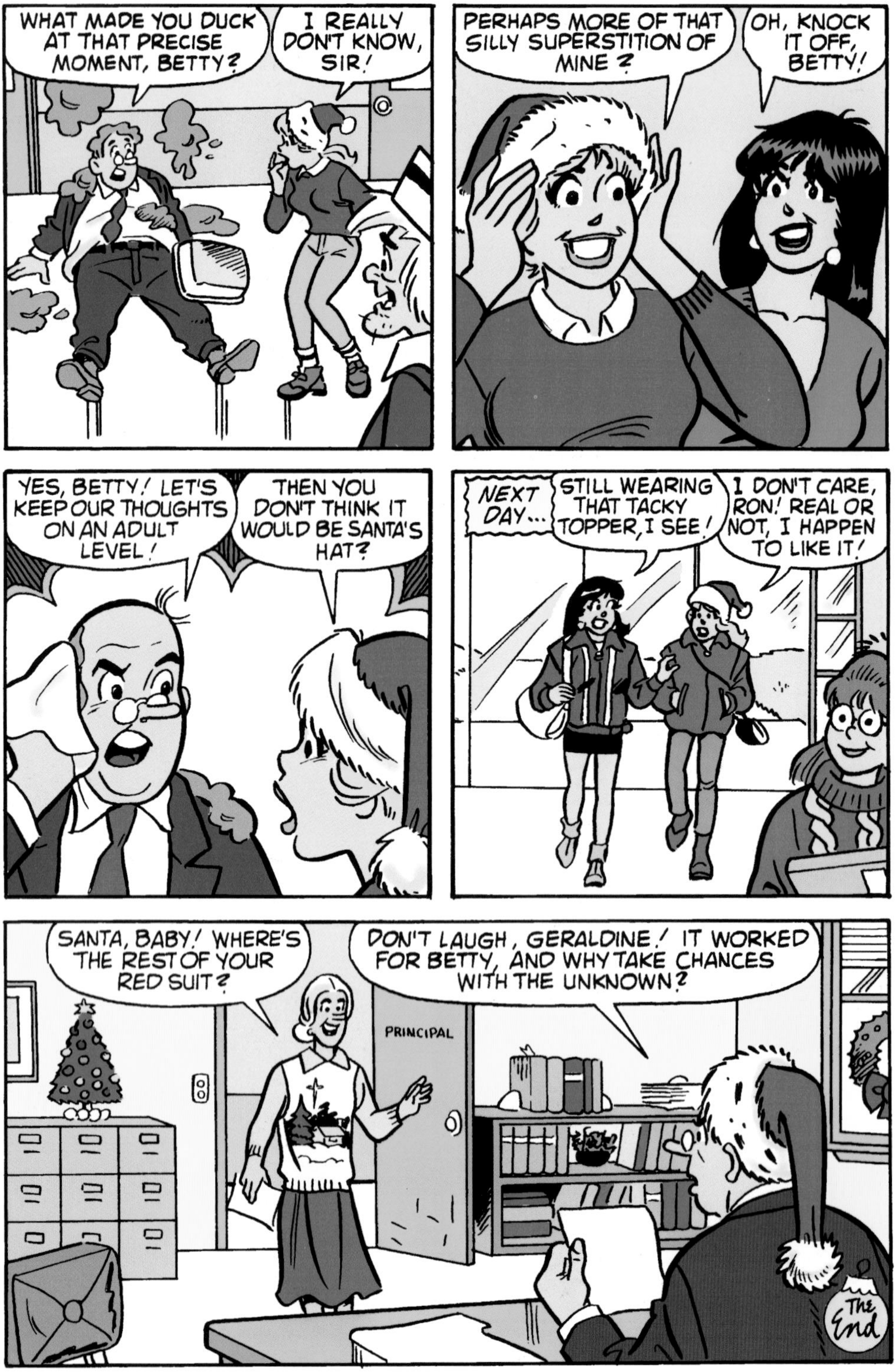
WHAT MADE YOU DUCK AT THAT PRECISE MOMENT, BETTY?
I REALLY DON'T KNOW, SIR!
PERHAPS MORE OF THAT SILLY SUPERSTITION OF MINE?
OH, KNOCK IT OFF, BETTY!
YES, BETTY! LET'S KEEP OUR THOUGHTS ON AN ADULT LEVEL!
THEN YOU DON'T THINK IT WOULD BE SANTA'S HAT?
NEXT DAY...
STILL WEARING THAT TACKY TOPPER, I SEE!
I DON'T CARE, RON! REAL OR NOT, I HAPPEN TO LIKE IT!
SANTA, BABY! WHERE'S THE REST OF YOUR RED SUIT?
DON'T LAUGH, GERALDINE! IT WORKED FOR BETTY, AND WHY TAKE CHANCES WITH THE UNKNOWN?
PRINCIPAL
THE End

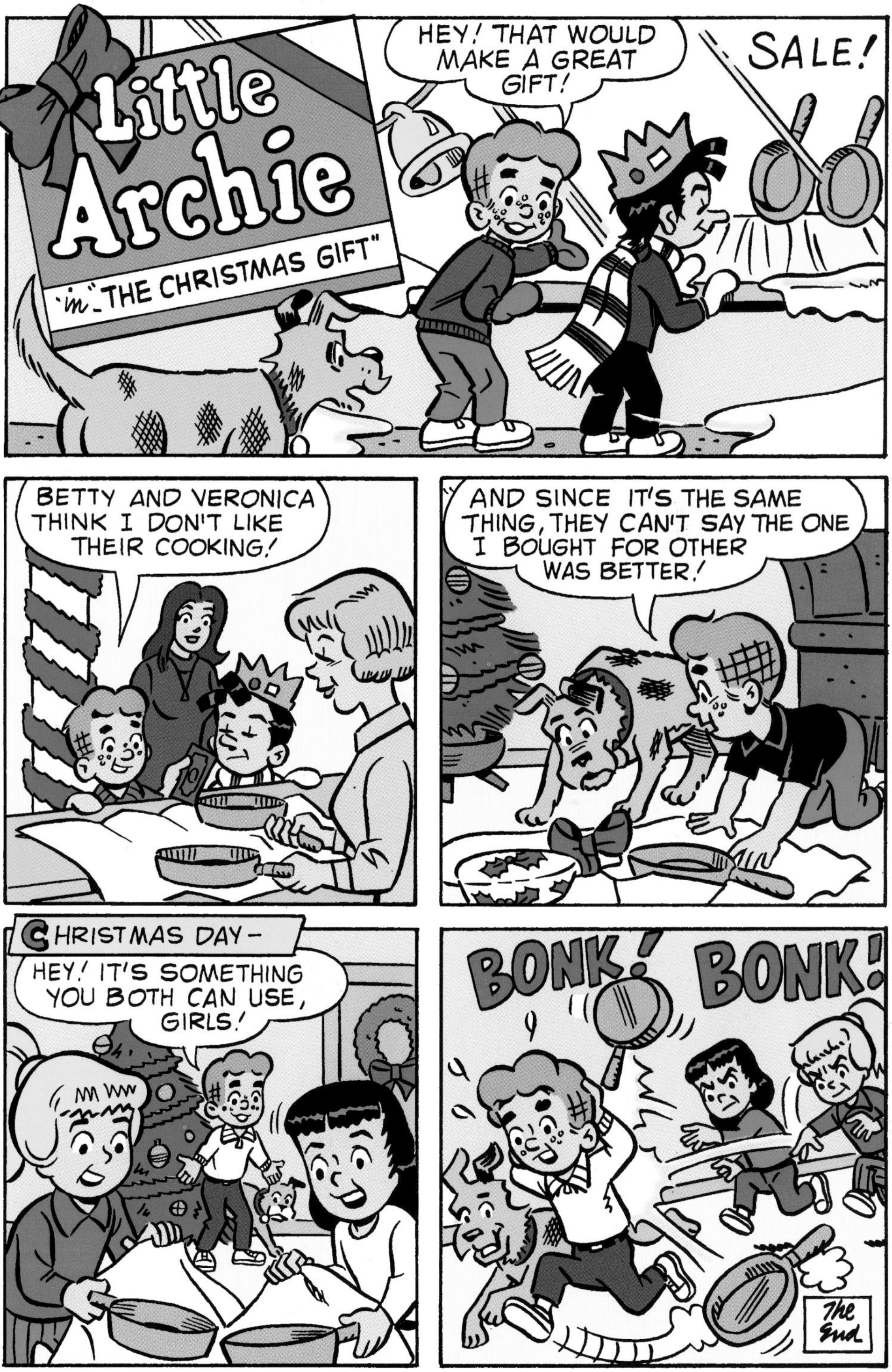
Little Archie
"in" "THE CHRISTMAS GIFT"
HEY! THAT WOULD MAKE A GREAT GIFT!
SALE!
BETTY AND VERONICA THINK I DON'T LIKE THEIR COOKING!
AND SINCE IT'S THE SAME THING, THEY CAN'T SAY THE ONE I BOUGHT FOR OTHER WAS BETTER!
CHRISTMAS DAY–
HEY! IT'S SOMETHING YOU BOTH CAN USE, GIRLS!
BONK! BONK!
The End

Dexter Taylor

Originally printed in ARCHIE'S HOLIDAY FUN DIGEST #3, 1999

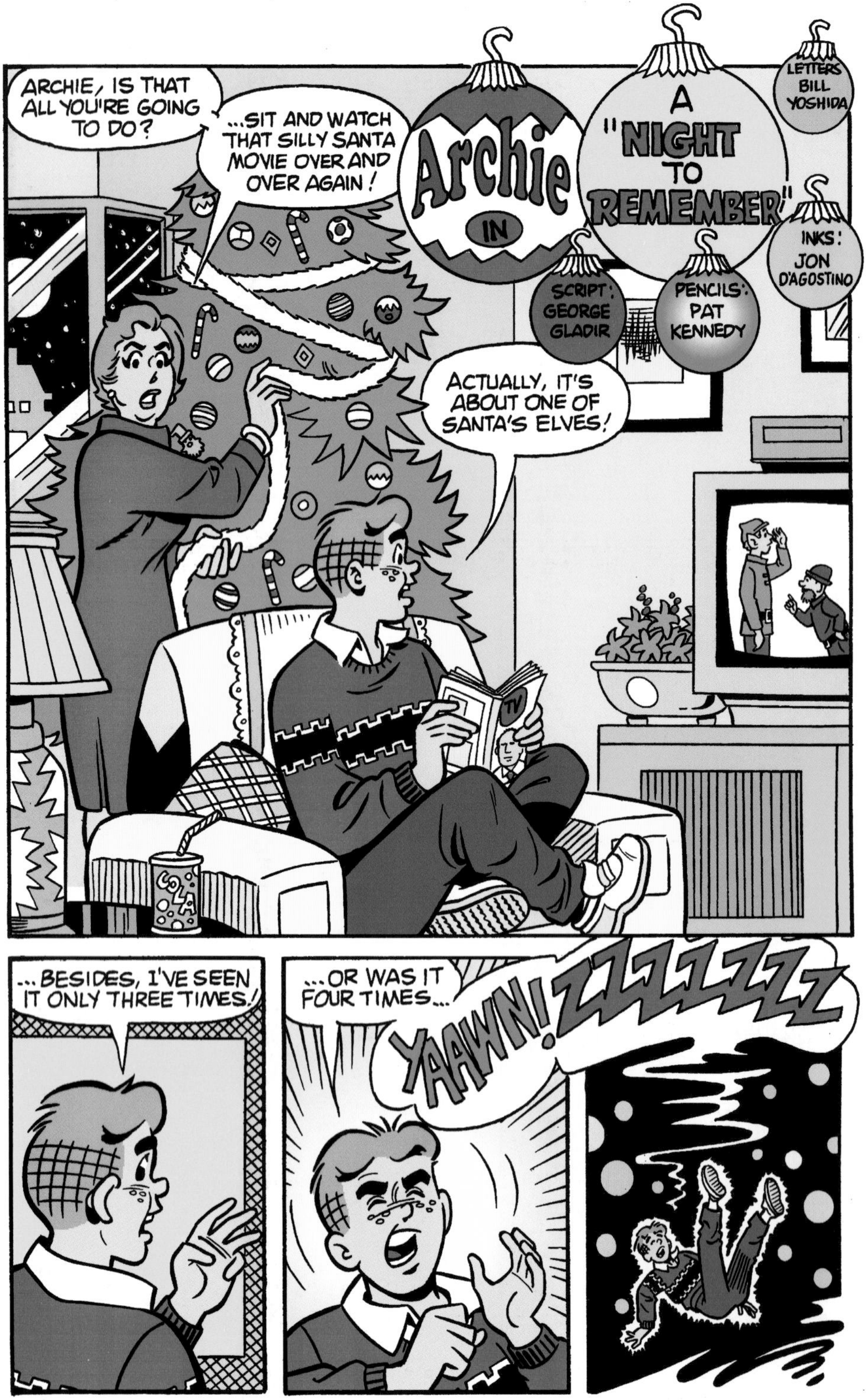
ARCHIE, IS THAT ALL YOU'RE GOING TO DO?
...SIT AND WATCH THAT SILLY SANTA MOVIE OVER AND OVER AGAIN!
Archie IN
A "NIGHT TO REMEMBER"
LETTERS BILL YOSHIDA
SCRIPT: GEORGE GLADIR
PENCILS: PAT KENNEDY
INKS: JON D'AGOSTINO
ACTUALLY, IT'S ABOUT ONE OF SANTA'S ELVES!
TV
COLA
...BESIDES, I'VE SEEN IT ONLY THREE TIMES!
...OR WAS IT FOUR TIMES...
YAAWN!
ZZZZZZZ

George Gladir • Pat Kennedy • Jon D'Agostino • Bill Yoshida

Originally printed in ARCHIE'S HOLIDAY FUN DIGEST #9, 2004

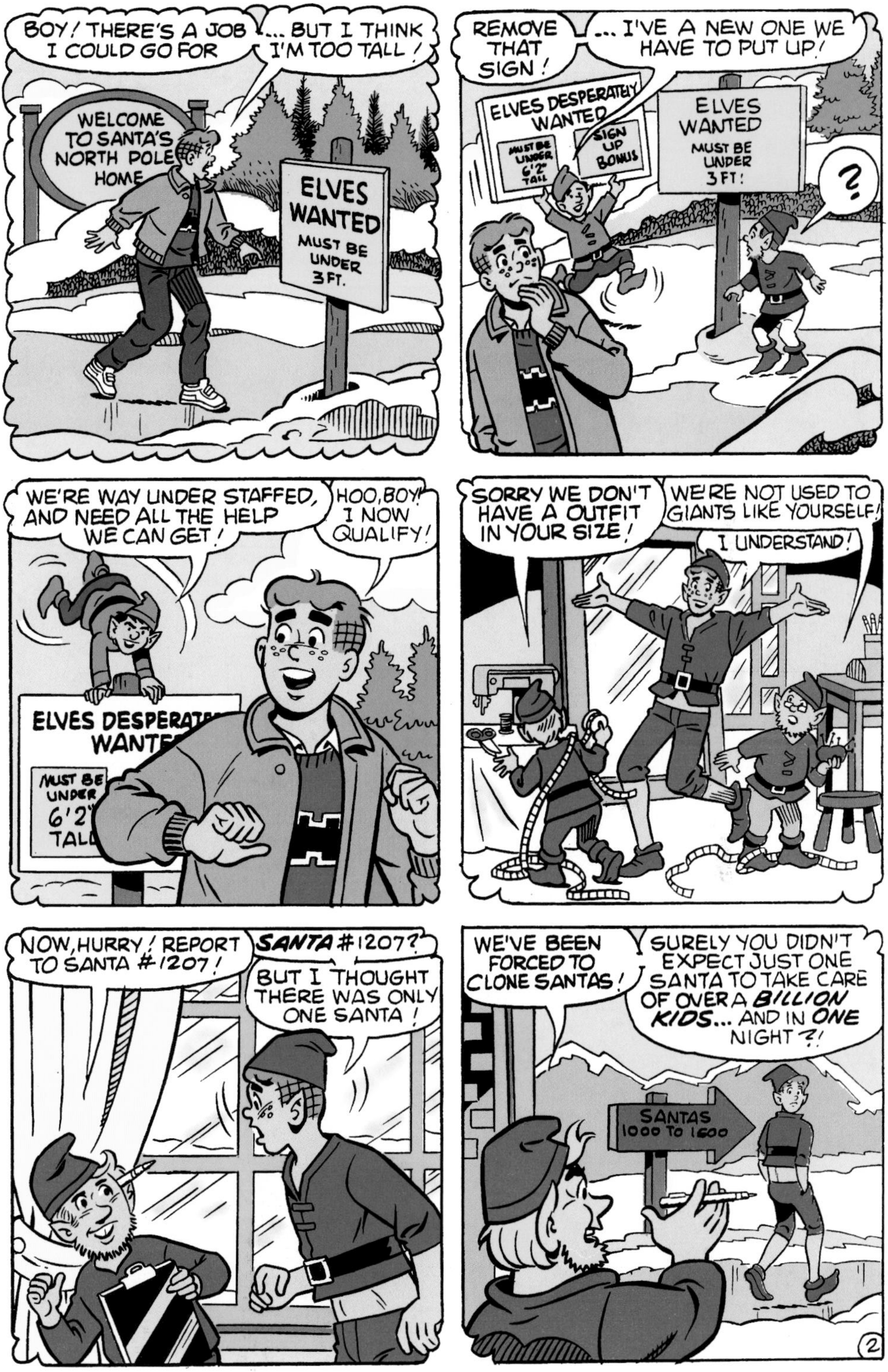
BOY! THERE'S A JOB I COULD GO FOR
... BUT I THINK I'M TOO TALL!
WELCOME TO SANTA'S NORTH POLE HOME
ELVES WANTED MUST BE UNDER 3 FT.
REMOVE THAT SIGN!
... I'VE A NEW ONE WE HAVE TO PUT UP!
ELVES DESPERATELY WANTED
MUST BE UNDER 6'2" TALL
SIGN UP BONUS
ELVES WANTED MUST BE UNDER 3 FT.
?
WE'RE WAY UNDER STAFFED, AND NEED ALL THE HELP WE CAN GET!
HOO, BOY! I NOW QUALIFY!
SORRY WE DON'T HAVE A OUTFIT IN YOUR SIZE!
WE'RE NOT USED TO GIANTS LIKE YOURSELF!
I UNDERSTAND!
NOW, HURRY! REPORT TO SANTA #1207!
SANTA #1207?
BUT I THOUGHT THERE WAS ONLY ONE SANTA!
WE'VE BEEN FORCED TO CLONE SANTAS!
SURELY YOU DIDN'T EXPECT JUST ONE SANTA TO TAKE CARE OF OVER A BILLION KIDS... AND IN ONE NIGHT?!
SANTAS 1000 TO 1600
2

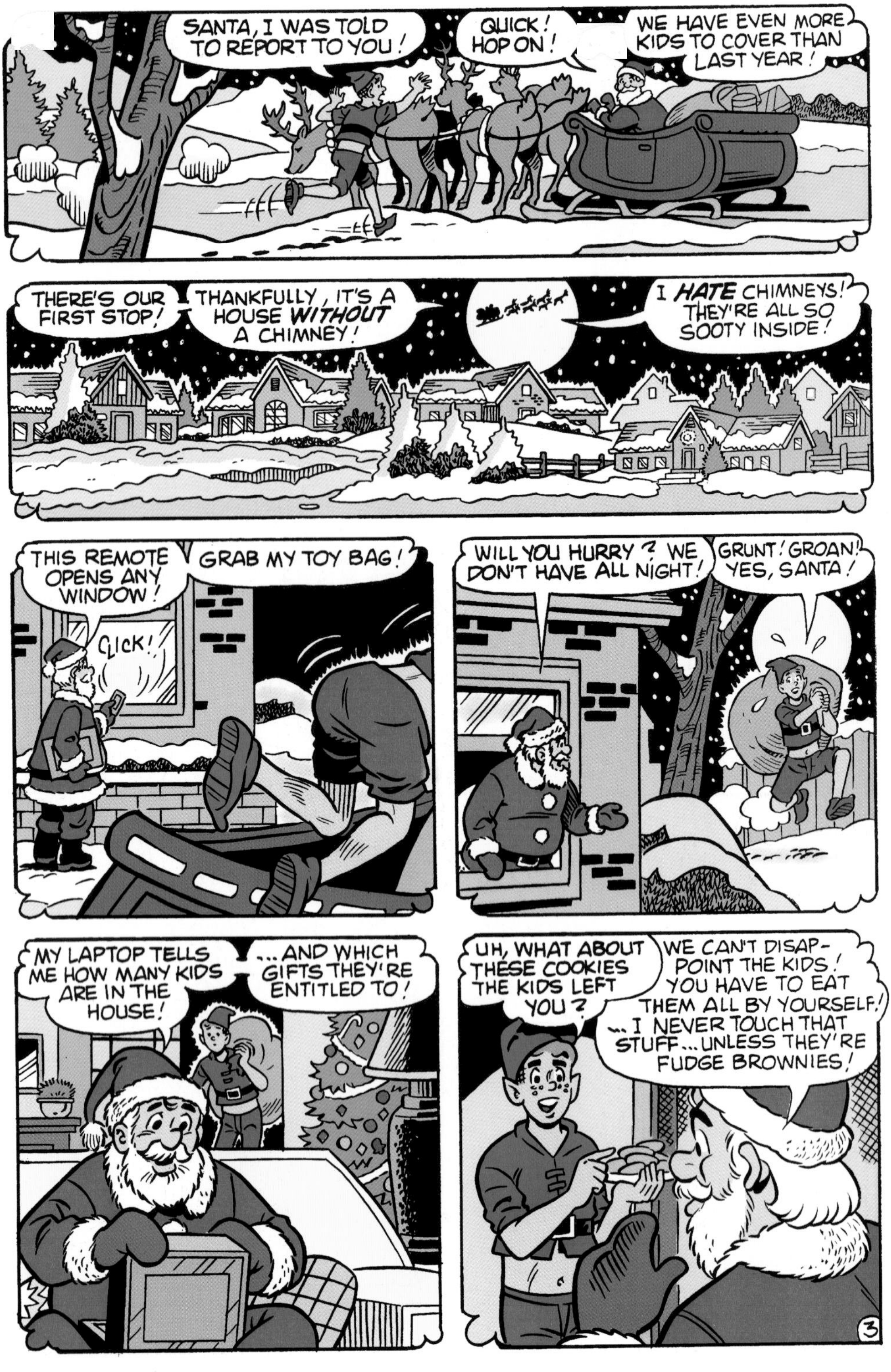
SANTA, I WAS TOLD TO REPORT TO YOU!
QUICK! HOP ON!
WE HAVE EVEN MORE KIDS TO COVER THAN LAST YEAR!
THERE'S OUR FIRST STOP!
THANKFULLY, IT'S A HOUSE WITHOUT A CHIMNEY!
I HATE CHIMNEYS! THEY'RE ALL SO SOOTY INSIDE!
THIS REMOTE OPENS ANY WINDOW!
CLICK!
GRAB MY TOY BAG!
WILL YOU HURRY? WE DON'T HAVE ALL NIGHT!
GRUNT! GROAN! YES, SANTA!
MY LAPTOP TELLS ME HOW MANY KIDS ARE IN THE HOUSE!
...AND WHICH GIFTS THEY'RE ENTITLED TO!
UH, WHAT ABOUT THESE COOKIES THE KIDS LEFT YOU?
WE CAN'T DISAPPOINT THE KIDS! YOU HAVE TO EAT THEM ALL BY YOURSELF!
...I NEVER TOUCH THAT STUFF...UNLESS THEY'RE FUDGE BROWNIES!
3

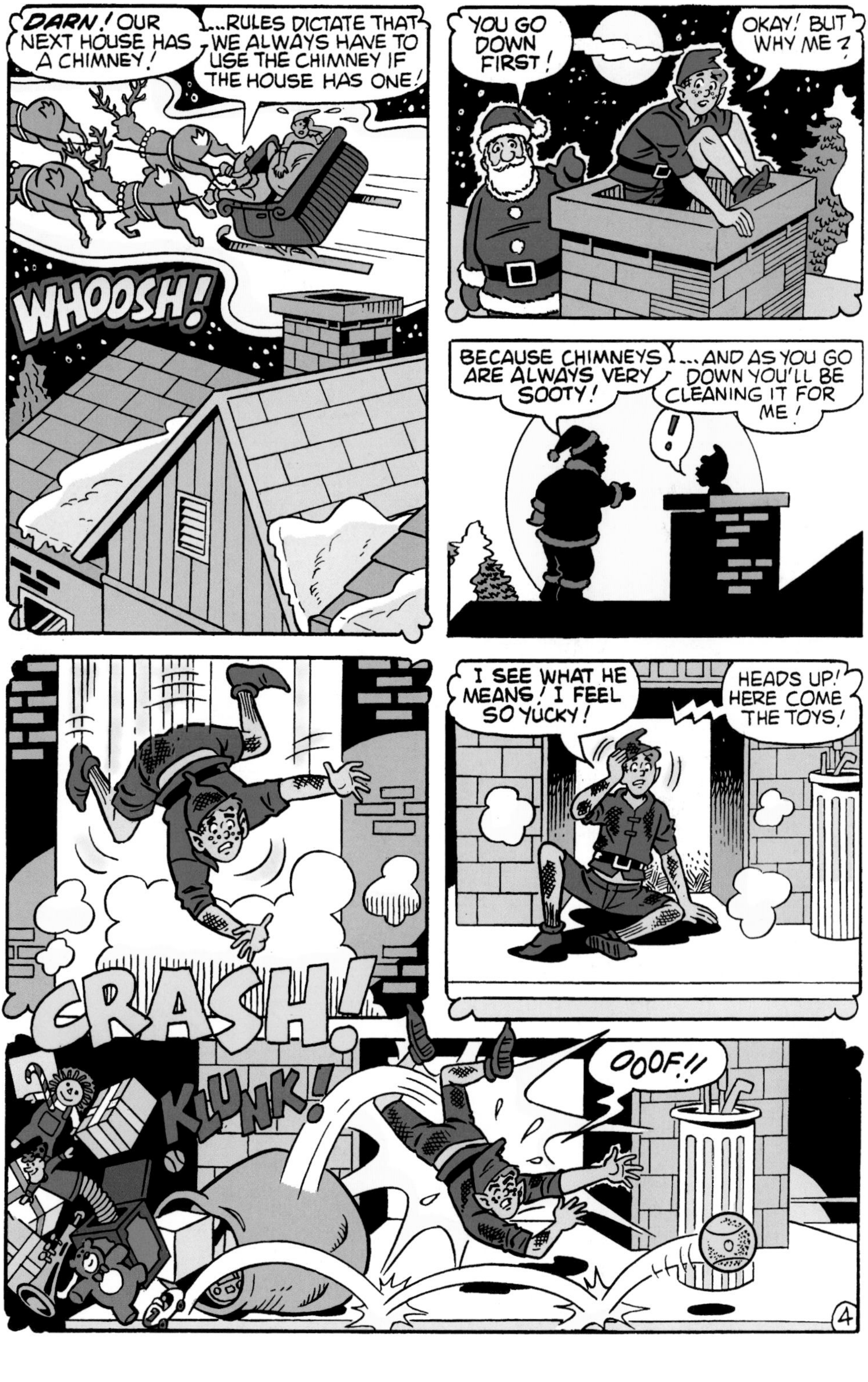
DARN! OUR NEXT HOUSE HAS A CHIMNEY!
...RULES DICTATE THAT WE ALWAYS HAVE TO USE THE CHIMNEY IF THE HOUSE HAS ONE!
WHOOSH!
YOU GO DOWN FIRST!
OKAY! BUT WHY ME?
BECAUSE CHIMNEYS ARE ALWAYS VERY SOOTY!
...AND AS YOU GO DOWN YOU'LL BE CLEANING IT FOR ME!
!
CRASH!
I SEE WHAT HE MEANS! I FEEL SO YUCKY!
HEADS UP! HERE COME THE TOYS!
KLUNK!
OOOF!!
4

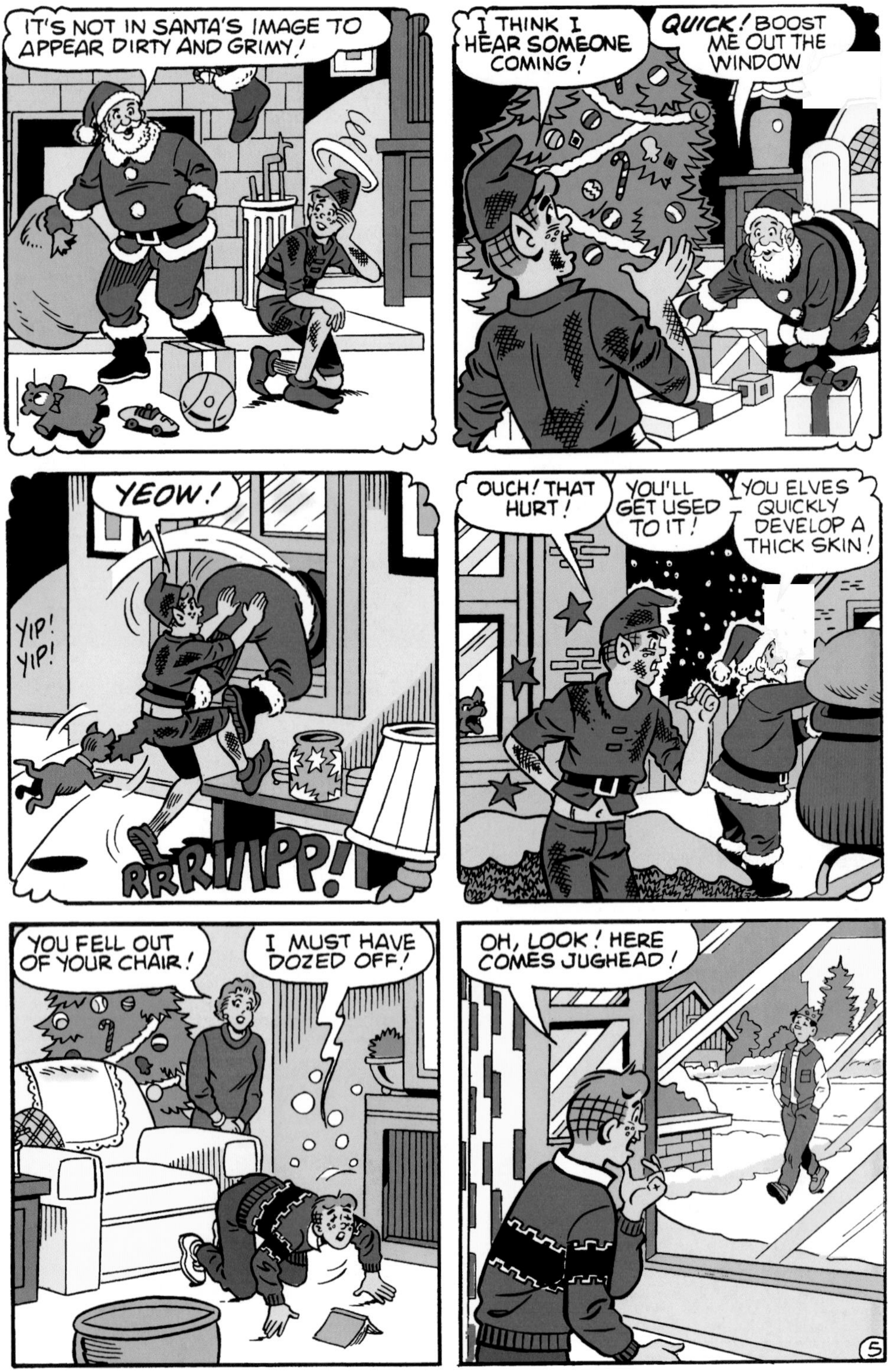
IT'S NOT IN SANTA'S IMAGE TO APPEAR DIRTY AND GRIMY!
I THINK I HEAR SOMEONE COMING!
QUICK! BOOST ME OUT THE WINDOW
YEOW!
YIP! YIP!
RRRIIIPP!
OUCH! THAT HURT!
YOU'LL GET USED TO IT!
YOU ELVES QUICKLY DEVELOP A THICK SKIN!
YOU FELL OUT OF YOUR CHAIR!
I MUST HAVE DOZED OFF!
OH, LOOK! HERE COMES JUGHEAD!
5

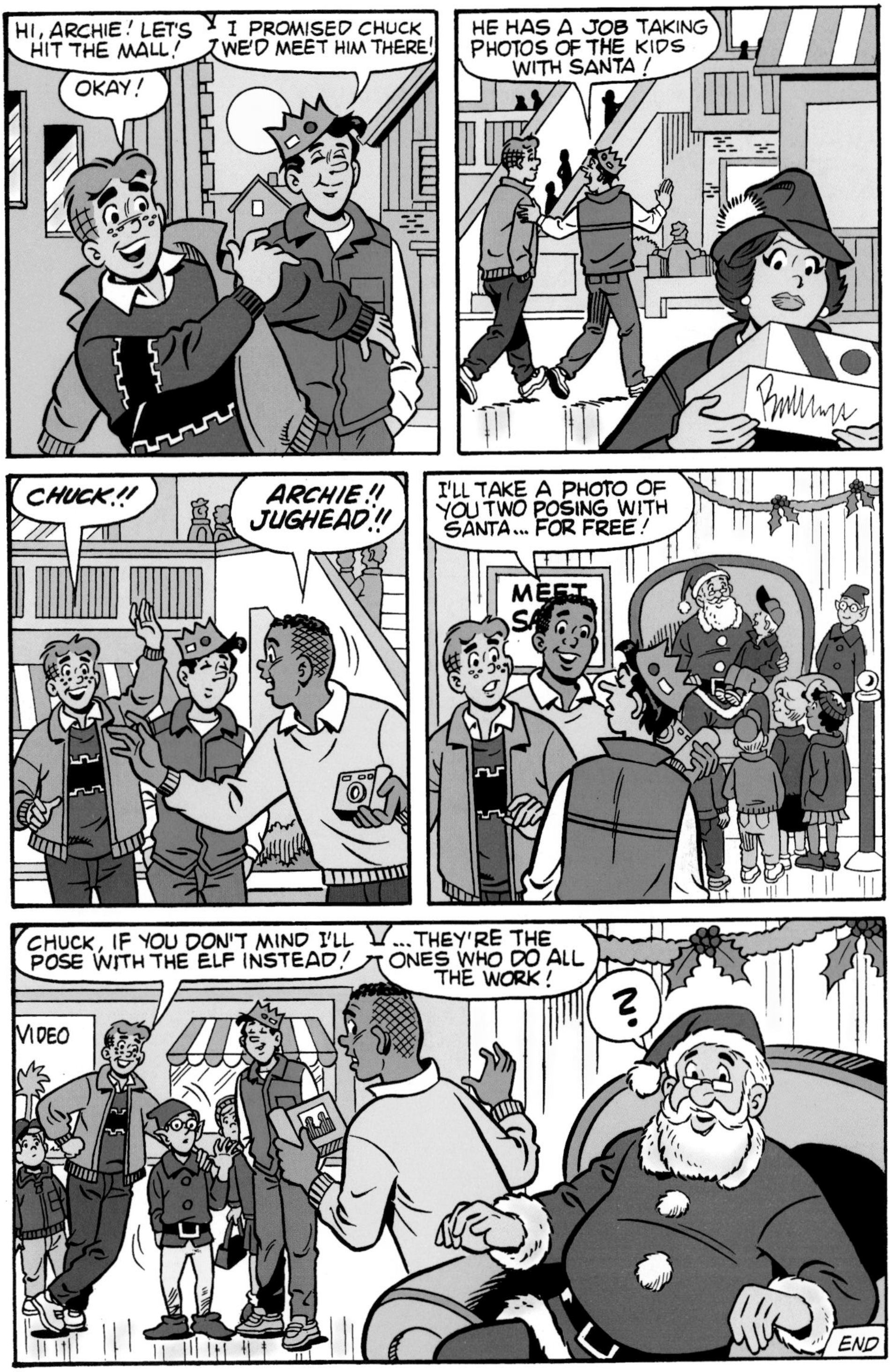
HI, ARCHIE! LET'S HIT THE MALL!
I PROMISED CHUCK WE'D MEET HIM THERE!
OKAY!
HE HAS A JOB TAKING PHOTOS OF THE KIDS WITH SANTA!
CHUCK!!
ARCHIE!! JUGHEAD!!
I'LL TAKE A PHOTO OF YOU TWO POSING WITH SANTA... FOR FREE!
MEET SA
CHUCK, IF YOU DON'T MIND I'LL POSE WITH THE ELF INSTEAD!
...THEY'RE THE ONES WHO DO ALL THE WORK!
?
VIDEO
END

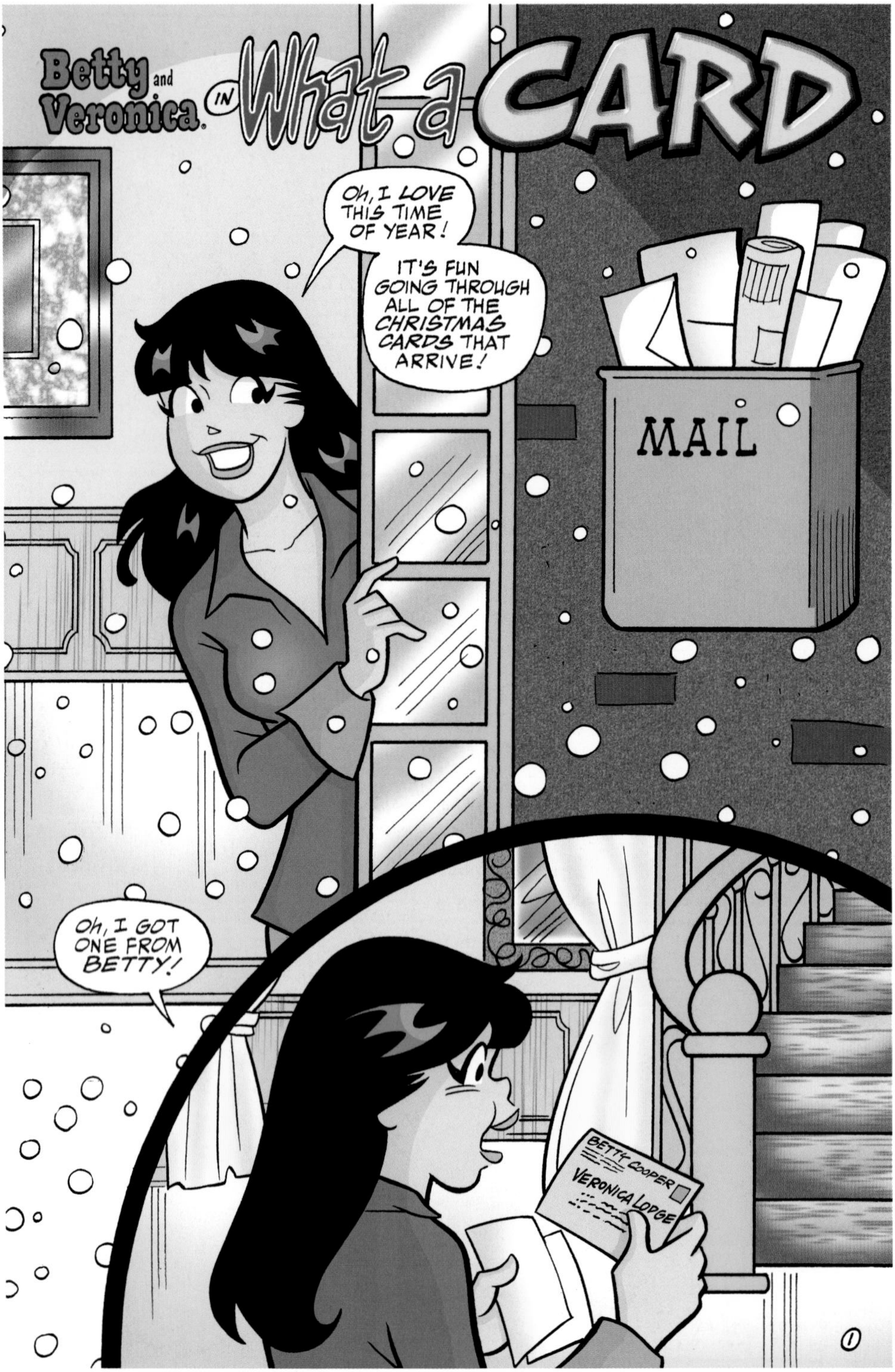
Betty and Veronica IN What a CARD
Oh, I LOVE THIS TIME OF YEAR!
IT'S FUN GOING THROUGH ALL OF THE CHRISTMAS CARDS THAT ARRIVE!
MAIL
Oh, I GOT ONE FROM BETTY!
BETTY COOPER
VERONICA LODGE
1

Dan Parent • Rich Koslowski • Jack Morelli

Originally printed in BETTY & VERONICA SPECTACULAR #72, 2006

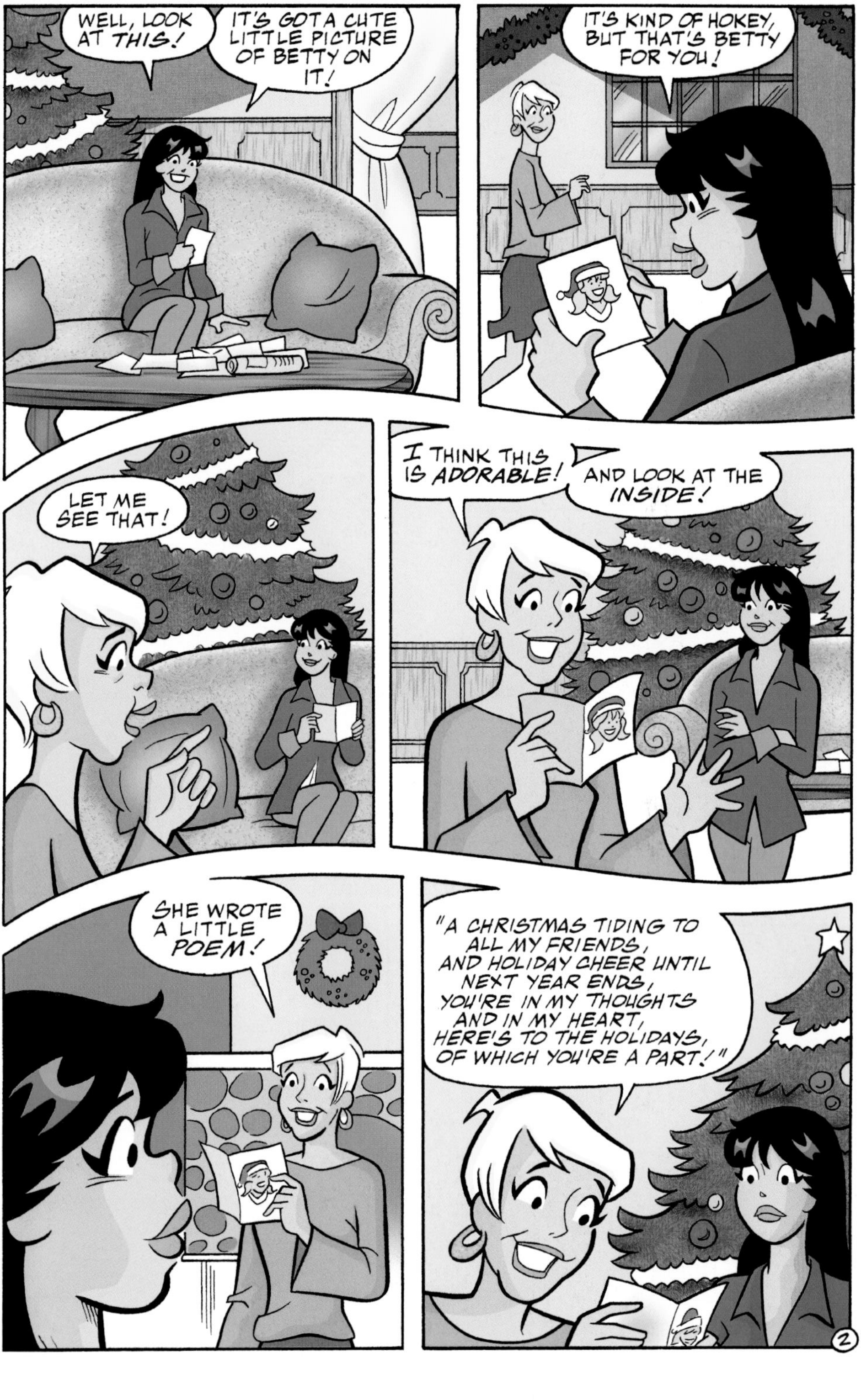
WELL, LOOK AT THIS!
IT'S GOT A CUTE LITTLE PICTURE OF BETTY ON IT!
IT'S KIND OF HOKEY, BUT THAT'S BETTY FOR YOU!
LET ME SEE THAT!
I THINK THIS IS ADORABLE!
AND LOOK AT THE INSIDE!
SHE WROTE A LITTLE POEM!
"A CHRISTMAS TIDING TO ALL MY FRIENDS, AND HOLIDAY CHEER UNTIL NEXT YEAR ENDS, YOU'RE IN MY THOUGHTS AND IN MY HEART, HERE'S TO THE HOLIDAYS, OF WHICH YOU'RE A PART!"
2

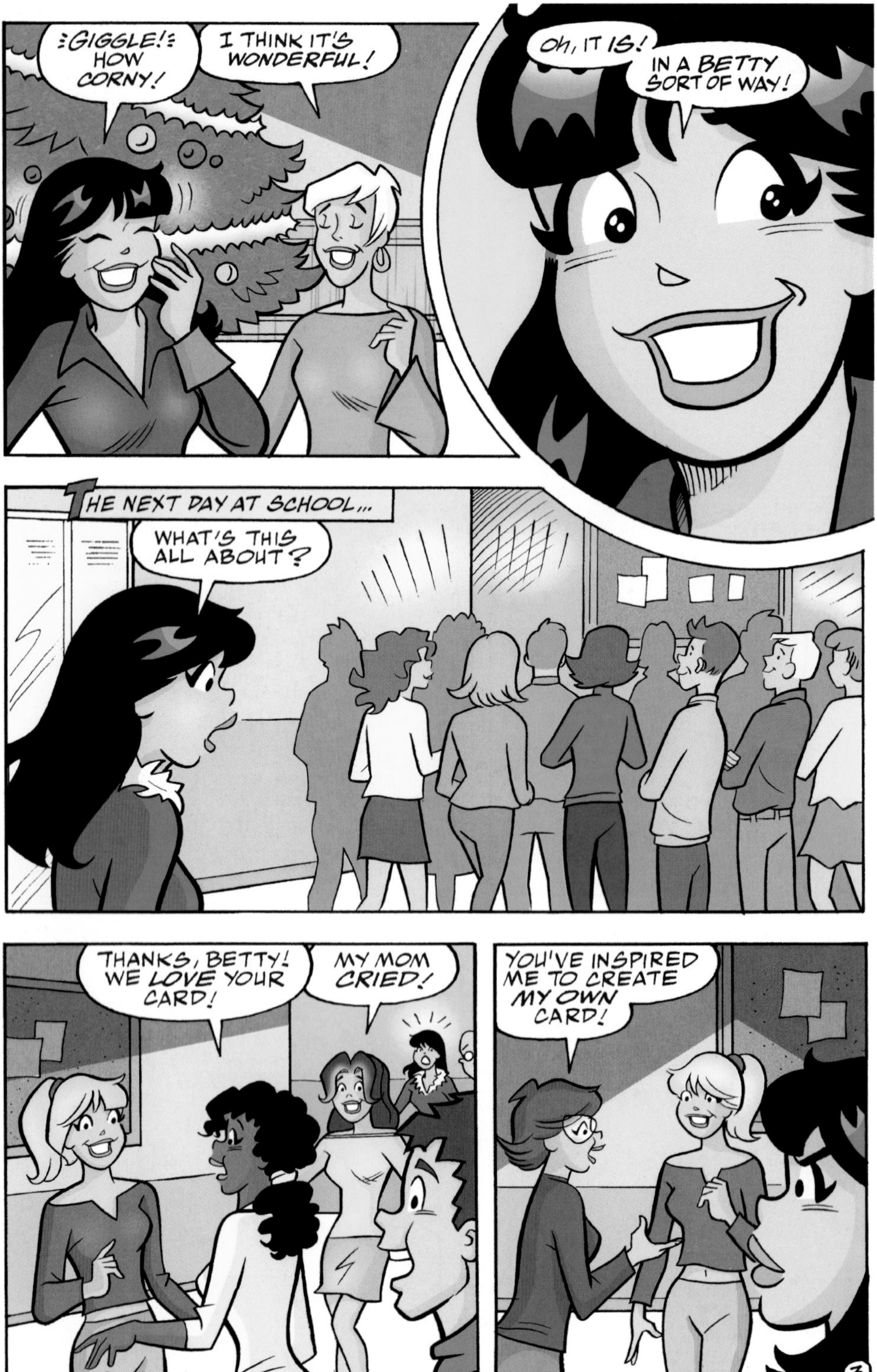

:GIGGLE!: HOW CORNY!
I THINK IT'S WONDERFUL!
Oh, IT IS!
IN A BETTY SORT OF WAY!
THE NEXT DAY AT SCHOOL...
WHAT'S THIS ALL ABOUT?
THANKS, BETTY! WE LOVE YOUR CARD!
MY MOM CRIED!
YOU'VE INSPIRED ME TO CREATE MY OWN CARD!
3

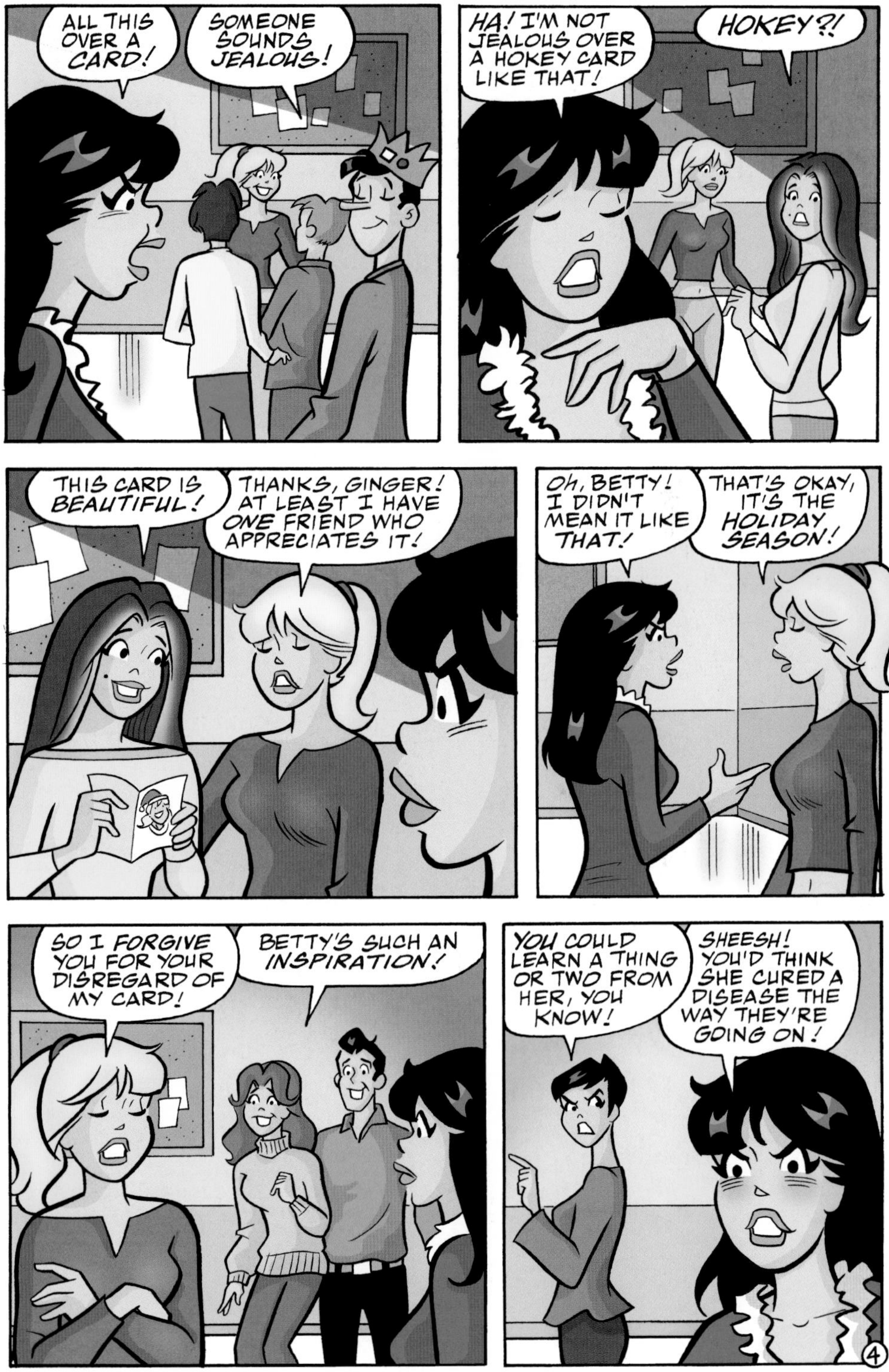
ALL THIS OVER A CARD!
SOMEONE SOUNDS JEALOUS!
HA! I'M NOT JEALOUS OVER A HOKEY CARD LIKE THAT!
HOKEY?!
THIS CARD IS BEAUTIFUL!
THANKS, GINGER! AT LEAST I HAVE ONE FRIEND WHO APPRECIATES IT!
OH, BETTY! I DIDN'T MEAN IT LIKE THAT!
THAT'S OKAY, IT'S THE HOLIDAY SEASON!
SO I FORGIVE YOU FOR YOUR DISREGARD OF MY CARD!
BETTY'S SUCH AN INSPIRATION!
YOU COULD LEARN A THING OR TWO FROM HER, YOU KNOW!
SHEESH! YOU'D THINK SHE CURED A DISEASE THE WAY THEY'RE GOING ON!
4

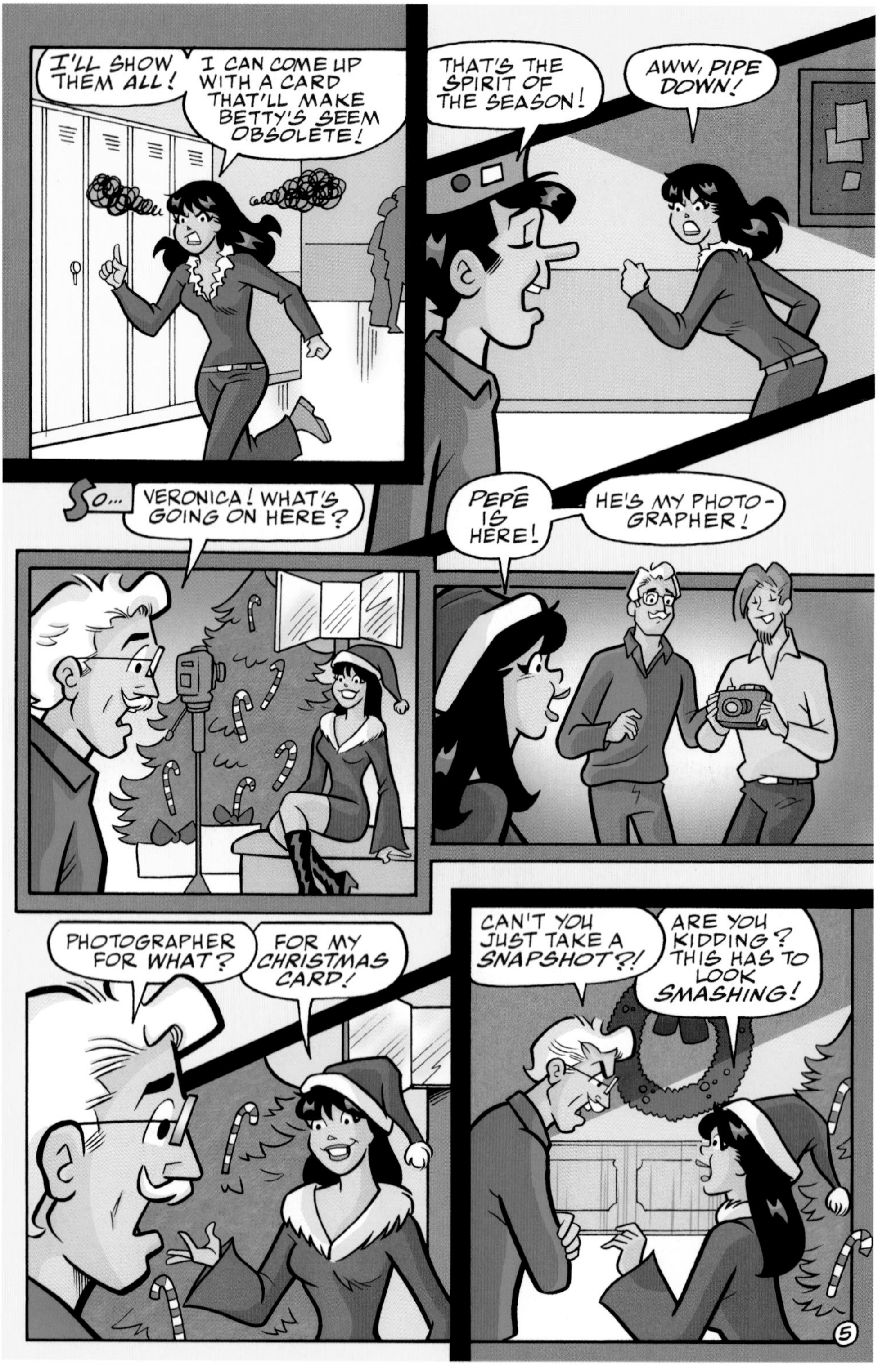
I'LL SHOW THEM ALL!
I CAN COME UP WITH A CARD THAT'LL MAKE BETTY'S SEEM OBSOLETE!
THAT'S THE SPIRIT OF THE SEASON!
AWW, PIPE DOWN!
SO...
VERONICA! WHAT'S GOING ON HERE?
PEPÉ IS HERE!
HE'S MY PHOTOGRAPHER!
PHOTOGRAPHER FOR WHAT?
FOR MY CHRISTMAS CARD!
CAN'T YOU JUST TAKE A SNAPSHOT?!
ARE YOU KIDDING? THIS HAS TO LOOK SMASHING!
5

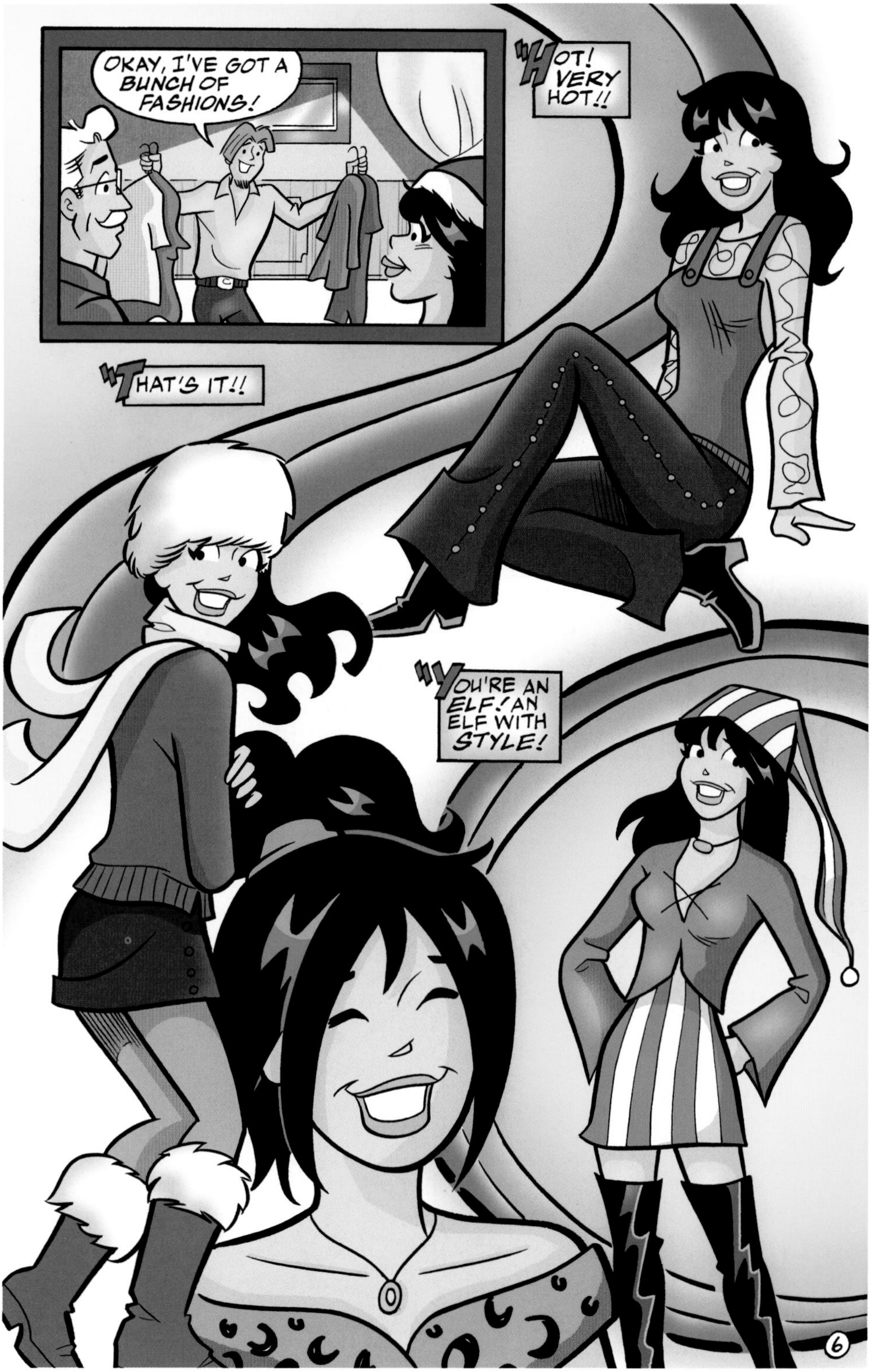
OKAY, I'VE GOT A BUNCH OF FASHIONS!
"HOT! VERY HOT!!
"THAT'S IT!!
"YOU'RE AN ELF! AN ELF WITH STYLE!
6

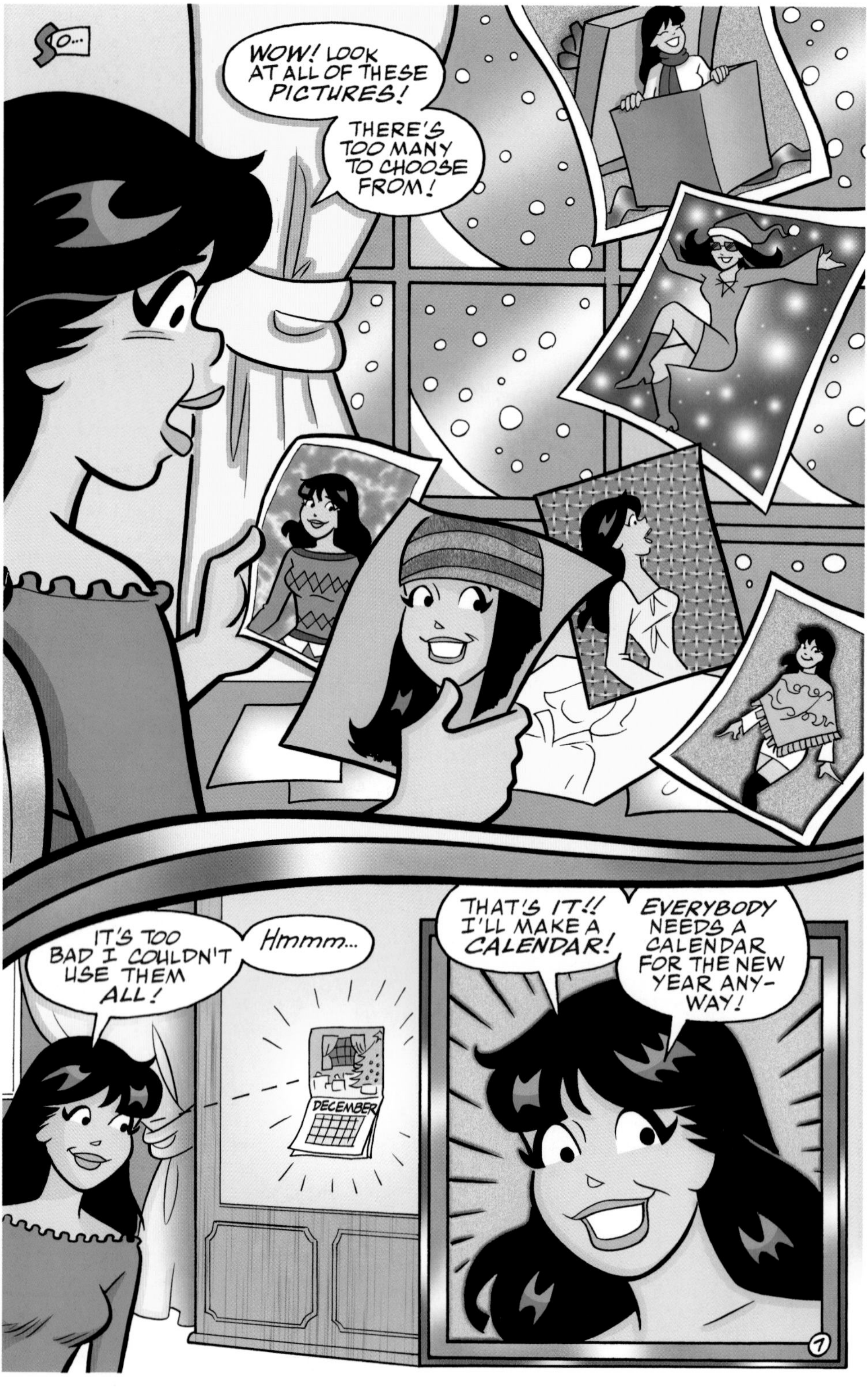
SO...
WOW! LOOK AT ALL OF THESE PICTURES!
THERE'S TOO MANY TO CHOOSE FROM!
IT'S TOO BAD I COULDN'T USE THEM ALL!
Hmmm...
DECEMBER
THAT'S IT!! I'LL MAKE A CALENDAR!
EVERYBODY NEEDS A CALENDAR FOR THE NEW YEAR ANYWAY!
7

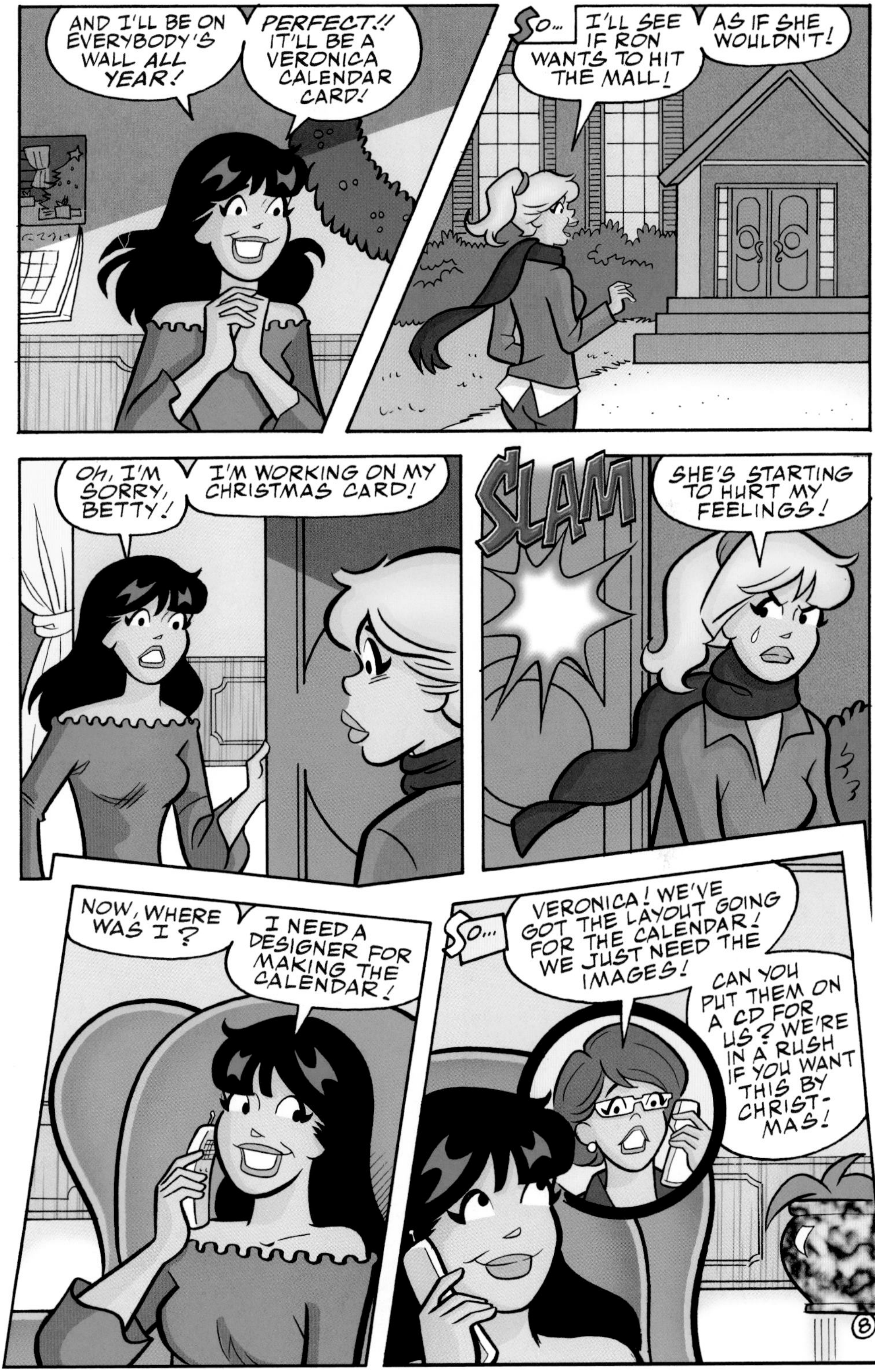
AND I'LL BE ON EVERYBODY'S WALL ALL YEAR!
PERFECT!! IT'LL BE A VERONICA CALENDAR CARD!
SO...
I'LL SEE IF RON WANTS TO HIT THE MALL!
AS IF SHE WOULDN'T!
Oh, I'M SORRY, BETTY!
I'M WORKING ON MY CHRISTMAS CARD!
SLAM
SHE'S STARTING TO HURT MY FEELINGS!
NOW, WHERE WAS I?
I NEED A DESIGNER FOR MAKING THE CALENDAR!
SO...
VERONICA! WE'VE GOT THE LAYOUT GOING FOR THE CALENDAR! WE JUST NEED THE IMAGES!
CAN YOU PUT THEM ON A CD FOR US? WE'RE IN A RUSH IF YOU WANT THIS BY CHRIST-MAS!
8

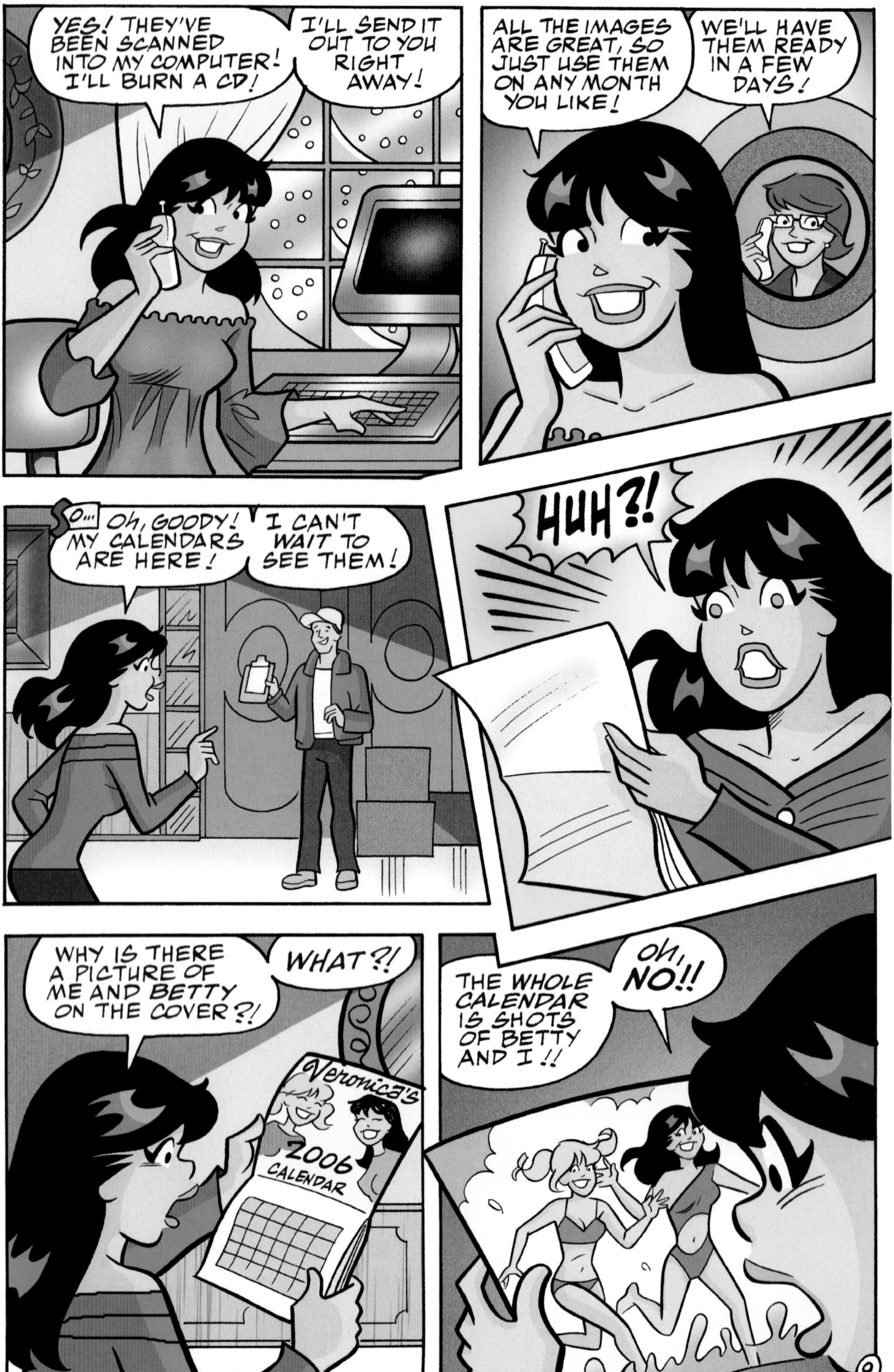
YES! THEY'VE BEEN SCANNED INTO MY COMPUTER! I'LL BURN A CD!
I'LL SEND IT OUT TO YOU RIGHT AWAY!
ALL THE IMAGES ARE GREAT, SO JUST USE THEM ON ANY MONTH YOU LIKE!
WE'LL HAVE THEM READY IN A FEW DAYS!
Oh, GOODY! MY CALENDARS ARE HERE!
I CAN'T WAIT TO SEE THEM!
HUH?!
WHY IS THERE A PICTURE OF ME AND BETTY ON THE COVER?!
WHAT?!
Veronica's
2006
CALENDAR
THE WHOLE CALENDAR IS SHOTS OF BETTY AND I!!
Oh, NO!!
9

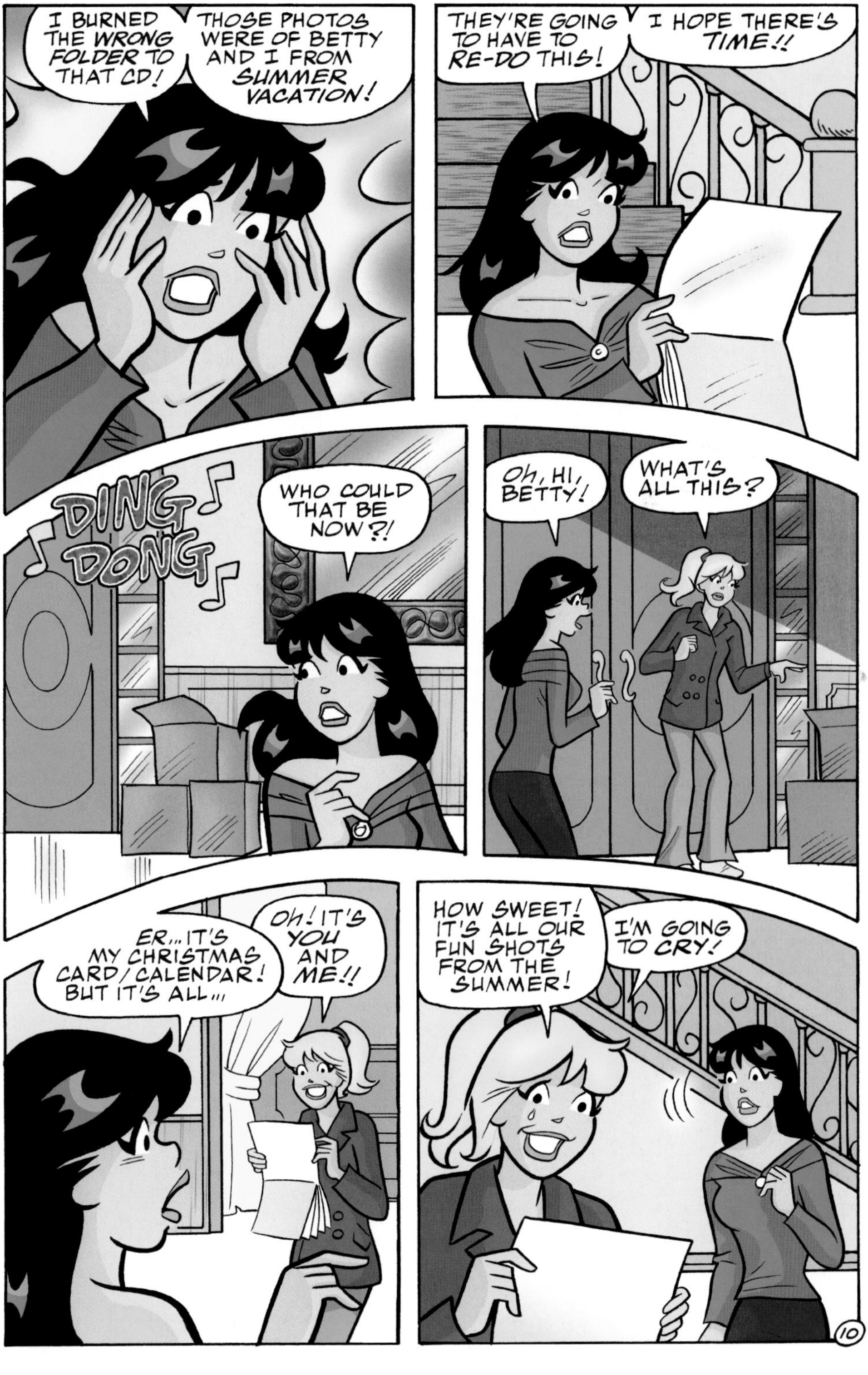
I BURNED THE WRONG FOLDER TO THAT CD!
THOSE PHOTOS WERE OF BETTY AND I FROM SUMMER VACATION!
THEY'RE GOING TO HAVE TO RE-DO THIS!
I HOPE THERE'S TIME!!
DING DONG
WHO COULD THAT BE NOW?!
Oh, HI, BETTY!
WHAT'S ALL THIS?
ER... IT'S MY CHRISTMAS CARD/CALENDAR! BUT IT'S ALL...
Oh! IT'S YOU AND ME!!
HOW SWEET! IT'S ALL OUR FUN SHOTS FROM THE SUMMER!
I'M GOING TO CRY!
10

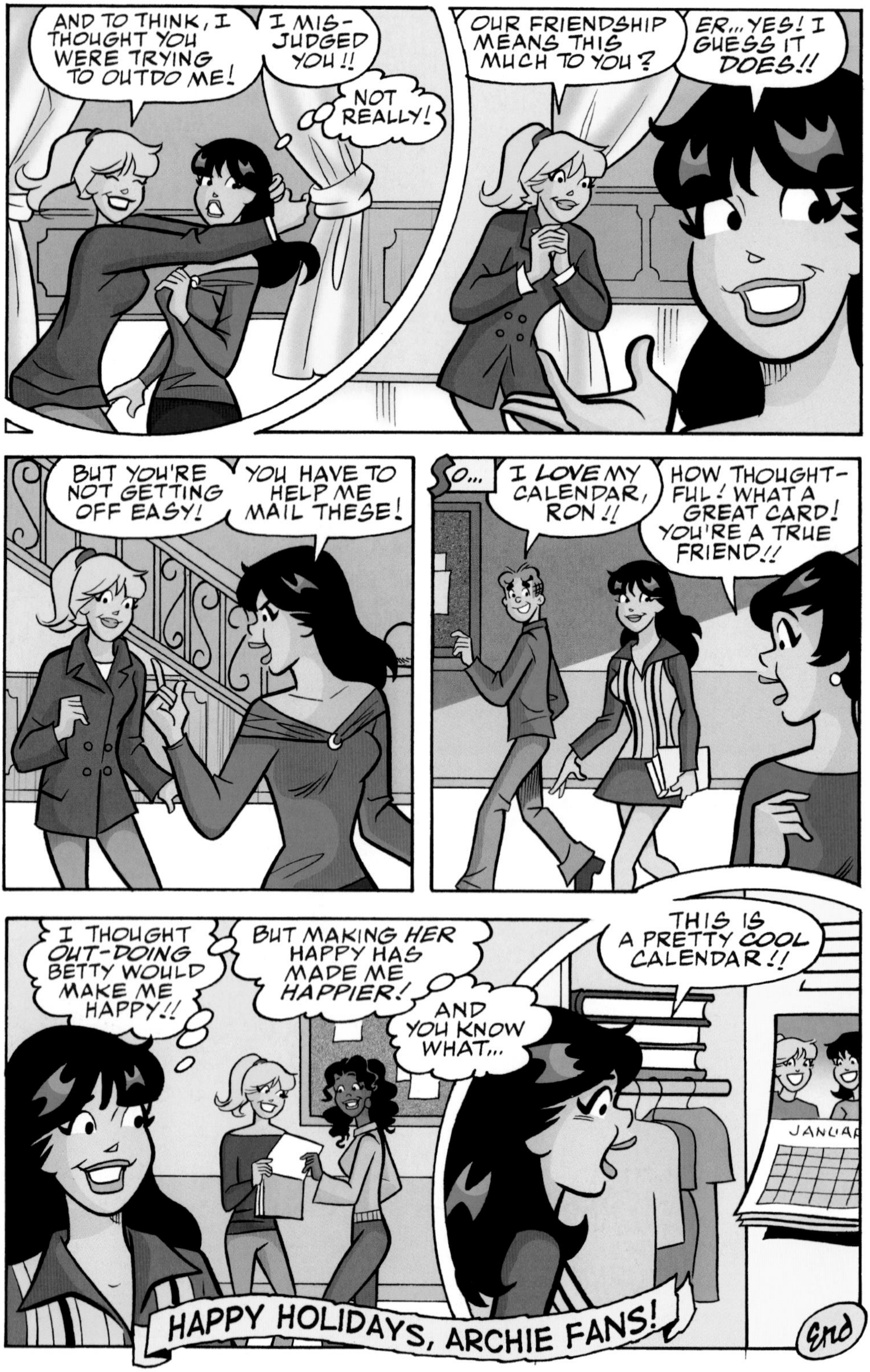
AND TO THINK, I THOUGHT YOU WERE TRYING TO OUTDO ME!
I MIS-JUDGED YOU!!
NOT REALLY!
OUR FRIENDSHIP MEANS THIS MUCH TO YOU?
ER... YES! I GUESS IT DOES!!
BUT YOU'RE NOT GETTING OFF EASY!
YOU HAVE TO HELP ME MAIL THESE!
SO...
I LOVE MY CALENDAR, RON!!
HOW THOUGHT-FUL! WHAT A GREAT CARD! YOU'RE A TRUE FRIEND!!
I THOUGHT OUT-DOING BETTY WOULD MAKE ME HAPPY!!
BUT MAKING HER HAPPY HAS MADE ME HAPPIER!
AND YOU KNOW WHAT...
THIS IS A PRETTY COOL CALENDAR!!
HAPPY HOLIDAYS, ARCHIE FANS!
End

Archie & Friends in Holiday on the High Seas

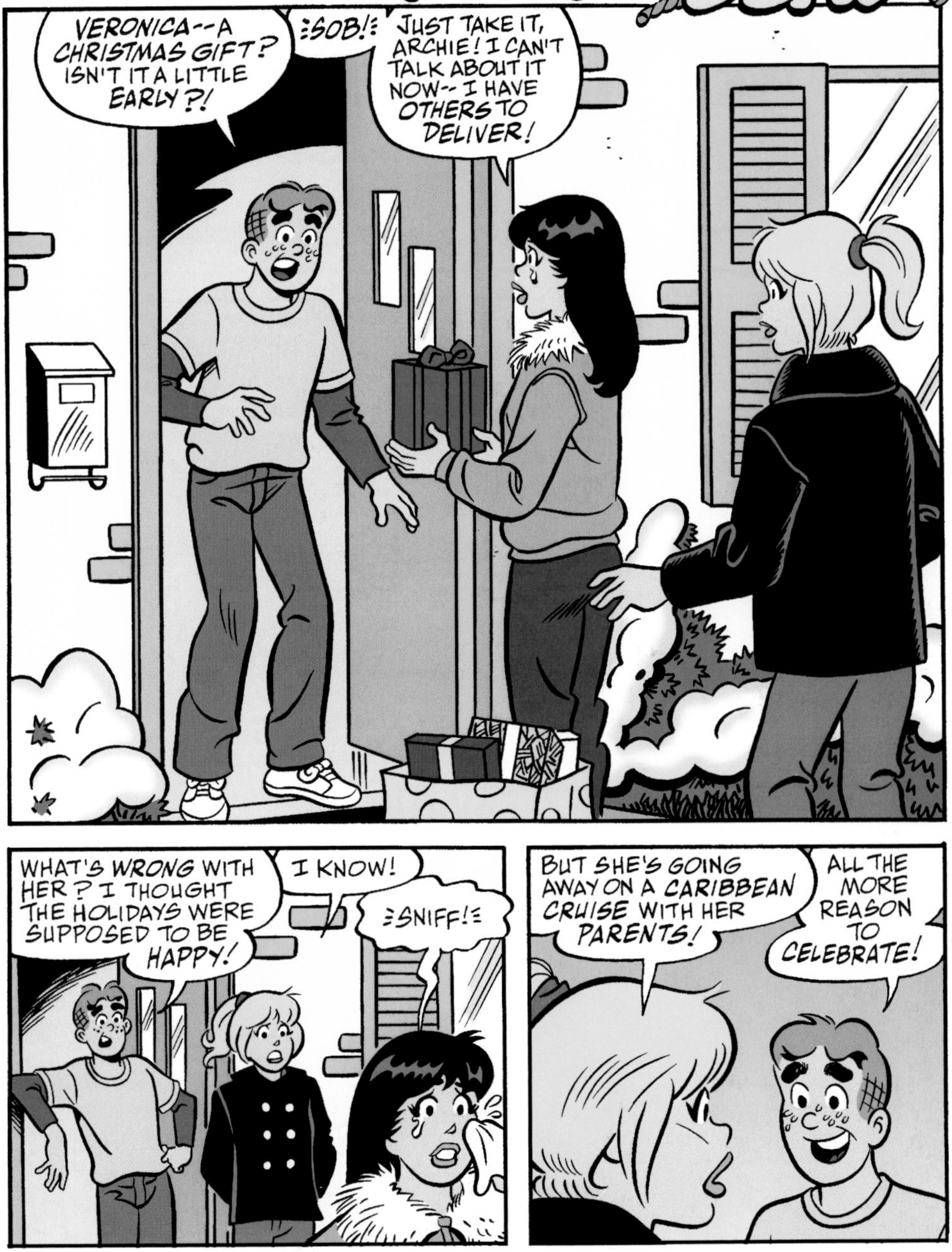
VERONICA--A CHRISTMAS GIFT? ISN'T IT A LITTLE EARLY?!
:SOB!:
JUST TAKE IT, ARCHIE! I CAN'T TALK ABOUT IT NOW-- I HAVE OTHERS TO DELIVER!
WHAT'S WRONG WITH HER? I THOUGHT THE HOLIDAYS WERE SUPPOSED TO BE HAPPY!
I KNOW!
:SNIFF!:
BUT SHE'S GOING AWAY ON A CARIBBEAN CRUISE WITH HER PARENTS!
ALL THE MORE REASON TO CELEBRATE!

Bill Golliher • Jeff Shultz • Al Milgrom • Jack Morelli

Originally printed in BETTY & VERONICA DOUBLE DIGEST MAGAZINE #156, 2008

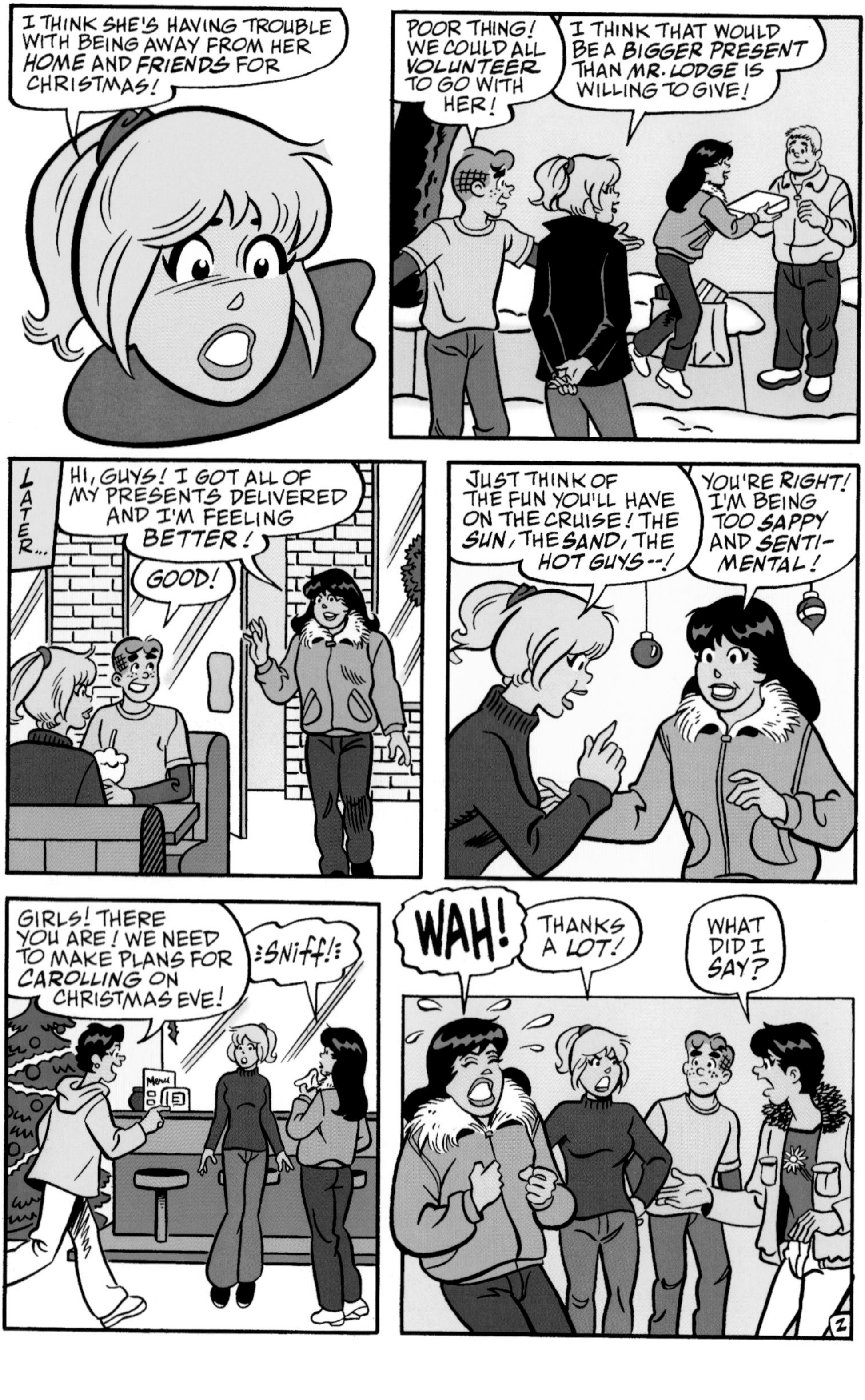
I THINK SHE'S HAVING TROUBLE WITH BEING AWAY FROM HER HOME AND FRIENDS FOR CHRISTMAS!
POOR THING! WE COULD ALL VOLUNTEER TO GO WITH HER!
I THINK THAT WOULD BE A BIGGER PRESENT THAN MR. LODGE IS WILLING TO GIVE!
LATER...
HI, GUYS! I GOT ALL OF MY PRESENTS DELIVERED AND I'M FEELING BETTER!
GOOD!
JUST THINK OF THE FUN YOU'LL HAVE ON THE CRUISE! THE SUN, THE SAND, THE HOT GUYS--!
YOU'RE RIGHT! I'M BEING TOO SAPPY AND SENTI-MENTAL!
GIRLS! THERE YOU ARE! WE NEED TO MAKE PLANS FOR CAROLLING ON CHRISTMAS EVE!
Sniff!
WAH!
THANKS A LOT!
WHAT DID I SAY?
2

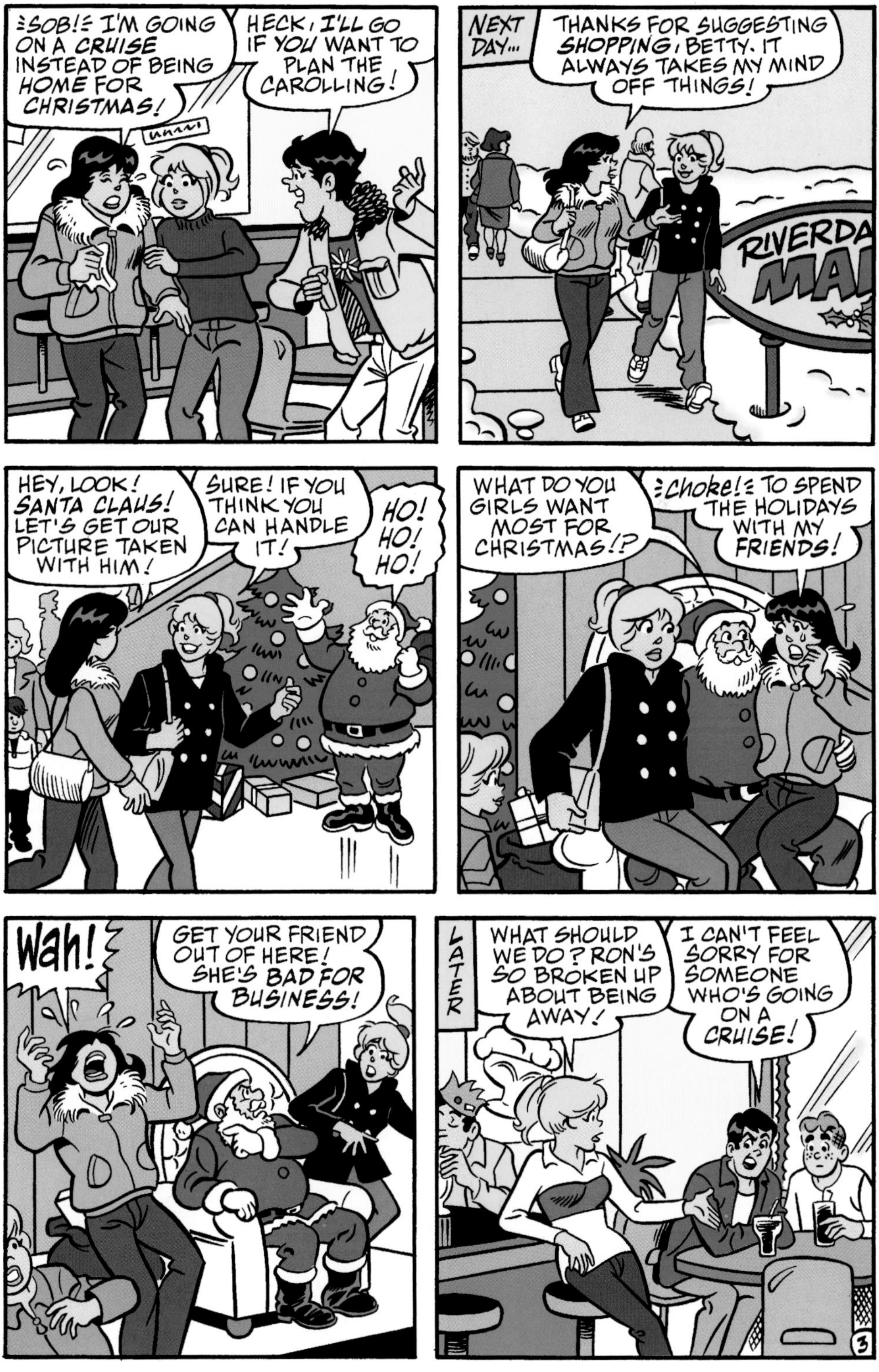

SOB! I'M GOING ON A CRUISE INSTEAD OF BEING HOME FOR CHRISTMAS!
HECK, I'LL GO IF YOU WANT TO PLAN THE CAROLLING!
NEXT DAY...
THANKS FOR SUGGESTING SHOPPING, BETTY. IT ALWAYS TAKES MY MIND OFF THINGS!
RIVERDA
MA
HEY, LOOK! SANTA CLAUS! LET'S GET OUR PICTURE TAKEN WITH HIM!
SURE! IF YOU THINK YOU CAN HANDLE IT!
HO! HO! HO!
WHAT DO YOU GIRLS WANT MOST FOR CHRISTMAS!?
CHOKE! TO SPEND THE HOLIDAYS WITH MY FRIENDS!
WAH!
GET YOUR FRIEND OUT OF HERE! SHE'S BAD FOR BUSINESS!
LATER
WHAT SHOULD WE DO? RON'S SO BROKEN UP ABOUT BEING AWAY!
I CAN'T FEEL SORRY FOR SOMEONE WHO'S GOING ON A CRUISE!
3

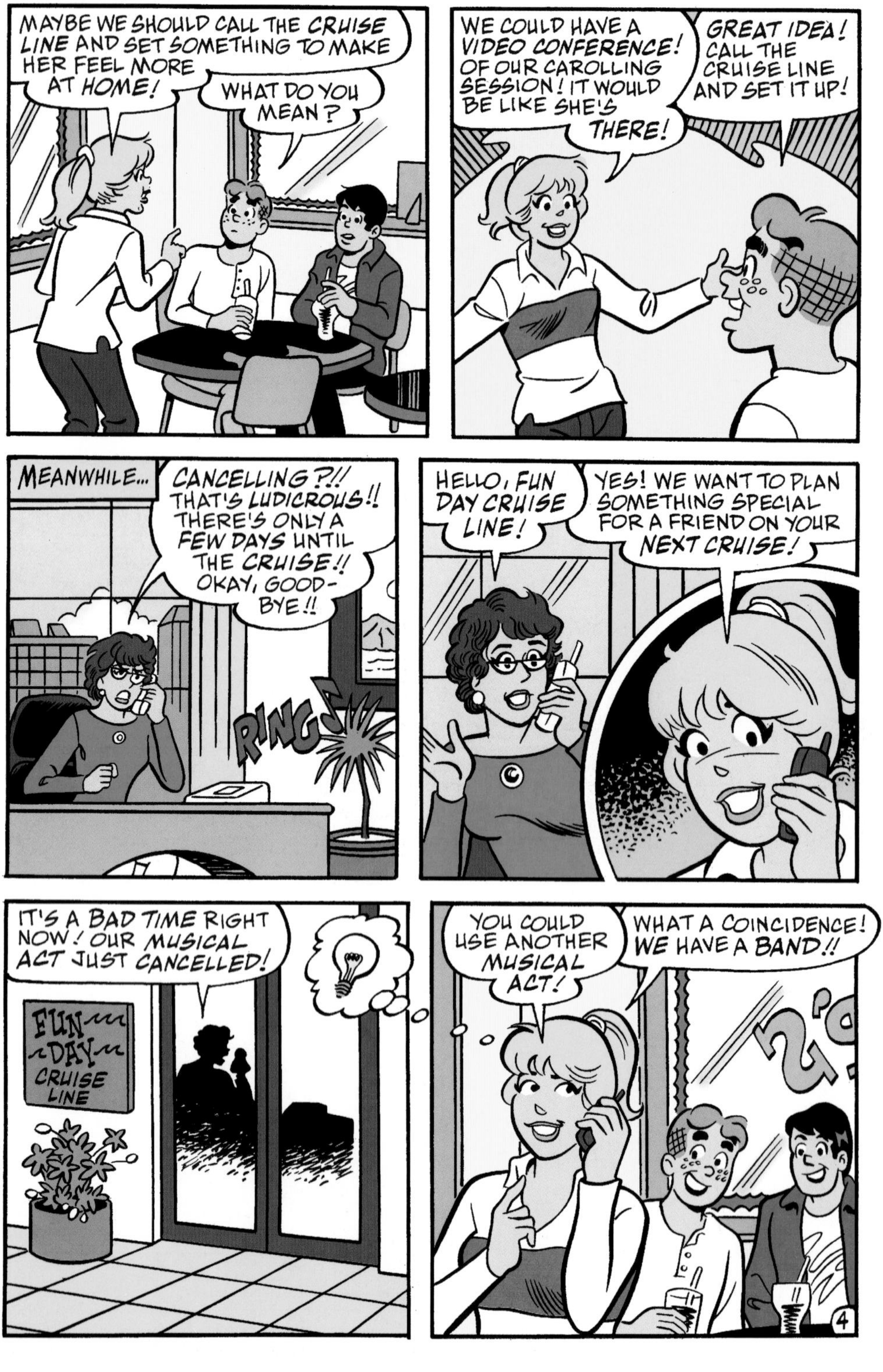
MAYBE WE SHOULD CALL THE CRUISE LINE AND SET SOMETHING TO MAKE HER FEEL MORE AT HOME!
WHAT DO YOU MEAN?
WE COULD HAVE A VIDEO CONFERENCE! OF OUR CAROLLING SESSION! IT WOULD BE LIKE SHE'S THERE!
GREAT IDEA! CALL THE CRUISE LINE AND SET IT UP!
MEANWHILE...
CANCELLING?!! THAT'S LUDICROUS!! THERE'S ONLY A FEW DAYS UNTIL THE CRUISE!! OKAY, GOOD-BYE!!
RING
HELLO, FUN DAY CRUISE LINE!
YES! WE WANT TO PLAN SOMETHING SPECIAL FOR A FRIEND ON YOUR NEXT CRUISE!
IT'S A BAD TIME RIGHT NOW! OUR MUSICAL ACT JUST CANCELLED!
FUN DAY CRUISE LINE
YOU COULD USE ANOTHER MUSICAL ACT!
WHAT A COINCIDENCE! WE HAVE A BAND!!
4

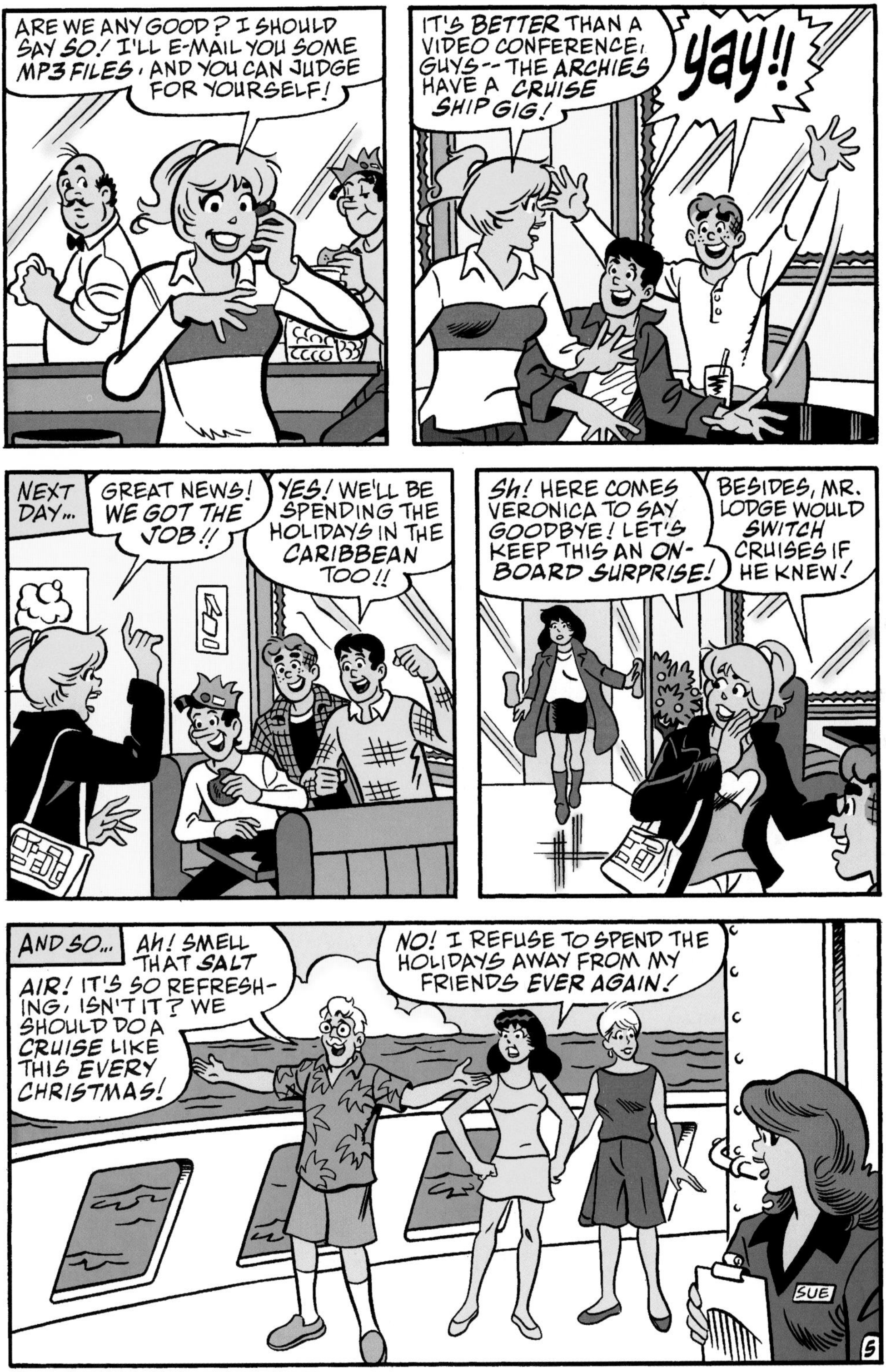
ARE WE ANY GOOD? I SHOULD SAY SO! I'LL E-MAIL YOU SOME MP3 FILES, AND YOU CAN JUDGE FOR YOURSELF!
IT'S BETTER THAN A VIDEO CONFERENCE, GUYS-- THE ARCHIES HAVE A CRUISE SHIP GIG!
yay!!
NEXT DAY...
GREAT NEWS! WE GOT THE JOB!!
YES! WE'LL BE SPENDING THE HOLIDAYS IN THE CARIBBEAN TOO!!
Sh! HERE COMES VERONICA TO SAY GOODBYE! LET'S KEEP THIS AN ON-BOARD SURPRISE!
BESIDES, MR. LODGE WOULD SWITCH CRUISES IF HE KNEW!
AND SO...
Ah! SMELL THAT SALT AIR! IT'S SO REFRESHING, ISN'T IT? WE SHOULD DO A CRUISE LIKE THIS EVERY CHRISTMAS!
NO! I REFUSE TO SPEND THE HOLIDAYS AWAY FROM MY FRIENDS EVER AGAIN!
SUE
5

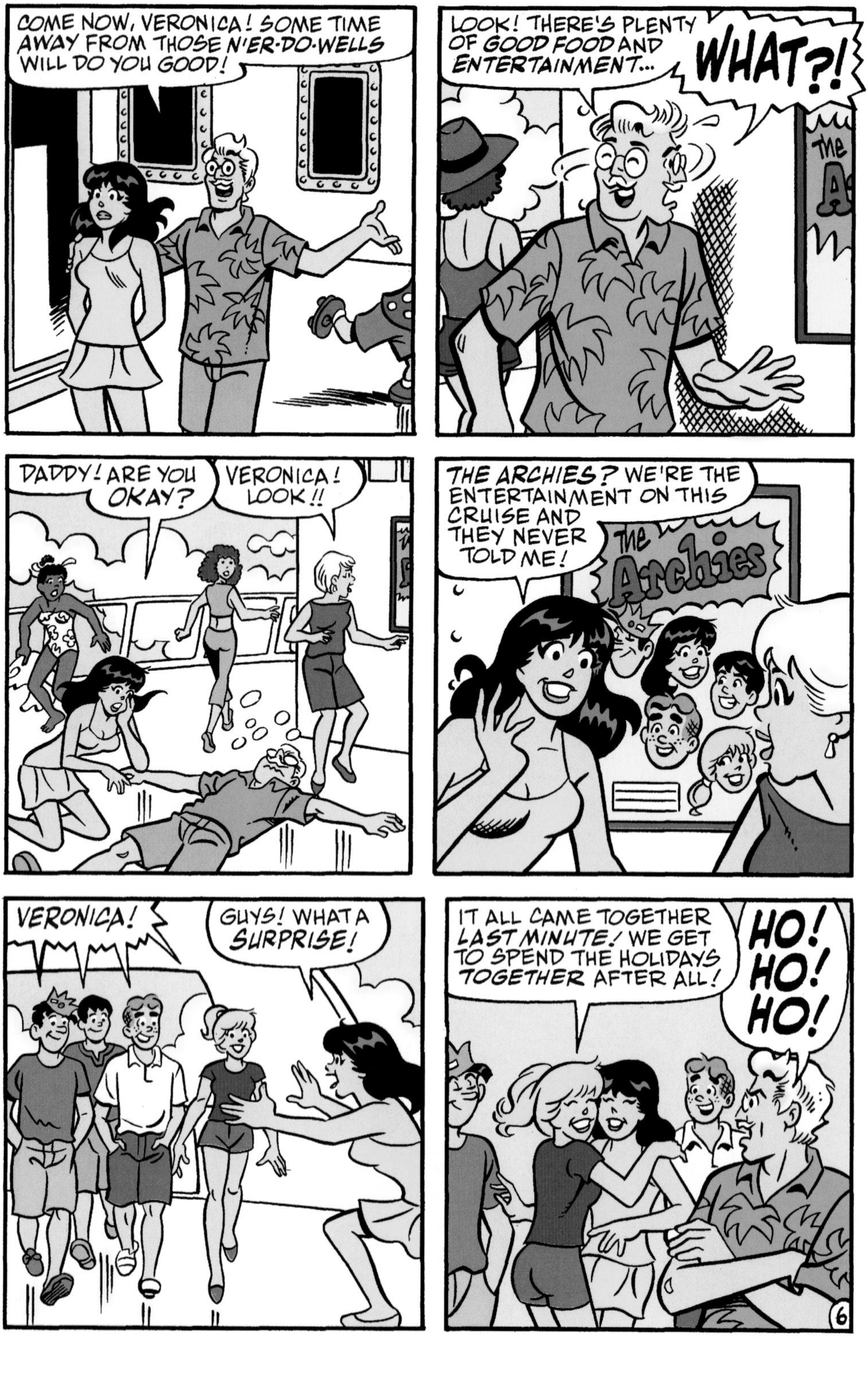
COME NOW, VERONICA! SOME TIME AWAY FROM THOSE N'ER-DO-WELLS WILL DO YOU GOOD!
LOOK! THERE'S PLENTY OF GOOD FOOD AND ENTERTAINMENT...
WHAT?!
DADDY! ARE YOU OKAY?
VERONICA! LOOK!!
THE ARCHIES? WE'RE THE ENTERTAINMENT ON THIS CRUISE AND THEY NEVER TOLD ME!
The Archies
VERONICA!
GUYS! WHAT A SURPRISE!
IT ALL CAME TOGETHER LAST MINUTE! WE GET TO SPEND THE HOLIDAYS TOGETHER AFTER ALL!
HO! HO! HO!
6

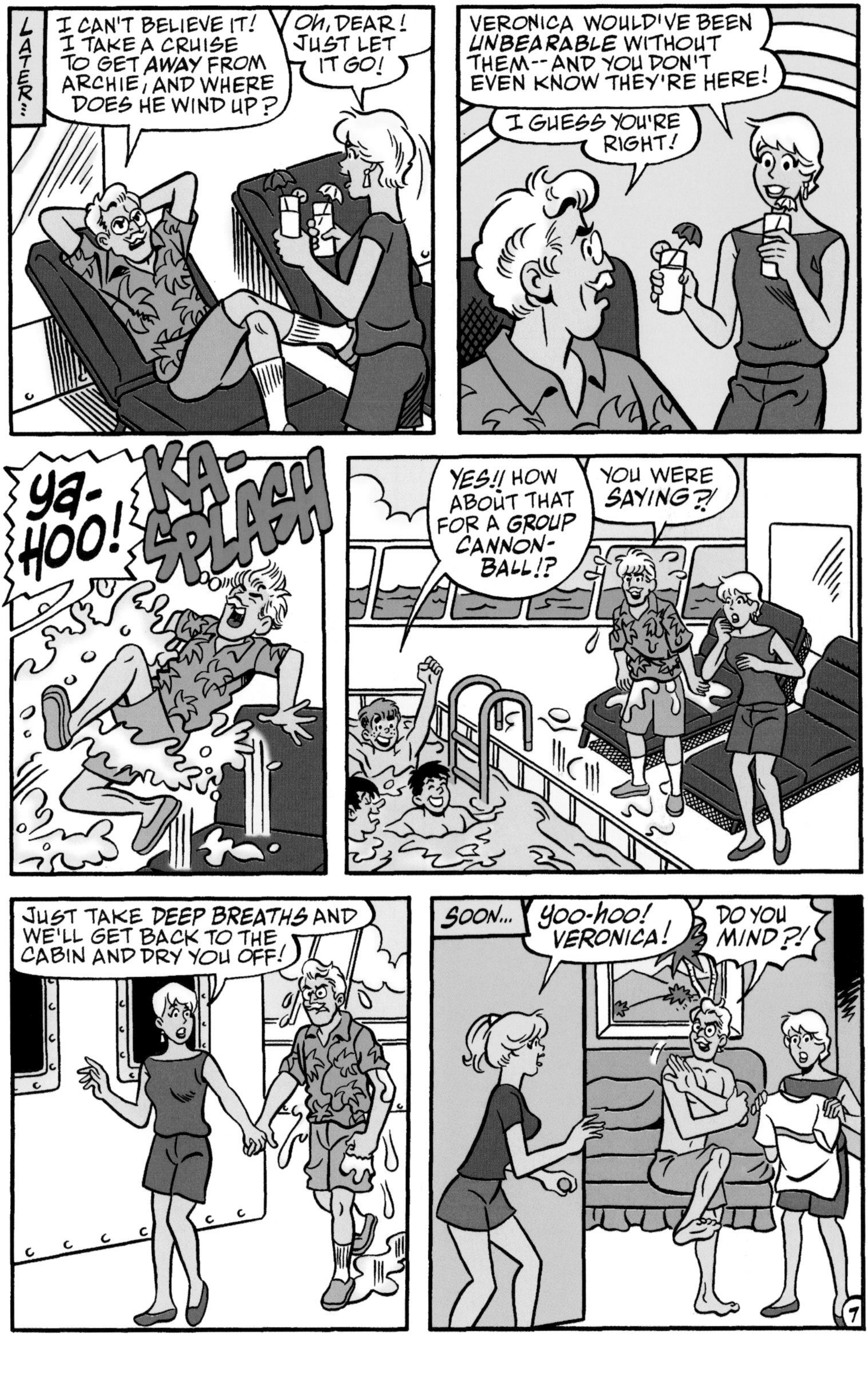
LATER...
I CAN'T BELIEVE IT! I TAKE A CRUISE TO GET AWAY FROM ARCHIE, AND WHERE DOES HE WIND UP?
OH, DEAR! JUST LET IT GO!
VERONICA WOULD'VE BEEN UNBEARABLE WITHOUT THEM--AND YOU DON'T EVEN KNOW THEY'RE HERE!
I GUESS YOU'RE RIGHT!
YA-HOO!
KA-SPLASH
YES!! HOW ABOUT THAT FOR A GROUP CANNON-BALL!?
YOU WERE SAYING?!
JUST TAKE DEEP BREATHS AND WE'LL GET BACK TO THE CABIN AND DRY YOU OFF!
SOON...
YOO-HOO! VERONICA!
DO YOU MIND?!
7

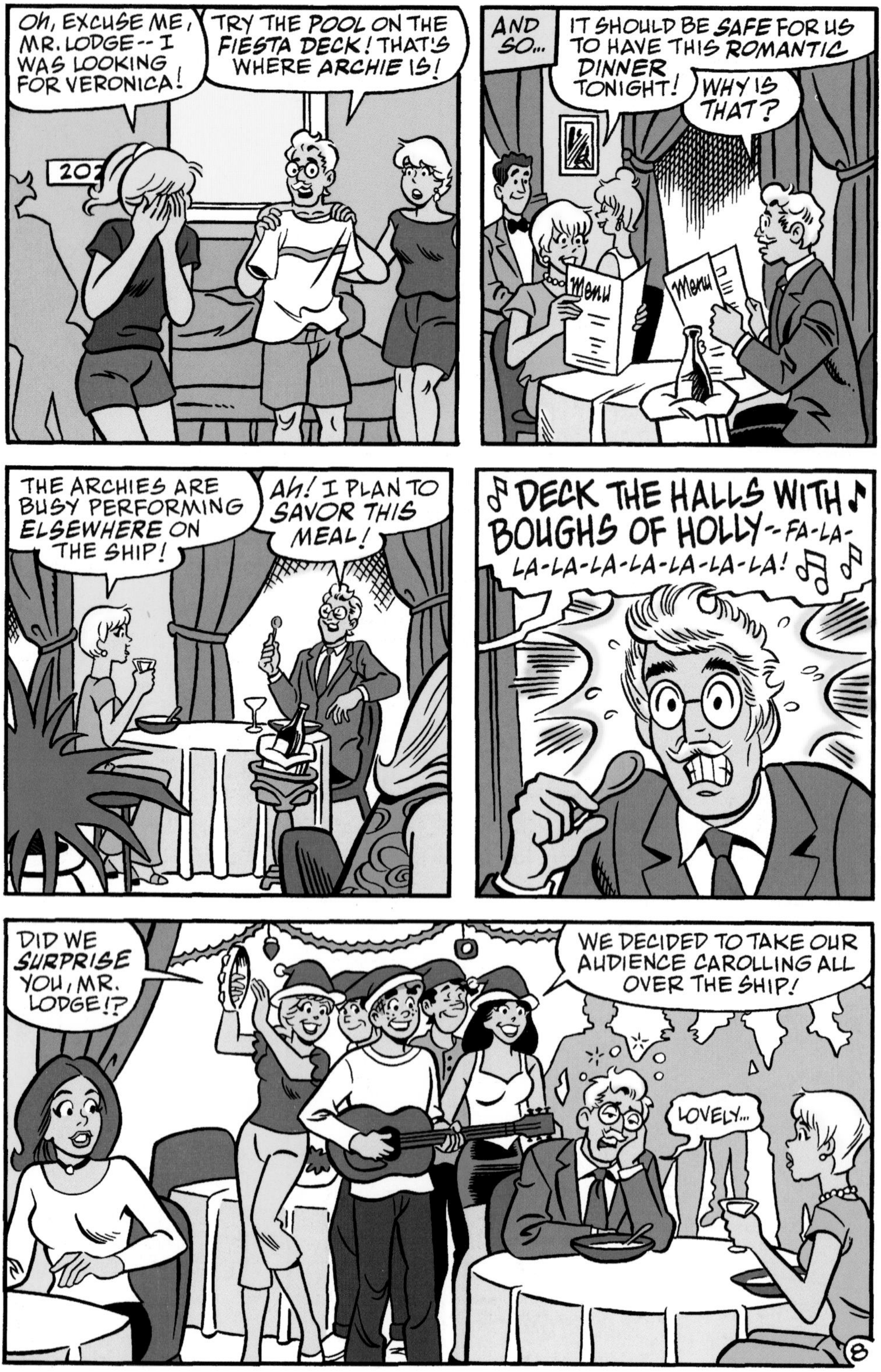
OH, EXCUSE ME, MR. LODGE -- I WAS LOOKING FOR VERONICA!
TRY THE POOL ON THE FIESTA DECK! THAT'S WHERE ARCHIE IS!
202
AND SO...
IT SHOULD BE SAFE FOR US TO HAVE THIS ROMANTIC DINNER TONIGHT!
WHY IS THAT?
MENU
MENU
THE ARCHIES ARE BUSY PERFORMING ELSEWHERE ON THE SHIP!
AH! I PLAN TO SAVOR THIS MEAL!
DECK THE HALLS WITH BOUGHS OF HOLLY -- FA-LA-LA-LA-LA-LA-LA-LA-LA!
DID WE SURPRISE YOU, MR. LODGE!?
WE DECIDED TO TAKE OUR AUDIENCE CAROLLING ALL OVER THE SHIP!
LOVELY...
8

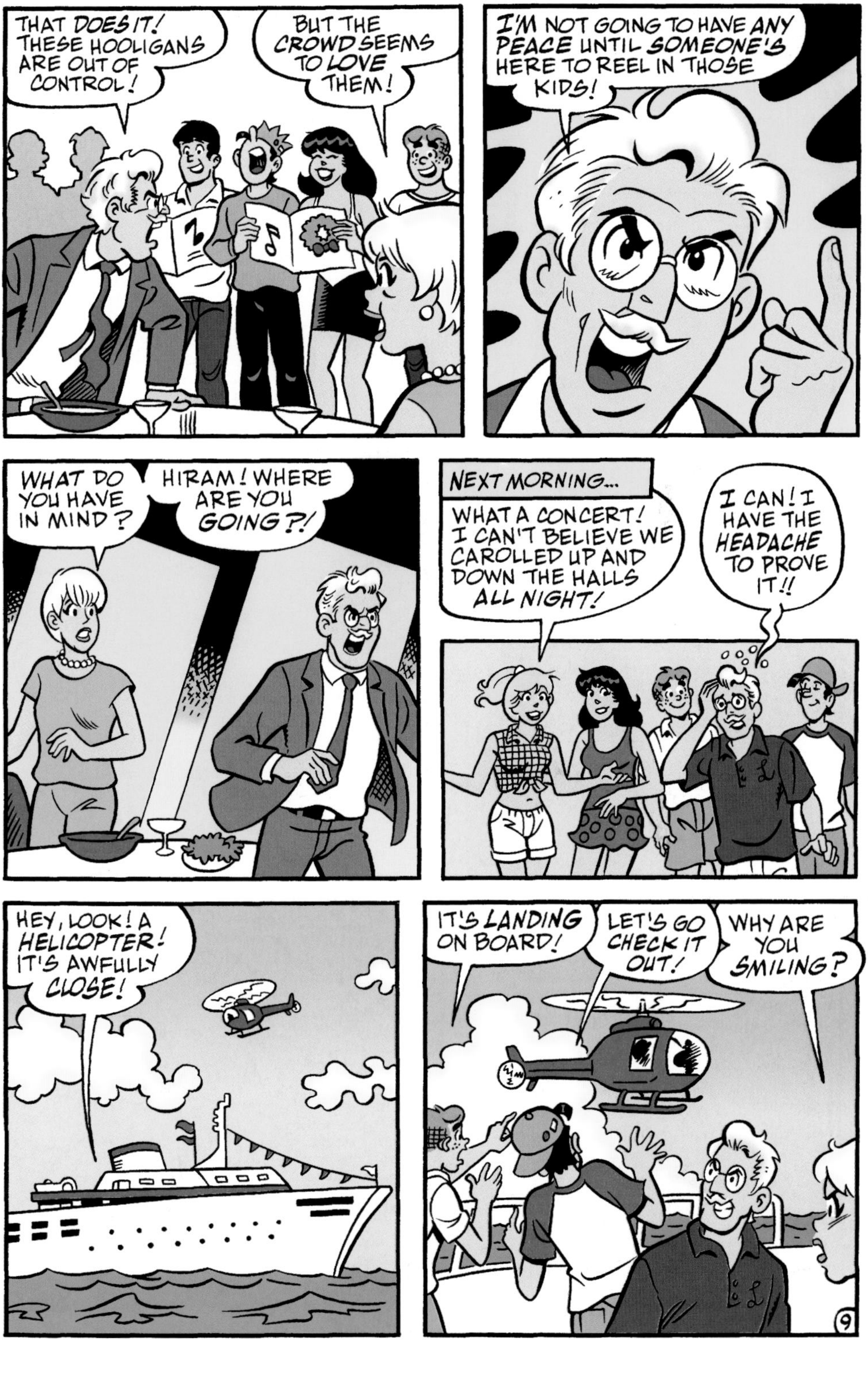
THAT DOES IT! THESE HOOLIGANS ARE OUT OF CONTROL!
BUT THE CROWD SEEMS TO LOVE THEM!
I'M NOT GOING TO HAVE ANY PEACE UNTIL SOMEONE'S HERE TO REEL IN THOSE KIDS!
WHAT DO YOU HAVE IN MIND?
HIRAM! WHERE ARE YOU GOING?!
NEXT MORNING...
WHAT A CONCERT! I CAN'T BELIEVE WE CAROLLED UP AND DOWN THE HALLS ALL NIGHT!
I CAN! I HAVE THE HEADACHE TO PROVE IT!!
HEY, LOOK! A HELICOPTER! IT'S AWFULLY CLOSE!
IT'S LANDING ON BOARD!
LET'S GO CHECK IT OUT!
WHY ARE YOU SMILING?
9

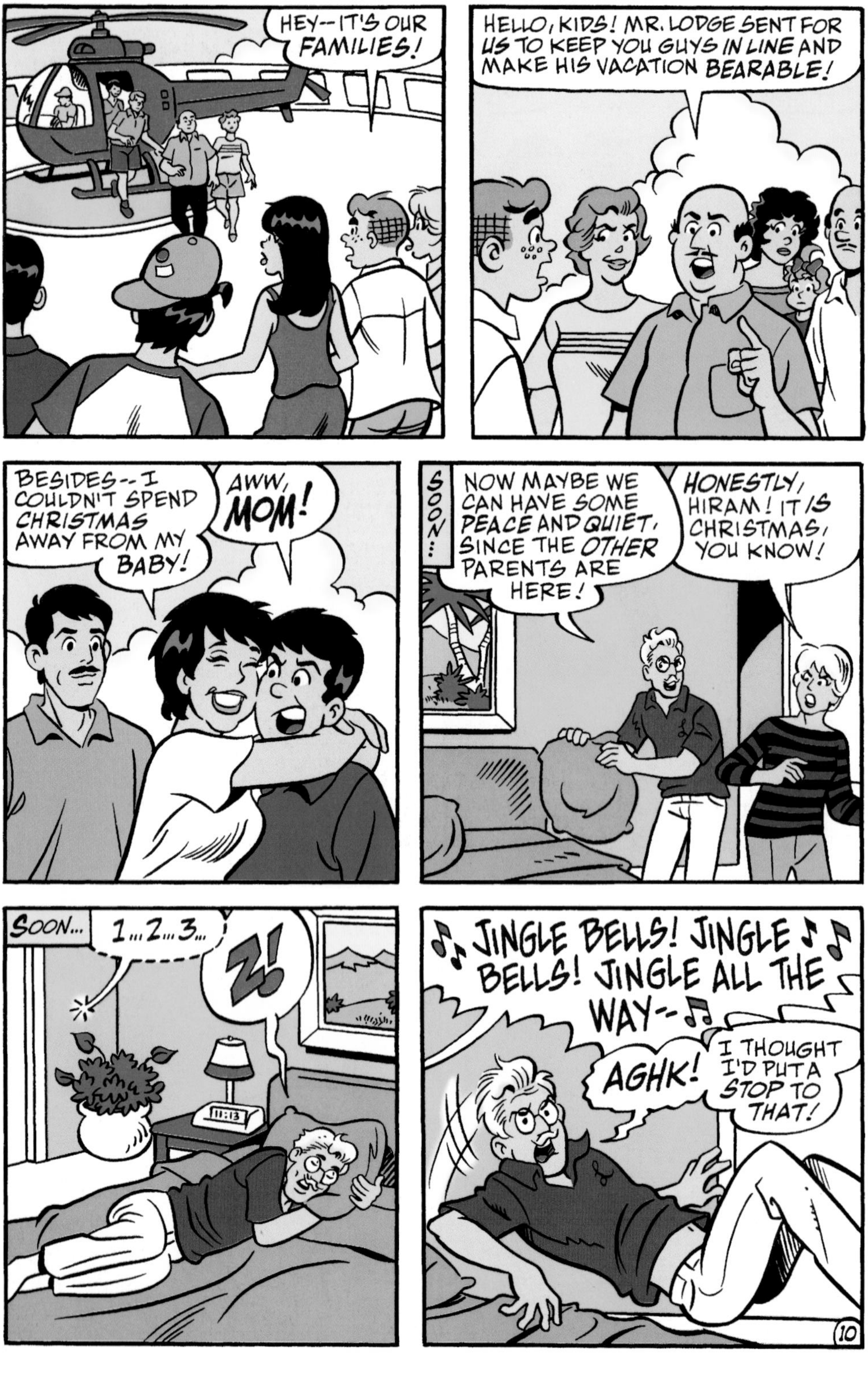
HEY--IT'S OUR FAMILIES!
HELLO, KIDS! MR. LODGE SENT FOR US TO KEEP YOU GUYS IN LINE AND MAKE HIS VACATION BEARABLE!
BESIDES--I COULDN'T SPEND CHRISTMAS AWAY FROM MY BABY!
AWW, MOM!
SOON...
NOW MAYBE WE CAN HAVE SOME PEACE AND QUIET, SINCE THE OTHER PARENTS ARE HERE!
HONESTLY, HIRAM! IT IS CHRISTMAS, YOU KNOW!
SOON...
1...2...3...
Z!
11:13
JINGLE BELLS! JINGLE BELLS! JINGLE ALL THE WAY--
AGHK!
I THOUGHT I'D PUT A STOP TO THAT!
10

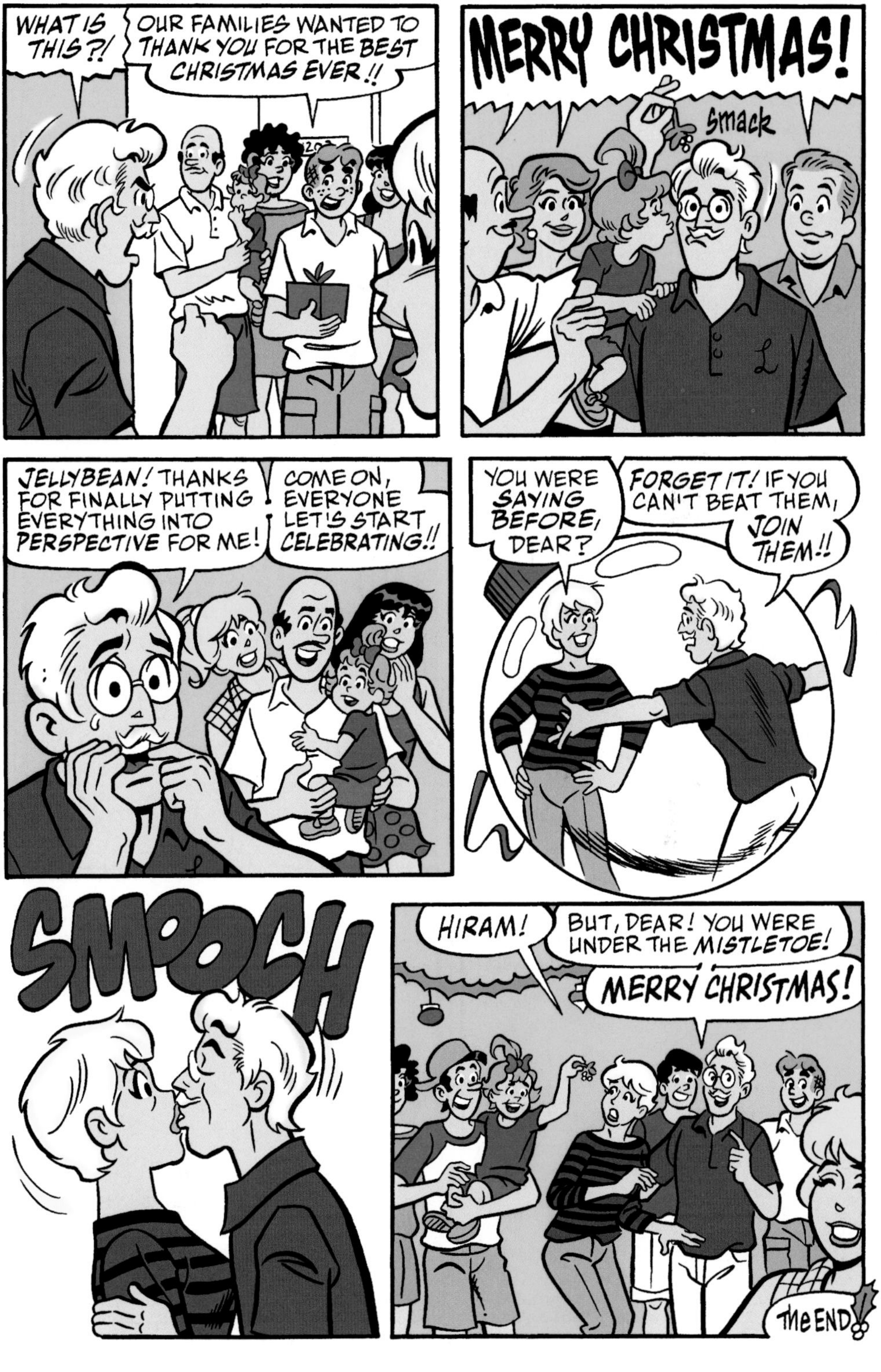
WHAT IS THIS?!
OUR FAMILIES WANTED TO THANK YOU FOR THE BEST CHRISTMAS EVER!!
MERRY CHRISTMAS!
Smack
JELLYBEAN! THANKS FOR FINALLY PUTTING EVERYTHING INTO PERSPECTIVE FOR ME!
COME ON, EVERYONE LET'S START CELEBRATING!!
YOU WERE SAYING BEFORE, DEAR?
FORGET IT! IF YOU CAN'T BEAT THEM, JOIN THEM!!
SMOOCH
HIRAM!
BUT, DEAR! YOU WERE UNDER THE MISTLETOE!
MERRY CHRISTMAS!
The END!

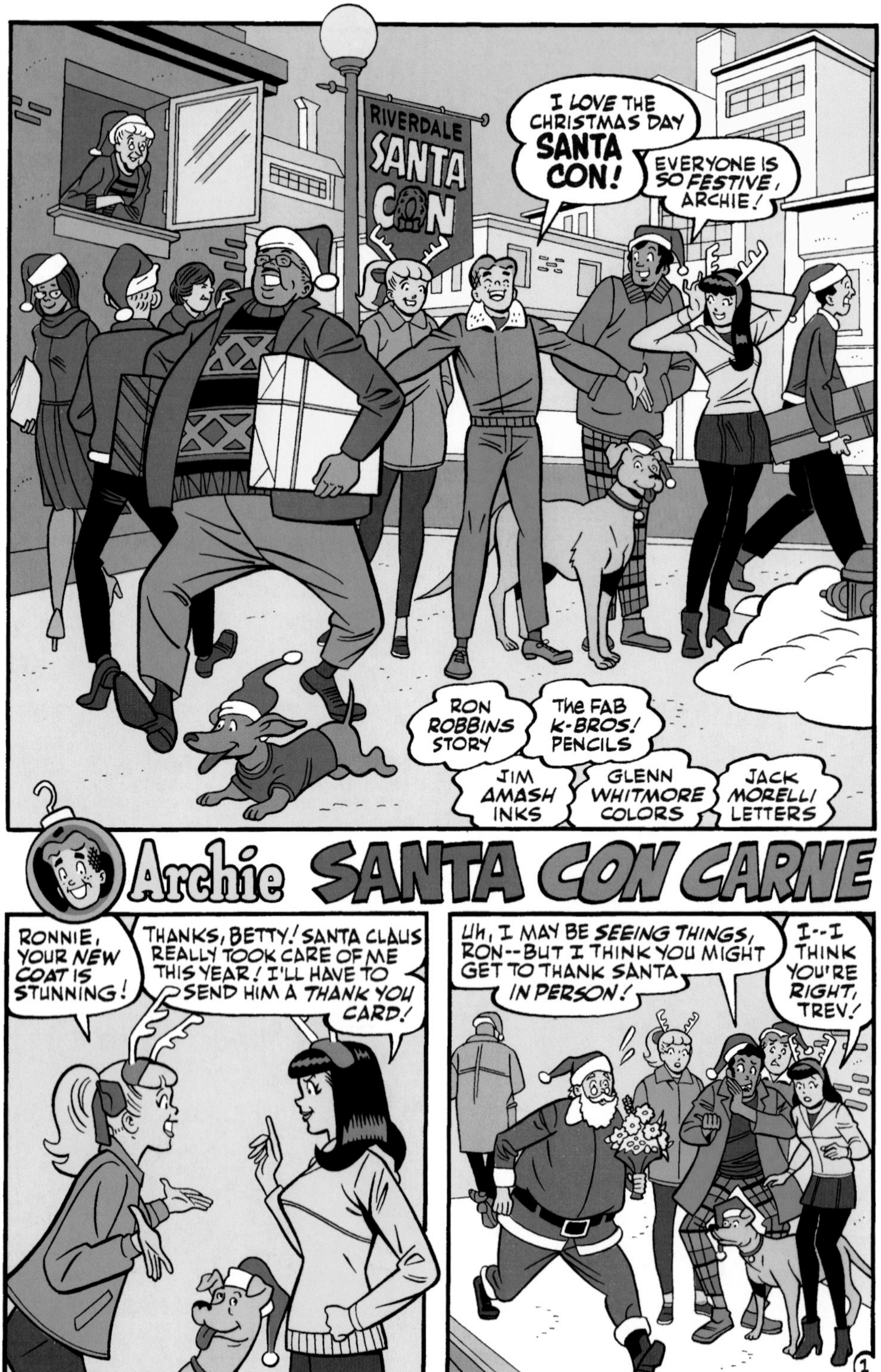
RIVERDALE SANTA CON
I LOVE THE CHRISTMAS DAY SANTA CON!
EVERYONE IS SO FESTIVE, ARCHIE!
RON ROBBINS STORY
The FAB K-BROS! PENCILS
JIM AMASH INKS
GLENN WHITMORE COLORS
JACK MORELLI LETTERS
Archie
SANTA CON CARNE
RONNIE, YOUR NEW COAT IS STUNNING!
THANKS, BETTY! SANTA CLAUS REALLY TOOK CARE OF ME THIS YEAR! I'LL HAVE TO SEND HIM A THANK YOU CARD!
UH, I MAY BE SEEING THINGS, RON--BUT I THINK YOU MIGHT GET TO THANK SANTA IN PERSON!
I--I THINK YOU'RE RIGHT, TREV!
1

Ron Robbins • Pat & Tim Kennedy • Jim Amash • Jack Morelli • Glenn Whitmore

Originally printed in WORLD OF ARCHIE DOUBLE DIGEST #115, 2021

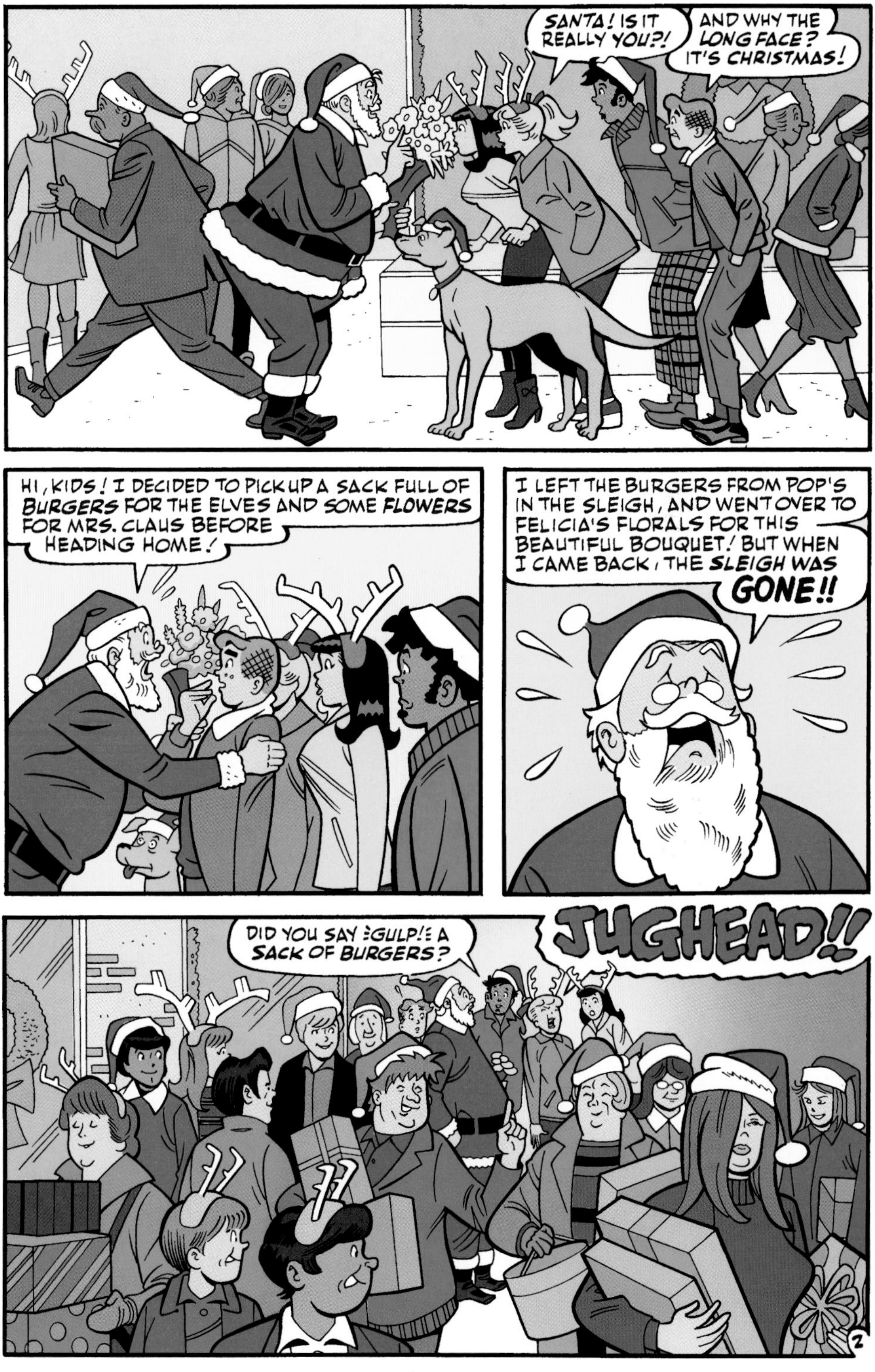
SANTA! IS IT REALLY YOU?!
AND WHY THE LONG FACE? IT'S CHRISTMAS!
HI, KIDS! I DECIDED TO PICK UP A SACK FULL OF BURGERS FOR THE ELVES AND SOME FLOWERS FOR MRS. CLAUS BEFORE HEADING HOME!
I LEFT THE BURGERS FROM POP'S IN THE SLEIGH, AND WENT OVER TO FELICIA'S FLORALS FOR THIS BEAUTIFUL BOUQUET! BUT WHEN I CAME BACK, THE SLEIGH WAS GONE!!
DID YOU SAY GULP! A SACK OF BURGERS?
JUGHEAD!!
2

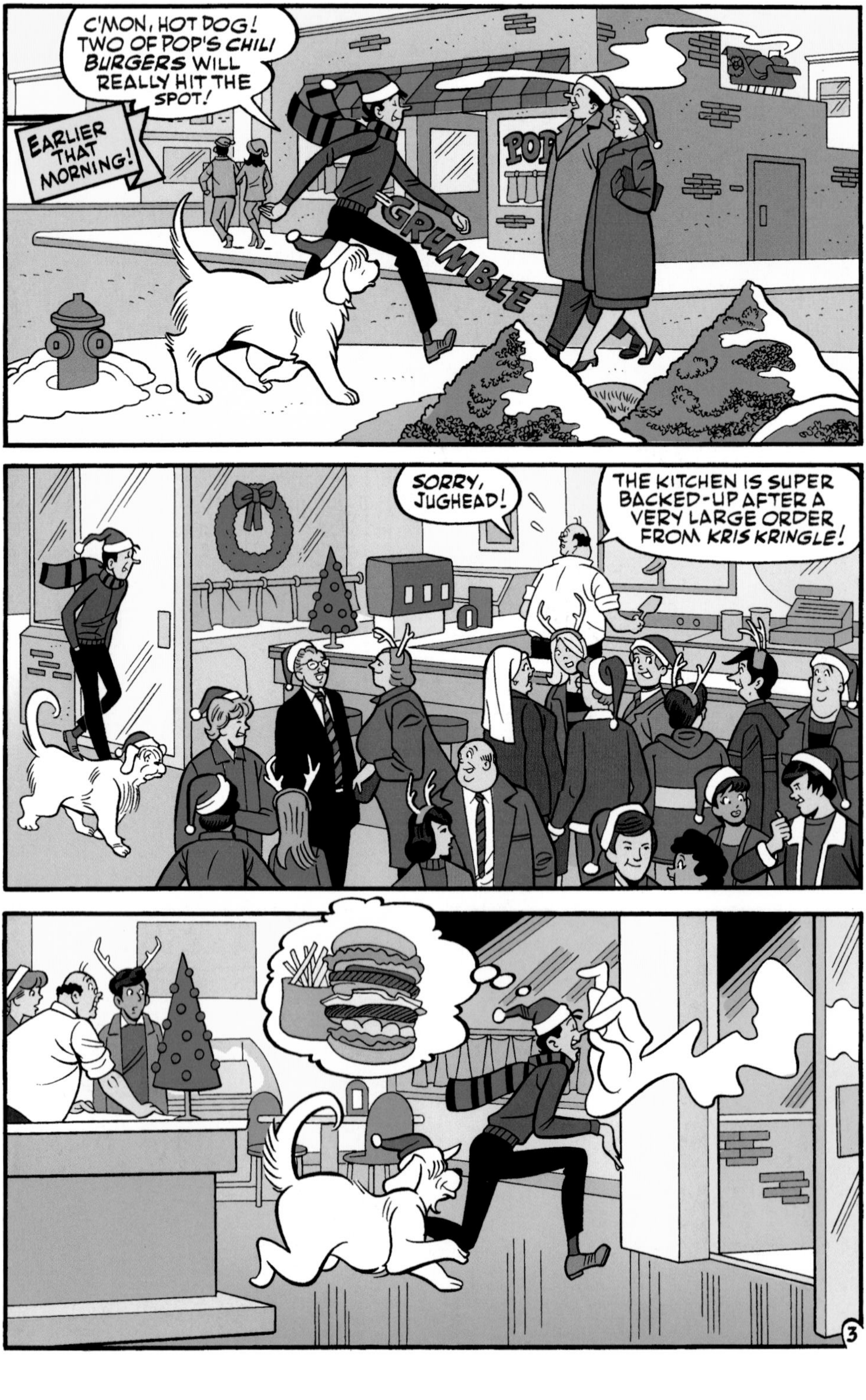
EARLIER THAT MORNING!
C'MON, HOT DOG! TWO OF POP'S *CHILI BURGERS* WILL REALLY HIT THE SPOT!
GRUMBLE
SORRY, JUGHEAD!
THE KITCHEN IS SUPER BACKED-UP AFTER A VERY LARGE ORDER FROM *KRIS KRINGLE*!
3

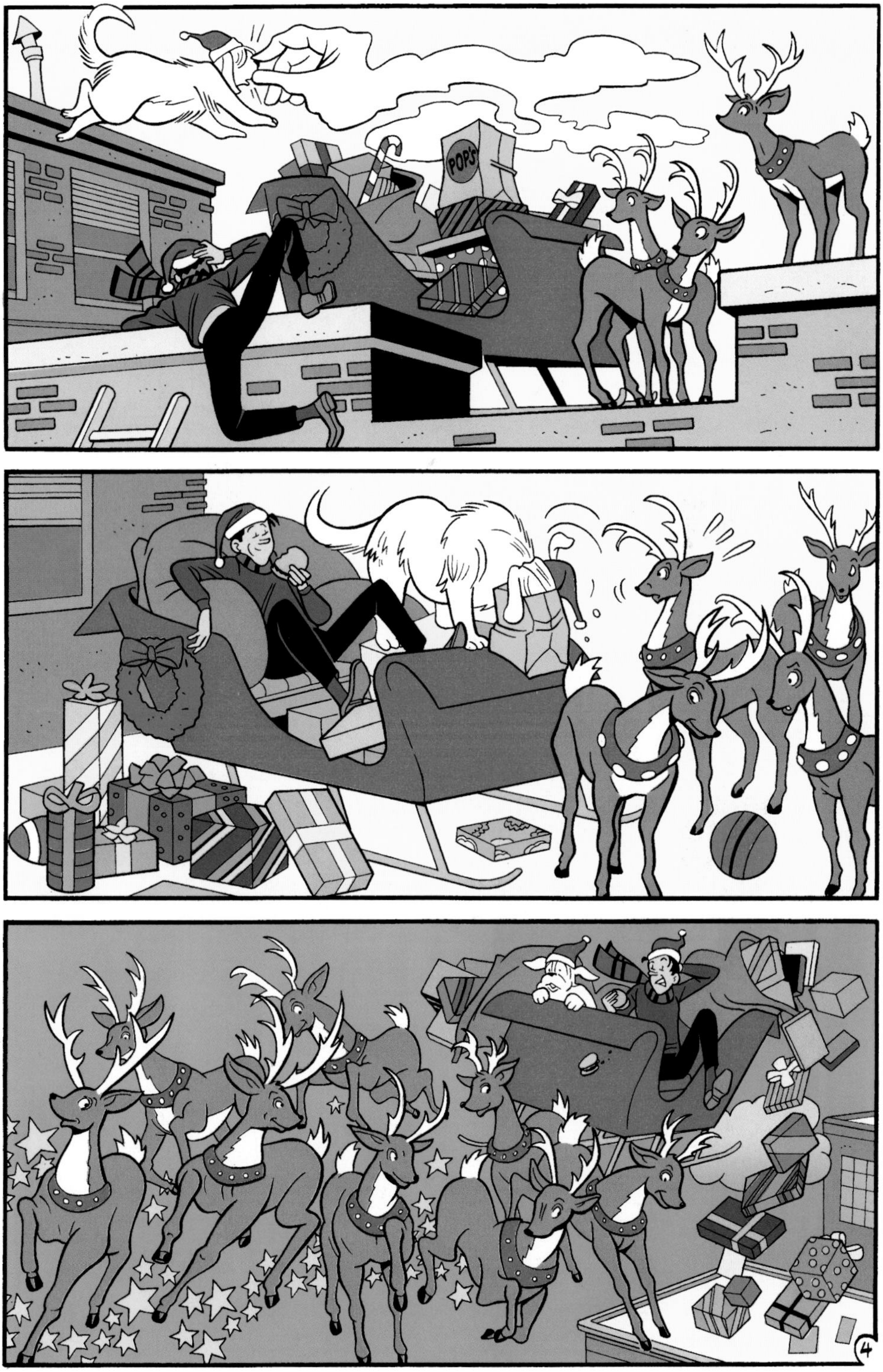
POP'S

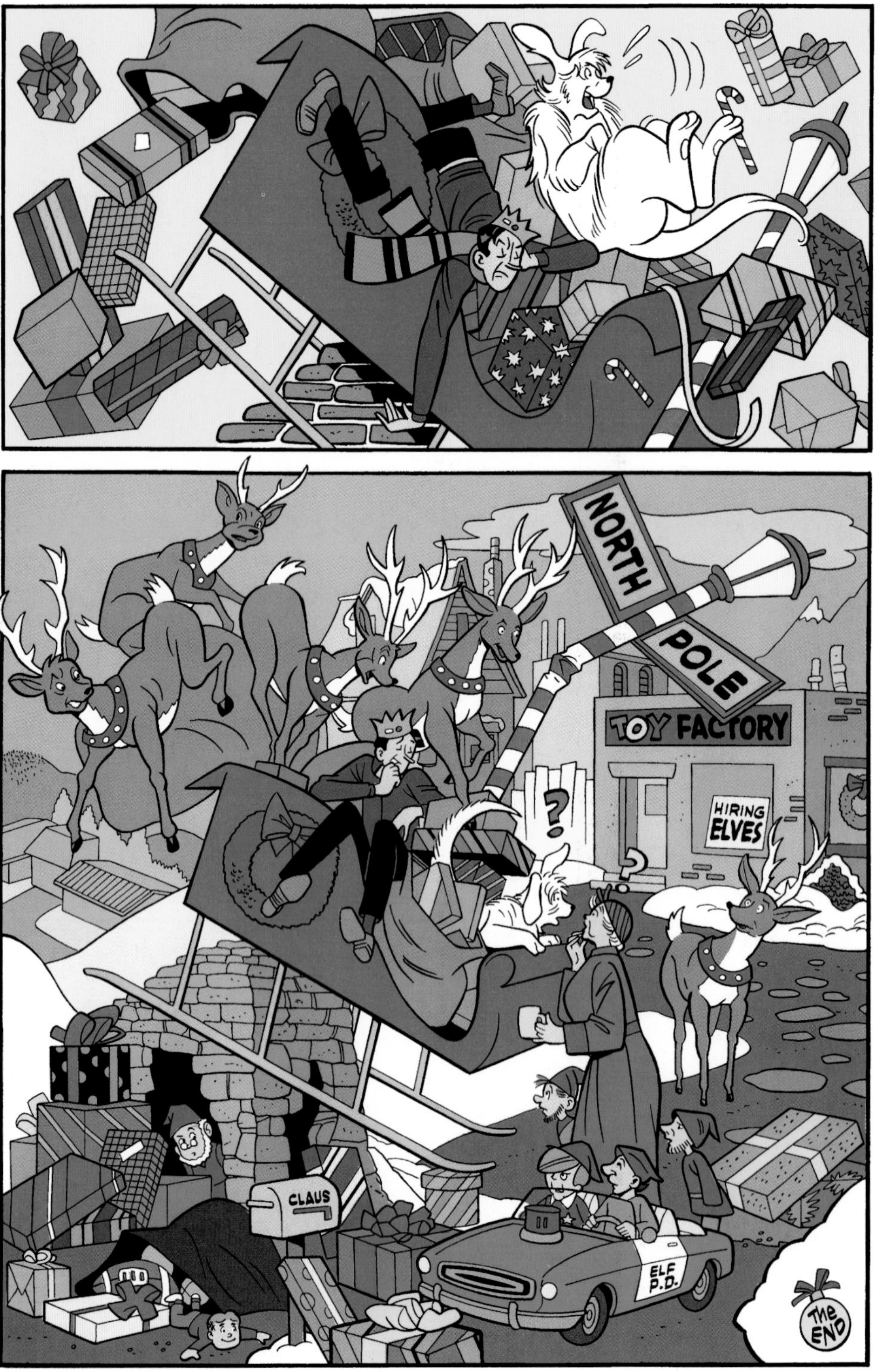
NORTH
POLE
TOY FACTORY
HIRING ELVES
?
?
CLAUS
ELF P.D.
THE END